Stephen Crane (November 1, 1871 – June 5, 1900) was an American poet, novelist, and short story writer. Prolific throughout his short life, he wrote notable works in the Realist tradition as well as early examples of American Naturalism and Impressionism. He is recognized by modern critics as one of the most innovative writers of his generation. The ninth surviving child of Methodist parents, Crane began writing at the age of four and had published several articles by the age of 16. Having little interest in university studies though he was active in a fraternity, he left Syracuse University in 1891 to work as a reporter and writer. Crane's first novel was the 1893 Bowery tale Maggie: A Girl of the Streets, generally considered by critics to be the first work of American literary Naturalism. He won international acclaim in 1895 for his Civil War novel The Red Badge of Courage, which he wrote without having any battle experience. (Source: Wikipedia)

Literary works:

Maggie: A Girl of the Streets (1893)
The Red Badge of Courage (1895)
The Black Riders and Other Lines (1895)
George's Mother (1896)
The Third Violet (1897)
The Open Boat and Other Tales of Adventure (1898)
War is Kind (1899)
Active Service (1899)
The Monster and Other Stories (1899)
Wounds in the Rain (1900)
Great Battles of the World
The O'Ruddy (1903)
The Monster. London
Last Words. London
Whilomville Stories

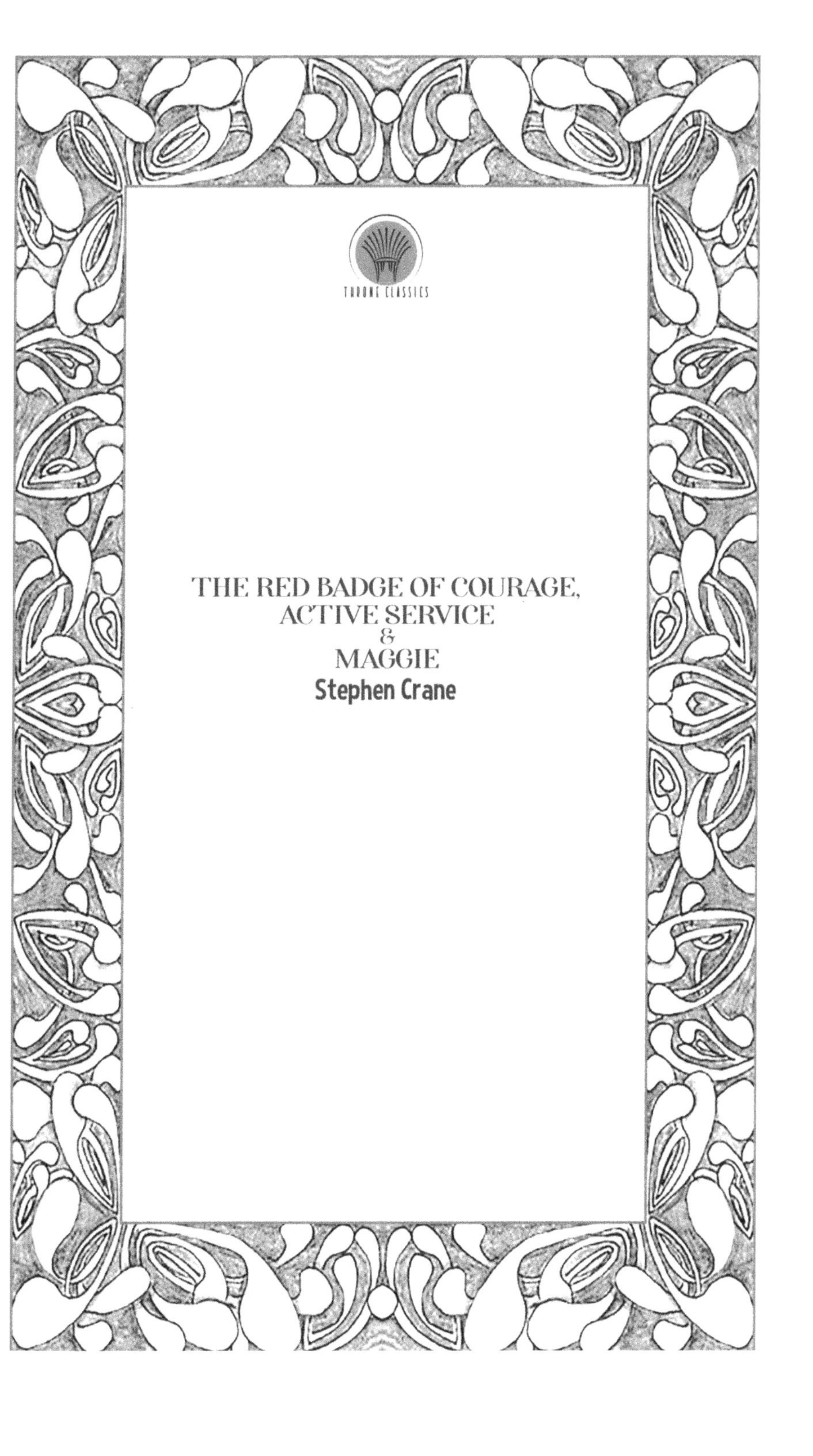

THE RED BADGE OF COURAGE, ACTIVE SERVICE & MAGGIE

Stephen Crane

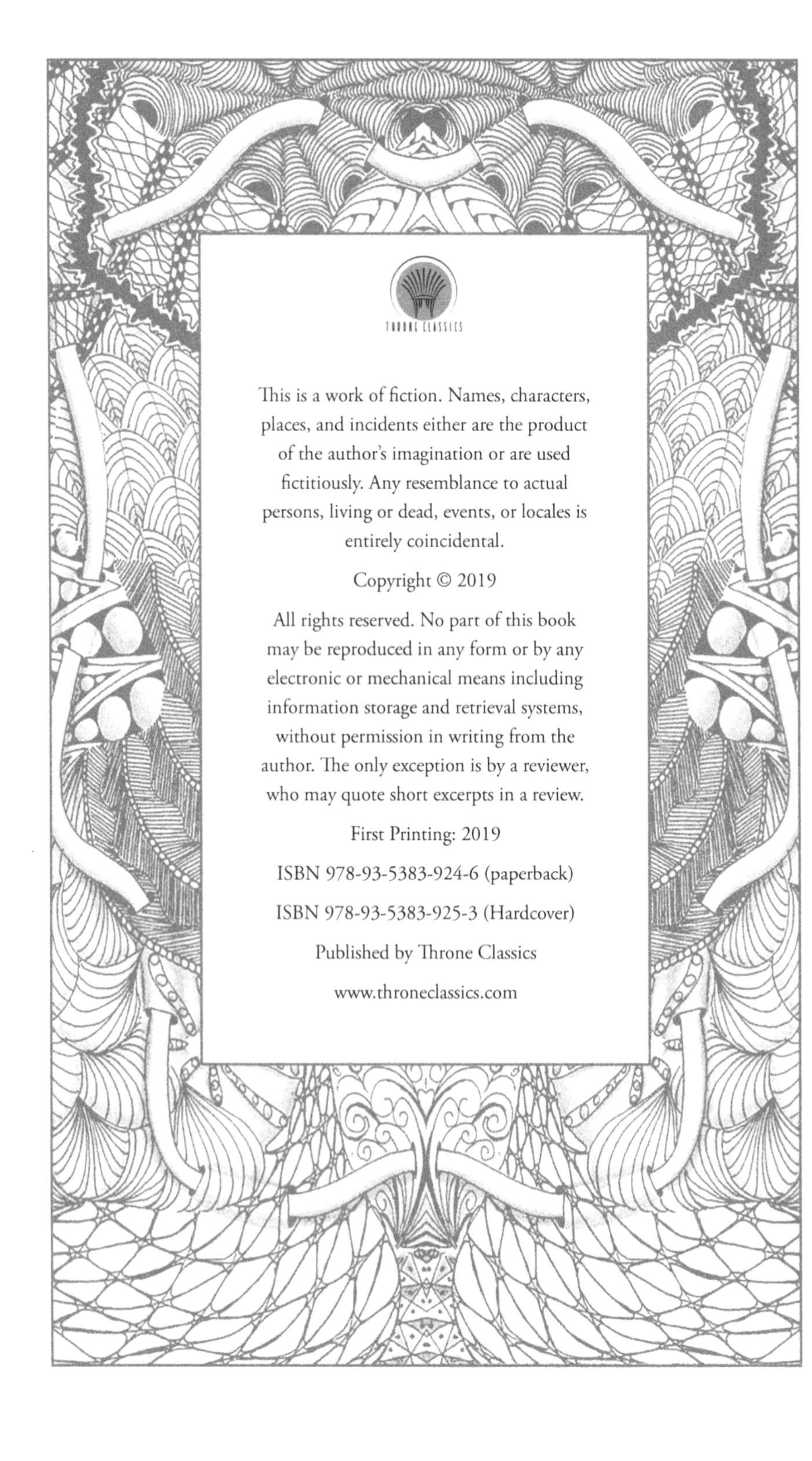

This is a work of fiction. Names, characters, places, and incidents either are the product of the author's imagination or are used fictitiously. Any resemblance to actual persons, living or dead, events, or locales is entirely coincidental.

First Printing: 2019

ISBN 978-93-5383-924-6 (paperback)

ISBN 978-93-5383-925-3 (Hardcover)

Published by Throne Classics

www.throneclassics.com

Contents

THE RED BADGE OF COURAGE **11**

Chapter 1 11

Chapter 2 21

Chapter 3 29

Chapter 4 38

Chapter 5 42

Chapter 6 49

Chapter 7 56

Chapter 8 60

Chapter 9 66

Chapter 10 72

Chapter 11 76

Chapter 12 82

Chapter 13 88

Chapter 14 94

Chapter 15 99

Chapter 16 103

Chapter 17 109

Chapter 18 114

Chapter 19 119

Chapter 20 125

Chapter 21 131

Chapter 22 137

Chapter 23 142

Chapter 24 147

ACTIVE SERVICE **153**
CHAPTER I. 153
CHAPTER II. 159
CHAPTER III. 164
CHAPTER IV. 174
CHAPTER V. 180
CHAPTER VI. 184
CHAPTER VII. 189
CHAPTER VIII. 198
CHAPTER IX. 206
CHAPTER X. 219
CHAPTER XI. 229
CHAPTER XII. 236
CHAPTER XIII. 242
CHAPTER XIV. 250
CHAPTER XV. 256
CHAPTER XVI. 264
CHAPTER XVII. 270
CHAPTER XVIII. 277
CHAPTER XIX. 285
CHAPTER XX. 293
CHAPTER XXI. 299
CHAPTER XXII. 305
CHAPTER XXIII 312
CHAPTER XXIV. 318
CHAPTER XXV. 327
CHAPTER XXVI. 333
CHAPTER XXVII. 342
CHAPTER XXVIII. 352
CHAPTER XXIX. 365
CHAPTER XXX 371

MAGGIE **377**
Chapter I 377
Chapter II 381
Chapter III 386
Chapter IV 390
Chapter V 394
Chapter VI 398
Chapter VII 402
Chapter VIII 407
Chapter IX 412
Chapter X 417
Chapter XI 421
Chapter XII 427
Chapter XIII 430
Chapter XIV 434
Chapter XV 440
Chapter XVI 444
Chapter XVII 448
Chapter XVIII 451
Chapter XIX 456
About Author 461

THE RED BADGE OF COURAGE, ACTIVE SERVICE & MAGGIE

THE RED BADGE OF COURAGE

Chapter 1

The cold passed reluctantly from the earth, and the retiring fogs revealed an army stretched out on the hills, resting. As the landscape changed from brown to green, the army awakened, and began to tremble with eagerness at the noise of rumors. It cast its eyes upon the roads, which were growing from long troughs of liquid mud to proper thoroughfares. A river, amber-tinted in the shadow of its banks, purled at the army's feet; and at night, when the stream had become of a sorrowful blackness, one could see across it the red, eyelike gleam of hostile camp-fires set in the low brows of distant hills.

Once a certain tall soldier developed virtues and went resolutely to wash a shirt. He came flying back from a brook waving his garment bannerlike. He was swelled with a tale he had heard from a reliable friend, who had heard it from a truthful cavalryman, who had heard it from his trustworthy brother, one of the orderlies at division headquarters. He adopted the important air of a herald in red and gold.

"We're goin' t' move t'morrah--sure," he said pompously to a group in the company street. "We're goin' 'way up the river, cut across, an' come around in behint 'em."

To his attentive audience he drew a loud and elaborate plan of a very brilliant campaign. When he had finished, the blue-clothed men scattered into small arguing groups between the rows of squat brown huts. A negro teamster who had been dancing upon a cracker box with the hilarious encouragement of twoscore soldiers was deserted. He sat mournfully down. Smoke drifted lazily from a multitude of quaint chimneys.

"It's a lie! that's all it is--a thunderin' lie!" said another private loudly. His smooth face was flushed, and his hands were thrust sulkily into his trouser's pockets. He took the matter as an affront to him. "I don't believe the derned old army's ever going to move. We're set. I've got ready to move eight times in the last two weeks, and we ain't moved yet."

The tall soldier felt called upon to defend the truth of a rumor he himself had introduced. He and the loud one came near to fighting over it.

A corporal began to swear before the assemblage. He had just put a costly board floor in his house, he said. During the early spring he had refrained from adding extensively to the comfort of his environment because he had felt that the army might start on the march at any moment. Of late, however, he had been impressed that they were in a sort of eternal camp.

Many of the men engaged in a spirited debate. One outlined in a peculiarly lucid manner all the plans of the commanding general. He was opposed by men who advocated that there were other plans of campaign. They clamored at each other, numbers making futile bids for the popular attention. Meanwhile, the soldier who had fetched the rumor bustled about with much importance. He was continually assailed by questions.

"What's up, Jim?"

"Th'army's goin' t' move."

"Ah, what yeh talkin' about? How yeh know it is?"

"Well, yeh kin b'lieve me er not, jest as yeh like. I don't care a hang."

There was much food for thought in the manner in which he replied. He came near to convincing them by disdaining to produce proofs. They grew much excited over it.

There was a youthful private who listened with eager ears to the words of the tall soldier and to the varied comments of his comrades. After receiving a fill of discussions concerning marches and attacks, he went to his hut and crawled through an intricate hole that served it as a door. He wished to be alone with some new thoughts that had lately come to him.

He lay down on a wide bunk that stretched across the end of the room. In the other end, cracker boxes were made to serve as furniture. They were grouped about the fireplace. A picture from an illustrated weekly was upon the log walls, and three rifles were paralleled on pegs. Equipments hung on handy projections, and some tin dishes lay upon a small pile of firewood. A folded tent was serving as a roof. The sunlight, without, beating upon it, made it glow a light yellow shade. A small window shot an oblique square of whiter light upon the cluttered floor. The smoke from the fire at times neglected the clay chimney and wreathed into the room, and this flimsy chimney of clay and sticks made endless threats to set ablaze the whole establishment.

The youth was in a little trance of astonishment. So they were at last going to fight. On the morrow, perhaps, there would be a battle, and he would be in it. For a time he was obliged to labor to make himself believe. He could not accept with assurance an omen that he was about to mingle in one of those great affairs of the earth.

He had, of course, dreamed of battles all his life--of vague and bloody conflicts that had thrilled him with their sweep and fire. In visions he had seen himself in many struggles. He had imagined peoples secure in the shadow of his eagle-eyed prowess. But awake he had regarded battles as crimson blotches on the pages of the past. He had put them as things of the bygone with his thought-images of heavy crowns and high castles. There was a portion of the world's history which he had regarded as the time of wars, but it, he thought, had been long gone over the horizon and had disappeared forever.

From his home his youthful eyes had looked upon the war in his own country with distrust. It must be some sort of a play affair. He had long despaired of witnessing a Greeklike struggle. Such would be no more, he had said. Men were better, or more timid. Secular and religious education had effaced the throat-grappling instinct, or else firm finance held in check the passions.

He had burned several times to enlist. Tales of great movements shook the land. They might not be distinctly Homeric, but there seemed to be much glory in them. He had read of marches, sieges, conflicts, and he had longed to see it all. His busy mind had drawn for him large pictures extravagant in color, lurid with breathless deeds.

But his mother had discouraged him. She had affected to look with some contempt upon the quality of his war ardor and patriotism. She could calmly seat herself and with no apparent difficulty give him many hundreds of reasons why he was of vastly more importance on the farm than on the field of battle. She had had certain ways of expression that told him that her statements on the subject came from a deep conviction. Moreover, on her side, was his belief that her ethical motive in the argument was impregnable.

At last, however, he had made firm rebellion against this yellow light thrown upon the color of his ambitions. The newspapers, the gossip of the village, his own picturings, had aroused him to an uncheckable degree. They were in truth fighting finely down there. Almost every day the newspaper printed accounts of a decisive victory.

One night, as he lay in bed, the winds had carried to him the clangoring of the church bell as some enthusiast jerked the rope frantically to tell the twisted news of a great battle. This voice of the people rejoicing in the night had made him shiver in a prolonged ecstasy of excitement. Later, he had gone down to his mother's room and had spoken thus: "Ma, I'm going to enlist."

"Henry, don't you be a fool," his mother had replied. She had then covered her face with the quilt. There was an end to the matter for that night.

Nevertheless, the next morning he had gone to a town that was near his mother's farm and had enlisted in a company that was forming there. When he had returned home his mother was milking the brindle cow. Four others stood waiting. "Ma, I've enlisted," he had said to her diffidently. There was a short silence. "The Lord's will be done, Henry," she had finally replied, and had then continued to milk the brindle cow.

When he had stood in the doorway with his soldier's clothes on his back, and with the light of excitement and expectancy in his eyes almost defeating the glow of regret for the home bonds, he had seen two tears leaving their trails on his mother's scarred cheeks.

Still, she had disappointed him by saying nothing whatever about returning with his shield or on it. He had privately primed himself for a beautiful scene. He had prepared certain sentences which he thought could be used with touching effect. But her words destroyed his plans. She had doggedly peeled potatoes and addressed him as follows: "You watch out, Henry, an' take good care of yerself in this here fighting business--you watch, an' take good care of yerself. Don't go a-thinkin' you can lick the hull rebel army at the start, because yeh can't. Yer jest one little feller amongst a hull lot of others, and yeh've got to keep quiet an' do what they tell yeh. I know how you are, Henry.

"I've knet yeh eight pair of socks, Henry, and I've put in all yer best shirts, because I want my boy to be jest as warm and comf'able as anybody in the army. Whenever they get holes in 'em, I want yeh to send 'em right-away back to me, so's I kin dern 'em.

"An' allus be careful an' choose yer comp'ny. There's lots of bad men in the army, Henry. The army makes 'em wild, and they like nothing better than the job of leading off a young feller like you, as ain't never been away from home much and has allus had a mother, an' a-learning 'em to drink and swear. Keep clear of them folks, Henry. I don't want yeh to ever do anything, Henry, that yeh would be 'shamed to let me know about. Jest think as if I was a-watchin' yeh. If yeh keep that in yer mind allus, I guess yeh'll come out about right.

"Yeh must allus remember yer father, too, child, an' remember he never drunk a drop of licker in his life, and seldom swore a cross oath.

"I don't know what else to tell yeh, Henry, excepting that yeh must never do no shirking, child, on my account. If so be a time comes when yeh have to be kilt or do a mean thing, why, Henry, don't think of anything 'cept what's right, because there's many a woman has to bear up 'ginst sech things these times, and the Lord 'll take keer of us all.

"Don't forgit about the socks and the shirts, child; and I've put a cup of blackberry jam with yer bundle, because I know yeh like it above all things. Good-by, Henry. Watch out, and be a good boy."

He had, of course, been impatient under the ordeal of this speech. It had not been quite what he expected, and he had borne it with an air of irritation. He departed feeling vague relief.

Still, when he had looked back from the gate, he had seen his mother kneeling among the potato parings. Her brown face, upraised, was stained with tears, and her spare form was quivering. He bowed his head and went on, feeling suddenly ashamed of his purposes.

From his home he had gone to the seminary to bid adieu to many schoolmates. They had thronged about him with wonder and admiration. He had felt the gulf now between them and had swelled with calm pride. He and some of his fellows who had donned blue were quite overwhelmed with privileges for all of one afternoon, and it had been a very delicious thing. They had strutted.

A certain light-haired girl had made vivacious fun at his martial spirit, but there was another and darker girl whom he had gazed at steadfastly, and he thought she grew demure and sad at sight of his blue and brass. As he had walked down the path between the rows of oaks, he had turned his head and detected her at a window watching his departure. As he perceived her, she had immediately begun to stare up through the high tree branches at the sky. He had seen a good deal of flurry and haste in her movement as she changed her attitude. He often thought of it.

On the way to Washington his spirit had soared. The regiment was fed and caressed at station after station until the youth had believed that he must be a hero. There was a lavish expenditure of bread and cold meats, coffee, and pickles and cheese. As he basked in the smiles of the girls and was patted and complimented by the old men, he had felt growing within him the strength to do mighty deeds of arms.

After complicated journeyings with many pauses, there had come months of monotonous life in a camp. He had had the belief that real war was a series of death struggles with small time in between for sleep and meals; but since his regiment had come to the field the army had done little but sit still and try to keep warm.

He was brought then gradually back to his old ideas. Greeklike struggles would be no more. Men were better, or more timid. Secular and religious education had effaced the throat-grappling instinct, or else firm finance held in check the passions.

He had grown to regard himself merely as a part of a vast blue demonstration. His province was to look out, as far as he could, for his personal comfort. For recreation he could twiddle his thumbs and speculate on the thoughts which must agitate the minds of the generals. Also, he was drilled and drilled and reviewed, and drilled and drilled and reviewed.

The only foes he had seen were some pickets along the river bank. They were a sun-tanned, philosophical lot, who sometimes shot reflectively at the blue pickets. When reproached for this afterward, they usually expressed sorrow, and swore by their gods that the guns had exploded without their permission. The youth, on guard duty one night, conversed across the stream with one of them. He was a slightly ragged man, who spat skillfully between his shoes and possessed a great fund of bland and infantile assurance. The youth liked him personally.

"Yank," the other had informed him, "yer a right dum good feller." This sentiment, floating to him upon the still air, had made him temporarily regret war.

Various veterans had told him tales. Some talked of gray, bewhiskered hordes who were advancing with relentless curses and chewing tobacco with unspeakable valor; tremendous bodies of fierce soldiery who were sweeping along like the Huns. Others spoke of tattered and eternally hungry men who fired despondent powders. "They'll charge through hell's fire an' brimstone t' git a holt on a haversack, an' sech stomachs ain't a'lastin' long," he was told. From the stories, the youth imagined the red, live bones sticking out through slits in the faded uniforms.

Still, he could not put a whole faith in veteran's tales, for recruits were their prey. They talked much of smoke, fire, and blood, but he could not tell how much might be lies. They persistently yelled "Fresh fish!" at him, and were in no wise to be trusted.

However, he perceived now that it did not greatly matter what kind of soldiers he was going to fight, so long as they fought, which fact no one disputed. There was a more serious problem. He lay in his bunk pondering upon it. He tried to mathematically prove to himself that he would not run from a battle.

Previously he had never felt obliged to wrestle too seriously with this question. In his life he had taken certain things for granted, never challenging his belief in ultimate success, and bothering little about means and roads. But here he was confronted with a thing of moment. It had suddenly appeared to him that perhaps in a battle he might run. He was forced to admit that as far as war was concerned he knew nothing of himself.

A sufficient time before he would have allowed the problem to kick its heels at the outer portals of his mind, but now he felt compelled to give serious attention to it.

A little panic-fear grew in his mind. As his imagination went forward to a fight, he saw hideous possibilities. He contemplated the lurking menaces of the future, and failed in an effort to see himself standing stoutly in the midst of them. He recalled his visions of broken-bladed glory, but in the shadow of the impending tumult he suspected them to be impossible pictures.

He sprang from the bunk and began to pace nervously to and fro. "Good Lord, what's th' matter with me?" he said aloud.

He felt that in this crisis his laws of life were useless. Whatever he had learned of himself was here of no avail. He was an unknown quantity. He saw that he would again be obliged to experiment as he had in early youth. He must accumulate information of himself, and meanwhile he resolved to remain close upon his guard lest those qualities of which he knew nothing should everlastingly disgrace him. "Good Lord!" he repeated in dismay.

After a time the tall soldier slid dexterously through the hole. The loud private followed. They were wrangling.

"That's all right," said the tall soldier as he entered. He waved his hand expressively. "You can believe me or not, jest as you like. All you got to do is sit down and wait as quiet as you can. Then pretty soon you'll find out I was right."

His comrade grunted stubbornly. For a moment he seemed to be searching for a formidable reply. Finally he said: "Well, you don't know everything in the world, do you?"

"Didn't say I knew everything in the world," retorted the other sharply. He began to stow various articles snugly into his knapsack.

The youth, pausing in his nervous walk, looked down at the busy figure. "Going to be a battle, sure, is there, Jim?" he asked.

"Of course there is," replied the tall soldier. "Of course there is. You jest wait 'til to-morrow, and you'll see one of the biggest battles ever was. You jest wait."

"Thunder!" said the youth.

"Oh, you'll see fighting this time, my boy, what'll be regular out-and-out fighting," added the tall soldier, with the air of a man who is about to exhibit a battle for the benefit of his friends.

"Huh!" said the loud one from a corner.

"Well," remarked the youth, "like as not this story'll turn out jest like them others did."

"Not much it won't," replied the tall soldier, exasperated. "Not much it won't. Didn't the cavalry all start this morning?" He glared about him. No one denied his statement. "The cavalry started this morning," he continued. "They say there ain't hardly any cavalry left in camp. They're going to Richmond, or some place, while we fight all the Johnnies. It's some dodge like that. The regiment's got orders, too. A feller what seen 'em go to headquarters told me a little while ago. And they're raising blazes all over camp--anybody can see that."

"Shucks!" said the loud one.

The youth remained silent for a time. At last he spoke to the tall soldier. "Jim!"

"What?"

"How do you think the reg'ment 'll do?"

"Oh, they'll fight all right, I guess, after they once get into it," said the other with cold judgment. He made a fine use of the third person. "There's been heaps of fun poked at 'em because they're new, of course, and all that; but they'll fight all right, I guess."

"Think any of the boys 'll run?" persisted the youth.

"Oh, there may be a few of 'em run, but there's them kind in every regiment, 'specially when they first goes under fire," said the other in a tolerant way. "Of course it might happen that the hull kit-and-boodle might start and run, if some big fighting came first-off, and then again they might stay and fight like fun. But you can't bet on nothing. Of course they ain't never been under fire yet, and it ain't likely they'll lick the hull rebel army all-to-oncet the first time; but I think they'll fight better than some, if worse than others. That's the way I figger. They call the reg'ment 'Fresh fish' and everything; but the boys come of good stock, and most of 'em 'll fight like sin after they oncet git shootin'," he added, with a mighty emphasis on the last four words.

"Oh, you think you know--" began the loud soldier with scorn.

The other turned savagely upon him. They had a rapid altercation, in which they fastened upon each other various strange epithets.

The youth at last interrupted them. "Did you ever think you might run yourself, Jim?" he asked. On concluding the sentence he laughed as if he had meant to aim a joke. The loud soldier also giggled.

The tall private waved his hand. "Well," said he profoundly, "I've thought it might get too hot for Jim Conklin in some of them scrimmages, and if a whole lot of boys started and run, why, I s'pose I'd start and run. And if I once started to run, I'd run like the devil, and no mistake. But if everybody was a-standing and a-fighting, why, I'd stand and fight. Be jiminey, I would. I'll bet on it."

"Huh!" said the loud one.

The youth of this tale felt gratitude for these words of his comrade. He had feared that all of the untried men possessed great and correct confidence. He now was in a measure reassured.

Chapter 2

The next morning the youth discovered that his tall comrade had been the fast-flying messenger of a mistake. There was much scoffing at the latter by those who had yesterday been firm adherents of his views, and there was even a little sneering by men who had never believed the rumor. The tall one fought with a man from Chatfield Corners and beat him severely.

The youth felt, however, that his problem was in no wise lifted from him. There was, on the contrary, an irritating prolongation. The tale had created in him a great concern for himself. Now, with the newborn question in his mind, he was compelled to sink back into his old place as part of a blue demonstration.

For days he made ceaseless calculations, but they were all wondrously unsatisfactory. He found that he could establish nothing. He finally concluded that the only way to prove himself was to go into the blaze, and then figuratively to watch his legs to discover their merits and faults. He reluctantly admitted that he could not sit still and with a mental slate and pencil derive an answer. To gain it, he must have blaze, blood, and danger, even as a chemist requires this, that, and the other. So he fretted for an opportunity.

Meanwhile, he continually tried to measure himself by his comrades. The tall soldier, for one, gave him some assurance. This man's serene unconcern dealt him a measure of confidence, for he had known him since childhood, and from his intimate knowledge he did not see how he could be capable of anything that was beyond him, the youth. Still, he thought that his comrade might be mistaken about himself. Or, on the other hand, he might be a man heretofore doomed to peace and obscurity, but, in reality, made to shine in war.

The youth would have liked to have discovered another who suspected himself. A sympathetic comparison of mental notes would have been a joy to him.

He occasionally tried to fathom a comrade with seductive sentences. He looked about to find men in the proper mood. All attempts failed to bring forth any statement which looked in any way like a confession to those doubts which he privately acknowledged in himself. He was afraid to make an open declaration of his concern, because he dreaded to place some unscrupulous confidant upon the high plane of the unconfessed from which elevation he could be derided.

In regard to his companions his mind wavered between two opinions, according to his mood. Sometimes he inclined to believing them all heroes. In fact, he usually admired in secret the superior development of the higher qualities in others. He could conceive of men going very insignificantly about the world bearing a load of courage unseen, and although he had known many of his comrades through boyhood, he began to fear that his judgment of them had been blind. Then, in other moments, he flouted these theories, and assured him that his fellows were all privately wondering and quaking.

His emotions made him feel strange in the presence of men who talked excitedly of a prospective battle as of a drama they were about to witness, with nothing but eagerness and curiosity apparent in their faces. It was often that he suspected them to be liars.

He did not pass such thoughts without severe condemnation of himself. He dinned reproaches at times. He was convicted by himself of many shameful crimes against the gods of traditions.

In his great anxiety his heart was continually clamoring at what he considered the intolerable slowness of the generals. They seemed content to perch tranquilly on the river bank, and leave him bowed down by the weight of a great problem. He wanted it settled forthwith. He could not long bear such a load, he said. Sometimes his anger at the commanders reached an acute stage, and he grumbled about the camp like a veteran.

One morning, however, he found himself in the ranks of his prepared regiment. The men were whispering speculations and recounting the old rumors. In the gloom before the break of the day their uniforms glowed a deep purple hue. From across the river the red eyes were still peering. In the eastern sky there was a yellow patch like a rug laid for the feet of the coming sun; and against it, black and patternlike, loomed the gigantic figure of the colonel on a gigantic horse.

From off in the darkness came the trampling of feet. The youth could occasionally see dark shadows that moved like monsters. The regiment stood at rest for what seemed a long time. The youth grew impatient. It was unendurable the way these affairs were managed. He wondered how long they were to be kept waiting.

As he looked all about him and pondered upon the mystic gloom, he began to believe that at any moment the ominous distance might be aflare, and the rolling crashes of an engagement come to his ears. Staring once at the red eyes across the river, he conceived them to be growing larger, as the orbs of a row of dragons advancing. He turned toward the colonel and saw him lift his gigantic arm and calmly stroke his mustache.

At last he heard from along the road at the foot of the hill the clatter of a horse's galloping hoofs. It must be the coming of orders. He bent forward, scarce breathing. The exciting clickety-click, as it grew louder and louder, seemed to be beating upon his soul. Presently a horseman with jangling equipment drew rein before the colonel of the regiment. The two held a short, sharp-worded conversation. The men in the foremost ranks craned their necks.

As the horseman wheeled his animal and galloped away he turned to shout over his shoulder, "Don't forget that box of cigars!" The colonel mumbled in reply. The youth wondered what a box of cigars had to do with war.

A moment later the regiment went swinging off into the darkness. It was now like one of those moving monsters wending with many feet. The air was heavy, and cold with dew. A mass of wet grass, marched upon, rustled like silk.

There was an occasional flash and glimmer of steel from the backs of all these huge crawling reptiles. From the road came creakings and grumblings as some surly guns were dragged away.

The men stumbled along still muttering speculations. There was a subdued debate. Once a man fell down, and as he reached for his rifle a comrade, unseeing, trod upon his hand. He of the injured fingers swore bitterly, and aloud. A low, tittering laugh went among his fellows.

Presently they passed into a roadway and marched forward with easy strides. A dark regiment moved before them, and from behind also came the tinkle of equipments on the bodies of marching men.

The rushing yellow of the developing day went on behind their backs. When the sunrays at last struck full and mellowingly upon the earth, the youth saw that the landscape was streaked with two long, thin, black columns which disappeared on the brow of a hill in front and rearward vanished in a wood. They were like two serpents crawling from the cavern of the night.

The river was not in view. The tall soldier burst into praises of what he thought to be his powers of perception.

Some of the tall one's companions cried with emphasis that they, too, had evolved the same thing, and they congratulated themselves upon it. But there were others who said that the tall one's plan was not the true one at all. They persisted with other theories. There was a vigorous discussion.

The youth took no part in them. As he walked along in careless line he was engaged with his own eternal debate. He could not hinder himself from dwelling upon it. He was despondent and sullen, and threw shifting glances about him. He looked ahead, often expecting to hear from the advance the rattle of firing.

But the long serpents crawled slowly from hill to hill without bluster of smoke. A dun-colored cloud of dust floated away to the right. The sky overhead was of a fairy blue.

The youth studied the faces of his companions, ever on the watch to detect kindred emotions. He suffered disappointment. Some ardor of the air which was causing the veteran commands to move with glee--almost with song--had infected the new regiment. The men began to speak of victory as of a thing they knew. Also, the tall soldier received his vindication. They were certainly going to come around in behind the enemy. They expressed commiseration for that part of the army which had been left upon the river bank, felicitating themselves upon being a part of a blasting host.

The youth, considering himself as separated from the others, was saddened by the blithe and merry speeches that went from rank to rank. The company wags all made their best endeavors. The regiment tramped to the tune of laughter.

The blatant soldier often convulsed whole files by his biting sarcasms aimed at the tall one.

And it was not long before all the men seemed to forget their mission. Whole brigades grinned in unison, and regiments laughed.

A rather fat soldier attempted to pilfer a horse from a dooryard. He planned to load his knapsack upon it. He was escaping with his prize when a young girl rushed from the house and grabbed the animal's mane. There followed a wrangle. The young girl, with pink cheeks and shining eyes, stood like a dauntless statue.

The observant regiment, standing at rest in the roadway, whooped at once, and entered whole-souled upon the side of the maiden. The men became so engrossed in this affair that they entirely ceased to remember their own large war. They jeered the piratical private, and called attention to various defects in his personal appearance; and they were wildly enthusiastic in support of the young girl.

To her, from some distance, came bold advice. "Hit him with a stick."

There were crows and catcalls showered upon him when he retreated without the horse. The regiment rejoiced at his downfall. Loud and vociferous congratulations were showered upon the maiden, who stood panting and regarding the troops with defiance.

At nightfall the column broke into regimental pieces, and the fragments went into the fields to camp. Tents sprang up like strange plants. Camp fires, like red, peculiar blossoms, dotted the night.

The youth kept from intercourse with his companions as much as circumstances would allow him. In the evening he wandered a few paces into the gloom. From this little distance the many fires, with the black forms of men passing to and fro before the crimson rays, made weird and satanic effects.

He lay down in the grass. The blades pressed tenderly against his cheek. The moon had been lighted and was hung in a treetop. The liquid stillness of the night enveloping him made him feel vast pity for himself. There was a caress in the soft winds; and the whole mood of the darkness, he thought, was one of sympathy for himself in his distress.

He wished, without reserve, that he was at home again making the endless rounds from the house to the barn, from the barn to the fields, from the fields to the barn, from the barn to the house. He remembered he had so often cursed the brindle cow and her mates, and had sometimes flung milking stools. But, from his present point of view, there was a halo of happiness about each of their heads, and he would have sacrificed all the brass buttons on the continent to have been enabled to return to them. He told himself that he was not formed for a soldier. And he mused seriously upon the radical differences between himself and those men who were dodging implike around the fires.

As he mused thus he heard the rustle of grass, and, upon turning his head, discovered the loud soldier. He called out, "Oh, Wilson!"

The latter approached and looked down. "Why, hello, Henry; is it you? What are you doing here?"

"Oh, thinking," said the youth.

The other sat down and carefully lighted his pipe. "You're getting blue my boy. You're looking thundering peek-ed. What the dickens is wrong with you?"

"Oh, nothing," said the youth.

The loud soldier launched then into the subject of the anticipated fight. "Oh, we've got 'em now!" As he spoke his boyish face was wreathed in a gleeful smile, and his voice had an exultant ring. "We've got 'em now. At last, by the eternal thunders, we'll lick 'em good!"

"If the truth was known," he added, more soberly, "they've licked us about every clip up to now; but this time--this time--we'll lick 'em good!"

"I thought you was objecting to this march a little while ago," said the youth coldly.

"Oh, it wasn't that," explained the other. "I don't mind marching, if there's going to be fighting at the end of it. What I hate is this getting moved here and moved there, with no good coming of it, as far as I can see, excepting sore feet and damned short rations."

"Well, Jim Conklin says we'll get plenty of fighting this time."

"He's right for once, I guess, though I can't see how it come. This time we're in for a big battle, and we've got the best end of it, certain sure. Gee rod! how we will thump 'em!"

He arose and began to pace to and fro excitedly. The thrill of his enthusiasm made him walk with an elastic step. He was sprightly, vigorous, fiery in his belief in success. He looked into the future with clear proud eye, and he swore with the air of an old soldier.

The youth watched him for a moment in silence. When he finally spoke his voice was as bitter as dregs. "Oh, you're going to do great things, I s'pose!"

The loud soldier blew a thoughtful cloud of smoke from his pipe. "Oh, I don't know," he remarked with dignity; "I don't know. I s'pose I'll do as well as the rest. I'm going to try like thunder." He evidently complimented himself upon the modesty of this statement.

"How do you know you won't run when the time comes?" asked the youth.

"Run?" said the loud one; "run?--of course not!" He laughed.

"Well," continued the youth, "lots of good-a-'nough men have thought they was going to do great things before the fight, but when the time come they skedaddled."

"Oh, that's all true, I s'pose," replied the other; "but I'm not going to skedaddle. The man that bets on my running will lose his money, that's all." He nodded confidently.

"Oh, shucks!" said the youth. "You ain't the bravest man in the world, are you?"

"No, I ain't," exclaimed the loud soldier indignantly; "and I didn't say I was the bravest man in the world, neither. I said I was going to do my share of fighting--that's what I said. And I am, too. Who are you, anyhow? You talk as if you thought you was Napoleon Bonaparte." He glared at the youth for a moment, and then strode away.

The youth called in a savage voice after his comrade: "Well, you needn't git mad about it!" But the other continued on his way and made no reply.

He felt alone in space when his injured comrade had disappeared. His failure to discover any mite of resemblance in their viewpoints made him more miserable than before. No one seemed to be wrestling with such a terrific personal problem. He was a mental outcast.

He went slowly to his tent and stretched himself on a blanket by the side of the snoring tall soldier. In the darkness he saw visions of a thousand-tongued fear that would babble at his back and cause him to flee, while others were going coolly about their country's business. He admitted that he would not be able to cope with this monster. He felt that every nerve in his body would be an ear to hear the voices, while other men would remain stolid and deaf.

And as he sweated with the pain of these thoughts, he could hear low, serene sentences. "I'll bid five." "Make it six." "Seven." "Seven goes."

He stared at the red, shivering reflection of a fire on the white wall of his tent until, exhausted and ill from the monotony of his suffering, he fell asleep.

Chapter 3

When another night came, the columns, changed to purple streaks, filed across two pontoon bridges. A glaring fire wine-tinted the waters of the river. Its rays, shining upon the moving masses of troops, brought forth here and there sudden gleams of silver or gold. Upon the other shore a dark and mysterious range of hills was curved against the sky. The insect voices of the night sang solemnly.

After this crossing the youth assured himself that at any moment they might be suddenly and fearfully assaulted from the caves of the lowering woods. He kept his eyes watchfully upon the darkness.

But his regiment went unmolested to a camping place, and its soldiers slept the brave sleep of wearied men. In the morning they were routed out with early energy, and hustled along a narrow road that led deep into the forest.

It was during this rapid march that the regiment lost many of the marks of a new command.

The men had begun to count the miles upon their fingers, and they grew tired. "Sore feet an' damned short rations, that's all," said the loud soldier. There was perspiration and grumblings. After a time they began to shed their knapsacks. Some tossed them unconcernedly down; others hid them carefully, asserting their plans to return for them at some convenient time. Men extricated themselves from thick shirts. Presently few carried anything but their necessary clothing, blankets, haversacks, canteens, and arms and ammunition. "You can now eat and shoot," said the tall soldier to the youth. "That's all you want to do."

There was sudden change from the ponderous infantry of theory to the light and speedy infantry of practice. The regiment, relieved of a burden, received a new impetus. But there was much loss of valuable knapsacks, and, on the whole, very good shirts.

But the regiment was not yet veteranlike in appearance. Veteran regiments in the army were likely to be very small aggregations of men. Once, when the command had first come to the field, some perambulating veterans, noting the length of their column, had accosted them thus: "Hey, fellers, what brigade is that?" And when the men had replied that they formed a regiment and not a brigade, the older soldiers had laughed, and said, "O Gawd!"

Also, there was too great a similarity in the hats. The hats of a regiment should properly represent the history of headgear for a period of years. And, moreover, there were no letters of faded gold speaking from the colors. They were new and beautiful, and the color bearer habitually oiled the pole.

Presently the army again sat down to think. The odor of the peaceful pines was in the men's nostrils. The sound of monotonous axe blows rang through the forest, and the insects, nodding upon their perches, crooned like old women. The youth returned to his theory of a blue demonstration.

One gray dawn, however, he was kicked in the leg by the tall soldier, and then, before he was entirely awake, he found himself running down a wood road in the midst of men who were panting from the first effects of speed. His canteen banged rythmically upon his thigh, and his haversack bobbed softly. His musket bounced a trifle from his shoulder at each stride and made his cap feel uncertain upon his head.

He could hear the men whisper jerky sentences: "Say--what's all this--about?" "What th' thunder--we--skedaddlin' this way fer?" "Billie--keep off m' feet. Yeh run--like a cow." And the loud soldier's shrill voice could be heard: "What th'devil they in sich a hurry for?"

The youth thought the damp fog of early morning moved from the rush of a great body of troops. From the distance came a sudden spatter of firing.

He was bewildered. As he ran with his comrades he strenuously tried to think, but all he knew was that if he fell down those coming behind would tread upon him. All his faculties seemed to be needed to guide him over and past obstructions. He felt carried along by a mob.

The sun spread disclosing rays, and, one by one, regiments burst into view like armed men just born of the earth. The youth perceived that the time had come. He was about to be measured. For a moment he felt in the face of his great trial like a babe, and the flesh over his heart seemed very thin. He seized time to look about him calculatingly.

But he instantly saw that it would be impossible for him to escape from the regiment. It inclosed him. And there were iron laws of tradition and law on four sides. He was in a moving box.

As he perceived this fact it occurred to him that he had never wished to come to the war. He had not enlisted of his free will. He had been dragged by the merciless government. And now they were taking him out to be slaughtered.

The regiment slid down a bank and wallowed across a little stream. The mournful current moved slowly on, and from the water, shaded black, some white bubble eyes looked at the men.

As they climbed the hill on the farther side artillery began to boom. Here the youth forgot many things as he felt a sudden impulse of curiosity. He scrambled up the bank with a speed that could not be exceeded by a bloodthirsty man.

He expected a battle scene.

There were some little fields girted and squeezed by a forest. Spread over the grass and in among the tree trunks, he could see knots and waving lines of skirmishers who were running hither and thither and firing at the landscape. A dark battle line lay upon a sunstruck clearing that gleamed orange color. A flag fluttered.

Other regiments floundered up the bank. The brigade was formed in line of battle, and after a pause started slowly through the woods in the rear of the receding skirmishers, who were continually melting into the scene to appear again farther on. They were always busy as bees, deeply absorbed in their little combats.

The youth tried to observe everything. He did not use care to avoid trees and branches, and his forgotten feet were constantly knocking against stones or getting entangled in briers. He was aware that these battalions with their commotions were woven red and startling into the gentle fabric of softened greens and browns. It looked to be a wrong place for a battle field.

The skirmishers in advance fascinated him. Their shots into thickets and at distant and prominent trees spoke to him of tragedies--hidden, mysterious, solemn.

Once the line encountered the body of a dead soldier. He lay upon his back staring at the sky. He was dressed in an awkward suit of yellowish brown. The youth could see that the soles of his shoes had been worn to the thinness of writing paper, and from a great rent in one the dead foot projected piteously. And it was as if fate had betrayed the soldier. In death it exposed to his enemies that poverty which in life he had perhaps concealed from his friends.

The ranks opened covertly to avoid the corpse. The invulnerable dead man forced a way for himself. The youth looked keenly at the ashen face. The wind raised the tawny beard. It moved as if a hand were stroking it. He vaguely desired to walk around and around the body and stare; the impulse of the living to try to read in dead eyes the answer to the Question.

During the march the ardor which the youth had acquired when out of view of the field rapidly faded to nothing. His curiosity was quite easily satisfied. If an intense scene had caught him with its wild swing as he came to the top of the bank, he might have gone roaring on. This advance upon Nature was too calm. He had opportunity to reflect. He had time in which to wonder about himself and to attempt to probe his sensations.

Absurd ideas took hold upon him. He thought that he did not relish the landscape. It threatened him. A coldness swept over his back, and it is true that his trousers felt to him that they were no fit for his legs at all.

A house standing placidly in distant fields had to him an ominous look. The shadows of the woods were formidable. He was certain that in this vista there lurked fierce-eyed hosts. The swift thought came to him that the generals did not know what they were about. It was all a trap. Suddenly those close forests would bristle with rifle barrels. Ironlike brigades would appear in the rear. They were all going to be sacrificed. The generals were stupids. The enemy would presently swallow the whole command. He glared about him, expecting to see the stealthy approach of his death.

He thought that he must break from the ranks and harangue his comrades. They must not all be killed like pigs; and he was sure it would come to pass unless they were informed of these dangers. The generals were idiots to send them marching into a regular pen. There was but one pair of eyes in the corps. He would step forth and make a speech. Shrill and passionate words came to his lips.

The line, broken into moving fragments by the ground, went calmly on through fields and woods. The youth looked at the men nearest him, and saw, for the most part, expressions of deep interest, as if they were investigating something that had fascinated them. One or two stepped with overvaliant airs as if they were already plunged into war. Others walked as upon thin ice. The greater part of the untested men appeared quiet and absorbed. They were going to look at war, the red animal--war, the blood-swollen god. And they were deeply engrossed in this march.

As he looked the youth gripped his outcry at his throat. He saw that even if the men were tottering with fear they would laugh at his warning. They would jeer him, and, if practicable, pelt him with missiles. Admitting that he might be wrong, a frenzied declamation of the kind would turn him into a worm.

He assumed, then, the demeanor of one who knows that he is doomed alone to unwritten responsibilities. He lagged, with tragic glances at the sky.

He was surprised presently by the young lieutenant of his company, who began heartily to beat him with a sword, calling out in a loud and insolent voice: "Come, young man, get up into ranks there. No skulking 'll do here." He mended his pace with suitable haste. And he hated the lieutenant, who had no appreciation of fine minds. He was a mere brute.

After a time the brigade was halted in the cathedral light of a forest. The busy skirmishers were still popping. Through the aisles of the wood could be seen the floating smoke from their rifles. Sometimes it went up in little balls, white and compact.

During this halt many men in the regiment began erecting tiny hills in front of them. They used stones sticks, earth, and anything they thought might turn a bullet. Some built comparatively large ones, while others seems content with little ones.

This procedure caused a discussion among the men. Some wished to fight like duelists, believing it to be correct to stand erect and be, from their feet to their foreheads, a mark. They said they scorned the devices of the cautious. But the others scoffed in reply, and pointed to the veterans on the flanks who were digging at the ground like terriers. In a short time there was quite a barricade along the regimental fronts. Directly, however, they were ordered to withdraw from that place.

This astounded the youth. He forgot his stewing over the advance movement. "Well, then, what did they march us out here for?" he demanded of the tall soldier. The latter with calm faith began a heavy explanation, although he had been compelled to leave a little protection of stones and dirt to which he had devoted much care and skill.

When the regiment was aligned in another position each man's regard for his safety caused another line of small intrenchments. They ate their noon meal behind a third one. They were moved from this one also. They were marched from place to place with apparent aimlessness.

The youth had been taught that a man became another thing in battle. He saw his salvation in such a change. Hence this waiting was an ordeal to him. He was in a fever of impatience. He considered that there was denoted a lack of purpose on the part of the generals. He began to complain to the tall soldier. "I can't stand this much longer," he cried. "I don't see what good it does to make us wear out our legs for nothin'." He wished to return to camp, knowing that this affair was a blue demonstration; or else to go into a battle and discover that he had been a fool in his doubts, and was, in truth, a man of traditional courage. The strain of present circumstances he felt to be intolerable.

The philosophical tall soldier measured a sandwich of cracker and pork and swallowed it in a nonchalant manner. "Oh, I suppose we must go reconnoitering around the country jest to keep 'em from getting too close, or to develop 'em, or something."

"Huh!" said the loud soldier.

"Well," cried the youth, still fidgeting, "I'd rather do anything 'most than go tramping 'round the country all day doing no good to nobody and jest tiring ourselves out."

"So would I," said the loud soldier. "It ain't right. I tell you if anybody with any sense was a-runnin' this army it--"

"Oh, shut up!" roared the tall private. "You little fool. You little damn' cuss. You ain't had that there coat and them pants on for six months, and yet you talk as if--"

"Well, I wanta do some fighting anyway," interrupted the other. "I didn't come here to walk. I could 'ave walked to home--'round an' 'round the barn, if I jest wanted to walk."

The tall one, red-faced, swallowed another sandwich as if taking poison in despair.

But gradually, as he chewed, his face became again quiet and contented. He could not rage in fierce argument in the presence of such sandwiches. During his meals he always wore an air of blissful contemplation of the food he had swallowed. His spirit seemed then to be communing with the viands.

He accepted new environment and circumstance with great coolness, eating from his haversack at every opportunity. On the march he went along with the stride of a hunter, objecting to neither gait nor distance. And he had not raised his voice when he had been ordered away from three little protective piles of earth and stone, each of which had been an engineering feat worthy of being made sacred to the name of his grandmother.

In the afternoon, the regiment went out over the same ground it had taken in the morning. The landscape then ceased to threaten the youth. He had been close to it and become familiar with it.

When, however, they began to pass into a new region, his old fears of stupidity and incompetence reassailed him, but this time he doggedly let them babble. He was occupied with his problem, and in his desperation he concluded that the stupidity did not greatly matter.

Once he thought he had concluded that it would be better to get killed directly and end his troubles. Regarding death thus out of the corner of his eye, he conceived it to be nothing but rest, and he was filled with a momentary astonishment that he should have made an extraordinary commotion over the mere matter of getting killed. He would die; he would go to some place where he would be understood. It was useless to expect appreciation of his profound and fine sense from such men as the lieutenant. He must look to the grave for comprehension.

The skirmish fire increased to a long clattering sound. With it was mingled far-away cheering. A battery spoke.

Directly the youth could see the skirmishers running. They were pursued by the sound of musketry fire. After a time the hot, dangerous flashes of the rifles were visible. Smoke clouds went slowly and insolently across the fields like observant phantoms. The din became crescendo, like the roar of an oncoming train.

A brigade ahead of them and on the right went into action with a rending roar. It was as if it had exploded. And thereafter it lay stretched in the distance behind a long gray wall, that one was obliged to look twice at to make sure that it was smoke.

The youth, forgetting his neat plan of getting killed, gazed spell bound. His eyes grew wide and busy with the action of the scene. His mouth was a little ways open.

Of a sudden he felt a heavy and sad hand laid upon his shoulder. Awakening from his trance of observation he turned and beheld the loud soldier.

"It's my first and last battle, old boy," said the latter, with intense gloom. He was quite pale and his girlish lip was trembling.

"Eh?" murmured the youth in great astonishment.

"It's my first and last battle, old boy," continued the loud soldier. "Something tells me--"

"What?"

"I'm a gone coon this first time and--and I w-want you to take these here things--to--my--folks." He ended in a quavering sob of pity for himself. He handed the youth a little packet done up in a yellow envelope.

"Why, what the devil--" began the youth again.

But the other gave him a glance as from the depths of a tomb, and raised his limp hand in a prophetic manner and turned away.

Chapter 4

The brigade was halted in the fringe of a grove. The men crouched among the trees and pointed their restless guns out at the fields. They tried to look beyond the smoke.

Out of this haze they could see running men. Some shouted information and gestured as the hurried.

The men of the new regiment watched and listened eagerly, while their tongues ran on in gossip of the battle. They mouthed rumors that had flown like birds out of the unknown.

"They say Perry has been driven in with big loss."

"Yes, Carrott went t' th' hospital. He said he was sick. That smart lieutenant is commanding 'G' Company. Th' boys say they won't be under Carrott no more if they all have t' desert. They allus knew he was a--"

"Hannises' batt'ry is took."

"It ain't either. I saw Hannises' batt'ry off on th' left not more'n fifteen minutes ago."

"Well--"

"Th' general, he ses he is goin' t' take th' hull command of th' 304th when we go inteh action, an' then he ses we'll do sech fightin' as never another one reg'ment done."

"They say we're catchin' it over on th' left. They say th' enemy driv' our line inteh a devil of a swamp an' took Hannises' batt'ry."

"No sech thing. Hannises' batt'ry was 'long here 'bout a minute ago."

"That young Hasbrouck, he makes a good off'cer. He ain't afraid 'a nothin'."

"I met one of th' 148th Maine boys an' he ses his brigade fit th' hull rebel army fer four hours over on th' turnpike road an' killed about five thousand of 'em. He ses one more sech fight as that an' th' war 'll be over."

"Bill wasn't scared either. No, sir! It wasn't that. Bill ain't a-gittin' scared easy. He was jest mad, that's what he was. When that feller trod on his hand, he up an' sed that he was willin' t' give his hand t' his country, but he be dumbed if he was goin' t' have every dumb bushwhacker in th' kentry walkin' 'round on it. So he went t' th' hospital disregardless of th' fight. Three fingers was crunched. Th' dern doctor wanted t' amputate 'm, an' Bill, he raised a heluva row, I hear. He's a funny feller."

The din in front swelled to a tremendous chorus. The youth and his fellows were frozen to silence. They could see a flag that tossed in the smoke angrily. Near it were the blurred and agitated forms of troops. There came a turbulent stream of men across the fields. A battery changing position at a frantic gallop scattered the stragglers right and left.

A shell screaming like a storm banshee went over the huddled heads of the reserves. It landed in the grove, and exploding redly flung the brown earth. There was a little shower of pine needles.

Bullets began to whistle among the branches and nip at the trees. Twigs and leaves came sailing down. It was as if a thousand axes, wee and invisible, were being wielded. Many of the men were constantly dodging and ducking their heads.

The lieutenant of the youth's company was shot in the hand. He began to swear so wondrously that a nervous laugh went along the regimental line. The officer's profanity sounded conventional. It relieved the tightened senses of the new men. It was as if he had hit his fingers with a tack hammer at home.

He held the wounded member carefully away from his side so that the blood would not drip upon his trousers.

The captain of the company, tucking his sword under his arm, produced a handkerchief and began to bind with it the lieutenant's wound. And they disputed as to how the binding should be done.

The battle flag in the distance jerked about madly. It seemed to be struggling to free itself from an agony. The billowing smoke was filled with horizontal flashes.

Men rushing swiftly emerged from it. They grew in numbers until it was seen that the whole command was fleeing. The flag suddenly sank down as if dying. Its motion as it fell was a gesture of despair.

Wild yells came from behind the walls of smoke. A sketch in gray and red dissolved into a moblike body of men who galloped like wild horses. The veteran regiments on the right and left of the 304th immediately began to jeer. With the passionate song of the bullets and the banshee shrieks of shells were mingled loud catcalls and bits of facetious advice concerning places of safety.

But the new regiment was breathless with horror. "Gawd! Saunders's got crushed!" whispered the man at the youth's elbow. They shrank back and crouched as if compelled to await a flood.

The youth shot a swift glance along the blue ranks of the regiment. The profiles were motionless, carven; and afterward he remembered that the color sergeant was standing with his legs apart, as if he expected to be pushed to the ground.

The following throng went whirling around the flank. Here and there were officers carried along on the stream like exasperated chips. They were striking about them with their swords and with their left fists, punching every head they could reach. They cursed like highwaymen.

A mounted officer displayed the furious anger of a spoiled child. He raged with his head, his arms, and his legs.

Another, the commander of the brigade, was galloping about bawling. His hat was gone and his clothes were awry. He resembled a man who has come from bed to go to a fire. The hoofs of his horse often threatened the heads of the running men, but they scampered with singular fortune. In this rush they were apparently all deaf and blind. They heeded not the largest and longest of the oaths that were thrown at them from all directions.

Frequently over this tumult could be heard the grim jokes of the critical veterans; but the retreating men apparently were not even conscious of the presence of an audience.

The battle reflection that shone for an instant in the faces on the mad current made the youth feel that forceful hands from heaven would not have been able to have held him in place if he could have got intelligent control of his legs.

There was an appalling imprint upon these faces. The struggle in the smoke had pictured an exaggeration of itself on the bleached cheeks and in the eyes wild with one desire.

The sight of this stampede exerted a floodlike force that seemed able to drag sticks and stones and men from the ground. They of the reserves had to hold on. They grew pale and firm, and red and quaking.

The youth achieved one little thought in the midst of this chaos. The composite monster which had caused the other troops to flee had not then appeared. He resolved to get a view of it, and then, he thought he might very likely run better than the best of them.

Chapter 5

There were moments of waiting. The youth thought of the village street at home before the arrival of the circus parade on a day in the spring. He remembered how he had stood, a small, thrillful boy, prepared to follow the dingy lady upon the white horse, or the band in its faded chariot. He saw the yellow road, the lines of expectant people, and the sober houses. He particularly remembered an old fellow who used to sit upon a cracker box in front of the store and feign to despise such exhibitions. A thousand details of color and form surged in his mind. The old fellow upon the cracker box appeared in middle prominence.

Some one cried, "Here they come!"

There was rustling and muttering among the men. They displayed a feverish desire to have every possible cartridge ready to their hands. The boxes were pulled around into various positions, and adjusted with great care. It was as if seven hundred new bonnets were being tried on.

The tall soldier, having prepared his rifle, produced a red handkerchief of some kind. He was engaged in knotting it about his throat with exquisite attention to its position, when the cry was repeated up and down the line in a muffled roar of sound.

"Here they come! Here they come!" Gun locks clicked.

Across the smoke-infested fields came a brown swarm of running men who were giving shrill yells. They came on, stooping and swinging their rifles at all angles. A flag, tilted forward, sped near the front.

As he caught sight of them the youth was momentarily startled by a thought that perhaps his gun was not loaded. He stood trying to rally his faltering intellect so that he might recollect the moment when he had loaded, but he could not.

A hatless general pulled his dripping horse to a stand near the colonel of the 304th. He shook his fist in the other's face. "You've got to hold 'em back!" he shouted, savagely; "you've got to hold 'em back!"

In his agitation the colonel began to stammer. "A-all r-right, General, all right, by Gawd! We-we 'll do our--we-we 'll d-d-do-do our best, General." The general made a passionate gesture and galloped away. The colonel, perchance to relieve his feelings, began to scold like a wet parrot. The youth, turning swiftly to make sure that the rear was unmolested, saw the commander regarding his men in a highly resentful manner, as if he regretted above everything his association with them.

The man at the youth's elbow was mumbling, as if to himself: "Oh, we 're in for it now! oh, we 're in for it now!"

The captain of the company had been pacing excitedly to and fro in the rear. He coaxed in schoolmistress fashion, as to a congregation of boys with primers. His talk was an endless repetition. "Reserve your fire, boys--don't shoot till I tell you--save your fire--wait till they get close up--don't be damned fools--"

Perspiration streamed down the youth's face, which was soiled like that of a weeping urchin. He frequently, with a nervous movement, wiped his eyes with his coat sleeve. His mouth was still a little ways open.

He got the one glance at the foe-swarming field in front of him, and instantly ceased to debate the question of his piece being loaded. Before he was ready to begin--before he had announced to himself that he was about to fight--he threw the obedient well-balanced rifle into position and fired a first wild shot. Directly he was working at his weapon like an automatic affair.

He suddenly lost concern for himself, and forgot to look at a menacing fate. He became not a man but a member. He felt that something of which he was a part--a regiment, an army, a cause, or a country--was in crisis. He was welded into a common personality which was dominated by a single desire. For some moments he could not flee no more than a little finger can commit a revolution from a hand.

If he had thought the regiment was about to be annihilated perhaps he could have amputated himself from it. But its noise gave him assurance. The regiment was like a firework that, once ignited, proceeds superior to circumstances until its blazing vitality fades. It wheezed and banged with a mighty power. He pictured the ground before it as strewn with the discomfited.

There was a consciousness always of the presence of his comrades about him. He felt the subtle battle brotherhood more potent even than the cause for which they were fighting. It was a mysterious fraternity born of the smoke and danger of death.

He was at a task. He was like a carpenter who has made many boxes, making still another box, only there was furious haste in his movements. He, in his thoughts, was careering off in other places, even as the carpenter who as he works whistles and thinks of his friend or his enemy, his home or a saloon. And these jolted dreams were never perfect to him afterward, but remained a mass of blurred shapes.

Presently he began to feel the effects of the war atmosphere--a blistering sweat, a sensation that his eyeballs were about to crack like hot stones. A burning roar filled his ears.

Following this came a red rage. He developed the acute exasperation of a pestered animal, a well-meaning cow worried by dogs. He had a mad feeling against his rifle, which could only be used against one life at a time. He wished to rush forward and strangle with his fingers. He craved a power that would enable him to make a world-sweeping gesture and brush all back. His impotency appeared to him, and made his rage into that of a driven beast.

Buried in the smoke of many rifles his anger was directed not so much against the men whom he knew were rushing toward him as against the swirling battle phantoms which were choking him, stuffing their smoke robes down his parched throat. He fought frantically for respite for his senses, for air, as a babe being smothered attacks the deadly blankets.

There was a blare of heated rage mingled with a certain expression of intentness on all faces. Many of the men were making low-toned noises with their mouths, and these subdued cheers, snarls, imprecations, prayers, made a wild, barbaric song that went as an undercurrent of sound, strange and chantlike with the resounding chords of the war march. The man at the youth's elbow was babbling. In it there was something soft and tender like the monologue of a babe. The tall soldier was swearing in a loud voice. From his lips came a black procession of curious oaths. Of a sudden another broke out in a querulous way like a man who has mislaid his hat. "Well, why don't they support us? Why don't they send supports? Do they think--"

The youth in his battle sleep heard this as one who dozes hears.

There was a singular absence of heroic poses. The men bending and surging in their haste and rage were in every impossible attitude. The steel ramrods clanked and clanged with incessant din as the men pounded them furiously into the hot rifle barrels. The flaps of the cartridge boxes were all unfastened, and bobbed idiotically with each movement. The rifles, once loaded, were jerked to the shoulder and fired without apparent aim into the smoke or at one of the blurred and shifting forms which upon the field before the regiment had been growing larger and larger like puppets under a magician's hand.

The officers, at their intervals, rearward, neglected to stand in picturesque attitudes. They were bobbing to and fro roaring directions and encouragements. The dimensions of their howls were extraordinary. They expended their lungs with prodigal wills. And often they nearly stood upon their heads in their anxiety to observe the enemy on the other side of the tumbling smoke.

The lieutenant of the youth's company had encountered a soldier who had fled screaming at the first volley of his comrades. Behind the lines these two were acting a little isolated scene. The man was blubbering and staring with sheeplike eyes at the lieutenant, who had seized him by the collar and was pommeling him. He drove him back into the ranks with many blows. The soldier went mechanically, dully, with his animal-like eyes upon the officer. Perhaps there was to him a divinity expressed in the voice of the other--stern, hard, with no reflection of fear in it. He tried to reload his gun, but his shaking hands prevented. The lieutenant was obliged to assist him.

The men dropped here and there like bundles. The captain of the youth's company had been killed in an early part of the action. His body lay stretched out in the position of a tired man resting, but upon his face there was an astonished and sorrowful look, as if he thought some friend had done him an ill turn. The babbling man was grazed by a shot that made the blood stream widely down his face. He clapped both hands to his head. "Oh!" he said, and ran. Another grunted suddenly as if he had been struck by a club in the stomach. He sat down and gazed ruefully. In his eyes there was mute, indefinite reproach. Farther up the line a man, standing behind a tree, had had his knee joint splintered by a ball. Immediately he had dropped his rifle and gripped the tree with both arms. And there he remained, clinging desperately and crying for assistance that he might withdraw his hold upon the tree.

At last an exultant yell went along the quivering line. The firing dwindled from an uproar to a last vindictive popping. As the smoke slowly eddied away, the youth saw that the charge had been repulsed. The enemy were scattered into reluctant groups. He saw a man climb to the top of the fence, straddle the rail, and fire a parting shot. The waves had receded, leaving bits of dark "debris" upon the ground.

Some in the regiment began to whoop frenziedly. Many were silent. Apparently they were trying to contemplate themselves.

After the fever had left his veins, the youth thought that at last he was going to suffocate. He became aware of the foul atmosphere in which he had been struggling. He was grimy and dripping like a laborer in a foundry. He grasped his canteen and took a long swallow of the warmed water.

A sentence with variations went up and down the line. "Well, we 've helt 'em back. We 've helt 'em back; derned if we haven't." The men said it blissfully, leering at each other with dirty smiles.

The youth turned to look behind him and off to the right and off to the left. He experienced the joy of a man who at last finds leisure in which to look about him.

Under foot there were a few ghastly forms motionless. They lay twisted in fantastic contortions. Arms were bent and heads were turned in incredible ways. It seemed that the dead men must have fallen from some great height to get into such positions. They looked to be dumped out upon the ground from the sky.

From a position in the rear of the grove a battery was throwing shells over it. The flash of the guns startled the youth at first. He thought they were aimed directly at him. Through the trees he watched the black figures of the gunners as they worked swiftly and intently. Their labor seemed a complicated thing. He wondered how they could remember its formula in the midst of confusion.

The guns squatted in a row like savage chiefs. They argued with abrupt violence. It was a grim pow-wow. Their busy servants ran hither and thither.

A small procession of wounded men were going drearily toward the rear. It was a flow of blood from the torn body of the brigade.

To the right and to the left were the dark lines of other troops. Far in front he thought he could see lighter masses protruding in points from the forest. They were suggestive of unnumbered thousands.

Once he saw a tiny battery go dashing along the line of the horizon. The tiny riders were beating the tiny horses.

From a sloping hill came the sound of cheerings and clashes. Smoke welled slowly through the leaves.

Batteries were speaking with thunderous oratorical effort. Here and there were flags, the red in the stripes dominating. They splashed bits of warm color upon the dark lines of troops.

The youth felt the old thrill at the sight of the emblems. They were like beautiful birds strangely undaunted in a storm.

As he listened to the din from the hillside, to a deep pulsating thunder that came from afar to the left, and to the lesser clamors which came from many directions, it occurred to him that they were fighting, too, over there, and over there, and over there. Heretofore he had supposed that all the battle was directly under his nose.

As he gazed around him the youth felt a flash of astonishment at the blue, pure sky and the sun gleamings on the trees and fields. It was surprising that Nature had gone tranquilly on with her golden process in the midst of so much devilment.

Chapter 6

The youth awakened slowly. He came gradually back to a position from which he could regard himself. For moments he had been scrutinizing his person in a dazed way as if he had never before seen himself. Then he picked up his cap from the ground. He wriggled in his jacket to make a more comfortable fit, and kneeling relaced his shoe. He thoughtfully mopped his reeking features.

So it was all over at last! The supreme trial had been passed. The red, formidable difficulties of war had been vanquished.

He went into an ecstasy of self-satisfaction. He had the most delightful sensations of his life. Standing as if apart from himself, he viewed that last scene. He perceived that the man who had fought thus was magnificent.

He felt that he was a fine fellow. He saw himself even with those ideals which he had considered as far beyond him. He smiled in deep gratification.

Upon his fellows he beamed tenderness and good will. "Gee! ain't it hot, hey?" he said affably to a man who was polishing his streaming face with his coat sleeves.

"You bet!" said the other, grinning sociably. "I never seen sech dumb hotness." He sprawled out luxuriously on the ground. "Gee, yes! An' I hope we don't have no more fightin' till a week from Monday."

There were some handshakings and deep speeches with men whose features were familiar, but with whom the youth now felt the bonds of tied hearts. He helped a cursing comrade to bind up a wound of the shin.

But, of a sudden, cries of amazement broke out along the ranks of the new regiment. "Here they come ag'in! Here they come ag'in!" The man who had sprawled upon the ground started up and said, "Gosh!"

The youth turned quick eyes upon the field. He discerned forms begin to swell in masses out of a distant wood. He again saw the tilted flag speeding forward.

The shells, which had ceased to trouble the regiment for a time, came swirling again, and exploded in the grass or among the leaves of the trees. They looked to be strange war flowers bursting into fierce bloom.

The men groaned. The luster faded from their eyes. Their smudged countenances now expressed a profound dejection. They moved their stiffened bodies slowly, and watched in sullen mood the frantic approach of the enemy. The slaves toiling in the temple of this god began to feel rebellion at his harsh tasks.

They fretted and complained each to each. "Oh, say, this is too much of a good thing! Why can't somebody send us supports?"

"We ain't never goin' to stand this second banging. I didn't come here to fight the hull damn' rebel army."

There was one who raised a doleful cry. "I wish Bill Smithers had trod on my hand, insteader me treddin' on his'n." The sore joints of the regiment creaked as it painfully floundered into position to repulse.

The youth stared. Surely, he thought, this impossible thing was not about to happen. He waited as if he expected the enemy to suddenly stop, apologize, and retire bowing. It was all a mistake.

But the firing began somewhere on the regimental line and ripped along in both directions. The level sheets of flame developed great clouds of smoke that tumbled and tossed in the mild wind near the ground for a moment, and then rolled through the ranks as through a gate. The clouds were tinged an earthlike yellow in the sunrays and in the shadow were a sorry blue. The flag was sometimes eaten and lost in this mass of vapor, but more often it projected, sun-touched, resplendent.

Into the youth's eyes there came a look that one can see in the orbs of a jaded horse. His neck was quivering with nervous weakness and the muscles of his arms felt numb and bloodless. His hands, too, seemed large and awkward as if he was wearing invisible mittens. And there was a great uncertainty about his knee joints.

The words that comrades had uttered previous to the firing began to recur to him. "Oh, say, this is too much of a good thing! What do they take us for--why don't they send supports? I didn't come here to fight the hull damned rebel army."

He began to exaggerate the endurance, the skill, and the valor of those who were coming. Himself reeling from exhaustion, he was astonished beyond measure at such persistency. They must be machines of steel. It was very gloomy struggling against such affairs, wound up perhaps to fight until sundown.

He slowly lifted his rifle and catching a glimpse of the thickspread field he blazed at a cantering cluster. He stopped then and began to peer as best as he could through the smoke. He caught changing views of the ground covered with men who were all running like pursued imps, and yelling.

To the youth it was an onslaught of redoubtable dragons. He became like the man who lost his legs at the approach of the red and green monster. He waited in a sort of a horrified, listening attitude. He seemed to shut his eyes and wait to be gobbled.

A man near him who up to this time had been working feverishly at his rifle suddenly stopped and ran with howls. A lad whose face had borne an expression of exalted courage, the majesty of he who dares give his life, was, at an instant, smitten abject. He blanched like one who has come to the edge of a cliff at midnight and is suddenly made aware. There was a revelation. He, too, threw down his gun and fled. There was no shame in his face. He ran like a rabbit.

Others began to scamper away through the smoke. The youth turned his head, shaken from his trance by this movement as if the regiment was leaving him behind. He saw the few fleeting forms.

He yelled then with fright and swung about. For a moment, in the great clamor, he was like a proverbial chicken. He lost the direction of safety. Destruction threatened him from all points.

Directly he began to speed toward the rear in great leaps. His rifle and cap were gone. His unbuttoned coat bulged in the wind. The flap of his cartridge box bobbed wildly, and his canteen, by its slender cord, swung out behind. On his face was all the horror of those things which he imagined.

The lieutenant sprang forward bawling. The youth saw his features wrathfully red, and saw him make a dab with his sword. His one thought of the incident was that the lieutenant was a peculiar creature to feel interested in such matters upon this occasion.

He ran like a blind man. Two or three times he fell down. Once he knocked his shoulder so heavily against a tree that he went headlong.

Since he had turned his back upon the fight his fears had been wondrously magnified. Death about to thrust him between the shoulder blades was far more dreadful than death about to smite him between the eyes. When he thought of it later, he conceived the impression that it is better to view the appalling than to be merely within hearing. The noises of the battle were like stones; he believed himself liable to be crushed.

As he ran on he mingled with others. He dimly saw men on his right and on his left, and he heard footsteps behind him. He thought that all the regiment was fleeing, pursued by those ominous crashes.

In his flight the sound of these following footsteps gave him his one meager relief. He felt vaguely that death must make a first choice of the men who were nearest; the initial morsels for the dragons would be then those who were following him. So he displayed the zeal of an insane sprinter in his purpose to keep them in the rear. There was a race.

As he, leading, went across a little field, he found himself in a region of shells. They hurtled over his head with long wild screams. As he listened he imagined them to have rows of cruel teeth that grinned at him. Once one lit before him and the livid lightning of the explosion effectually barred the way in his chosen direction. He groveled on the ground and then springing up went careering off through some bushes.

He experienced a thrill of amazement when he came within view of a battery in action. The men there seemed to be in conventional moods, altogether unaware of the impending annihilation. The battery was disputing with a distant antagonist and the gunners were wrapped in admiration of their shooting. They were continually bending in coaxing postures over the guns. They seemed to be patting them on the back and encouraging them with words. The guns, stolid and undaunted, spoke with dogged valor.

The precise gunners were coolly enthusiastic. They lifted their eyes every chance to the smoke-wreathed hillock from whence the hostile battery addressed them. The youth pitied them as he ran. Methodical idiots! Machine-like fools! The refined joy of planting shells in the midst of the other battery's formation would appear a little thing when the infantry came swooping out of the woods.

The face of a youthful rider, who was jerking his frantic horse with an abandon of temper he might display in a placid barnyard, was impressed deeply upon his mind. He knew that he looked upon a man who would presently be dead.

Too, he felt a pity for the guns, standing, six good comrades, in a bold row.

He saw a brigade going to the relief of its pestered fellows. He scrambled upon a wee hill and watched it sweeping finely, keeping formation in difficult places. The blue of the line was crusted with steel color, and the brilliant flags projected. Officers were shouting.

This sight also filled him with wonder. The brigade was hurrying briskly to be gulped into the infernal mouths of the war god. What manner of men were they, anyhow? Ah, it was some wondrous breed! Or else they didn't comprehend--the fools.

A furious order caused commotion in the artillery. An officer on a bounding horse made maniacal motions with his arms. The teams went swinging up from the rear, the guns were whirled about, and the battery scampered away. The cannon with their noses poked slantingly at the ground grunted and grumbled like stout men, brave but with objections to hurry.

The youth went on, moderating his pace since he had left the place of noises.

Later he came upon a general of division seated upon a horse that pricked its ears in an interested way at the battle. There was a great gleaming of yellow and patent leather about the saddle and bridle. The quiet man astride looked mouse-colored upon such a splendid charger.

A jingling staff was galloping hither and thither. Sometimes the general was surrounded by horsemen and at other times he was quite alone. He looked to be much harassed. He had the appearance of a business man whose market is swinging up and down.

The youth went slinking around this spot. He went as near as he dared trying to overhear words. Perhaps the general, unable to comprehend chaos, might call upon him for information. And he could tell him. He knew all concerning it. Of a surety the force was in a fix, and any fool could see that if they did not retreat while they had opportunity--why--

He felt that he would like to thrash the general, or at least approach and tell him in plain words exactly what he thought him to be. It was criminal to stay calmly in one spot and make no effort to stay destruction. He loitered in a fever of eagerness for the division commander to apply to him.

As he warily moved about, he heard the general call out irritably: "Tompkins, go over an' see Taylor, an' tell him not t' be in such an all-fired hurry; tell him t' halt his brigade in th' edge of th' woods; tell him t' detach a reg'ment--say I think th' center 'll break if we don't help it out some; tell him t' hurry up."

A slim youth on a fine chestnut horse caught these swift words from the mouth of his superior. He made his horse bound into a gallop almost from a walk in his haste to go upon his mission. There was a cloud of dust.

A moment later the youth saw the general bounce excitedly in his saddle.

"Yes, by heavens, they have!" The officer leaned forward. His face was aflame with excitement. "Yes, by heavens, they 've held 'im! They 've held 'im!"

He began to blithely roar at his staff: "We 'll wallop 'im now. We 'll wallop 'im now. We 've got 'em sure." He turned suddenly upon an aide: "Here--you--Jones--quick--ride after Tompkins--see Taylor--tell him t' go in--everlastingly--like blazes--anything."

As another officer sped his horse after the first messenger, the general beamed upon the earth like a sun. In his eyes was a desire to chant a paean. He kept repeating, "They 've held 'em, by heavens!"

His excitement made his horse plunge, and he merrily kicked and swore at it. He held a little carnival of joy on horseback.

Chapter 7

The youth cringed as if discovered in a crime. By heavens, they had won after all! The imbecile line had remained and become victors. He could hear cheering.

He lifted himself upon his toes and looked in the direction of the fight. A yellow fog lay wallowing on the treetops. From beneath it came the clatter of musketry. Hoarse cries told of an advance.

He turned away amazed and angry. He felt that he had been wronged.

He had fled, he told himself, because annihilation approached. He had done a good part in saving himself, who was a little piece of the army. He had considered the time, he said, to be one in which it was the duty of every little piece to rescue itself if possible. Later the officers could fit the little pieces together again, and make a battle front. If none of the little pieces were wise enough to save themselves from the flurry of death at such a time, why, then, where would be the army? It was all plain that he had proceeded according to very correct and commendable rules. His actions had been sagacious things. They had been full of strategy. They were the work of a master's legs.

Thoughts of his comrades came to him. The brittle blue line had withstood the blows and won. He grew bitter over it. It seemed that the blind ignorance and stupidity of those little pieces had betrayed him. He had been overturned and crushed by their lack of sense in holding the position, when intelligent deliberation would have convinced them that it was impossible. He, the enlightened man who looks afar in the dark, had fled because of his superior perceptions and knowledge. He felt a great anger against his comrades. He knew it could be proved that they had been fools.

He wondered what they would remark when later he appeared in camp. His mind heard howls of derision. Their density would not enable them to understand his sharper point of view.

He began to pity himself acutely. He was ill used. He was trodden beneath the feet of an iron injustice. He had proceeded with wisdom and from the most righteous motives under heaven's blue only to be frustrated by hateful circumstances.

A dull, animal-like rebellion against his fellows, war in the abstract, and fate grew within him. He shambled along with bowed head, his brain in a tumult of agony and despair. When he looked loweringly up, quivering at each sound, his eyes had the expression of those of a criminal who thinks his guilt little and his punishment great, and knows that he can find no words.

He went from the fields into a thick woods, as if resolved to bury himself. He wished to get out of hearing of the crackling shots which were to him like voices.

The ground was cluttered with vines and bushes, and the trees grew close and spread out like bouquets. He was obliged to force his way with much noise. The creepers, catching against his legs, cried out harshly as their sprays were torn from the barks of trees. The swishing saplings tried to make known his presence to the world. He could not conciliate the forest. As he made his way, it was always calling out protestations. When he separated embraces of trees and vines the disturbed foliages waved their arms and turned their face leaves toward him. He dreaded lest these noisy motions and cries should bring men to look at him. So he went far, seeking dark and intricate places.

After a time the sound of musketry grew faint and the cannon boomed in the distance. The sun, suddenly apparent, blazed among the trees. The insects were making rhythmical noises. They seemed to be grinding their teeth in unison. A woodpecker stuck his impudent head around the side of a tree. A bird flew on lighthearted wing.

Off was the rumble of death. It seemed now that Nature had no ears.

This landscape gave him assurance. A fair field holding life. It was the religion of peace. It would die if its timid eyes were compelled to see blood. He conceived Nature to be a woman with a deep aversion to tragedy.

He threw a pine cone at a jovial squirrel, and he ran with chattering fear. High in a treetop he stopped, and, poking his head cautiously from behind a branch, looked down with an air of trepidation.

The youth felt triumphant at this exhibition. There was the law, he said. Nature had given him a sign. The squirrel, immediately upon recognizing danger, had taken to his legs without ado. He did not stand stolidly baring his furry belly to the missile, and die with an upward glance at the sympathetic heavens. On the contrary, he had fled as fast as his legs could carry him; and he was but an ordinary squirrel, too--doubtless no philosopher of his race. The youth wended, feeling that Nature was of his mind. She re-enforced his argument with proofs that lived where the sun shone.

Once he found himself almost into a swamp. He was obliged to walk upon bog tufts and watch his feet to keep from the oily mire. Pausing at one time to look about him he saw, out at some black water, a small animal pounce in and emerge directly with a gleaming fish.

The youth went again into the deep thickets. The brushed branches made a noise that drowned the sounds of cannon. He walked on, going from obscurity into promises of a greater obscurity.

At length he reached a place where the high, arching boughs made a chapel. He softly pushed the green doors aside and entered. Pine needles were a gentle brown carpet. There was a religious half light.

Near the threshold he stopped, horror-stricken at the sight of a thing.

He was being looked at by a dead man who was seated with his back against a columnlike tree. The corpse was dressed in a uniform that had once been blue, but was now faded to a melancholy shade of green. The eyes, staring at the youth, had changed to the dull hue to be seen on the side of a dead fish. The mouth was open. Its red had changed to an appalling yellow. Over the gray skin of the face ran little ants. One was trundling some sort of bundle along the upper lip.

The youth gave a shriek as he confronted the thing. He was for moments turned to stone before it. He remained staring into the liquid-looking eyes. The dead man and the living man exchanged a long look. Then the youth cautiously put one hand behind him and brought it against a tree. Leaning upon this he retreated, step by step, with his face still toward the thing. He feared that if he turned his back the body might spring up and stealthily pursue him.

The branches, pushing against him, threatened to throw him over upon it. His unguided feet, too, caught aggravatingly in brambles; and with it all he received a subtle suggestion to touch the corpse. As he thought of his hand upon it he shuddered profoundly.

At last he burst the bonds which had fastened him to the spot and fled, unheeding the underbrush. He was pursued by the sight of black ants swarming greedily upon the gray face and venturing horribly near to the eyes.

After a time he paused, and, breathless and panting, listened. He imagined some strange voice would come from the dead throat and squawk after him in horrible menaces.

The trees about the portal of the chapel moved soughingly in a soft wind. A sad silence was upon the little guarding edifice.

Chapter 8

The trees began softly to sing a hymn of twilight. The sun sank until slanted bronze rays struck the forest. There was a lull in the noises of insects as if they had bowed their beaks and were making a devotional pause. There was silence save for the chanted chorus of the trees.

Then, upon this stillness, there suddenly broke a tremendous clangor of sounds. A crimson roar came from the distance.

The youth stopped. He was transfixed by this terrific medley of all noises. It was as if worlds were being rended. There was the ripping sound of musketry and the breaking crash of the artillery.

His mind flew in all directions. He conceived the two armies to be at each other panther fashion. He listened for a time. Then he began to run in the direction of the battle. He saw that it was an ironical thing for him to be running thus toward that which he had been at such pains to avoid. But he said, in substance, to himself that if the earth and the moon were about to clash, many persons would doubtless plan to get upon the roofs to witness the collision.

As he ran, he became aware that the forest had stopped its music, as if at last becoming capable of hearing the foreign sounds. The trees hushed and stood motionless. Everything seemed to be listening to the crackle and clatter and earthshaking thunder. The chorus peaked over the still earth.

It suddenly occurred to the youth that the fight in which he had been was, after all, but perfunctory popping. In the hearing of this present din he was doubtful if he had seen real battle scenes. This uproar explained a celestial battle; it was tumbling hordes a-struggle in the air.

Reflecting, he saw a sort of a humor in the point of view of himself and his fellows during the late encounter. They had taken themselves and the enemy very seriously and had imagined that they were deciding the war. Individuals must have supposed that they were cutting the letters of their names deep into everlasting tablets of brass, or enshrining their reputations forever in the hearts of their countrymen, while, as to fact, the affair would appear in printed reports under a meek and immaterial title. But he saw that it was good, else, he said, in battle every one would surely run save forlorn hopes and their ilk.

He went rapidly on. He wished to come to the edge of the forest that he might peer out.

As he hastened, there passed through his mind pictures of stupendous conflicts. His accumulated thought upon such subjects was used to form scenes. The noise was as the voice of an eloquent being, describing.

Sometimes the brambles formed chains and tried to hold him back. Trees, confronting him, stretched out their arms and forbade him to pass. After its previous hostility this new resistance of the forest filled him with a fine bitterness. It seemed that Nature could not be quite ready to kill him.

But he obstinately took roundabout ways, and presently he was where he could see long gray walls of vapor where lay battle lines. The voices of cannon shook him. The musketry sounded in long irregular surges that played havoc with his ears. He stood regardant for a moment. His eyes had an awestruck expression. He gawked in the direction of the fight.

Presently he proceeded again on his forward way. The battle was like the grinding of an immense and terrible machine to him. Its complexities and powers, its grim processes, fascinated him. He must go close and see it produce corpses.

He came to a fence and clambered over it. On the far side, the ground was littered with clothes and guns. A newspaper, folded up, lay in the dirt. A dead soldier was stretched with his face hidden in his arm. Farther off there was a group of four or five corpses keeping mournful company. A hot sun had blazed upon this spot.

In this place the youth felt that he was an invader. This forgotten part of the battle ground was owned by the dead men, and he hurried, in the vague apprehension that one of the swollen forms would rise and tell him to begone.

He came finally to a road from which he could see in the distance dark and agitated bodies of troops, smoke-fringed. In the lane was a blood-stained crowd streaming to the rear. The wounded men were cursing, groaning, and wailing. In the air, always, was a mighty swell of sound that it seemed could sway the earth. With the courageous words of the artillery and the spiteful sentences of the musketry mingled red cheers. And from this region of noises came the steady current of the maimed.

One of the wounded men had a shoeful of blood. He hopped like a schoolboy in a game. He was laughing hysterically.

One was swearing that he had been shot in the arm through the commanding general's mismanagement of the army. One was marching with an air imitative of some sublime drum major. Upon his features was an unholy mixture of merriment and agony. As he marched he sang a bit of doggerel in a high and quavering voice:

"Sing a song 'a vic'try,

A pocketful 'a bullets,

Five an' twenty dead men

Baked in a--pie."

Parts of the procession limped and staggered to this tune.

Another had the gray seal of death already upon his face. His lips were curled in hard lines and his teeth were clinched. His hands were bloody from where he had pressed them upon his wound. He seemed to be awaiting the moment when he should pitch headlong. He stalked like the specter of a soldier, his eyes burning with the power of a stare into the unknown.

There were some who proceeded sullenly, full of anger at their wounds, and ready to turn upon anything as an obscure cause.

An officer was carried along by two privates. He was peevish. "Don't joggle so, Johnson, yeh fool," he cried. "Think m' leg is made of iron? If yeh can't carry me decent, put me down an' let some one else do it."

He bellowed at the tottering crowd who blocked the quick march of his bearers. "Say, make way there, can't yeh? Make way, dickens take it all."

They sulkily parted and went to the roadsides. As he was carried past they made pert remarks to him. When he raged in reply and threatened them, they told him to be damned.

The shoulder of one of the tramping bearers knocked heavily against the spectral soldier who was staring into the unknown.

The youth joined this crowd and marched along with it. The torn bodies expressed the awful machinery in which the men had been entangled.

Orderlies and couriers occasionally broke through the throng in the roadway, scattering wounded men right and left, galloping on followed by howls. The melancholy march was continually disturbed by the messengers, and sometimes by bustling batteries that came swinging and thumping down upon them, the officers shouting orders to clear the way.

There was a tattered man, fouled with dust, blood and powder stain from hair to shoes, who trudged quietly at the youth's side. He was listening with eagerness and much humility to the lurid descriptions of a bearded sergeant. His lean features wore an expression of awe and admiration. He was like a listener in a country store to wondrous tales told among the sugar barrels. He eyed the story-teller with unspeakable wonder. His mouth was agape in yokel fashion.

The sergeant, taking note of this, gave pause to his elaborate history while he administered a sardonic comment. "Be keerful, honey, you 'll be a-ketchin' flies," he said.

The tattered man shrank back abashed.

After a time he began to sidle near to the youth, and in a diffident way try to make him a friend. His voice was gentle as a girl's voice and his eyes were pleading. The youth saw with surprise that the soldier had two wounds, one in the head, bound with a blood-soaked rag, and the other in the arm, making that member dangle like a broken bough.

After they had walked together for some time the tattered man mustered sufficient courage to speak. "Was pretty good fight, wa'n't it?" he timidly said. The youth, deep in thought, glanced up at the bloody and grim figure with its lamblike eyes. "What?"

"Was pretty good fight, wa'n't it?"

"Yes," said the youth shortly. He quickened his pace.

But the other hobbled industriously after him. There was an air of apology in his manner, but he evidently thought that he needed only to talk for a time, and the youth would perceive that he was a good fellow.

"Was pretty good fight, wa'n't it?" he began in a small voice, and the he achieved the fortitude to continue. "Dern me if I ever see fellers fight so. Laws, how they did fight! I knowed th' boys 'd like it when they onct got square at it. Th' boys ain't had no fair chanct up t' now, but this time they showed what they was. I knowed it 'd turn out this way. Yeh can't lick them boys. No, sir! They 're fighters, they be."

He breathed a deep breath of humble admiration. He had looked at the youth for encouragement several times. He received none, but gradually he seemed to get absorbed in his subject.

"I was talkin' 'cross pickets with a boy from Georgie, onct, an' that boy, he ses, 'Your fellers 'll all run like hell when they onct hearn a gun,' he ses. 'Mebbe they will,' I ses, 'but I don't b'lieve none of it,' I ses; 'an' b'jiminey,' I ses back t' 'um, 'mebbe your fellers 'll all run like hell when they onct hearn a gun,' I ses. He larfed. Well, they didn't run t' day, did they, hey? No, sir! They fit, an' fit, an' fit."

His homely face was suffused with a light of love for the army which was to him all things beautiful and powerful.

After a time he turned to the youth. "Where yeh hit, ol' boy?" he asked in a brotherly tone.

The youth felt instant panic at this question, although at first its full import was not borne in upon him.

“What?” he asked.

“Where yeh hit?” repeated the tattered man.

“Why,” began the youth, “I--I--that is--why--I--”

He turned away suddenly and slid through the crowd. His brow was heavily flushed, and his fingers were picking nervously at one of his buttons. He bent his head and fastened his eyes studiously upon the button as if it were a little problem.

The tattered man looked after him in astonishment.

Chapter 9

The youth fell back in the procession until the tattered soldier was not in sight. Then he started to walk on with the others.

But he was amid wounds. The mob of men was bleeding. Because of the tattered soldier's question he now felt that his shame could be viewed. He was continually casting sidelong glances to see if the men were contemplating the letters of guilt he felt burned into his brow.

At times he regarded the wounded soldiers in an envious way. He conceived persons with torn bodies to be peculiarly happy. He wished that he, too, had a wound, a red badge of courage.

The spectral soldier was at his side like a stalking reproach. The man's eyes were still fixed in a stare into the unknown. His gray, appalling face had attracted attention in the crowd, and men, slowing to his dreary pace, were walking with him. They were discussing his plight, questioning him and giving him advice. In a dogged way he repelled them, signing to them to go on and leave him alone. The shadows of his face were deepening and his tight lips seemed holding in check the moan of great despair. There could be seen a certain stiffness in the movements of his body, as if he were taking infinite care not to arouse the passion of his wounds. As he went on, he seemed always looking for a place, like one who goes to choose a grave.

Something in the gesture of the man as he waved the bloody and pitying soldiers away made the youth start as if bitten. He yelled in horror. Tottering forward he laid a quivering hand upon the man's arm. As the latter slowly turned his waxlike features toward him the youth screamed:

"Gawd! Jim Conklin!"

The tall soldier made a little commonplace smile. "Hello, Henry," he said.

The youth swayed on his legs and glared strangely. He stuttered and stammered. "Oh, Jim--oh, Jim--oh, Jim--"

The tall soldier held out his gory hand. There was a curious red and black combination of new blood and old blood upon it. "Where yeh been, Henry?" he asked. He continued in a monotonous voice, "I thought mebbe yeh got keeled over. There 's been thunder t' pay t'-day. I was worryin' about it a good deal."

The youth still lamented. "Oh, Jim--oh, Jim--oh, Jim--"

"Yeh know," said the tall soldier, "I was out there." He made a careful gesture. "An', Lord, what a circus! An', b'jiminey, I got shot--I got shot. Yes, b'jiminey, I got shot." He reiterated this fact in a bewildered way, as if he did not know how it came about.

The youth put forth anxious arms to assist him, but the tall soldier went firmly as if propelled. Since the youth's arrival as a guardian for his friend, the other wounded men had ceased to display much interest. They occupied themselves again in dragging their own tragedies toward the rear.

Suddenly, as the two friends marched on, the tall soldier seemed to be overcome by a tremor. His face turned to a semblance of gray paste. He clutched the youth's arm and looked all about him, as if dreading to be overheard. Then he began to speak in a shaking whisper:

"I tell yeh what I'm 'fraid of, Henry--I'll tell yeh what I'm 'fraid of. I 'm 'fraid I 'll fall down--an' them yeh know--them damned artillery wagons--they like as not 'll run over me. That 's what I 'm 'fraid of--"

The youth cried out to him hysterically: "I 'll take care of yeh, Jim! I 'll take care of yeh! I swear t' Gawd I will!"

"Sure--will yeh, Henry?" the tall soldier beseeched.

"Yes--yes--I tell yeh--I'll take care of yeh, Jim!" protested the youth. He could not speak accurately because of the gulpings in his throat.

But the tall soldier continued to beg in a lowly way. He now hung babelike to the youth's arm. His eyes rolled in the wildness of his terror. "I was allus a good friend t' yeh, wa'n't I, Henry? I 've allus been a pretty good feller, ain't I? An' it ain't much t' ask, is it? Jest t' pull me along outer th' road? I'd do it fer you, wouldn't I, Henry?"

He paused in piteous anxiety to await his friend's reply.

The youth had reached an anguish where the sobs scorched him. He strove to express his loyalty, but he could only make fantastic gestures.

However, the tall soldier seemed suddenly to forget all those fears. He became again the grim, stalking specter of a soldier. He went stonily forward. The youth wished his friend to lean upon him, but the other always shook his head and strangely protested. "No--no--no--leave me be--leave me be--"

His look was fixed again upon the unknown. He moved with mysterious purpose, and all of the youth's offers he brushed aside. "No--no--leave me be--leave me be--"

The youth had to follow.

Presently the latter heard a voice talking softly near his shoulder. Turning he saw that it belonged to the tattered soldier. "Ye'd better take 'im outa th' road, pardner. There's a batt'ry comin' helitywhoop down th' road an' he 'll git runned over. He 's a goner anyhow in about five minutes--yeh kin see that. Ye 'd better take 'im outa th' road. Where th' blazes does hi git his stren'th from?"

"Lord knows!" cried the youth. He was shaking his hands helplessly.

He ran forward presently and grasped the tall soldier by the arm. "Jim! Jim!" he coaxed, "come with me."

The tall soldier weakly tried to wrench himself free. "Huh," he said vacantly. He stared at the youth for a moment. At last he spoke as if dimly comprehending. "Oh! Inteh th' fields? Oh!"

He started blindly through the grass.

The youth turned once to look at the lashing riders and jouncing guns of the battery. He was startled from this view by a shrill outcry from the tattered man.

"Gawd! He's runnin'!"

Turning his head swiftly, the youth saw his friend running in a staggering and stumbling way toward a little clump of bushes. His heart seemed to wrench itself almost free from his body at this sight. He made a noise of pain. He and the tattered man began a pursuit. There was a singular race.

When he overtook the tall soldier he began to plead with all the words he could find. "Jim--Jim--what are you doing--what makes you do this way--you'll hurt yerself."

The same purpose was in the tall soldier's face. He protested in a dulled way, keeping his eyes fastened on the mystic place of his intentions. "No--no--don't tech me--leave me be--leave me be--"

The youth, aghast and filled with wonder at the tall soldier, began quaveringly to question him. "Where yeh goin', Jim? What you thinking about? Where you going? Tell me, won't you, Jim?"

The tall soldier faced about as upon relentless pursuers. In his eyes there was a great appeal. "Leave me be, can't yeh? Leave me be for a minnit."

The youth recoiled. "Why, Jim," he said, in a dazed way, "what 's the matter with you?"

The tall soldier turned and, lurching dangerously, went on. The youth and the tattered soldier followed, sneaking as if whipped, feeling unable to face the stricken man if he should again confront them. They began to have thoughts of a solemn ceremony. There was something rite-like in these movements of the doomed soldier. And there was a resemblance in him to a devotee of a mad religion, blood-sucking, muscle-wrenching, bone-crushing. They were awed and afraid. They hung back lest he have at command a dreadful weapon.

At last, they saw him stop and stand motionless. Hastening up, they perceived that his face wore an expression telling that he had at last found the place for which he had struggled. His spare figure was erect; his bloody hands were quietly at his side. He was waiting with patience for something that he had come to meet. He was at the rendezvous. They paused and stood, expectant.

There was a silence.

Finally, the chest of the doomed soldier began to heave with a strained motion. It increased in violence until it was as if an animal was within and was kicking and tumbling furiously to be free.

This spectacle of gradual strangulation made the youth writhe, and once as his friend rolled his eyes, he saw something in them that made him sink wailing to the ground. He raised his voice in a last supreme call.

"Jim--Jim--Jim--"

The tall soldier opened his lips and spoke. He made a gesture. "Leave me be--don't tech me--leave me be--"

There was another silence while he waited.

Suddenly his form stiffened and straightened. Then it was shaken by a prolonged ague. He stared into space. To the two watchers there was a curious and profound dignity in the firm lines of his awful face.

He was invaded by a creeping strangeness that slowly enveloped him. For a moment the tremor of his legs caused him to dance a sort of hideous hornpipe. His arms beat wildly about his head in expression of implike enthusiasm.

His tall figure stretched itself to its full height. There was a slight rending sound. Then it began to swing forward, slow and straight, in the manner of a falling tree. A swift muscular contortion made the left shoulder strike the ground first.

The body seemed to bounce a little way from the earth. "God!" said the tattered soldier.

The youth had watched, spellbound, this ceremony at the place of meeting. His face had been twisted into an expression of every agony he had imagined for his friend.

He now sprang to his feet and, going closer, gazed upon the pastelike face. The mouth was open and the teeth showed in a laugh.

As the flap of the blue jacket fell away from the body, he could see that the side looked as if it had been chewed by wolves.

The youth turned, with sudden, livid rage, toward the battlefield. He shook his fist. He seemed about to deliver a philippic.

"Hell--"

The red sun was pasted in the sky like a wafer.

Chapter 10

The tattered man stood musing.

"Well, he was a reg'lar jim-dandy fer nerve, wa'n't he," said he finally in a little awestruck voice. "A reg'lar jim-dandy." He thoughtfully poked one of the docile hands with his foot. "I wonner where he got 'is stren'th from? I never seen a man do like that before. It was a funny thing. Well, he was a reg'lar jim-dandy."

The youth desired to screech out his grief. He was stabbed, but his tongue lay dead in the tomb of his mouth. He threw himself again upon the ground and began to brood.

The tattered man stood musing.

"Look-a-here, pardner," he said, after a time. He regarded the corpse as he spoke. "He 's up an' gone, ain't 'e, an' we might as well begin t' look out fer ol' number one. This here thing is all over. He 's up an' gone, ain't 'e? An' he 's all right here. Nobody won't bother 'im. An' I must say I ain't enjoying any great health m'self these days."

The youth, awakened by the tattered soldier's tone, looked quickly up. He saw that he was swinging uncertainly on his legs and that his face had turned to a shade of blue.

"Good Lord!" he cried, "you ain't goin' t'--not you, too."

The tattered man waved his hand. "Nary die," he said. "All I want is some pea soup an' a good bed. Some pea soup," he repeated dreamfully.

The youth arose from the ground. "I wonder where he came from. I left him over there." He pointed. "And now I find 'im here. And he was coming from over there, too." He indicated a new direction. They both turned toward the body as if to ask of it a question.

"Well," at length spoke the tattered man, "there ain't no use in our stayin' here an' tryin' t' ask him anything."

The youth nodded an assent wearily. They both turned to gaze for a moment at the corpse.

The youth murmured something.

"Well, he was a jim-dandy, wa'n't 'e?" said the tattered man as if in response.

They turned their backs upon it and started away. For a time they stole softly, treading with their toes. It remained laughing there in the grass.

"I'm commencin' t' feel pretty bad," said the tattered man, suddenly breaking one of his little silences. "I'm commencin' t' feel pretty damn' bad."

The youth groaned. "Oh Lord!" He wondered if he was to be the tortured witness of another grim encounter.

But his companion waved his hand reassuringly. "Oh, I'm not goin' t' die yit! There too much dependin' on me fer me t' die yit. No, sir! Nary die! I CAN'T! Ye'd oughta see th' swad a' chil'ren I've got, an' all like that."

The youth glancing at his companion could see by the shadow of a smile that he was making some kind of fun.

As they plodded on the tattered soldier continued to talk. "Besides, if I died, I wouldn't die th' way that feller did. That was th' funniest thing. I'd jest flop down, I would. I never seen a feller die th' way that feller did.

"Yeh know Tom Jamison, he lives next door t' me up home. He's a nice feller, he is, an' we was allus good friends. Smart, too. Smart as a steel trap. Well, when we was a-fightin' this atternoon, all-of-a-sudden he begin t' rip up an' cuss an' beller at me. 'Yer shot, yeh blamed infernal!'--he swear horrible--he ses t' me. I put up m' hand t' m' head an' when I looked at m' fingers, I seen, sure 'nough, I was shot. I give a holler an' begin t' run, but b'fore I could git away another one hit me in th' arm an' whirl' me clean 'round. I got skeared when they was all a-shootin' b'hind me an' I run t' beat all, but I cotch it pretty bad. I've an idee I'd a been fightin' yit, if t'was n't fer Tom Jamison."

Then he made a calm announcement: "There's two of 'em--little ones--but they 're beginnin' t' have fun with me now. I don't b'lieve I kin walk much furder."

They went slowly on in silence. "Yeh look pretty peek'ed yerself," said the tattered man at last. "I bet yeh 've got a worser one than yeh think. Ye'd better take keer of yer hurt. It don't do t' let sech things go. It might be inside mostly, an' them plays thunder. Where is it located?" But he continued his harangue without waiting for a reply. "I see a feller git hit plum in th' head when my reg'ment was a-standin' at ease onct. An' everybody yelled to 'im: 'Hurt, John? Are yeh hurt much?' 'No,' ses he. He looked kinder surprised, an' he went on tellin' 'em how he felt. He sed he didn't feel nothin'. But, by dad, th' first thing that feller knowed he was dead. Yes, he was dead--stone dead. So, yeh wanta watch out. Yeh might have some queer kind 'a hurt yerself. Yeh can't never tell. Where is your'n located?"

The youth had been wriggling since the introduction of this topic. He now gave a cry of exasperation and made a furious motion with his hand. "Oh, don't bother me!" he said. He was enraged against the tattered man, and could have strangled him. His companions seemed ever to play intolerable parts. They were ever upraising the ghost of shame on the stick of their curiosity. He turned toward the tattered man as one at bay. "Now, don't bother me," he repeated with desperate menace.

"Well, Lord knows I don't wanta bother anybody," said the other. There was a little accent of despair in his voice as he replied, "Lord knows I 've gota 'nough m' own t' tend to."

The youth, who had been holding a bitter debate with himself and casting glances of hatred and contempt at the tattered man, here spoke in a hard voice. "Good-by," he said.

The tattered man looked at him in gaping amazement. "Why--why, pardner, where yeh goin'?" he asked unsteadily. The youth looking at him, could see that he, too, like that other one, was beginning to act dumb and animal-like. His thoughts seemed to be floundering about in his head. "Now--now--look--a--here, you Tom Jamison--now--I won't have this--this here won't do. Where--where yeh goin'?"

The youth pointed vaguely. "Over there," he replied.

"Well, now look--a--here--now," said the tattered man, rambling on in idiot fashion. His head was hanging forward and his words were slurred. "This thing won't do, now, Tom Jamison. It won't do. I know yeh, yeh pig-headed devil. Yeh wanta go trompin' off with a bad hurt. It ain't right--now--Tom Jamison--it ain't. Yeh wanta leave me take keer of yeh, Tom Jamison. It ain't--right--it ain't--fer yeh t' go--trompin' off--with a bad hurt--it ain't--ain't--ain't right--it ain't."

In reply the youth climbed a fence and started away. He could hear the tattered man bleating plaintively.

Once he faced about angrily. "What?"

"Look--a--here, now, Tom Jamison--now--it ain't--"

The youth went on. Turning at a distance he saw the tattered man wandering about helplessly in the field.

He now thought that he wished he was dead. He believed he envied those men whose bodies lay strewn over the grass of the fields and on the fallen leaves of the forest.

The simple questions of the tattered man had been knife thrusts to him. They asserted a society that probes pitilessly at secrets until all is apparent. His late companion's chance persistency made him feel that he could not keep his crime concealed in his bosom. It was sure to be brought plain by one of those arrows which cloud the air and are constantly pricking, discovering, proclaiming those things which are willed to be forever hidden. He admitted that he could not defend himself against this agency. It was not within the power of vigilance.

Chapter 11

He became aware that the furnace roar of the battle was growing louder. Great blown clouds had floated to the still heights of air before him. The noise, too, was approaching. The woods filtered men and the fields became dotted.

As he rounded a hillock, he perceived that the roadway was now a crying mass of wagons, teams, and men. From the heaving tangle issued exhortations, commands, imprecations. Fear was sweeping it all along. The cracking whips bit and horses plunged and tugged. The white-topped wagons strained and stumbled in their exertions like fat sheep.

The youth felt comforted in a measure by this sight. They were all retreating. Perhaps, then, he was not so bad after all. He seated himself and watched the terror-stricken wagons. They fled like soft, ungainly animals. All the roarers and lashers served to help him to magnify the dangers and horrors of the engagement that he might try to prove to himself that the thing with which men could charge him was in truth a symmetrical act. There was an amount of pleasure to him in watching the wild march of this vindication.

Presently the calm head of a forward-going column of infantry appeared in the road. It came swiftly on. Avoiding the obstructions gave it the sinuous movement of a serpent. The men at the head butted mules with their musket stocks. They prodded teamsters indifferent to all howls. The men forced their way through parts of the dense mass by strength. The blunt head of the column pushed. The raving teamsters swore many strange oaths.

The commands to make way had the ring of a great importance in them. The men were going forward to the heart of the din. They were to confront the eager rush of the enemy. They felt the pride of their onward movement when the remainder of the army seemed trying to dribble down this road. They tumbled teams about with a fine feeling that it was no matter so long as their column got to the front in time. This importance made their faces grave and stern. And the backs of the officers were very rigid.

As the youth looked at them the black weight of his woe returned to him. He felt that he was regarding a procession of chosen beings. The separation was as great to him as if they had marched with weapons of flame and banners of sunlight. He could never be like them. He could have wept in his longings.

He searched about in his mind for an adequate malediction for the indefinite cause, the thing upon which men turn the words of final blame. It--whatever it was--was responsible for him, he said. There lay the fault.

The haste of the column to reach the battle seemed to the forlorn young man to be something much finer than stout fighting. Heroes, he thought, could find excuses in that long seething lane. They could retire with perfect self-respect and make excuses to the stars.

He wondered what those men had eaten that they could be in such haste to force their way to grim chances of death. As he watched his envy grew until he thought that he wished to change lives with one of them. He would have liked to have used a tremendous force, he said, throw off himself and become a better. Swift pictures of himself, apart, yet in himself, came to him--a blue desperate figure leading lurid charges with one knee forward and a broken blade high--a blue, determined figure standing before a crimson and steel assault, getting calmly killed on a high place before the eyes of all. He thought of the magnificent pathos of his dead body.

These thoughts uplifted him. He felt the quiver of war desire. In his ears, he heard the ring of victory. He knew the frenzy of a rapid successful charge. The music of the trampling feet, the sharp voices, the clanking arms of the column near him made him soar on the red wings of war. For a few moments he was sublime.

He thought that he was about to start for the front. Indeed, he saw a picture of himself, dust-stained, haggard, panting, flying to the front at the proper moment to seize and throttle the dark, leering witch of calamity.

Then the difficulties of the thing began to drag at him. He hesitated, balancing awkwardly on one foot.

He had no rifle; he could not fight with his hands, said he resentfully to his plan. Well, rifles could be had for the picking. They were extraordinarily profuse.

Also, he continued, it would be a miracle if he found his regiment. Well, he could fight with any regiment.

He started forward slowly. He stepped as if he expected to tread upon some explosive thing. Doubts and he were struggling.

He would truly be a worm if any of his comrades should see him returning thus, the marks of his flight upon him. There was a reply that the intent fighters did not care for what happened rearward saving that no hostile bayonets appeared there. In the battle-blur his face would, in a way, be hidden, like the face of a cowled man.

But then he said that his tireless fate would bring forth, when the strife lulled for a moment, a man to ask of him an explanation. In imagination he felt the scrutiny of his companions as he painfully labored through some lies.

Eventually, his courage expended itself upon these objections. The debates drained him of his fire.

He was not cast down by this defeat of his plan, for, upon studying the affair carefully, he could not but admit that the objections were very formidable.

Furthermore, various ailments had begun to cry out. In their presence he could not persist in flying high with the wings of war; they rendered it almost impossible for him to see himself in a heroic light. He tumbled headlong.

He discovered that he had a scorching thirst. His face was so dry and grimy that he thought he could feel his skin crackle. Each bone of his body had an ache in it, and seemingly threatened to break with each movement. His feet were like two sores. Also, his body was calling for food. It was more powerful than a direct hunger. There was a dull, weight-like feeling in his stomach, and, when he tried to walk, his head swayed and he tottered. He could not see with distinctness. Small patches of green mist floated before his vision.

While he had been tossed by many emotions, he had not been aware of ailments. Now they beset him and made clamor. As he was at last compelled to pay attention to them, his capacity for self-hate was multiplied. In despair, he declared that he was not like those others. He now conceded it to be impossible that he should ever become a hero. He was a craven loon. Those pictures of glory were piteous things. He groaned from his heart and went staggering off.

A certain mothlike quality within him kept him in the vicinity of the battle. He had a great desire to see, and to get news. He wished to know who was winning.

He told himself that, despite his unprecedented suffering, he had never lost his greed for a victory, yet, he said, in a half-apologetic manner to his conscience, he could not but know that a defeat for the army this time might mean many favorable things for him. The blows of the enemy would splinter regiments into fragments. Thus, many men of courage, he considered, would be obliged to desert the colors and scurry like chickens. He would appear as one of them. They would be sullen brothers in distress, and he could then easily believe he had not run any farther or faster than they. And if he himself could believe in his virtuous perfection, he conceived that there would be small trouble in convincing all others.

He said, as if in excuse for this hope, that previously the army had encountered great defeats and in a few months had shaken off all blood and tradition of them, emerging as bright and valiant as a new one; thrusting out of sight the memory of disaster, and appearing with the valor and confidence of unconquered legions. The shrilling voices of the people at home would pipe dismally for a time, but various generals were usually compelled to listen to these ditties. He of course felt no compunctions for proposing a general as a sacrifice. He could not tell who the chosen for the barbs might be, so he could center no direct sympathy upon him. The people were afar and he did not conceive public opinion to be accurate at long range. It was quite probable they would hit the wrong man who, after he had recovered from his amazement would perhaps spend the rest of his days in writing replies to the songs of his alleged failure. It would be very unfortunate, no doubt, but in this case a general was of no consequence to the youth.

In a defeat there would be a roundabout vindication of himself. He thought it would prove, in a manner, that he had fled early because of his superior powers of perception. A serious prophet upon predicting a flood should be the first man to climb a tree. This would demonstrate that he was indeed a seer.

A moral vindication was regarded by the youth as a very important thing. Without salve, he could not, he thought, wear the sore badge of his dishonor through life. With his heart continually assuring him that he was despicable, he could not exist without making it, through his actions, apparent to all men.

If the army had gone gloriously on he would be lost. If the din meant that now his army's flags were tilted forward he was a condemned wretch. He would be compelled to doom himself to isolation. If the men were advancing, their indifferent feet were trampling upon his chances for a successful life.

As these thoughts went rapidly through his mind, he turned upon them and tried to thrust them away. He denounced himself as a villain. He said that he was the most unutterably selfish man in existence. His mind pictured the soldiers who would place their defiant bodies before the spear of the yelling battle fiend, and as he saw their dripping corpses on an imagined field, he said that he was their murderer.

Again he thought that he wished he was dead. He believed that he envied a corpse. Thinking of the slain, he achieved a great contempt for some of them, as if they were guilty for thus becoming lifeless. They might have been killed by lucky chances, he said, before they had had opportunities to flee or before they had been really tested. Yet they would receive laurels from tradition. He cried out bitterly that their crowns were stolen and their robes of glorious memories were shams. However, he still said that it was a great pity he was not as they.

A defeat of the army had suggested itself to him as a means of escape from the consequences of his fall. He considered, now, however, that it was useless to think of such a possibility. His education had been that success for that mighty blue machine was certain; that it would make victories as a contrivance turns out buttons. He presently discarded all his speculations in the other direction. He returned to the creed of soldiers.

When he perceived again that it was not possible for the army to be defeated, he tried to bethink him of a fine tale which he could take back to his regiment, and with it turn the expected shafts of derision.

But, as he mortally feared these shafts, it became impossible for him to invent a tale he felt he could trust. He experimented with many schemes, but threw them aside one by one as flimsy. He was quick to see vulnerable places in them all.

Furthermore, he was much afraid that some arrow of scorn might lay him mentally low before he could raise his protecting tale.

He imagined the whole regiment saying: "Where's Henry Fleming? He run, didn't 'e? Oh, my!" He recalled various persons who would be quite sure to leave him no peace about it. They would doubtless question him with sneers, and laugh at his stammering hesitation. In the next engagement they would try to keep watch of him to discover when he would run.

Wherever he went in camp, he would encounter insolent and lingeringly cruel stares. As he imagined himself passing near a crowd of comrades, he could hear one say, "There he goes!"

Then, as if the heads were moved by one muscle, all the faces were turned toward him with wide, derisive grins. He seemed to hear some one make a humorous remark in a low tone. At it the others all crowed and cackled. He was a slang phrase.

Chapter 12

The column that had butted stoutly at the obstacles in the roadway was barely out of the youth's sight before he saw dark waves of men come sweeping out of the woods and down through the fields. He knew at once that the steel fibers had been washed from their hearts. They were bursting from their coats and their equipments as from entanglements. They charged down upon him like terrified buffaloes.

Behind them blue smoke curled and clouded above the treetops, and through the thickets he could sometimes see a distant pink glare. The voices of the cannon were clamoring in interminable chorus.

The youth was horrorstricken. He stared in agony and amazement. He forgot that he was engaged in combating the universe. He threw aside his mental pamphlets on the philosophy of the retreated and rules for the guidance of the damned.

The fight was lost. The dragons were coming with invincible strides. The army, helpless in the matted thickets and blinded by the overhanging night, was going to be swallowed. War, the red animal, war, the blood-swollen god, would have bloated fill.

Within him something bade to cry out. He had the impulse to make a rallying speech, to sing a battle hymn, but he could only get his tongue to call into the air: "Why--why--what--what 's th' matter?"

Soon he was in the midst of them. They were leaping and scampering all about him. Their blanched faces shone in the dusk. They seemed, for the most part, to be very burly men. The youth turned from one to another of them as they galloped along. His incoherent questions were lost. They were heedless of his appeals. They did not seem to see him.

They sometimes gabbled insanely. One huge man was asking of the sky: "Say, where de plank road? Where de plank road!" It was as if he had lost a child. He wept in his pain and dismay.

Presently, men were running hither and thither in all ways. The artillery booming, forward, rearward, and on the flanks made jumble of ideas of direction. Landmarks had vanished into the gathered gloom. The youth began to imagine that he had got into the center of the tremendous quarrel, and he could perceive no way out of it. From the mouths of the fleeing men came a thousand wild questions, but no one made answers.

The youth, after rushing about and throwing interrogations at the heedless bands of retreating infantry, finally clutched a man by the arm. They swung around face to face.

"Why--why--" stammered the youth struggling with his balking tongue.

The man screamed: "Let go me! Let go me!" His face was livid and his eyes were rolling uncontrolled. He was heaving and panting. He still grasped his rifle, perhaps having forgotten to release his hold upon it. He tugged frantically, and the youth being compelled to lean forward was dragged several paces.

"Let go me! Let go me!"

"Why--why--" stuttered the youth.

"Well, then!" bawled the man in a lurid rage. He adroitly and fiercely swung his rifle. It crushed upon the youth's head. The man ran on.

The youth's fingers had turned to paste upon the other's arm. The energy was smitten from his muscles. He saw the flaming wings of lightning flash before his vision. There was a deafening rumble of thunder within his head.

Suddenly his legs seemed to die. He sank writhing to the ground. He tried to arise. In his efforts against the numbing pain he was like a man wrestling with a creature of the air.

There was a sinister struggle.

Sometimes he would achieve a position half erect, battle with the air for a moment, and then fall again, grabbing at the grass. His face was of a clammy pallor. Deep groans were wrenched from him.

At last, with a twisting movement, he got upon his hands and knees, and from thence, like a babe trying to walk, to his feet. Pressing his hands to his temples he went lurching over the grass.

He fought an intense battle with his body. His dulled senses wished him to swoon and he opposed them stubbornly, his mind portraying unknown dangers and mutilations if he should fall upon the field. He went tall soldier fashion. He imagined secluded spots where he could fall and be unmolested. To search for one he strove against the tide of pain.

Once he put his hand to the top of his head and timidly touched the wound. The scratching pain of the contact made him draw a long breath through his clinched teeth. His fingers were dabbled with blood. He regarded them with a fixed stare.

Around him he could hear the grumble of jolted cannon as the scurrying horses were lashed toward the front. Once, a young officer on a besplashed charger nearly ran him down. He turned and watched the mass of guns, men, and horses sweeping in a wide curve toward a gap in a fence. The officer was making excited motions with a gauntleted hand. The guns followed the teams with an air of unwillingness, of being dragged by the heels.

Some officers of the scattered infantry were cursing and railing like fishwives. Their scolding voices could be heard above the din. Into the unspeakable jumble in the roadway rode a squadron of cavalry. The faded yellow of their facings shone bravely. There was a mighty altercation.

The artillery were assembling as if for a conference.

The blue haze of evening was upon the field. The lines of forest were long purple shadows. One cloud lay along the western sky partly smothering the red.

As the youth left the scene behind him, he heard the guns suddenly roar out. He imagined them shaking in black rage. They belched and howled like brass devils guarding a gate. The soft air was filled with the tremendous remonstrance. With it came the shattering peal of opposing infantry. Turning to look behind him, he could see sheets of orange light illumine the shadowy distance. There were subtle and sudden lightnings in the far air. At times he thought he could see heaving masses of men.

He hurried on in the dusk. The day had faded until he could barely distinguish place for his feet. The purple darkness was filled with men who lectured and jabbered. Sometimes he could see them gesticulating against the blue and somber sky. There seemed to be a great ruck of men and munitions spread about in the forest and in the fields.

The little narrow roadway now lay lifeless. There were overturned wagons like sun-dried bowlders. The bed of the former torrent was choked with the bodies of horses and splintered parts of war machines.

It had come to pass that his wound pained him but little. He was afraid to move rapidly, however, for a dread of disturbing it. He held his head very still and took many precautions against stumbling. He was filled with anxiety, and his face was pinched and drawn in anticipation of the pain of any sudden mistake of his feet in the gloom.

His thoughts, as he walked, fixed intently upon his hurt. There was a cool, liquid feeling about it and he imagined blood moving slowly down under his hair. His head seemed swollen to a size that made him think his neck to be inadequate.

The new silence of his wound made much worriment. The little blistering voices of pain that had called out from his scalp were, he thought, definite in their expression of danger. By them he believed he could measure his plight. But when they remained ominously silent he became frightened and imagined terrible fingers that clutched into his brain.

Amid it he began to reflect upon various incidents and conditions of the past. He bethought him of certain meals his mother had cooked at home, in which those dishes of which he was particularly fond had occupied prominent positions. He saw the spread table. The pine walls of the kitchen were glowing in the warm light from the stove. Too, he remembered how he and his companions used to go from the school-house to the bank of a shaded pool. He saw his clothes in disorderly array upon the grass of the bank. He felt the swash of the fragrant water upon his body. The leaves of the overhanging maple rustled with melody in the wind of youthful summer.

He was overcome presently by a dragging weariness. His head hung forward and his shoulders were stooped as if he were bearing a great bundle. His feet shuffled along the ground.

He held continuous arguments as to whether he should lie down and sleep at some near spot, or force himself on until he reached a certain haven. He often tried to dismiss the question, but his body persisted in rebellion and his senses nagged at him like pampered babies.

At last he heard a cheery voice near his shoulder: "Yeh seem t' be in a pretty bad way, boy?"

The youth did not look up, but he assented with thick tongue. "Uh!"

The owner of the cheery voice took him firmly by the arm. "Well," he said, with a round laugh, "I'm goin' your way. Th' hull gang is goin' your way. An' I guess I kin give yeh a lift." They began to walk like a drunken man and his friend.

As they went along, the man questioned the youth and assisted him with the replies like one manipulating the mind of a child. Sometimes he interjected anecdotes. "What reg'ment do yeh b'long teh? Eh? What 's that? Th' 304th N' York? Why, what corps is that in? Oh, it is? Why, I thought they wasn't engaged t'-day-they 're 'way over in th' center. Oh, they was, eh? Well pretty nearly everybody got their share 'a fightin' t'-day. By dad, I give myself up fer dead any number 'a times. There was shootin' here an' shootin' there, an' hollerin' here an' hollerin' there, in th' damn' darkness, until I couldn't tell t' save m' soul which side I was on. Sometimes I thought I was sure 'nough from Ohier, an' other times I could 'a swore I was from th' bitter end of Florida. It was th' most mixed up dern thing I ever see. An' these here hull woods is a reg'lar mess. It 'll be a miracle if we find our reg'ments t'-night. Pretty soon, though, we 'll meet a-plenty of guards an' provost-guards, an' one thing an' another. Ho! there they go with an off'cer, I guess. Look at his hand a-draggin'. He 's got all th' war he wants, I bet. He won't be talkin' so big about his reputation an' all when they go t' sawin' off his leg. Poor feller! My brother 's got whiskers jest like that. How did yeh git 'way over here, anyhow? Your reg'ment is a long way from here, ain't it? Well, I guess we can find it. Yeh know there was a boy killed in my comp'ny t'-day that I thought th' world an' all of. Jack was a nice feller. By ginger, it hurt like thunder t' see ol' Jack jest git knocked flat. We was a-standin' purty peaceable fer a spell, 'though there was men runnin' ev'ry way all 'round us, an' while we was a-standin' like that, 'long come a big fat feller. He began t' peck at Jack's elbow, an' he ses: 'Say, where 's th' road t' th' river?' An' Jack, he never paid no attention, an' th' feller kept on a-peckin' at his elbow an' sayin': 'Say, where 's th' road t' th' river?' Jack was a-lookin' ahead all th' time tryin' t' see th' Johnnies comin' through th' woods, an' he never paid no attention t' this big fat feller fer a long time, but at last he turned 'round an' he ses: 'Ah, go t' hell an' find th' road t' th' river!' An' jest then a shot slapped him bang on th' side th' head. He was a sergeant, too. Them was his last words. Thunder, I wish we was sure 'a findin' our reg'ments t'-night. It 's goin' t' be long huntin'. But I guess we kin do it."

In the search which followed, the man of the cheery voice seemed to the youth to possess a wand of a magic kind. He threaded the mazes of the tangled forest with a strange fortune. In encounters with guards and patrols he displayed the keenness of a detective and the valor of a gamin. Obstacles fell before him and became of assistance. The youth, with his chin still on his breast, stood woodenly by while his companion beat ways and means out of sullen things.

The forest seemed a vast hive of men buzzing about in frantic circles, but the cheery man conducted the youth without mistakes, until at last he began to chuckle with glee and self-satisfaction. "Ah, there yeh are! See that fire?"

The youth nodded stupidly.

"Well, there 's where your reg'ment is. An' now, good-by, ol' boy, good luck t' yeh."

A warm and strong hand clasped the youth's languid fingers for an instant, and then he heard a cheerful and audacious whistling as the man strode away. As he who had so befriended him was thus passing out of his life, it suddenly occurred to the youth that he had not once seen his face.

Chapter 13

The youth went slowly toward the fire indicated by his departed friend. As he reeled, he bethought him of the welcome his comrades would give him. He had a conviction that he would soon feel in his sore heart the barbed missiles of ridicule. He had no strength to invent a tale; he would be a soft target.

He made vague plans to go off into the deeper darkness and hide, but they were all destroyed by the voices of exhaustion and pain from his body. His ailments, clamoring, forced him to seek the place of food and rest, at whatever cost.

He swung unsteadily toward the fire. He could see the forms of men throwing black shadows in the red light, and as he went nearer it became known to him in some way that the ground was strewn with sleeping men.

Of a sudden he confronted a black and monstrous figure. A rifle barrel caught some glinting beams. "Halt! halt!" He was dismayed for a moment, but he presently thought that he recognized the nervous voice. As he stood tottering before the rifle barrel, he called out: "Why, hello, Wilson, you--you here?"

The rifle was lowered to a position of caution and the loud soldier came slowly forward. He peered into the youth's face. "That you, Henry?"

"Yes, it's--it's me."

"Well, well, ol' boy," said the other, "by ginger, I'm glad t' see yeh! I give yeh up fer a goner. I thought yeh was dead sure enough." There was husky emotion in his voice.

The youth found that now he could barely stand upon his feet. There was a sudden sinking of his forces. He thought he must hasten to produce his tale to protect him from the missiles already on the lips of his redoubtable comrades. So, staggering before the loud soldier, he began: "Yes, yes. I've--I've had an awful time. I've been all over. Way over on th' right. Ter'ble fightin' over there. I had an awful time. I got separated from the reg'ment. Over on th' right, I got shot. In th' head. I never see sech fightin'. Awful time. I don't see how I could a' got separated from th' reg'ment. I got shot, too."

His friend had stepped forward quickly. "What? Got shot? Why didn't yeh say so first? Poor ol' boy, we must--hol' on a minnit; what am I doin'. I'll call Simpson."

Another figure at that moment loomed in the gloom. They could see that it was the corporal. "Who yeh talkin' to, Wilson?" he demanded. His voice was anger-toned. "Who yeh talkin' to? Yeh th' derndest sentinel--why--hello, Henry, you here? Why, I thought you was dead four hours ago! Great Jerusalem, they keep turnin' up every ten minutes or so! We thought we'd lost forty-two men by straight count, but if they keep on a-comin' this way, we'll git th' comp'ny all back by mornin' yit. Where was yeh?"

"Over on th' right. I got separated"--began the youth with considerable glibness.

But his friend had interrupted hastily. "Yes, an' he got shot in th' head an' he's in a fix, an' we must see t' him right away." He rested his rifle in the hollow of his left arm and his right around the youth's shoulder.

"Gee, it must hurt like thunder!" he said.

The youth leaned heavily upon his friend. "Yes, it hurts--hurts a good deal," he replied. There was a faltering in his voice.

"Oh," said the corporal. He linked his arm in the youth's and drew him forward. "Come on, Henry. I'll take keer 'a yeh."

As they went on together the loud private called out after them: "Put 'im t' sleep in my blanket, Simpson. An'--hol' on a minnit--here's my canteen. It's full 'a coffee. Look at his head by th' fire an' see how it looks. Maybe it's a pretty bad un. When I git relieved in a couple 'a minnits, I'll be over an' see t' him."

The youth's senses were so deadened that his friend's voice sounded from afar and he could scarcely feel the pressure of the corporal's arm. He submitted passively to the latter's directing strength. His head was in the old manner hanging forward upon his breast. His knees wobbled.

The corporal led him into the glare of the fire. "Now, Henry," he said, "let's have look at yer ol' head."

The youth sat obediently and the corporal, laying aside his rifle, began to fumble in the bushy hair of his comrade. He was obliged to turn the other's head so that the full flush of the fire light would beam upon it. He puckered his mouth with a critical air. He drew back his lips and whistled through his teeth when his fingers came in contact with the splashed blood and the rare wound.

"Ah, here we are!" he said. He awkwardly made further investigations. "Jest as I thought," he added, presently. "Yeh've been grazed by a ball. It's raised a queer lump jest as if some feller had lammed yeh on th' head with a club. It stopped a-bleedin' long time ago. Th' most about it is that in th' mornin' yeh'll fell that a number ten hat wouldn't fit yeh. An' your head'll be all het up an' feel as dry as burnt pork. An' yeh may git a lot 'a other sicknesses, too, by mornin'. Yeh can't never tell. Still, I don't much think so. It's jest a damn' good belt on th' head, an' nothin' more. Now, you jest sit here an' don't move, while I go rout out th' relief. Then I'll send Wilson t' take keer 'a yeh."

The corporal went away. The youth remained on the ground like a parcel. He stared with a vacant look into the fire.

After a time he aroused, for some part, and the things about him began to take form. He saw that the ground in the deep shadows was cluttered with men, sprawling in every conceivable posture. Glancing narrowly into the more distant darkness, he caught occasional glimpses of visages that loomed pallid and ghostly, lit with a phosphorescent glow. These faces expressed in their lines the deep stupor of the tired soldiers. They made them appear like men drunk with wine. This bit of forest might have appeared to an ethereal wanderer as a scene of the result of some frightful debauch.

On the other side of the fire the youth observed an officer asleep, seated bolt upright, with his back against a tree. There was something perilous in his position. Badgered by dreams, perhaps, he swayed with little bounces and starts, like an old, toddy-stricken grandfather in a chimney corner. Dust and stains were upon his face. His lower jaw hung down as if lacking strength to assume its normal position. He was the picture of an exhausted soldier after a feast of war.

He had evidently gone to sleep with his sword in his arms. These two had slumbered in an embrace, but the weapon had been allowed in time to fall unheeded to the ground. The brass-mounted hilt lay in contact with some parts of the fire.

Within the gleam of rose and orange light from the burning sticks were other soldiers, snoring and heaving, or lying deathlike in slumber. A few pairs of legs were stuck forth, rigid and straight. The shoes displayed the mud or dust of marches and bits of rounded trousers, protruding from the blankets, showed rents and tears from hurried pitchings through the dense brambles.

The fire cackled musically. From it swelled light smoke. Overhead the foliage moved softly. The leaves, with their faces turned toward the blaze, were colored shifting hues of silver, often edged with red. Far off to the right, through a window in the forest could be seen a handful of stars lying, like glittering pebbles, on the black level of the night.

Occasionally, in this low-arched hall, a soldier would arouse and turn his body to a new position, the experience of his sleep having taught him of uneven and objectionable places upon the ground under him. Or, perhaps, he would lift himself to a sitting posture, blink at the fire for an unintelligent moment, throw a swift glance at his prostrate companion, and then cuddle down again with a grunt of sleepy content.

The youth sat in a forlorn heap until his friend the loud young soldier came, swinging two canteens by their light strings. "Well, now, Henry, ol' boy," said the latter, "we'll have yeh fixed up in jest about a minnit."

He had the bustling ways of an amateur nurse. He fussed around the fire and stirred the sticks to brilliant exertions. He made his patient drink largely from the canteen that contained the coffee. It was to the youth a delicious draught. He tilted his head afar back and held the canteen long to his lips. The cool mixture went caressingly down his blistered throat. Having finished, he sighed with comfortable delight.

The loud young soldier watched his comrade with an air of satisfaction. He later produced an extensive handkerchief from his pocket. He folded it into a manner of bandage and soused water from the other canteen upon the middle of it. This crude arrangement he bound over the youth's head, tying the ends in a queer knot at the back of the neck.

"There," he said, moving off and surveying his deed, "yeh look like th' devil, but I bet yeh feel better."

The youth contemplated his friend with grateful eyes. Upon his aching and swelling head the cold cloth was like a tender woman's hand.

"Yeh don't holler ner say nothin'," remarked his friend approvingly. "I know I'm a blacksmith at takin' keer 'a sick folks, an' yeh never squeaked. Yer a good un, Henry. Most 'a men would a' been in th' hospital long ago. A shot in th' head ain't foolin' business."

The youth made no reply, but began to fumble with the buttons of his jacket.

"Well, come, now," continued his friend, "come on. I must put yeh t' bed an' see that yeh git a good night's rest."

The other got carefully erect, and the loud young soldier led him among the sleeping forms lying in groups and rows. Presently he stooped and picked up his blankets. He spread the rubber one upon the ground and placed the woolen one about the youth's shoulders.

"There now," he said, "lie down an' git some sleep."

The youth, with his manner of doglike obedience, got carefully down like a crone stooping. He stretched out with a murmur of relief and comfort. The ground felt like the softest couch.

But of a sudden he ejaculated: "Hol' on a minnit! Where you goin' t' sleep?"

His friend waved his hand impatiently. "Right down there by yeh."

"Well, but hol' on a minnit," continued the youth. "What yeh goin' t' sleep in? I've got your--"

The loud young soldier snarled: "Shet up an' go on t' sleep. Don't be makin' a damn' fool 'a yerself," he said severely.

After the reproof the youth said no more. An exquisite drowsiness had spread through him. The warm comfort of the blanket enveloped him and made a gentle langour. His head fell forward on his crooked arm and his weighted lids went softly down over his eyes. Hearing a splatter of musketry from the distance, he wondered indifferently if those men sometimes slept. He gave a long sigh, snuggled down into his blanket, and in a moment was like his comrades.

Chapter 14

When the youth awoke it seemed to him that he had been asleep for a thousand years, and he felt sure that he opened his eyes upon an unexpected world. Gray mists were slowly shifting before the first efforts of the sun rays. An impending splendor could be seen in the eastern sky. An icy dew had chilled his face, and immediately upon arousing he curled farther down into his blanket. He stared for a while at the leaves overhead, moving in a heraldic wind of the day.

The distance was splintering and blaring with the noise of fighting. There was in the sound an expression of a deadly persistency, as if it had not began and was not to cease.

About him were the rows and groups of men that he had dimly seen the previous night. They were getting a last draught of sleep before the awakening. The gaunt, careworn features and dusty figures were made plain by this quaint light at the dawning, but it dressed the skin of the men in corpse-like hues and made the tangled limbs appear pulseless and dead. The youth started up with a little cry when his eyes first swept over this motionless mass of men, thick-spread upon the ground, pallid, and in strange postures. His disordered mind interpreted the hall of the forest as a charnel place. He believed for an instant that he was in the house of the dead, and he did not dare to move lest these corpses start up, squalling and squawking. In a second, however, he achieved his proper mind. He swore a complicated oath at himself. He saw that this somber picture was not a fact of the present, but a mere prophecy.

He heard then the noise of a fire crackling briskly in the cold air, and, turning his head, he saw his friend pottering busily about a small blaze. A few other figures moved in the fog, and he heard the hard cracking of axe blows.

Suddenly there was a hollow rumble of drums. A distant bugle sang faintly. Similar sounds, varying in strength, came from near and far over the forest. The bugles called to each other like brazen gamecocks. The near thunder of the regimental drums rolled.

The body of men in the woods rustled. There was a general uplifting of heads. A murmuring of voices broke upon the air. In it there was much bass of grumbling oaths. Strange gods were addressed in condemnation of the early hours necessary to correct war. An officer's peremptory tenor rang out and quickened the stiffened movement of the men. The tangled limbs unraveled. The corpse-hued faces were hidden behind fists that twisted slowly in the eye sockets.

The youth sat up and gave vent to an enormous yawn. "Thunder!" he remarked petulantly. He rubbed his eyes, and then putting up his hand felt carefully the bandage over his wound. His friend, perceiving him to be awake, came from the fire. "Well, Henry, ol' man, how do yeh feel this mornin'?" he demanded.

The youth yawned again. Then he puckered his mouth to a little pucker. His head, in truth, felt precisely like a melon, and there was an unpleasant sensation at his stomach.

"Oh, Lord, I feel pretty bad," he said.

"Thunder!" exclaimed the other. "I hoped ye'd feel all right this mornin'. Let's see th' bandage--I guess it's slipped." He began to tinker at the wound in rather a clumsy way until the youth exploded.

"Gosh-dern it!" he said in sharp irritation; "you're the hangdest man I ever saw! You wear muffs on your hands. Why in good thunderation can't you be more easy? I'd rather you'd stand off an' throw guns at it. Now, go slow, an' don't act as if you was nailing down carpet."

He glared with insolent command at his friend, but the latter answered soothingly. "Well, well, come now, an' git some grub," he said. "Then, maybe, yeh'll feel better."

At the fireside the loud young soldier watched over his comrade's wants with tenderness and care. He was very busy marshaling the little black vagabonds of tin cups and pouring into them the streaming iron colored mixture from a small and sooty tin pail. He had some fresh meat, which he roasted hurriedly on a stick. He sat down then and contemplated the youth's appetite with glee.

The youth took note of a remarkable change in his comrade since those days of camp life upon the river bank. He seemed no more to be continually regarding the proportions of his personal prowess. He was not furious at small words that pricked his conceits. He was no more a loud young soldier. There was about him now a fine reliance. He showed a quiet belief in his purposes and his abilities. And this inward confidence evidently enabled him to be indifferent to little words of other men aimed at him.

The youth reflected. He had been used to regarding his comrade as a blatant child with an audacity grown from his inexperience, thoughtless, headstrong, jealous, and filled with a tinsel courage. A swaggering babe accustomed to strut in his own dooryard. The youth wondered where had been born these new eyes; when his comrade had made the great discovery that there were many men who would refuse to be subjected by him. Apparently, the other had now climbed a peak of wisdom from which he could perceive himself as a very wee thing. And the youth saw that ever after it would be easier to live in his friend's neighborhood.

His comrade balanced his ebony coffee-cup on his knee. "Well, Henry," he said, "what d'yeh think th' chances are? D'yeh think we'll wallop 'em?"

The youth considered for a moment. "Day-b'fore-yesterday," he finally replied, with boldness, "you would 'a' bet you'd lick the hull kit-an'-boodle all by yourself."

His friend looked a trifle amazed. "Would I?" he asked. He pondered. "Well, perhaps I would," he decided at last. He stared humbly at the fire.

The youth was quite disconcerted at this surprising reception of his remarks. "Oh, no, you wouldn't either," he said, hastily trying to retrace.

But the other made a deprecating gesture. "Oh, yeh needn't mind, Henry," he said. "I believe I was a pretty big fool in those days." He spoke as after a lapse of years.

There was a little pause.

"All th' officers say we've got th' rebs in a pretty tight box," said the friend, clearing his throat in a commonplace way. "They all seem t' think we've got 'em jest where we want 'em."

"I don't know about that," the youth replied. "What I seen over on th' right makes me think it was th' other way about. From where I was, it looked as if we was gettin' a good poundin' yestirday."

"D'yeh think so?" inquired the friend. "I thought we handled 'em pretty rough yestirday."

"Not a bit," said the youth. "Why, lord, man, you didn't see nothing of the fight. Why!" Then a sudden thought came to him. "Oh! Jim Conklin's dead."

His friend started. "What? Is he? Jim Conklin?"

The youth spoke slowly. "Yes. He's dead. Shot in th' side."

"Yeh don't say so. Jim Conklin. . .poor cuss!"

All about them were other small fires surrounded by men with their little black utensils. From one of these near came sudden sharp voices in a row. It appeared that two light-footed soldiers had been teasing a huge, bearded man, causing him to spill coffee upon his blue knees. The man had gone into a rage and had sworn comprehensively. Stung by his language, his tormentors had immediately bristled at him with a great show of resenting unjust oaths. Possibly there was going to be a fight.

The friend arose and went over to them, making pacific motions with his arms. "Oh, here, now, boys, what's th' use?" he said. "We'll be at th' rebs in less'n an hour. What's th' good fightin' 'mong ourselves?"

One of the light-footed soldiers turned upon him red-faced and violent. "Yeh needn't come around here with yer preachin'. I s'pose yeh don't approve 'a fightin' since Charley Morgan licked yeh; but I don't see what business this here is 'a yours or anybody else."

"Well, it ain't," said the friend mildly. "Still I hate t' see--"

There was a tangled argument.

"Well, he--," said the two, indicating their opponent with accusative forefingers.

The huge soldier was quite purple with rage. He pointed at the two soldiers with his great hand, extended clawlike. "Well, they--"

But during this argumentative time the desire to deal blows seemed to pass, although they said much to each other. Finally the friend returned to his old seat. In a short while the three antagonists could be seen together in an amiable bunch.

"Jimmie Rogers ses I'll have t' fight him after th' battle t'-day," announced the friend as he again seated himself. "He ses he don't allow no interferin' in his business. I hate t' see th' boys fightin' 'mong themselves."

The youth laughed. "Yer changed a good bit. Yeh ain't at all like yeh was. I remember when you an' that Irish feller--" He stopped and laughed again.

"No, I didn't use t' be that way," said his friend thoughtfully. "That's true 'nough."

"Well, I didn't mean--" began the youth.

The friend made another deprecatory gesture. "Oh, yeh needn't mind, Henry."

There was another little pause.

"Th' reg'ment lost over half th' men yestirday," remarked the friend eventually. "I thought 'a course they was all dead, but, laws, they kep' a-comin' back last night until it seems, after all, we didn't lose but a few. They'd been scattered all over, wanderin' around in th' woods, fightin' with other reg'ments, an' everything. Jest like you done."

"So?" said the youth.

Chapter 15

The regiment was standing at order arms at the side of a lane, waiting for the command to march, when suddenly the youth remembered the little packet enwrapped in a faded yellow envelope which the loud young soldier with lugubrious words had intrusted to him. It made him start. He uttered an exclamation and turned toward his comrade.

"Wilson!"

"What?"

His friend, at his side in the ranks, was thoughtfully staring down the road. From some cause his expression was at that moment very meek. The youth, regarding him with sidelong glances, felt impelled to change his purpose. "Oh, nothing," he said.

His friend turned his head in some surprise, "Why, what was yeh goin' t' say?"

"Oh, nothing," repeated the youth.

He resolved not to deal the little blow. It was sufficient that the fact made him glad. It was not necessary to knock his friend on the head with the misguided packet.

He had been possessed of much fear of his friend, for he saw how easily questionings could make holes in his feelings. Lately, he had assured himself that the altered comrade would not tantalize him with a persistent curiosity, but he felt certain that during the first period of leisure his friend would ask him to relate his adventures of the previous day.

He now rejoiced in the possession of a small weapon with which he could prostrate his comrade at the first signs of a cross-examination. He was master. It would now be he who could laugh and shoot the shafts of derision.

The friend had, in a weak hour, spoken with sobs of his own death. He had delivered a melancholy oration previous to his funeral, and had doubtless in the packet of letters, presented various keepsakes to relatives. But he had not died, and thus he had delivered himself into the hands of the youth.

The latter felt immensely superior to his friend, but he inclined to condescension. He adopted toward him an air of patronizing good humor.

His self-pride was now entirely restored. In the shade of its flourishing growth he stood with braced and self-confident legs, and since nothing could now be discovered he did not shrink from an encounter with the eyes of judges, and allowed no thoughts of his own to keep him from an attitude of manfulness. He had performed his mistakes in the dark, so he was still a man.

Indeed, when he remembered his fortunes of yesterday, and looked at them from a distance he began to see something fine there. He had license to be pompous and veteranlike.

His panting agonies of the past he put out of his sight.

In the present, he declared to himself that it was only the doomed and the damned who roared with sincerity at circumstance. Few but they ever did it. A man with a full stomach and the respect of his fellows had no business to scold about anything that he might think to be wrong in the ways of the universe, or even with the ways of society. Let the unfortunates rail; the others may play marbles.

He did not give a great deal of thought to these battles that lay directly before him. It was not essential that he should plan his ways in regard to them. He had been taught that many obligations of a life were easily avoided. The lessons of yesterday had been that retribution was a laggard and blind. With these facts before him he did not deem it necessary that he should become feverish over the possibilities of the ensuing twenty-four hours. He could leave much to chance. Besides, a faith in himself had secretly blossomed. There was a little flower of confidence growing within him. He was now a man of experience. He had been out among the dragons, he said, and he assured himself that they were not so hideous as he had imagined them. Also, they were inaccurate; they did not sting with precision. A stout heart often defied, and defying, escaped.

And, furthermore, how could they kill him who was the chosen of gods and doomed to greatness?

He remembered how some of the men had run from the battle. As he recalled their terror-struck faces he felt a scorn for them. They had surely been more fleet and more wild than was absolutely necessary. They were weak mortals. As for himself, he had fled with discretion and dignity.

He was aroused from this reverie by his friend, who, having hitched about nervously and blinked at the trees for a time, suddenly coughed in an introductory way, and spoke.

"Fleming!"

"What?"

The friend put his hand up to his mouth and coughed again. He fidgeted in his jacket.

"Well," he gulped at last, "I guess yeh might as well give me back them letters." Dark, prickling blood had flushed into his cheeks and brow.

"All right, Wilson," said the youth. He loosened two buttons of his coat, thrust in his hand, and brought forth the packet. As he extended it to his friend the latter's face was turned from him.

He had been slow in the act of producing the packet because during it he had been trying to invent a remarkable comment on the affair. He could conjure up nothing of sufficient point. He was compelled to allow his friend to escape unmolested with his packet. And for this he took unto himself considerable credit. It was a generous thing.

His friend at his side seemed suffering great shame. As he contemplated him, the youth felt his heart grow more strong and stout. He had never been compelled to blush in such manner for his acts; he was an individual of extraordinary virtues.

He reflected, with condescending pity: "Too bad! Too bad! The poor devil, it makes him feel tough!"

After this incident, and as he reviewed the battle pictures he had seen, he felt quite competent to return home and make the hearts of the people glow with stories of war. He could see himself in a room of warm tints telling tales to listeners. He could exhibit laurels. They were insignificant; still, in a district where laurels were infrequent, they might shine.

He saw his gaping audience picturing him as the central figure in blazing scenes. And he imagined the consternation and the ejaculations of his mother and the young lady at the seminary as they drank his recitals. Their vague feminine formula for beloved ones doing brave deeds on the field of battle without risk of life would be destroyed.

Chapter 16

A sputtering of musketry was always to be heard. Later, the cannon had entered the dispute. In the fog-filled air their voices made a thudding sound. The reverberations were continual. This part of the world led a strange, battleful existence.

The youth's regiment was marched to relieve a command that had lain long in some damp trenches. The men took positions behind a curving line of rifle pits that had been turned up, like a large furrow, along the line of woods. Before them was a level stretch, peopled with short, deformed stumps. From the woods beyond came the dull popping of the skirmishers and pickets, firing in the fog. From the right came the noise of a terrific fracas.

The men cuddled behind the small embankment and sat in easy attitudes awaiting their turn. Many had their backs to the firing. The youth's friend lay down, buried his face in his arms, and almost instantly, it seemed, he was in a deep sleep.

The youth leaned his breast against the brown dirt and peered over at the woods and up and down the line. Curtains of trees interfered with his ways of vision. He could see the low line of trenches but for a short distance. A few idle flags were perched on the dirt hills. Behind them were rows of dark bodies with a few heads sticking curiously over the top.

Always the noise of skirmishers came from the woods on the front and left, and the din on the right had grown to frightful proportions. The guns were roaring without an instant's pause for breath. It seemed that the cannon had come from all parts and were engaged in a stupendous wrangle. It became impossible to make a sentence heard.

The youth wished to launch a joke--a quotation from newspapers. He desired to say, "All quiet on the Rappahannock," but the guns refused to permit even a comment upon their uproar. He never successfully concluded the sentence. But at last the guns stopped, and among the men in the rifle pits rumors again flew, like birds, but they were now for the most part black creatures who flapped their wings drearily near to the ground and refused to rise on any wings of hope. The men's faces grew doleful from the interpreting of omens. Tales of hesitation and uncertainty on the part of those high in place and responsibility came to their ears. Stories of disaster were borne into their minds with many proofs. This din of musketry on the right, growing like a released genie of sound, expressed and emphasized the army's plight.

The men were disheartened and began to mutter. They made gestures expressive of the sentence: "Ah, what more can we do?" And it could always be seen that they were bewildered by the alleged news and could not fully comprehend a defeat.

Before the gray mists had been totally obliterated by the sun rays, the regiment was marching in a spread column that was retiring carefully through the woods. The disordered, hurrying lines of the enemy could sometimes be seen down through the groves and little fields. They were yelling, shrill and exultant.

At this sight the youth forgot many personal matters and became greatly enraged. He exploded in loud sentences. "B'jiminey, we're generaled by a lot 'a lunkheads."

"More than one feller has said that t'-day," observed a man.

His friend, recently aroused, was still very drowsy. He looked behind him until his mind took in the meaning of the movement. Then he sighed. "Oh, well, I s'pose we got licked," he remarked sadly.

The youth had a thought that it would not be handsome for him to freely condemn other men. He made an attempt to restrain himself, but the words upon his tongue were too bitter. He presently began a long and intricate denunciation of the commander of the forces.

"Mebbe, it wa'n't all his fault--not all together. He did th' best he knowed. It's our luck t' git licked often," said his friend in a weary tone. He was trudging along with stooped shoulders and shifting eyes like a man who has been caned and kicked.

"Well, don't we fight like the devil? Don't we do all that men can?" demanded the youth loudly.

He was secretly dumfounded at this sentiment when it came from his lips. For a moment his face lost its valor and he looked guiltily about him. But no one questioned his right to deal in such words, and presently he recovered his air of courage. He went on to repeat a statement he had heard going from group to group at the camp that morning. "The brigadier said he never saw a new reg'ment fight the way we fought yestirday, didn't he? And we didn't do better than many another reg'ment, did we? Well, then, you can't say it's th' army's fault, can you?"

In his reply, the friend's voice was stern. "'A course not," he said. "No man dare say we don't fight like th' devil. No man will ever dare say it. Th' boys fight like hell-roosters. But still--still, we don't have no luck."

"Well, then, if we fight like the devil an' don't ever whip, it must be the general's fault," said the youth grandly and decisively. "And I don't see any sense in fighting and fighting and fighting, yet always losing through some derned old lunkhead of a general."

A sarcastic man who was tramping at the youth's side, then spoke lazily. "Mebbe yeh think yeh fit th' hull battle yestirday, Fleming," he remarked.

The speech pierced the youth. Inwardly he was reduced to an abject pulp by these chance words. His legs quaked privately. He cast a frightened glance at the sarcastic man.

"Why, no," he hastened to say in a conciliating voice "I don't think I fought the whole battle yesterday."

But the other seemed innocent of any deeper meaning. Apparently, he had no information. It was merely his habit. "Oh!" he replied in the same tone of calm derision.

The youth, nevertheless, felt a threat. His mind shrank from going near to the danger, and thereafter he was silent. The significance of the sarcastic man's words took from him all loud moods that would make him appear prominent. He became suddenly a modest person.

There was low-toned talk among the troops. The officers were impatient and snappy, their countenances clouded with the tales of misfortune. The troos, sifting through the forest, were sullen. In the youth's company once a man's laugh rang out. A dozen soldiers turned their faces quickly toward him and frowned with vague displeasure.

The noise of firing dogged their footsteps. Sometimes, it seemed to be driven a little way, but it always returned again with increased insolence. The men muttered and cursed, throwing black looks in its direction.

In a clear space the troops were at last halted. Regiments and brigades, broken and detached through their encounters with thickets, grew together again and lines were faced toward the pursuing bark of the enemy's infantry.

This noise, following like the yelpings of eager, metallic hounds, increased to a loud and joyous burst, and then, as the sun went serenely up the sky, throwing illuminating rays into the gloomy thickets, it broke forth into prolonged pealings. The woods began to crackle as if afire.

"Whoop-a-dadee," said a man, "here we are! Everybody fightin'. Blood an' destruction."

"I was willin' t' bet they'd attack as soon as th' sun got fairly up," savagely asserted the lieutenant who commanded the youth's company. He jerked without mercy at his little mustache. He strode to and fro with dark dignity in the rear of his men, who were lying down behind whatever protection they had collected.

A battery had trundled into position in the rear and was thoughtfully shelling the distance. The regiment, unmolested as yet, awaited the moment when the gray shadows of the woods before them should be slashed by the lines of flame. There was much growling and swearing.

"Good Gawd," the youth grumbled, "we're always being chased around like rats! It makes me sick. Nobody seems to know where we go or why we go. We just get fired around from pillar to post and get licked here and get licked there, and nobody knows what it's done for. It makes a man feel like a damn' kitten in a bag. Now, I'd like to know what the eternal thunders we was marched into these woods for anyhow, unless it was to give the rebs a regular pot shot at us. We came in here and got our legs all tangled up in these cussed briers, and then we begin to fight and the rebs had an easy time of it. Don't tell me it's just luck! I know better. It's this derned old--"

The friend seemed jaded, but he interrupted his comrade with a voice of calm confidence. "It'll turn out all right in th' end," he said.

"Oh, the devil it will! You always talk like a dog-hanged parson. Don't tell me! I know--"

At this time there was an interposition by the savage-minded lieutenant, who was obliged to vent some of his inward dissatisfaction upon his men. "You boys shut right up! There no need 'a your wastin' your breath in long-winded arguments about this an' that an' th' other. You've been jawin' like a lot 'a old hens. All you've got t' do is to fight, an' you'll get plenty 'a that t' do in about ten minutes. Less talkin' an' more fightin' is what's best for you boys. I never saw sech gabbling jackasses."

He paused, ready to pounce upon any man who might have the temerity to reply. No words being said, he resumed his dignified pacing.

"There's too much chin music an' too little fightin' in this war, anyhow," he said to them, turning his head for a final remark.

The day had grown more white, until the sun shed his full radiance upon the thronged forest. A sort of a gust of battle came sweeping toward that part of the line where lay the youth's regiment. The front shifted a trifle to meet it squarely. There was a wait. In this part of the field there passed slowly the intense moments that precede the tempest.

A single rifle flashed in a thicket before the regiment. In an instant it was joined by many others. There was a mighty song of clashes and crashes that went sweeping through the woods. The guns in the rear, aroused and enraged by shells that had been thrown burr-like at them, suddenly involved themselves in a hideous altercation with another band of guns. The battle roar settled to a rolling thunder, which was a single, long explosion.

In the regiment there was a peculiar kind of hesitation denoted in the attitudes of the men. They were worn, exhausted, having slept but little and labored much. They rolled their eyes toward the advancing battle as they stood awaiting the shock. Some shrank and flinched. They stood as men tied to stakes.

Chapter 17

This advance of the enemy had seemed to the youth like a ruthless hunting. He began to fume with rage and exasperation. He beat his foot upon the ground, and scowled with hate at the swirling smoke that was approaching like a phantom flood. There was a maddening quality in this seeming resolution of the foe to give him no rest, to give him no time to sit down and think. Yesterday he had fought and had fled rapidly. There had been many adventures. For to-day he felt that he had earned opportunities for contemplative repose. He could have enjoyed portraying to uninitiated listeners various scenes at which he had been a witness or ably discussing the processes of war with other proved men. Too it was important that he should have time for physical recuperation. He was sore and stiff from his experiences. He had received his fill of all exertions, and he wished to rest.

But those other men seemed never to grow weary; they were fighting with their old speed. He had a wild hate for the relentless foe. Yesterday, when he had imagined the universe to be against him, he had hated it, little gods and big gods; to-day he hated the army of the foe with the same great hatred. He was not going to be badgered of his life, like a kitten chased by boys, he said. It was not well to drive men into final corners; at those moments they could all develop teeth and claws.

He leaned and spoke into his friend's ear. He menaced the woods with a gesture. "If they keep on chasing us, by Gawd, they'd better watch out. Can't stand TOO much."

The friend twisted his head and made a calm reply. "If they keep on a-chasin' us they'll drive us all inteh th' river."

The youth cried out savagely at this statement. He crouched behind a little tree, with his eyes burning hatefully and his teeth set in a curlike snarl. The awkward bandage was still about his head, and upon it, over his wound, there was a spot of dry blood. His hair was wondrously tousled, and some straggling, moving locks hung over the cloth of the bandage down toward his forehead. His jacket and shirt were open at the throat, and exposed his young bronzed neck. There could be seen spasmodic gulpings at his throat.

His fingers twined nervously about his rifle. He wished that it was an engine of annihilating power. He felt that he and his companions were being taunted and derided from sincere convictions that they were poor and puny. His knowledge of his inability to take vengeance for it made his rage into a dark and stormy specter, that possessed him and made him dream of abominable cruelties. The tormentors were flies sucking insolently at his blood, and he thought that he would have given his life for a revenge of seeing their faces in pitiful plights.

The winds of battle had swept all about the regiment, until the one rifle, instantly followed by others, flashed in its front. A moment later the regiment roared forth its sudden and valiant retort. A dense wall of smoke settled down. It was furiously slit and slashed by the knifelike fire from the rifles.

To the youth the fighters resembled animals tossed for a death struggle into a dark pit. There was a sensation that he and his fellows, at bay, were pushing back, always pushing fierce onslaughts of creatures who were slippery. Their beams of crimson seemed to get no purchase upon the bodies of their foes; the latter seemed to evade them with ease, and come through, between, around, and about with unopposed skill.

When, in a dream, it occurred to the youth that his rifle was an impotent stick, he lost sense of everything but his hate, his desire to smash into pulp the glittering smile of victory which he could feel upon the faces of his enemies.

The blue smoke-swallowed line curled and writhed like a snake stepped upon. It swung its ends to and fro in an agony of fear and rage.

The youth was not conscious that he was erect upon his feet. He did not know the direction of the ground. Indeed, once he even lost the habit of balance and fell heavily. He was up again immediately. One thought went through the chaos of his brain at the time. He wondered if he had fallen because he had been shot. But the suspicion flew away at once. He did not think more of it.

He had taken up a first position behind the little tree, with a direct determination to hold it against the world. He had not deemed it possible that his army could that day succeed, and from this he felt the ability to fight harder. But the throng had surged in all ways, until he lost directions and locations, save that he knew where lay the enemy.

The flames bit him, and the hot smoke broiled his skin. His rifle barrel grew so hot that ordinarily he could not have borne it upon his palms; but he kept on stuffing cartridges into it, and pounding them with his clanking, bending ramrod. If he aimed at some changing form through the smoke, he pulled the trigger with a fierce grunt, as if he were dealing a blow of the fist with all his strength.

When the enemy seemed falling back before him and his fellows, he went instantly forward, like a dog who, seeing his foes lagging, turns and insists upon being pursued. And when he was compelled to retire again, he did it slowly, sullenly, taking steps of wrathful despair.

Once he, in his intent hate, was almost alone, and was firing, when all those near him had ceased. He was so engrossed in his occupation that he was not aware of a lull.

He was recalled by a hoarse laugh and a sentence that came to his ears in a voice of contempt and amazement. "Yeh infernal fool, don't yeh know enough t' quit when there ain't anything t' shoot at? Good Gawd!"

He turned then and, pausing with his rifle thrown half into position, looked at the blue line of his comrades. During this moment of leisure they seemed all to be engaged in staring with astonishment at him. They had become spectators. Turning to the front again he saw, under the lifted smoke, a deserted ground.

He looked bewildered for a moment. Then there appeared upon the glazed vacancy of his eyes a diamond point of intelligence. "Oh," he said, comprehending.

He returned to his comrades and threw himself upon the ground. He sprawled like a man who had been thrashed. His flesh seemed strangely on fire, and the sounds of the battle continued in his ears. He groped blindly for his canteen.

The lieutenant was crowing. He seemed drunk with fighting. He called out to the youth: "By heavens, if I had ten thousand wild cats like you I could tear th' stomach outa this war in less'n a week!" He puffed out his chest with large dignity as he said it.

Some of the men muttered and looked at the youth in awestruck ways. It was plain that as he had gone on loading and firing and cursing without proper intermission, they had found time to regard him. And they now looked upon him as a war devil.

The friend came staggering to him. There was some fright and dismay in his voice. "Are yeh all right, Fleming? Do yeh feel all right? There ain't nothin' th' matter with yeh, Henry, is there?"

"No," said the youth with difficulty. His throat seemed full of knobs and burrs.

These incidents made the youth ponder. It was revealed to him that he had been a barbarian, a beast. He had fought like a pagan who defends his religion. Regarding it, he saw that it was fine, wild, and, in some ways, easy. He had been a tremendous figure, no doubt. By this struggle he had overcome obstacles which he had admitted to be mountains. They had fallen like paper peaks, and he was now what he called a hero. And he had not been aware of the process. He had slept, and, awakening, found himself a knight.

He lay and basked in the occasional stares of his comrades. Their faces were varied in degrees of blackness from the burned powder. Some were utterly smudged. They were reeking with perspiration, and their breaths came hard and wheezing. And from these soiled expanses they peered at him.

"Hot work! Hot work!" cried the lieutenant deliriously. He walked up and down, restless and eager. Sometimes his voice could be heard in a wild, incomprehensible laugh.

When he had a particularly profound thought upon the science of war he always unconsciously addressed himself to the youth.

There was some grim rejoicing by the men. "By thunder, I bet this army'll never see another new reg'ment like us!"

"You bet!"

"A dog, a woman, an' a walnut tree

Th' more yeh beat 'em, th' better they be!

That's like us."

"Lost a piler men, they did. If an ol' woman swep' up th' woods she'd git a dustpanful."

"Yes, an' if she'll come around ag'in in 'bout an hour she'll get a pile more."

The forest still bore its burden of clamor. From off under the trees came the rolling clatter of the musketry. Each distant thicket seemed a strange porcupine with quills of flame. A cloud of dark smoke, as from smoldering ruins, went up toward the sun now bright and gay in the blue, enameled sky.

Chapter 18

The ragged line had respite for some minutes, but during its pause the struggle in the forest became magnified until the trees seemed to quiver from the firing and the ground to shake from the rushing of men. The voices of the cannon were mingled in a long and interminable row. It seemed difficult to live in such an atmosphere. The chests of the men strained for a bit of freshness, and their throats craved water.

There was one shot through the body, who raised a cry of bitter lamentation when came this lull. Perhaps he had been calling out during the fighting also, but at that time no one had heard him. But now the men turned at the woeful complaints of him upon the ground.

"Who is it? Who is it?"

"Its Jimmie Rogers. Jimmie Rogers."

When their eyes first encountered him there was a sudden halt, as if they feared to go near. He was thrashing about in the grass, twisting his shuddering body into many strange postures. He was screaming loudly. This instant's hesitation seemed to fill him with a tremendous, fantastic contempt, and he damned them in shrieked sentences.

The youth's friend had a geographical illusion concerning a stream, and he obtained permission to go for some water. Immediately canteens were showered upon him. "Fill mine, will yeh?" "Bring me some, too." "And me, too." He departed, ladened. The youth went with his friend, feeling a desire to throw his heated body into the stream and, soaking there, drink quarts.

They made a hurried search for the supposed stream, but did not find it. "No water here," said the youth. They turned without delay and began to retrace their steps.

From their position as they again faced toward the place of the fighting, they could comprehend a greater amount of the battle than when their visions had been blurred by the hurling smoke of the line. They could see dark stretches winding along the land, and on one cleared space there was a row of guns making gray clouds, which were filled with large flashes of orange-colored flame. Over some foliage they could see the roof of a house. One window, glowing a deep murder red, shone squarely through the leaves. From the edifice a tall leaning tower of smoke went far into the sky.

Looking over their own troops, they saw mixed masses slowly getting into regular form. The sunlight made twinkling points of the bright steel. To the rear there was a glimpse of a distant roadway as it curved over a slope. It was crowded with retreating infantry. From all the interwoven forest arose the smoke and bluster of the battle. The air was always occupied by a blaring.

Near where they stood shells were flip-flapping and hooting. Occasional bullets buzzed in the air and spanged into tree trunks. Wounded men and other stragglers were slinking through the woods.

Looking down an aisle of the grove, the youth and his companion saw a jangling general and his staff almost ride upon a wounded man, who was crawling on his hands and knees. The general reined strongly at his charger's opened and foamy mouth and guided it with dexterous horsemanship past the man. The latter scrambled in wild and torturing haste. His strength evidently failed him as he reached a place of safety. One of his arms suddenly weakened, and he fell, sliding over upon his back. He lay stretched out, breathing gently.

A moment later the small, creaking cavalcade was directly in front of the two soldiers. Another officer, riding with the skillful abandon of a cowboy, galloped his horse to a position directly before the general. The two unnoticed foot soldiers made a little show of going on, but they lingered near in the desire to overhear the conversation. Perhaps, they thought, some great inner historical things would be said.

The general, whom the boys knew as the commander of their division, looked at the other officer and spoke coolly, as if he were criticising his clothes. "Th' enemy's formin' over there for another charge," he said. "It'll be directed against Whiterside, an' I fear they'll break through unless we work like thunder t' stop them."

The other swore at his restive horse, and then cleared his throat. He made a gesture toward his cap. "It'll be hell t' pay stoppin' them," he said shortly.

"I presume so," remarked the general. Then he began to talk rapidly and in a lower tone. He frequently illustrated his words with a pointing finger. The two infantrymen could hear nothing until finally he asked: "What troops can you spare?"

The officer who rode like a cowboy reflected for an instant. "Well," he said, "I had to order in th' 12th to help th' 76th, an' I haven't really got any. But there's th' 304th. They fight like a lot 'a mule drivers. I can spare them best of any."

The youth and his friend exchanged glances of astonishment.

The general spoke sharply. "Get 'em ready, then. I'll watch developments from here, an' send you word when t' start them. It'll happen in five minutes."

As the other officer tossed his fingers toward his cap and wheeling his horse, started away, the general called out to him in a sober voice: "I don't believe many of your mule drivers will get back."

The other shouted something in reply. He smiled.

With scared faces, the youth and his companion hurried back to the line.

These happenings had occupied an incredibly short time, yet the youth felt that in them he had been made aged. New eyes were given to him. And the most startling thing was to learn suddenly that he was very insignificant. The officer spoke of the regiment as if he referred to a broom. Some part of the woods needed sweeping, perhaps, and he merely indicated a broom in a tone properly indifferent to its fate. It was war, no doubt, but it appeared strange.

As the two boys approached the line, the lieutenant perceived them and swelled with wrath. "Fleming--Wilson--how long does it take yeh to git water, anyhow--where yeh been to."

But his oration ceased as he saw their eyes, which were large with great tales. "We're goin' t' charge--we're goin' t' charge!" cried the youth's friend, hastening with his news.

"Charge?" said the lieutenant. "Charge? Well, b'Gawd! Now, this is real fightin'." Over his soiled countenance there went a boastful smile. "Charge? Well, b'Gawd!"

A little group of soldiers surrounded the two youths. "Are we, sure 'nough? Well, I'll be derned! Charge? What fer? What at? Wilson, you're lyin'."

"I hope to die," said the youth, pitching his tones to the key of angry remonstrance. "Sure as shooting, I tell you."

And his friend spoke in re-enforcement. "Not by a blame sight, he ain't lyin'. We heard 'em talkin'."

They caught sight of two mounted figures a short distance from them. One was the colonel of the regiment and the other was the officer who had received orders from the commander of the division. They were gesticulating at each other. The soldier, pointing at them, interpreted the scene.

One man had a final objection: "How could yeh hear 'em talkin'?" But the men, for a large part, nodded, admitting that previously the two friends had spoken truth.

They settled back into reposeful attitudes with airs of having accepted the matter. And they mused upon it, with a hundred varieties of expression. It was an engrossing thing to think about. Many tightened their belts carefully and hitched at their trousers.

A moment later the officers began to bustle among the men, pushing them into a more compact mass and into a better alignment. They chased those that straggled and fumed at a few men who seemed to show by their attitudes that they had decided to remain at that spot. They were like critical shepherds, struggling with sheep.

Presently, the regiment seemed to draw itself up and heave a deep breath. None of the men's faces were mirrors of large thoughts. The soldiers were bended and stooped like sprinters before a signal. Many pairs of glinting eyes peered from the grimy faces toward the curtains of the deeper woods. They seemed to be engaged in deep calculations of time and distance.

They were surrounded by the noises of the monstrous altercation between the two armies. The world was fully interested in other matters. Apparently, the regiment had its small affair to itself.

The youth, turning, shot a quick, inquiring glance at his friend. The latter returned to him the same manner of look. They were the only ones who possessed an inner knowledge. "Mule drivers--hell t' pay--don't believe many will get back." It was an ironical secret. Still, they saw no hesitation in each other's faces, and they nodded a mute and unprotesting assent when a shaggy man near them said in a meek voice: "We'll git swallowed."

Chapter 19

The youth stared at the land in front of him. Its foliages now seemed to veil powers and horrors. He was unaware of the machinery of orders that started the charge, although from the corners of his eyes he saw an officer, who looked like a boy a-horseback, come galloping, waving his hat. Suddenly he felt a straining and heaving among the men. The line fell slowly forward like a toppling wall, and, with a convulsive gasp that was intended for a cheer, the regiment began its journey. The youth was pushed and jostled for a moment before he understood the movement at all, but directly he lunged ahead and began to run.

He fixed his eye upon a distant and prominent clump of trees where he had concluded the enemy were to be met, and he ran toward it as toward a goal. He had believed throughout that it was a mere question of getting over an unpleasant matter as quickly as possible, and he ran desperately, as if pursued for a murder. His face was drawn hard and tight with the stress of his endeavor. His eyes were fixed in a lurid glare. And with his soiled and disordered dress, his red and inflamed features surmounted by the dingy rag with its spot of blood, his wildly swinging rifle, and banging accouterments, he looked to be an insane soldier.

As the regiment swung from its position out into a cleared space the woods and thickets before it awakened. Yellow flames leaped toward it from many directions. The forest made a tremendous objection.

The line lurched straight for a moment. Then the right wing swung forward; it in turn was surpassed by the left. Afterward the center careered to the front until the regiment was a wedge-shaped mass, but an instant later the opposition of the bushes, trees, and uneven places on the ground split the command and scattered it into detached clusters.

The youth, light-footed, was unconsciously in advance. His eyes still kept note of the clump of trees. From all places near it the clannish yell of the enemy could be heard. The little flames of rifles leaped from it. The song of the bullets was in the air and shells snarled among the treetops. One tumbled directly into the middle of a hurrying group and exploded in crimson fury. There was an instant spectacle of a man, almost over it, throwing up his hands to shield his eyes.

Other men, punched by bullets, fell in grotesque agonies. The regiment left a coherent trail of bodies.

They had passed into a clearer atmosphere. There was an effect like a revelation in the new appearance of the landscape. Some men working madly at a battery were plain to them, and the opposing infantry's lines were defined by the gray walls and fringes of smoke.

It seemed to the youth that he saw everything. Each blade of the green grass was bold and clear. He thought that he was aware of every change in the thin, transparent vapor that floated idly in sheets. The brown or gray trunks of the trees showed each roughness of their surfaces. And the men of the regiment, with their starting eyes and sweating faces, running madly, or falling, as if thrown headlong, to queer, heaped-up corpses--all were comprehended. His mind took a mechanical but firm impression, so that afterward everything was pictured and explained to him, save why he himself was there.

But there was a frenzy made from this furious rush. The men, pitching forward insanely, had burst into cheerings, moblike and barbaric, but tuned in strange keys that can arouse the dullard and the stoic. It made a mad enthusiasm that, it seemed, would be incapable of checking itself before granite and brass. There was the delirium that encounters despair and death, and is heedless and blind to the odds. It is a temporary but sublime absence of selfishness. And because it was of this order was the reason, perhaps, why the youth wondered, afterward, what reasons he could have had for being there.

Presently the straining pace ate up the energies of the men. As if by agreement, the leaders began to slacken their speed. The volleys directed against them had had a seeming windlike effect. The regiment snorted and blew. Among some stolid trees it began to falter and hesitate. The men, staring intently, began to wait for some of the distant walls of smoke to move and disclose to them the scene. Since much of their strength and their breath had vanished, they returned to caution. They were become men again.

The youth had a vague belief that he had run miles, and he thought, in a way, that he was now in some new and unknown land.

The moment the regiment ceased its advance the protesting splutter of musketry became a steadied roar. Long and accurate fringes of smoke spread out. From the top of a small hill came level belchings of yellow flame that caused an inhuman whistling in the air.

The men, halted, had opportunity to see some of their comrades dropping with moans and shrieks. A few lay under foot, still or wailing. And now for an instant the men stood, their rifles slack in their hands, and watched the regiment dwindle. They appeared dazed and stupid. This spectacle seemed to paralyze them, overcome them with a fatal fascination. They stared woodenly at the sights, and, lowering their eyes, looked from face to face. It was a strange pause, and a strange silence.

Then, above the sounds of the outside commotion, arose the roar of the lieutenant. He strode suddenly forth, his infantile features black with rage.

"Come on, yeh fools!" he bellowed. "Come on! Yeh can't stay here. Yeh must come on." He said more, but much of it could not be understood.

He started rapidly forward, with his head turned toward the men, "Come on," he was shouting. The men stared with blank and yokel-like eyes at him. He was obliged to halt and retrace his steps. He stood then with his back to the enemy and delivered gigantic curses into the faces of the men. His body vibrated from the weight and force of his imprecations. And he could string oaths with the facility of a maiden who strings beads.

The friend of the youth aroused. Lurching suddenly forward and dropping to his knees, he fired an angry shot at the persistent woods. This action awakened the men. They huddled no more like sheep. They seemed suddenly to bethink themselves of their weapons, and at once commenced firing. Belabored by their officers, they began to move forward. The regiment, involved like a cart involved in mud and muddle, started unevenly with many jolts and jerks. The men stopped now every few paces to fire and load, and in this manner moved slowly on from trees to trees.

The flaming opposition in their front grew with their advance until it seemed that all forward ways were barred by the thin leaping tongues, and off to the right an ominous demonstration could sometimes be dimly discerned. The smoke lately generated was in confusing clouds that made it difficult for the regiment to proceed with intelligence. As he passed through each curling mass the youth wondered what would confront him on the farther side.

The command went painfully forward until an open space interposed between them and the lurid lines. Here, crouching and cowering behind some trees, the men clung with desperation, as if threatened by a wave. They looked wild-eyed, and as if amazed at this furious disturbance they had stirred. In the storm there was an ironical expression of their importance. The faces of the men, too, showed a lack of a certain feeling of responsibility for being there. It was as if they had been driven. It was the dominant animal failing to remember in the supreme moments the forceful causes of various superficial qualities. The whole affair seemed incomprehensible to many of them.

As they halted thus the lieutenant again began to bellow profanely. Regardless of the vindictive threats of the bullets, he went about coaxing, berating, and bedamning. His lips, that were habitually in a soft and childlike curve, were now writhed into unholy contortions. He swore by all possible deities.

Once he grabbed the youth by the arm. "Come on, yeh lunkhead!" he roared. "Come on! We'll all git killed if we stay here. We've on'y got t' go across that lot. An' then"--the remainder of his idea disappeared in a blue haze of curses.

The youth stretched forth his arm. "Cross there?" His mouth was puckered in doubt and awe.

"Certainly. Jest 'cross th' lot! We can't stay here," screamed the lieutenant. He poked his face close to the youth and waved his bandaged hand. "Come on!" Presently he grappled with him as if for a wrestling bout. It was as if he planned to drag the youth by the ear on to the assault.

The private felt a sudden unspeakable indignation against his officer. He wrenched fiercely and shook him off.

"Come on yerself, then," he yelled. There was a bitter challenge in his voice.

They galloped together down the regimental front. The friend scrambled after them. In front of the colors the three men began to bawl: "Come on! come on!" They danced and gyrated like tortured savages.

The flag, obedient to these appeals, bended its glittering form and swept toward them. The men wavered in indecision for a moment, and then with a long, wailful cry the dilapidated regiment surged forward and began its new journey.

Over the field went the scurrying mass. It was a handful of men splattered into the faces of the enemy. Toward it instantly sprang the yellow tongues. A vast quantity of blue smoke hung before them. A mighty banging made ears valueless.

The youth ran like a madman to reach the woods before a bullet could discover him. He ducked his head low, like a football player. In his haste his eyes almost closed, and the scene was a wild blur. Pulsating saliva stood at the corners of his mouth.

Within him, as he hurled himself forward, was born a love, a despairing fondness for this flag which was near him. It was a creation of beauty and invulnerability. It was a goddess, radiant, that bended its form with an imperious gesture to him. It was a woman, red and white, hating and loving, that called him with the voice of his hopes. Because no harm could come to it he endowed it with power. He kept near, as if it could be a saver of lives, and an imploring cry went from his mind.

In the mad scramble he was aware that the color sergeant flinched suddenly, as if struck by a bludgeon. He faltered, and then became motionless, save for his quivering knees. He made a spring and a clutch at the pole. At the same instant his friend grabbed it from the other side. They jerked at it, stout and furious, but the color sergeant was dead, and the corpse would not relinquish its trust. For a moment there was a grim encounter. The dead man, swinging with bended back, seemed to be obstinately tugging, in ludicrous and awful ways, for the possession of the flag.

It was past in an instant of time. They wrenched the flag furiously from the dead man, and, as they turned again, the corpse swayed forward with bowed head. One arm swung high, and the curved hand fell with heavy protest on the friend's unheeding shoulder.

Chapter 20

When the two youths turned with the flag they saw that much of the regiment had crumbled away, and the dejected remnant was coming slowly back. The men, having hurled themselves in projectile fashion, had presently expended their forces. They slowly retreated, with their faces still toward the spluttering woods, and their hot rifles still replying to the din. Several officers were giving orders, their voices keyed to screams.

"Where in hell yeh goin'?" the lieutenant was asking in a sarcastic howl. And a red-bearded officer, whose voice of triple brass could plainly be heard, was commanding: "Shoot into 'em! Shoot into 'em, Gawd damn their souls!" There was a melee of screeches, in which the men were ordered to do conflicting and impossible things.

The youth and his friend had a small scuffle over the flag. "Give it t' me!" "No, let me keep it!" Each felt satisfied with the other's possession of it, but each felt bound to declare, by an offer to carry the emblem, his willingness to further risk himself. The youth roughly pushed his friend away.

The regiment fell back to the stolid trees. There it halted for a moment to blaze at some dark forms that had begun to steal upon its track. Presently it resumed its march again, curving among the tree trunks. By the time the depleted regiment had again reached the first open space they were receiving a fast and merciless fire. There seemed to be mobs all about them.

The greater part of the men, discouraged, their spirits worn by the turmoil, acted as if stunned. They accepted the pelting of the bullets with bowed and weary heads. It was of no purpose to strive against walls. It was of no use to batter themselves against granite. And from this consciousness that they had attempted to conquer an unconquerable thing there seemed to arise a feeling that they had been betrayed. They glowered with bent brows, but dangerously, upon some of the officers, more particularly upon the red-bearded one with the voice of triple brass.

However, the rear of the regiment was fringed with men, who continued to shoot irritably at the advancing foes. They seemed resolved to make every trouble. The youthful lieutenant was perhaps the last man in the disordered mass. His forgotten back was toward the enemy. He had been shot in the arm. It hung straight and rigid. Occasionally he would cease to remember it, and be about to emphasize an oath with a sweeping gesture. The multiplied pain caused him to swear with incredible power.

The youth went along with slipping uncertain feet. He kept watchful eyes rearward. A scowl of mortification and rage was upon his face. He had thought of a fine revenge upon the officer who had referred to him and his fellows as mule drivers. But he saw that it could not come to pass. His dreams had collapsed when the mule drivers, dwindling rapidly, had wavered and hesitated on the little clearing, and then had recoiled. And now the retreat of the mule drivers was a march of shame to him.

A dagger-pointed gaze from without his blackened face was held toward the enemy, but his greater hatred was riveted upon the man, who, not knowing him, had called him a mule driver.

When he knew that he and his comrades had failed to do anything in successful ways that might bring the little pangs of a kind of remorse upon the officer, the youth allowed the rage of the baffled to possess him. This cold officer upon a monument, who dropped epithets unconcernedly down, would be finer as a dead man, he thought. So grievous did he think it that he could never possess the secret right to taunt truly in answer.

He had pictured red letters of curious revenge. "We ARE mule drivers, are we?" And now he was compelled to throw them away.

He presently wrapped his heart in the cloak of his pride and kept the flag erect. He harangued his fellows, pushing against their chests with his free hand. To those he knew well he made frantic appeals, beseeching them by name. Between him and the lieutenant, scolding and near to losing his mind with rage, there was felt a subtle fellowship and equality. They supported each other in all manner of hoarse, howling protests.

But the regiment was a machine run down. The two men babbled at a forceless thing. The soldiers who had heart to go slowly were continually shaken in their resolves by a knowledge that comrades were slipping with speed back to the lines. It was difficult to think of reputation when others were thinking of skins. Wounded men were left crying on this black journey.

The smoke fringes and flames blustered always. The youth, peering once through a sudden rift in a cloud, saw a brown mass of troops, interwoven and magnified until they appeared to be thousands. A fierce-hued flag flashed before his vision.

Immediately, as if the uplifting of the smoke had been prearranged, the discovered troops burst into a rasping yell, and a hundred flames jetted toward the retreating band. A rolling gray cloud again interposed as the regiment doggedly replied. The youth had to depend again upon his misused ears, which were trembling and buzzing from the melee of musketry and yells.

The way seemed eternal. In the clouded haze men became panic-stricken with the thought that the regiment had lost its path, and was proceeding in a perilous direction. Once the men who headed the wild procession turned and came pushing back against their comrades, screaming that they were being fired upon from points which they had considered to be toward their own lines. At this cry a hysterical fear and dismay beset the troops. A soldier, who heretofore had been ambitious to make the regiment into a wise little band that would proceed calmly amid the huge-appearing difficulties, suddenly sank down and buried his face in his arms with an air of bowing to a doom. From another a shrill lamentation rang out filled with profane allusions to a general. Men ran hither and thither, seeking with their eyes roads of escape. With serene regularity, as if controlled by a schedule, bullets buffed into men.

The youth walked stolidly into the midst of the mob, and with his flag in his hands took a stand as if he expected an attempt to push him to the ground. He unconsciously assumed the attitude of the color bearer in the fight of the preceding day. He passed over his brow a hand that trembled. His breath did not come freely. He was choking during this small wait for the crisis.

His friend came to him. "Well, Henry, I guess this is good-by-John."

"Oh, shut up, you damned fool!" replied the youth, and he would not look at the other.

The officers labored like politicians to beat the mass into a proper circle to face the menaces. The ground was uneven and torn. The men curled into depressions and fitted themselves snugly behind whatever would frustrate a bullet. The youth noted with vague surprise that the lieutenant was standing mutely with his legs far apart and his sword held in the manner of a cane. The youth wondered what had happened to his vocal organs that he no more cursed.

There was something curious in this little intent pause of the lieutenant. He was like a babe which, having wept its fill, raises its eyes and fixes upon a distant toy. He was engrossed in this contemplation, and the soft under lip quivered from self-whispered words.

Some lazy and ignorant smoke curled slowly. The men, hiding from the bullets, waited anxiously for it to lift and disclose the plight of the regiment.

The silent ranks were suddenly thrilled by the eager voice of the youthful lieutenant bawling out: "Here they come! Right onto us, b'Gawd!" His further words were lost in a roar of wicked thunder from the men's rifles.

The youth's eyes had instantly turned in the direction indicated by the awakened and agitated lieutenant, and he had seen the haze of treachery disclosing a body of soldiers of the enemy. They were so near that he could see their features. There was a recognition as he looked at the types of faces. Also he perceived with dim amazement that their uniforms were rather gay in effect, being light gray, accented with a brilliant-hued facing. Too, the clothes seemed new.

These troops had apparently been going forward with caution, their rifles held in readiness, when the youthful lieutenant had discovered them and their movement had been interrupted by the volley from the blue regiment. From the moment's glimpse, it was derived that they had been unaware of the proximity of their dark-suited foes or had mistaken the direction. Almost instantly they were shut utterly from the youth's sight by the smoke from the energetic rifles of his companions. He strained his vision to learn the accomplishment of the volley, but the smoke hung before him.

The two bodies of troops exchanged blows in the manner of a pair of boxers. The fast angry firings went back and forth. The men in blue were intent with the despair of their circumstances and they seized upon the revenge to be had at close range. Their thunder swelled loud and valiant. Their curving front bristled with flashes and the place resounded with the clangor of their ramrods. The youth ducked and dodged for a time and achieved a few unsatisfactory views of the enemy. There appeared to be many of them and they were replying swiftly. They seemed moving toward the blue regiment, step by step. He seated himself gloomily on the ground with his flag between his knees.

As he noted the vicious, wolflike temper of his comrades he had a sweet thought that if the enemy was about to swallow the regimental broom as a large prisoner, it could at least have the consolation of going down with bristles forward.

But the blows of the antagonist began to grow more weak. Fewer bullets ripped the air, and finally, when the men slackened to learn of the fight, they could see only dark, floating smoke. The regiment lay still and gazed. Presently some chance whim came to the pestering blur, and it began to coil heavily away. The men saw a ground vacant of fighters. It would have been an empty stage if it were not for a few corpses that lay thrown and twisted into fantastic shapes upon the sward.

At sight of this tableau, many of the men in blue sprang from behind their covers and made an ungainly dance of joy. Their eyes burned and a hoarse cheer of elation broke from their dry lips.

It had begun to seem to them that events were trying to prove that they were impotent. These little battles had evidently endeavored to demonstrate that the men could not fight well. When on the verge of submission to these opinions, the small duel had showed them that the proportions were not impossible, and by it they had revenged themselves upon their misgivings and upon the foe.

The impetus of enthusiasm was theirs again. They gazed about them with looks of uplifted pride, feeling new trust in the grim, always confident weapons in their hands. And they were men.

Chapter 21

Presently they knew that no firing threatened them. All ways seemed once more opened to them. The dusty blue lines of their friends were disclosed a short distance away. In the distance there were many colossal noises, but in all this part of the field there was a sudden stillness.

They perceived that they were free. The depleted band drew a long breath of relief and gathered itself into a bunch to complete its trip.

In this last length of journey the men began to show strange emotions. They hurried with nervous fear. Some who had been dark and unfaltering in the grimmest moments now could not conceal an anxiety that made them frantic. It was perhaps that they dreaded to be killed in insignificant ways after the times for proper military deaths had passed. Or, perhaps, they thought it would be too ironical to get killed at the portals of safety. With backward looks of perturbation, they hastened.

As they approached their own lines there was some sarcasm exhibited on the part of a gaunt and bronzed regiment that lay resting in the shade of the trees. Questions were wafted to them.

"Where th' hell yeh been?"

"What yeh comin' back fer?"

"Why didn't yeh stay there?"

"Was it warm out there, sonny?"

"Goin' home now, boys?"

One shouted in taunting mimicry: "Oh, mother, come quick an' look at th' sojers!"

There was no reply from the bruised and battered regiment, save that one man made broadcast challenges to fist fights and the red-bearded officer walked rather near and glared in great swashbuckler style at a tall captain in the other regiment. But the lieutenant suppressed the man who wished to fist fight, and the tall captain, flushing at the little fanfare of the red-bearded one, was obliged to look intently at some trees.

The youth's tender flesh was deeply stung by these remarks. From under his creased brows he glowered with hate at the mockers. He meditated upon a few revenges. Still, many in the regiment hung their heads in criminal fashion, so that it came to pass that the men trudged with sudden heaviness, as if they bore upon their bended shoulders the coffin of their honor. And the youthful lieutenant, recollecting himself, began to mutter softly in black curses.

They turned when they arrived at their old position to regard the ground over which they had charged.

The youth in this contemplation was smitten with a large astonishment. He discovered that the distances, as compared with the brilliant measurings of his mind, were trivial and ridiculous. The stolid trees, where much had taken place, seemed incredibly near. The time, too, now that he reflected, he saw to have been short. He wondered at the number of emotions and events that had been crowded into such little spaces. Elfin thoughts must have exaggerated and enlarged everything, he said.

It seemed, then, that there was bitter justice in the speeches of the gaunt and bronzed veterans. He veiled a glance of disdain at his fellows who strewed the ground, choking with dust, red from perspiration, misty-eyed, disheveled.

They were gulping at their canteens, fierce to wring every mite of water from them, and they polished at their swollen and watery features with coat sleeves and bunches of grass.

However, to the youth there was a considerable joy in musing upon his performances during the charge. He had had very little time previously in which to appreciate himself, so that there was now much satisfaction in quietly thinking of his actions. He recalled bits of color that in the flurry had stamped themselves unawares upon his engaged senses.

As the regiment lay heaving from its hot exertions the officer who had named them as mule drivers came galloping along the line. He had lost his cap. His tousled hair streamed wildly, and his face was dark with vexation and wrath. His temper was displayed with more clearness by the way in which he managed his horse. He jerked and wrenched savagely at his bridle, stopping the hard-breathing animal with a furious pull near the colonel of the regiment. He immediately exploded in reproaches which came unbidden to the ears of the men. They were suddenly alert, being always curious about black words between officers.

"Oh, thunder, MacChesnay, what an awful bull you made of this thing!" began the officer. He attempted low tones, but his indignation caused certain of the men to learn the sense of his words. "What an awful mess you made! Good Lord, man, you stopped about a hundred feet this side of a very pretty success! If your men had gone a hundred feet farther you would have made a great charge, but as it is--what a lot of mud diggers you've got anyway!"

The men, listening with bated breath, now turned their curious eyes upon the colonel. They had a ragamuffin interest in this affair.

The colonel was seen to straighten his form and put one hand forth in oratorical fashion. He wore an injured air; it was as if a deacon had been accused of stealing. The men were wiggling in an ecstasy of excitement.

But of a sudden the colonel's manner changed from that of a deacon to that of a Frenchman. He shrugged his shoulders. "Oh, well, general, we went as far as we could," he said calmly.

"As far as you could? Did you, b'Gawd?" snorted the other. "Well, that wasn't very far, was it?" he added, with a glance of cold contempt into the other's eyes. "Not very far, I think. You were intended to make a diversion in favor of Whiterside. How well you succeeded your own ears can now tell you." He wheeled his horse and rode stiffly away.

The colonel, bidden to hear the jarring noises of an engagement in the woods to the left, broke out in vague damnations.

The lieutenant, who had listened with an air of impotent rage to the interview, spoke suddenly in firm and undaunted tones. "I don't care what a man is--whether he is a general or what--if he says th' boys didn't put up a good fight out there he's a damned fool."

"Lieutenant," began the colonel, severely, "this is my own affair, and I'll trouble you--"

The lieutenant made an obedient gesture. "All right, colonel, all right," he said. He sat down with an air of being content with himself.

The news that the regiment had been reproached went along the line. For a time the men were bewildered by it. "Good thunder!" they ejaculated, staring at the vanishing form of the general. They conceived it to be a huge mistake.

Presently, however, they began to believe that in truth their efforts had been called light. The youth could see this conviction weigh upon the entire regiment until the men were like cuffed and cursed animals, but withal rebellious.

The friend, with a grievance in his eye, went to the youth. "I wonder what he does want," he said. "He must think we went out there an' played marbles! I never see sech a man!"

The youth developed a tranquil philosophy for these moments of irritation. "Oh, well," he rejoined, "he probably didn't see nothing of it at all and god mad as blazes, and concluded we were a lot of sheep, just because we didn't do what he wanted done. It's a pity old Grandpa Henderson got killed yestirday--he'd have known that we did our best and fought good. It's just our awful luck, that's what."

"I should say so," replied the friend. He seemed to be deeply wounded at an injustice. "I should say we did have awful luck! There's no fun in fightin' fer people when everything yeh do--no matter what--ain't done right. I have a notion t' stay behind next time an' let 'em take their ol' charge an' go t' th' devil with it."

The youth spoke soothingly to his comrade. "Well, we both did good. I'd like to see the fool what'd say we both didn't do as good as we could!"

"Of course we did," declared the friend stoutly. "An' I'd break th' feller's neck if he was as big as a church. But we're all right, anyhow, for I heard one feller say that we two fit th' best in th' reg'ment, an' they had a great argument 'bout it. Another feller, 'a course, he had t' up an' say it was a lie--he seen all what was goin' on an' he never seen us from th' beginnin' t' th' end. An' a lot more stuck in an' ses it wasn't a lie--we did fight like thunder, an' they give us quite a sendoff. But this is what I can't stand--these everlastin' ol' soldiers, titterin' an' laughin', an then that general, he's crazy."

The youth exclaimed with sudden exasperation: "He's a lunkhead! He makes me mad. I wish he'd come along next time. We'd show 'im what--"

He ceased because several men had come hurrying up. Their faces expressed a bringing of great news.

"O Flem, yeh jest oughta heard!" cried one, eagerly.

"Heard what?" said the youth.

"Yeh jest oughta heard!" repeated the other, and he arranged himself to tell his tidings. The others made an excited circle. "Well, sir, th' colonel met your lieutenant right by us--it was damnedest thing I ever heard--an' he ses: 'Ahem! ahem!' he ses. 'Mr. Hasbrouck!' he ses, 'by th' way, who was that lad what carried th' flag?' he ses. There, Flemin', what d' yeh think 'a that? 'Who was th' lad what carried th' flag?' he ses, an' th' lieutenant, he speaks up right away: 'That's Flemin', an' he's a jimhickey,' he ses, right away. What? I say he did. 'A jimhickey,' he ses--those 'r his words. He did, too. I say he did. If you kin tell this story better than I kin, go ahead an' tell it. Well, then, keep yer mouth shet. Th' lieutenant, he ses: 'He's a jimhickey,' and th' colonel, he ses: 'Ahem! ahem! he is, indeed, a very good man t' have, ahem! He kep' th' flag 'way t' th' front. I saw 'im. He's a good un,' ses th' colonel. 'You bet,' ses th' lieutenant, 'he an' a feller named Wilson was at th' head 'a th' charge, an' howlin' like Indians all th' time,' he ses. 'Head 'a th' charge all th' time,' he ses. 'A feller named Wilson,' he ses. There, Wilson, m'boy, put that in a letter an' send it hum t' yer mother, hay? 'A feller named Wilson,' he ses. An' th' colonel, he ses: 'Were they, indeed? Ahem! ahem! My sakes!' he ses. 'At th' head 'a th' reg'ment?' he ses. 'They were,' ses th' lieutenant. 'My sakes!' ses th' colonel. He ses: 'Well, well, well,' he ses. 'They deserve t' be major-generals.'"

The youth and his friend had said: "Huh!" "Yer lyin' Thompson." "Oh, go t' blazes!" "He never sed it." "Oh, what a lie!" "Huh!" But despite these youthful scoffings and embarrassments, they knew that their faces were deeply flushing from thrills of pleasure. They exchanged a secret glance of joy and congratulation.

They speedily forgot many things. The past held no pictures of error and disappointment. They were very happy, and their hearts swelled with grateful affection for the colonel and the youthful lieutenant.

Chapter 22

When the woods again began to pour forth the dark-hued masses of the enemy the youth felt serene self-confidence. He smiled briefly when he saw men dodge and duck at the long screechings of shells that were thrown in giant handfuls over them. He stood, erect and tranquil, watching the attack begin against apart of the line that made a blue curve along the side of an adjacent hill. His vision being unmolested by smoke from the rifles of his companions, he had opportunities to see parts of the hard fight. It was a relief to perceive at last from whence came some of these noises which had been roared into his ears.

Off a short way he saw two regiments fighting a little separate battle with two other regiments. It was in a cleared space, wearing a set-apart look. They were blazing as if upon a wager, giving and taking tremendous blows. The firings were incredibly fierce and rapid. These intent regiments apparently were oblivious of all larger purposes of war, and were slugging each other as if at a matched game.

In another direction he saw a magnificent brigade going with the evident intention of driving the enemy from a wood. They passed in out of sight and presently there was a most awe-inspiring racket in the wood. The noise was unspeakable. Having stirred this prodigious uproar, and, apparently, finding it too prodigious, the brigade, after a little time, came marching airily out again with its fine formation in nowise disturbed. There were no traces of speed in its movements. The brigade was jaunty and seemed to point a proud thumb at the yelling wood.

On a slope to the left there was a long row of guns, gruff and maddened, denouncing the enemy, who, down through the woods, were forming for another attack in the pitiless monotony of conflicts. The round red discharges from the guns made a crimson flare and a high, thick smoke. Occasional glimpses could be caught of groups of the toiling artillerymen. In the rear of this row of guns stood a house, calm and white, amid bursting shells. A congregation of horses, tied to a long railing, were tugging frenziedly at their bridles. Men were running hither and thither.

The detached battle between the four regiments lasted for some time. There chanced to be no interference, and they settled their dispute by themselves. They struck savagely and powerfully at each other for a period of minutes, and then the lighter-hued regiments faltered and drew back, leaving the dark-blue lines shouting. The youth could see the two flags shaking with laughter amid the smoke remnants.

Presently there was a stillness, pregnant with meaning. The blue lines shifted and changed a trifle and stared expectantly at the silent woods and fields before them. The hush was solemn and churchlike, save for a distant battery that, evidently unable to remain quiet, sent a faint rolling thunder over the ground. It irritated, like the noises of unimpressed boys. The men imagined that it would prevent their perched ears from hearing the first words of the new battle.

Of a sudden the guns on the slope roared out a message of warning. A spluttering sound had begun in the woods. It swelled with amazing speed to a profound clamor that involved the earth in noises. The splitting crashes swept along the lines until an interminable roar was developed. To those in the midst of it it became a din fitted to the universe. It was the whirring and thumping of gigantic machinery, complications among the smaller stars. The youth's ears were filled cups. They were incapable of hearing more.

On an incline over which a road wound he saw wild and desperate rushes of men perpetually backward and forward in riotous surges. These parts of the opposing armies were two long waves that pitched upon each other madly at dictated points. To and fro they swelled. Sometimes, one side by its yells and cheers would proclaim decisive blows, but a moment later the other side would be all yells and cheers. Once the youth saw a spray of light forms go in houndlike leaps toward the waving blue lines. There was much howling, and presently it went away with a vast mouthful of prisoners. Again, he saw a blue wave dash with such thunderous force against a gray obstruction that it seemed to clear the earth of it and leave nothing but trampled sod. And always in their swift and deadly rushes to and fro the men screamed and yelled like maniacs.

Particular pieces of fence or secure positions behind collections of trees were wrangled over, as gold thrones or pearl bedsteads. There were desperate lunges at these chosen spots seemingly every instant, and most of them were bandied like light toys between the contending forces. The youth could not tell from the battle flags flying like crimson foam in many directions which color of cloth was winning.

His emaciated regiment bustled forth with undiminished fierceness when its time came. When assaulted again by bullets, the men burst out in a barbaric cry of rage and pain. They bent their heads in aims of intent hatred behind the projected hammers of their guns. Their ramrods clanged loud with fury as their eager arms pounded the cartridges into the rifle barrels. The front of the regiment was a smoke-wall penetrated by the flashing points of yellow and red.

Wallowing in the fight, they were in an astonishingly short time resmudged. They surpassed in stain and dirt all their previous appearances. Moving to and fro with strained exertion, jabbering all the while, they were, with their swaying bodies, black faces, and glowing eyes, like strange and ugly fiends jigging heavily in the smoke.

The lieutenant, returning from a tour after a bandage, produced from a hidden receptacle of his mind new and portentous oaths suited to the emergency. Strings of expletives he swung lashlike over the backs of his men, and it was evident that his previous efforts had in nowise impaired his resources.

The youth, still the bearer of the colors, did not feel his idleness. He was deeply absorbed as a spectator. The crash and swing of the great drama made him lean forward, intent-eyed, his face working in small contortions. Sometimes he prattled, words coming unconsciously from him in grotesque exclamations. He did not know that he breathed; that the flag hung silently over him, so absorbed was he.

A formidable line of the enemy came within dangerous range. They could be seen plainly--tall, gaunt men with excited faces running with long strides toward a wandering fence.

At sight of this danger the men suddenly ceased their cursing monotone. There was an instant of strained silence before they threw up their rifles and fired a plumping volley at the foes. There had been no order given; the men, upon recognizing the menace, had immediately let drive their flock of bullets without waiting for word of command.

But the enemy were quick to gain the protection of the wandering line of fence. They slid down behind it with remarkable celerity, and from this position they began briskly to slice up the blue men.

These latter braced their energies for a great struggle. Often, white clinched teeth shone from the dusky faces. Many heads surged to and fro, floating upon a pale sea of smoke. Those behind the fence frequently shouted and yelped in taunts and gibelike cries, but the regiment maintained a stressed silence. Perhaps, at this new assault the men recalled the fact that they had been named mud diggers, and it made their situation thrice bitter. They were breathlessly intent upon keeping the ground and thrusting away the rejoicing body of the enemy. They fought swiftly and with a despairing savageness denoted in their expressions.

The youth had resolved not to budge whatever should happen. Some arrows of scorn that had buried themselves in his heart had generated strange and unspeakable hatred. It was clear to him that his final and absolute revenge was to be achieved by his dead body lying, torn and gluttering, upon the field. This was to be a poignant retaliation upon the officer who had said "mule drivers," and later "mud diggers," for in all the wild graspings of his mind for a unit responsible for his sufferings and commotions he always seized upon the man who had dubbed him wrongly. And it was his idea, vaguely formulated, that his corpse would be for those eyes a great and salt reproach.

The regiment bled extravagantly. Grunting bundles of blue began to drop. The orderly sergeant of the youth's company was shot through the cheeks. Its supports being injured, his jaw hung afar down, disclosing in the wide cavern of his mouth a pulsing mass of blood and teeth. And with it all he made attempts to cry out. In his endeavor there was a dreadful earnestness, as if he conceived that one great shriek would make him well.

The youth saw him presently go rearward. His strength seemed in nowise impaired. He ran swiftly, casting wild glances for succor.

Others fell down about the feet of their companions. Some of the wounded crawled out and away, but many lay still, their bodies twisted into impossible shapes.

The youth looked once for his friend. He saw a vehement young man, powder-smeared and frowzled, whom he knew to be him. The lieutenant, also, was unscathed in his position at the rear. He had continued to curse, but it was now with the air of a man who was using his last box of oaths.

For the fire of the regiment had begun to wane and drip. The robust voice, that had come strangely from the thin ranks, was growing rapidly weak.

Chapter 23

The colonel came running along the back of the line. There were other officers following him. "We must charge'm!" they shouted. "We must charge'm!" they cried with resentful voices, as if anticipating a rebellion against this plan by the men.

The youth, upon hearing the shouts, began to study the distance between him and the enemy. He made vague calculations. He saw that to be firm soldiers they must go forward. It would be death to stay in the present place, and with all the circumstances to go backward would exalt too many others. Their hope was to push the galling foes away from the fence.

He expected that his companions, weary and stiffened, would have to be driven to this assault, but as he turned toward them he perceived with a certain surprise that they were giving quick and unqualified expressions of assent. There was an ominous, clanging overture to the charge when the shafts of the bayonets rattled upon the rifle barrels. At the yelled words of command the soldiers sprang forward in eager leaps. There was new and unexpected force in the movement of the regiment. A knowledge of its faded and jaded condition made the charge appear like a paroxysm, a display of the strength that comes before a final feebleness. The men scampered in insane fever of haste, racing as if to achieve a sudden success before an exhilarating fluid should leave them. It was a blind and despairing rush by the collection of men in dusty and tattered blue, over a green sward and under a sapphire sky, toward a fence, dimly outlined in smoke, from behind which sputtered the fierce rifles of enemies.

The youth kept the bright colors to the front. He was waving his free arm in furious circles, the while shrieking mad calls and appeals, urging on those that did not need to be urged, for it seemed that the mob of blue men hurling themselves on the dangerous group of rifles were again grown suddenly wild with an enthusiasm of unselfishness. From the many firings starting toward them, it looked as if they would merely succeed in making a great sprinkling of corpses on the grass between their former position and the fence. But they were in a state of frenzy, perhaps because of forgotten vanities, and it made an exhibition of sublime recklessness. There was no obvious questioning, nor figurings, nor diagrams. There was, apparently, no considered loopholes. It appeared that the swift wings of their desires would have shattered against the iron gates of the impossible.

He himself felt the daring spirit of a savage, religion-mad. He was capable of profound sacrifices, a tremendous death. He had no time for dissections, but he knew that he thought of the bullets only as things that could prevent him from reaching the place of his endeavor. There were subtle flashings of joy within him that thus should be his mind.

He strained all his strength. His eyesight was shaken and dazzled by the tension of thought and muscle. He did not see anything excepting the mist of smoke gashed by the little knives of fire, but he knew that in it lay the aged fence of a vanished farmer protecting the snuggled bodies of the gray men.

As he ran a thought of the shock of contact gleamed in his mind. He expected a great concussion when the two bodies of troops crashed together. This became a part of his wild battle madness. He could feel the onward swing of the regiment about him and he conceived of a thunderous, crushing blow that would prostrate the resistance and spread consternation and amazement for miles. The flying regiment was going to have a catapultian effect. This dream made him run faster among his comrades, who were giving vent to hoarse and frantic cheers.

But presently he could see that many of the men in gray did not intend to abide the blow. The smoke, rolling, disclosed men who ran, their faces still turned. These grew to a crowd, who retired stubbornly. Individuals wheeled frequently to send a bullet at the blue wave.

But at one part of the line there was a grim and obdurate group that made no movement. They were settled firmly down behind posts and rails. A flag, ruffled and fierce, waved over them and their rifles dinned fiercely.

The blue whirl of men got very near, until it seemed that in truth there would be a close and frightful scuffle. There was an expressed disdain in the opposition of the little group, that changed the meaning of the cheers of the men in blue. They became yells of wrath, directed, personal. The cries of the two parties were now in sound an interchange of scathing insults.

They in blue showed their teeth; their eyes shone all white. They launched themselves as at the throats of those who stood resisting. The space between dwindled to an insignificant distance.

The youth had centered the gaze of his soul upon that other flag. Its possession would be high pride. It would express bloody minglings, near blows. He had a gigantic hatred for those who made great difficulties and complications. They caused it to be as a craved treasure of mythology, hung amid tasks and contrivances of danger.

He plunged like a mad horse at it. He was resolved it should not escape if wild blows and darings of blows could seize it. His own emblem, quivering and aflare, was winging toward the other. It seemed there would shortly be an encounter of strange beaks and claws, as of eagles.

The swirling body of blue men came to a sudden halt at close and disastrous range and roared a swift volley. The group in gray was split and broken by this fire, but its riddled body still fought. The men in blue yelled again and rushed in upon it.

The youth, in his leapings, saw, as through a mist, a picture of four or five men stretched upon the ground or writhing upon their knees with bowed heads as if they had been stricken by bolts from the sky. Tottering among them was the rival color bearer, whom the youth saw had been bitten vitally by the bullets of the last formidable volley. He perceived this man fighting a last struggle, the struggle of one whose legs are grasped by demons. It was a ghastly battle. Over his face was the bleach of death, but set upon it was the dark and hard lines of desperate purpose. With this terrible grin of resolution he hugged his precious flag to him and was stumbling and staggering in his design to go the way that led to safety for it.

But his wounds always made it seem that his feet were retarded, held, and he fought a grim fight, as with invisible ghouls fastened greedily upon his limbs. Those in advance of the scampering blue men, howling cheers, leaped at the fence. The despair of the lost was in his eyes as he glanced back at them.

The youth's friend went over the obstruction in a tumbling heap and sprang at the flag as a panther at prey. He pulled at it and, wrenching it free, swung up its red brilliancy with a mad cry of exultation even as the color bearer, gasping, lurched over in a final throe and, stiffening convulsively, turned his dead face to the ground. There was much blood upon the grass blades.

At the place of success there began more wild clamorings of cheers. The men gesticulated and bellowed in an ecstasy. When they spoke it was as if they considered their listener to be a mile away. What hats and caps were left to them they often slung high in the air.

At one part of the line four men had been swooped upon, and they now sat as prisoners. Some blue men were about them in an eager and curious circle. The soldiers had trapped strange birds, and there was an examination. A flurry of fast questions was in the air.

One of the prisoners was nursing a superficial wound in the foot. He cuddled it, baby-wise, but he looked up from it often to curse with an astonishing utter abandon straight at the noses of his captors. He consigned them to red regions; he called upon the pestilential wrath of strange gods. And with it all he was singularly free from recognition of the finer points of the conduct of prisoners of war. It was as if a clumsy clod had trod upon his toe and he conceived it to be his privilege, his duty, to use deep, resentful oaths.

Another, who was a boy in years, took his plight with great calmness and apparent good nature. He conversed with the men in blue, studying their faces with his bright and keen eyes. They spoke of battles and conditions. There was an acute interest in all their faces during this exchange of view points. It seemed a great satisfaction to hear voices from where all had been darkness and speculation.

The third captive sat with a morose countenance. He preserved a stoical and cold attitude. To all advances he made one reply without variation, "Ah, go t' hell!"

The last of the four was always silent and, for the most part, kept his face turned in unmolested directions. From the views the youth received he seemed to be in a state of absolute dejection. Shame was upon him, and with it profound regret that he was, perhaps, no more to be counted in the ranks of his fellows. The youth could detect no expression that would allow him to believe that the other was giving a thought to his narrowed future, the pictured dungeons, perhaps, and starvations and brutalities, liable to the imagination. All to be seen was shame for captivity and regret for the right to antagonize.

After the men had celebrated sufficiently they settled down behind the old rail fence, on the opposite side to the one from which their foes had been driven. A few shot perfunctorily at distant marks.

There was some long grass. The youth nestled in it and rested, making a convenient rail support the flag. His friend, jubilant and glorified, holding his treasure with vanity, came to him there. They sat side by side and congratulated each other.

Chapter 24

The roarings that had stretched in a long line of sound across the face of the forest began to grow intermittent and weaker. The stentorian speeches of the artillery continued in some distant encounter, but the crashes of the musketry had almost ceased. The youth and his friend of a sudden looked up, feeling a deadened form of distress at the waning of these noises, which had become a part of life. They could see changes going on among the troops. There were marchings this way and that way. A battery wheeled leisurely. On the crest of a small hill was the thick gleam of many departing muskets.

The youth arose. "Well, what now, I wonder?" he said. By his tone he seemed to be preparing to resent some new monstrosity in the way of dins and smashes. He shaded his eyes with his grimy hand and gazed over the field.

His friend also arose and stared. "I bet we're goin' t' git along out of this an' back over th' river," said he.

"Well, I swan!" said the youth.

They waited, watching. Within a little while the regiment received orders to retrace its way. The men got up grunting from the grass, regretting the soft repose. They jerked their stiffened legs, and stretched their arms over their heads. One man swore as he rubbed his eyes. They all groaned "O Lord!" They had as many objections to this change as they would have had to a proposal for a new battle.

They trampled slowly back over the field across which they had run in a mad scamper.

The regiment marched until it had joined its fellows. The reformed brigade, in column, aimed through a wood at the road. Directly they were in a mass of dust-covered troops, and were trudging along in a way parallel to the enemy's lines as these had been defined by the previous turmoil.

They passed within view of a stolid white house, and saw in front of it groups of their comrades lying in wait behind a neat breastwork. A row of guns were booming at a distant enemy. Shells thrown in reply were raising clouds of dust and splinters. Horsemen dashed along the line of intrenchments.

At this point of its march the division curved away from the field and went winding off in the direction of the river. When the significance of this movement had impressed itself upon the youth he turned his head and looked over his shoulder toward the trampled and debris-strewed ground. He breathed a breath of new satisfaction. He finally nudged his friend. "Well, it's all over," he said to him.

His friend gazed backward. "B'Gawd, it is," he assented. They mused.

For a time the youth was obliged to reflect in a puzzled and uncertain way. His mind was undergoing a subtle change. It took moments for it to cast off its battleful ways and resume its accustomed course of thought. Gradually his brain emerged from the clogged clouds, and at last he was enabled to more closely comprehend himself and circumstance.

He understood then that the existence of shot and countershot was in the past. He had dwelt in a land of strange, squalling upheavals and had come forth. He had been where there was red of blood and black of passion, and he was escaped. His first thoughts were given to rejoicings at this fact.

Later he began to study his deeds, his failures, and his achievements. Thus, fresh from scenes where many of his usual machines of reflection had been idle, from where he had proceeded sheeplike, he struggled to marshal all his acts.

At last they marched before him clearly. From this present view point he was enabled to look upon them in spectator fashion and criticise them with some correctness, for his new condition had already defeated certain sympathies.

Regarding his procession of memory he felt gleeful and unregretting, for in it his public deeds were paraded in great and shining prominence. Those performances which had been witnessed by his fellows marched now in wide purple and gold, having various deflections. They went gayly with music. It was pleasure to watch these things. He spent delightful minutes viewing the gilded images of memory.

He saw that he was good. He recalled with a thrill of joy the respectful comments of his fellows upon his conduct.

Nevertheless, the ghost of his flight from the first engagement appeared to him and danced. There were small shoutings in his brain about these matters. For a moment he blushed, and the light of his soul flickered with shame.

A specter of reproach came to him. There loomed the dogging memory of the tattered soldier--he who, gored by bullets and faint of blood, had fretted concerning an imagined wound in another; he who had loaned his last of strength and intellect for the tall soldier; he who, blind with weariness and pain, had been deserted in the field.

For an instant a wretched chill of sweat was upon him at the thought that he might be detected in the thing. As he stood persistently before his vision, he gave vent to a cry of sharp irritation and agony.

His friend turned. "What's the matter, Henry?" he demanded. The youth's reply was an outburst of crimson oaths.

As he marched along the little branch-hung roadway among his prattling companions this vision of cruelty brooded over him. It clung near him always and darkened his view of these deeds in purple and gold. Whichever way his thoughts turned they were followed by the somber phantom of the desertion in the fields. He looked stealthily at his companions, feeling sure that they must discern in his face evidences of this pursuit. But they were plodding in ragged array, discussing with quick tongues the accomplishments of the late battle.

"Oh, if a man should come up an' ask me, I'd say we got a dum good lickin'."

"Lickin'--in yer eye! We ain't licked, sonny. We're goin' down here aways, swing aroun', an' come in behint 'em."

"Oh, hush, with your comin' in behint 'em. I've seen all 'a that I wanta. Don't tell me about comin' in behint--"

"Bill Smithers, he ses he'd rather been in ten hundred battles than been in that heluva hospital. He ses they got shootin' in th' nighttime, an' shells dropped plum among 'em in th' hospital. He ses sech hollerin' he never see."

"Hasbrouck? He's th' best off'cer in this here reg'ment. He's a whale."

"Didn't I tell yeh we'd come aroun' in behint 'em? Didn't I tell yeh so? We--"

"Oh, shet yeh mouth!"

For a time this pursuing recollection of the tattered man took all elation from the youth's veins. He saw his vivid error, and he was afraid that it would stand before him all his life. He took no share in the chatter of his comrades, nor did he look at them or know them, save when he felt sudden suspicion that they were seeing his thoughts and scrutinizing each detail of the scene with the tattered soldier.

Yet gradually he mustered force to put the sin at a distance. And at last his eyes seemed to open to some new ways. He found that he could look back upon the brass and bombast of his earlier gospels and see them truly. He was gleeful when he discovered that he now despised them.

With this conviction came a store of assurance. He felt a quiet manhood, nonassertive but of sturdy and strong blood. He knew that he would no more quail before his guides wherever they should point. He had been to touch the great death, and found that, after all, it was but the great death. He was a man.

So it came to pass that as he trudged from the place of blood and wrath his soul changed. He came from hot plowshares to prospects of clover tranquilly, and it was as if hot plowshares were not. Scars faded as flowers.

It rained. The procession of weary soldiers became a bedraggled train, despondent and muttering, marching with churning effort in a trough of liquid brown mud under a low, wretched sky. Yet the youth smiled, for he saw that the world was a world for him, though many discovered it to be made of oaths and walking sticks. He had rid himself of the red sickness of battle. The sultry nightmare was in the past. He had been an animal blistered and sweating in the heat and pain of war. He turned now with a lover's thirst to images of tranquil skies, fresh meadows, cool brooks--an existence of soft and eternal peace.

Over the river a golden ray of sun came through the hosts of leaden rain clouds.

THE END.

ACTIVE SERVICE

CHAPTER I.

MARJORY walked pensively along the hall. In the cool shadows made by the palms on the window ledge, her face wore the expression of thoughtful melancholy expected on the faces of the devotees who pace in cloistered gloom. She halted before a door at the end of the hall and laid her hand on the knob. She stood hesitating, her head bowed. It was evident that this mission was to require great fortitude.

At last she opened the door. " Father," she began at once. There was disclosed an elderly, narrow-faced man seated at a large table and surrounded by manuscripts and books. The sunlight flowing through curtains of Turkey red fell sanguinely upon the bust of dead-eyed Pericles on the mantle. A little clock was ticking, hidden somewhere among the countless leaves of writing, the maps and broad heavy tomes that swarmed upon the table.

Her father looked up quickly with an ogreish scowl.

Go away! " he cried in a rage. " Go away. Go away. Get out " " He seemed on the point of arising to eject the visitor. It was plain to her that he had been interrupted in the writing of one of his sentences, ponderous, solemn and endless, in which wandered multitudes of homeless and friendless prepositions, adjectives looking for a parent, and quarrelling nouns, sentences which no longer symbolised the languageform of thought but which had about them a quaint aroma from the dens of long-dead scholars. " Get out," snarled the professor.

Father," faltered the girl. Either because his formulated thought was now completely knocked out of his mind by his own emphasis in defending it, or because he detected something of portent in her expression, his manner suddenly changed, and with a petulant glance at his writing he laid down his pen and sank back in his chair to listen. " Well, what is it, my child ? "

The girl took a chair near the window and gazed out upon the snow-stricken campus, where at the moment a group of students returning from a class room were festively hurling snow-balls. " I've got something important to tell you, father," said she, but I don't quite know how to say it."

"Something important ? " repeated the professor. He was not habitually interested in the affairs of his family, but this proclamation that something important could be connected with them, filled his mind with a capricious interest. "Well, what is it, Marjory? "

She replied calmly: " Rufus Coleman wants to marry me."

"What?" demanded the professor loudly. "Rufus Coleman.

What do you mean? "

The girl glanced furtively at him. She did not seem to be able to frame a suitable sentence.

As for the professor, he had, like all men both thoughtless and thoughtful, told himself that one day his daughter would come to him with a tale of this kind. He had never forgotten that the little girl was to be a woman, and he had never forgotten that this tall, lithe creature, the present Marjory, was a woman. He had been entranced and confident or entranced and apprehensive according' to the time. A man focussed upon astronomy, the pig market or social progression, may nevertheless have a secondary mind which hovers like a spirit over his dahlia tubers and dreams upon the mystery of their slow and tender revelations. The professor's secondary mind had dwelt always with his daughter and watched with a faith and delight the changing to a woman of a certain fat and mumbling babe. However, he now saw this machine, this self- sustaining, self-operative love, which had run with the ease of a clock, suddenly crumble to ashes and leave the mind of a great scholar staring at a calamity. " Rufus Coleman," he repeated, stunned. Here was his daughter, very obviously desirous of marrying Rufus Coleman. " Marjory," he cried in amazement and fear, "what possesses, you? Marry Rufus Colman?"

The girl seemed to feel a strong sense of relief at his prompt recognition of a fact. Being freed from the necessity of making a flat declaration, she simply hung her head and blushed impressively. A hush fell upon them. The professor stared long at his daughter. The shadow of unhappiness deepened upon his face. " Marjory, Marjory," he murmured at last. He had tramped heroically upon his panic and devoted his strength to bringing thought into some kind of attitude toward this terrible fact. " I am-I am surprised," he began. Fixing her then with a stern eye, he asked: "Why do you wish to marry this man? You, with your opportunities of meeting persons of intelligence. And you want to marry-" His voice grew tragic. "You want to marry the Sunday editor of the New York Eclipse."

" It is not so very terrible, is it?" said Marjory sullenly.

"Wait a moment; don't talk," cried the professor. He arose and walked nervously to and fro, his hands flying in the air. He was very red behind the ears as when in the Classroom some student offended him. " A gambler, a sporter of fine clothes, an expert on champagne, a polite loafer, a witness knave who edits the Sunday edition of a great outrage upon our sensibilities. You want to marry him, this man? Marjory, you are insane. This fraud who asserts that his work is intelligent, this fool comes here to my house and-"

He became aware that his daughter was regarding him coldly. "I thought we had best have all this part of it over at once," she remarked.

He confronted her in a new kind of surprise. The little keen- eyed professor was at this time imperial, on the verge of a majestic outburst. " Be still," he said. "Don't be clever with your father. Don't be a dodger. Or, if you are, don't speak of it to me. I suppose this fine young man expects to see me personally? "

" He was coming to-morrow," replied Marjory. She began to weep. " He was coming to-morrow."

" Um," said the professor. He continued his pacing while Marjory wept with her head bowed to the arm of the chair. His brow made the three dark vertical crevices well known to his students. Some. times he glowered murderously at the photographs of ancient temples which adorned the walls. "My poor child," he said once, as he paused near her, " to think I never knew you were a fool. I have been deluding myself. It has been my fault as much as it has been yours. I will not readily forgive myself."

The girl raised her face and looked at him. Finally, resolved to disregard the dishevelment wrought by tears, she presented a desperate front with her wet eyes and flushed cheeks. Her hair was disarrayed. "I don't see why you can call me a fool," she said. The pause before this sentence had been so portentous of a wild and rebellious speech that the professor almost laughed now. But still the father for the first time knew that he was being un-dauntedly faced by his child in his own library, in the presence Of 372 pages of the book that was to be his masterpiece. At the back of his mind he felt a great awe as if his own youthful spirit had come from the past and challenged him with a glance. For a moment he was almost a defeated man. He dropped into a chair. " Does your mother know of this " " he asked mournfully.

"Yes," replied the girl. "She knows. She has been trying to make me give up Rufus."

"Rufus," cried the professor rejuvenated by anger.

"Well, his name is Rufus," said the girl.

"But please don't call him so before me," said the father with icy dignity. " I do not recognise him as being named Rufus. That is a contention of yours which does not arouse my interest. I know him very well as a gambler and a drunkard, and if incidentally, he is named Rufus, I fail to see any importance to it."

" He is not a gambler and he is not a drunkard," she said.

" Um. He drinks heavily-that is well known. He gambles. He plays cards for money—more than he possesses-at least he did when he was in college."

" You said you liked him when he was in college."

" So I did. So I did," answered the professor sharply. " I often find myself liking that kind of a boy in college. Don't I know them-those lads with their beer and their poker games in the dead of the night with a towel hung over the keyhole. Their habits are often vicious enough, but something remains in them through it all and they may go away and do great things. This happens. We know it. It happens with confusing insistence. It destroys theo- ries. There-there isn't much to say about it. And sometimes we like this kind of a boy better than we do the-the others. For my part I know of many a pure, pious and fine- minded student that I have positively loathed from a personal point-of-view. But," he added, " this Rufus Coleman, his life in college and his life since, go to prove how often we get off the track. There is no gauge of collegiate conduct whatever, until we can get evidence of the man's work in the world. Your precious scoundrel's evidence is now all in and he is a failure, or worse."

" You are not habitually so fierce in judging people," said the girl.

"I would be if they all wanted to marry my daughter," rejoined the professor. " Rather than let that man make love to you-or even be within a short railway journey of you, I'll cart you off to Europe this winter and keep you there until you forget. If you persist in this silly fancy, I shall at once become medieval."

Marjory had evidently recovered much of her composure. "Yes, father, new climates are alway's supposed to cure one," she remarked with a kind of lightness.

" It isn't so much the old expedient," said the professor musingly, "as it is that I would be afraid to leave you herewith no protection against that drinking gambler and gambling drunkard."

" Father, I have to ask you not to use such terms in speaking of the man that I shall marry."

There was a silence. To all intents, the professor remained unmoved. He smote the tips of his fingers thoughtfully together. " Ye-es," he observed. "That sounds reasonable from your standpoint." His eyes studied her face in a long and steady glance. He arose and went into the hall. When he returned he wore his hat and great coat. He took a book and some papers from the table and went away.

Marjory walked slowly through the halls and up to her room. From a window she could see her father making his way across the campus labouriously against the wind and whirling snow. She watched it, this little black figure, bent forward, patient, steadfast. It was an inferior fact that her father was one of the famous scholars of the generation. To her, he was now a little old man facing the wintry winds. Recollect. ing herself and Rufus Coleman she began to weep again, wailing amid the ruins of her tumbled hopes. Her skies had turned to paper and her trees were mere bits of green sponge. But amid all this woe appeared the little black image of her father making its way against the storm.

CHAPTER II.

IN a high-walled corrider of one of the college buildings, a crowd of students waited amid jostlings and a loud buzz of talk. Suddenly a huge pair of doors flew open and a wedge of young men inserted itself boisterously and deeply into the throng. There was a great scuffle attended by a general banging of books upon heads. The two lower classes engaged in herculean play while members of the two higher classes, standing aloof, devoted themselves strictly to the encouragement of whichever party for a moment lost ground or heart. This was in order to prolong the conflict.

The combat, waged in the desperation of proudest youth, waxed hot and hotter. The wedge had been instantly smitten into a kind of block of men. It had crumpled into an irregular square and on three sides it was now assailed with remarkable ferocity.

It was a matter of wall meet wall in terrific rushes, during which lads could feel their very hearts leaving them in the compress of friends and foes. They on the outskirts upheld the honour of their classes by squeezing into paper thickness the lungs of those of their fellows who formed the centre of the melee

In some way it resembled a panic at a theatre.

The first lance-like attack of the Sophomores had been formidable, but the Freshmen outnumbering their enemies and smarting from continual Sophomoric oppression, had swarmed to the front like drilled collegians and given the arrogant foe the first serious check of the year. Therefore the tall Gothic windows which lined one side of the corridor looked down upon as incomprehensible and enjoyable a tumult as could mark the steps of advanced education. The Seniors and juniors cheered themselves ill. Long freed from the joy of such meetings, their only means for this kind of recreation was to involve the lower classes, and they had never seen the victims fall to with such vigour and courage. Bits of printed leaves, torn note-books, dismantled collars and cravats, all floated to the floor beneath the feet of the warring hordes. There were no blows; it was a battle of pressure. It was a deadly pushing where the leaders on either side often suffered the most cruel and sickening agony caught thus between phalanxes of shoulders with friend as well as foe contributing to the pain.

Charge after charge of Freshmen beat upon the now compact and organised Sophomores. Then, finally, the rock began to give slow way. A roar came from the Freshmen and they hurled themselves in a frenzy upon their betters.

To be under the gaze of the juniors and Seniors is to be in sight of all men, and so the Sophomores at this important moment laboured with the desperation of the half- doomed to stem the terrible Freshmen.

In the kind of game, it was the time when bad tempers came strongly to the front, and in many Sophomores' minds a thought arose of the incomparable insolence of the Freshmen. A blow was struck; an infuriated Sophomore had swung an arm high and smote a Freshman.

Although it had seemed that no greater noise could be made by the given numbers, the din that succeeded this manifestation surpassed everything. The juniors and Seniors immediately set up an angry howl. These veteran classes projected themselves into the middle of the fight, buffeting everybody with small thought as to merit. This method of bringing peace was as militant as a landslide, but they had much trouble before they could separate the central clump of antagonists into its parts. A score of Freshmen had cried out: "It was Coke. Coke punched him. Coke." A dozen of them were tempestuously endeavouring to register their protest against fisticuffs by means of an introduction of more fisticuffs.

The upper classmen were swift, harsh and hard. "Come, now, Freshies, quit it. Get back, get back, d'y'hear?" With a wrench of muscles they forced themselves in front of Coke, who was being blindly defended by his classmates from intensely earnest attacks by outraged Freshmen.

These meetings between the lower classes at the door of a recitation room were accounted quite comfortable and idle affairs, and a blow delivered openly and in hatred fractured a sharply defined rule of conduct. The corridor was in a hubbub. Many Seniors and Juniors, bursting from old and iron discipline, wildly clamoured that some Freshman should be given the privilege of a single encounter with Coke. The Freshmen themselves were frantic. They besieged the tight and dauntless circle of men that encompassed Coke. None dared confront the Seniors openly, but by headlong rushes at auspicious moments they tried to come to quarters with the rings of dark-browed Sophomores. It was no longer a festival, a game; it was a riot. Coke, wild-eyed, pallid with fury, a ribbon of blood on his chin, swayed in the middle of the mob of his classmates, comrades who waived the ethics of the blow under the circumstance of being obliged as a corps to stand against the scorn of the whole college, as well as against the tremendous assaults of the Freshmen. Shamed by their own man, but knowing full well the right time and the wrong time for a palaver of regret and disavowal, this battalion struggled in the desperation of despair. Once they were upon the verge of making unholy campaign against the interfering Seniors. This fiery impertinence was the measure of their state.

It was a critical moment in the play of the college. Four or five defeats from the Sophomores during the fall had taught the Freshmen much. They had learned the comparative measurements, and they knew now that their prowess was ripe to enable them to amply revenge what was, according to their standards, an execrable deed by a man who had not the virtue to play the rough game, but was obliged to resort to uncommon methods. In short, the Freshmen were almost out of control, and the Sophomores debased but defiant, were quite out of control. The Senior and junior classes which, in American colleges dictate in these affrays, found their dignity toppling, and in consequence there was a sudden oncome of the entire force of upper classmen football players naturally in advance. All distinctions were dissolved at once in a general fracas. The stiff and still Gothic windows surveyed a scene of dire carnage.

Suddenly a voice rang brazenly through the tumult. It was not loud, but it was different. " Gentlemen! Gentlemen!"" Instantly there was a remarkable number of haltings, abrupt replacements, quick changes. Prof. Wainwright stood at the door of his recitation room, looking into the eyes of each member of the mob of three hundred. "Ssh! " said the mob. " Ssh! Quit! Stop! It's the Embassador! Stop!" He had once been minister to Austro-Hungary, and forever now to the students of the college his name was Embassador. He stepped into the corridor, and they cleared for him a little respectful zone of floor. He looked about him coldly. " It seems quite a general dishevelment. The Sophomores display an energy in the halls which I do not detect in the class room." A feeble murmur of appreciation arose from the outskirts of the throng. While he had been speaking several remote groups of battling men had been violently signaled and suppressed by other students. The professor gazed into terraces of faces that were still inflamed. " I needn't say that I am surprised," he remarked in the accepted rhetoric of his kind. He added musingly: " There seems to be a great deal of torn linen. Who is the young gentleman with blood on his chin?"

The throng moved restlessly. A manful silence, such as might be in the tombs of stern and honourable knights, fell upon the shadowed corridor. The subdued rustling had fainted to nothing. Then out of the crowd Coke, pale and desperate, delivered himself.

" Oh, Mr. Coke," said the professor, "I would be glad if you would tell the gentlemen they may retire to their dormitories." He waited while the students passed out to the campus.

The professor returned to his room for some books, and then began his own march across the snowy campus. The wind twisted his coat-tails fantastically, and he was obliged to keep one hand firmly on the top of his hat. When he arrived home he met his wife in the hall. " Look here, Mary," he cried. She followed him into the library. " Look here," he said. "What is this all about? Marjory tells me she wants to marry Rufus Coleman."

Mrs. Wainwright was a fat woman who was said to pride herself upon being very wise and if necessary, sly. In addition she laughed continually in an inexplicably personal way, which apparently made everybody who heard her feel offended. Mrs. Wainwright laughed.

"Well," said the professor, bristling, " what do you mean by that? "

"Oh, Harris," she replied. " Oh, Harris."

The professor straightened in his chair. " I do not see any

illumination in those remarks, Mary. I understand from

Marjory's manner that she is bent upon marrying Rufus

Coleman. She said you knew of it."

" Why, of course I knew. It was as plain—-"

" Plain !" scoffed the professor. " Plain !"

Why, of course," she cried. "I knew it all along."

There was nothing in her tone which proved that she admired the event itself. She was evidently carried away by the triumph of her penetration. " I knew it all along," she added, nodding.

The professor looked at her affectionately. "You knew it all along, then, Mary? Why didn't you tell me, dear? "

" Because you ought to have known it," she answered blatantly.

The professor was glaring. Finally he spoke in tones of grim reproach. "Mary, whenever you happen to know anything, dear, it seems only a matter of partial recompense that you should tell me."

The wife had been taught in a terrible school that she should never invent any inexpensive retorts concerning bookworms and so she yawed at once. "Really, Harris. Really, I didn't suppose the affair was serious. You could have knocked me down with a feather. Of course he has been here very often, but then Marjory gets a great deal of attention. A great deal of attention." The professor had been thinking. " Rather than let my girl marry that scalawag, I'll take you and her to Greece this winter with the class. Separation. It is a sure cure that has the sanction of antiquity."

"Well," said Mrs. Wainwright, "you know best, Harris. You know best." It was a common remark with her, and it probably meant either approbation or disapprobation if it did not mean simple discretion.

CHAPTER III.

THERE had been a babe with no arms born in one of the western counties of Massachusetts. In place of upper limbs the child had growing from its chest a pair of fin-like hands, mere bits of skin-covered bone. Furthermore, it had only one eye. This phenomenon lived four days, but the news of the birth had travelled up this country road and through that village until it reached the ears of the editor of the Michaelstown Tribune. He was also a correspondent of the New York Eclipse. On the third day he appeared at the home of the parents accompanied by a photographer. While the latter arranged his, instrument, the correspondent talked to the father and mother, two coweyed and yellow-faced people who seemed to suffer a primitive fright of the strangers. Afterwards as the correspondent and the photographer were climbing into their buggy, the mother crept furtively down to the gate and asked, in a foreigner's dialect, if they would send her a copy of the photograph. The correspondent carelessly indulgent, promised it. As the buggy swung away, the father came from behind an apple tree, and the two semi-humans watched it with its burden of glorious strangers until it rumbled across the bridge and disappeared. The correspondent was elate; he told the photographer that the Eclipse would probably pay fifty dollars for the article and the photograph.

The office of the New York Eclipse was at the top of the immense building on Broadway. It was a sheer mountain to the heights of which the interminable thunder of the streets arose faintly. The Hudson was a broad path of silver in the distance. Its edge was marked by the tracery of sailing ships' rigging and by the huge and many-coloured stacks of ocean liners. At the foot of the cliff lay City Hall Park. It seemed no larger than a quilt. The grey walks patterned the snow-covering into triangles and ovals and upon them many tiny people scurried here and there, without sound, like a fish at the bottom of a pool. It was only the vehicles that sent high, unmistakable, the deep bass of their movement. And yet after listening one seemed to hear a singular murmurous note, a pulsation, as if the crowd made noise by its mere living, a mellow hum of the eternal strife. Then suddenly out of the deeps might ring a human voice, a newsboy shout perhaps, the cry of a faraway jackal at night.

From the level of the ordinary roofs, combined in many plateaus, dotted with short iron chimneys from which curled wisps of steam, arose other mountains like the Eclipse Building. They were great peaks, ornate, glittering with paint or polish. Northward they subsided to sun-crowned ranges.

From some of the windows of the Eclipse office dropped the walls of a terrible chasm in the darkness of which could be seen vague struggling figures. Looking down into this appalling crevice one discovered only the tops of hats and knees which in spasmodic jerks seemed to touch the rims of the hats. The scene represented some weird fight or dance or carouse. It was not an exhibition of men hurrying along a narrow street.

It was good to turn one's eyes from that place to the vista of the city's splendid reaches, with spire and spar shining in the clear atmosphere and the marvel of the Jersey shore, pearl- misted or brilliant with detail. From this height the sweep of a snow-storm was defined and majestic. Even a slight summer shower, with swords of lurid yellow sunlight piercing its edges as if warriors were contesting every foot of its advance, was from the Eclipse office something so inspiring that the chance pilgrim felt a sense of exultation as if from this peak he was surveying the worldwide war of the elements and life. The staff of the Eclipse usually worked without coats and amid the smoke from pipes.

To one of the editorial chambers came a photograph and an article from Michaelstown, Massachusetts. A boy placed the packet and many others upon the desk of a young man who was standing before a window and thoughtfully drumming upon the pane. He turned at the thudding of the packets upon his desk. " Blast you," he remarked amiably. " Oh, I guess it won't hurt you to work," answered the boy, grinning with a comrade's Insolence. Baker, an assistant editor for the Sunday paper, took scat at his desk and began the task of examining the packets. His face could not display any particular interest because he had been at the same work for nearly a fortnight.

The first long envelope he opened was from a woman. There was a neat little manuscript accompanied by a letter which explained that the writer was a widow who was trying to make her living by her pen and who, further, hoped that the generosity of the editor of the Eclipse would lead him to give her article the opportunity which she was sure it deserved. She hoped that the editor would pay her as well as possible for it, as she needed the money greatly. She added that her brother was a reporter on the Little Rock Sentinel and he had declared that her literary style was excellent. Baker really did not read this note. His vast experience of a fortnight had enabled him to detect its kind in two glances. He unfolded the manuscript, looked at it woodenly and then tossed it with the letter to the top of his desk, where it lay with the other corpses. None could think of widows in Arkansas, ambitious from the praise of the reporter on the Little Rock Sentinel, waiting for a crown of literary glory and money. In the next envelope a man using the note-paper of a Boston journal begged to know if the accompanying article would be acceptable; if not it was to be kindly returned in the enclosed stamped envelope. It was a humourous essay on trolley cars. Adventuring through the odd scraps that were come to the great mill, Baker paused occasionally to relight his pipe.

As he went through envelope after envelope, the desks about him gradually were occupied by young men who entered from the hall with their faces still red from the cold of the streets. For the most part they bore the unmistakable stamp of the American college. They had that confident poise which is easily brought from the athletic field. Moreover, their clothes were quite in the way of being of the newest fashion. There was an air of precision about their cravats and linen. But on the other hand there might be with them some indifferent westerner who was obliged to resort to irregular means and harangue startled shop-keepers in order to provide himself with collars of a strange kind. He was usually very quick and brave of eye and noted for his inability to perceive a distinction between his own habit and the habit of others, his western character preserving itself inviolate amid a confusion of manners.

The men, coming one and one, or two and two, flung badinage to all corners of the room. Afterward, as they wheeled from time to time in their chairs, they bitterly insulted each other with the utmost good-nature, taking unerring aim at faults and riddling personalities with the quaint and cynical humour of a newspaper office. Throughout this banter, it was strange to note how infrequently the men smiled, particularly when directly engaged in an encounter.

A wide door opened into another apartment where were many little slanted tables, each under an electric globe with a green shade. Here a curly-headed scoundrel with a corncob pipe was hurling paper balls the size of apples at the head of an industrious man who, under these difficulties, was trying to draw a picture of an awful wreck with ghastly-faced sailors frozen in the rigging. Near this pair a lady was challenging a German artist who resembled Napoleon III. with having been publicly drunk at a music hall on the previous night. Next to the great gloomy corridor of this sixteenth floor was a little office presided over by an austere boy, and here waited in enforced patience a little dismal band of people who wanted to see the Sunday editor.

Baker took a manuscript and after glancing about the room, walked over to a man at another desk, Here is something that. I think might do," he said. The man at the desk read the first two pages. " But where is the photograph " " he asked then. "There should be a photograph with this thing."

" Oh, I forgot," said Baker. He brought from his desk a photograph of the babe that had been born lacking arms and one eye. Baker's superior braced a knee against his desk and settled back to a judicial attitude. He took the photograph and looked at it impassively. " Yes," he said, after a time, " that's a pretty good thing. You better show that to Coleman when he comes in."

In the little office where the dismal band waited, there had been a sharp hopeful stir when Rufus Coleman, the Sunday editor, passed rapidly from door to door and vanished within the holy precincts. It had evidently been in the minds of some to accost him then, but his eyes did not turn once in their direction. It was as if he had not seen them. Many experiences had taught him that the proper manner of passing through this office was at a blind gallop.

The dismal band turned then upon the austere office boy. Some demanded with terrible dignity that he should take in their cards at once. Others sought to ingratiate themselves by smiles of tender friendliness. He for his part employed what we would have called his knowledge of men and women upon the group, and in consequence blundered and bungled vividly, freezing with a glance an annoyed and importunate Arctic explorer who was come to talk of illustrations for an article that had been lavishly paid for in advance. The hero might have thought he was again in the northern seas. At the next moment the boy was treating almost courteously a German from the cast side who wanted the Eclipse to print a grand full page advertising description of his invention, a gun which was supposed to have a range of forty miles and to be able to penetrate anything with equanimity and joy. The gun, as a matter of fact, had once been induced to go off when it had hurled itself passionately upon its back, incidentally breaking its inventor's leg. The projectile had wandered some four hundred yards seaward, where it dug a hole in the water which was really a menace to navigation. Since then there had been nothing tangible save the inventor, in splints and out of splints, as the fortunes of science decreed. In short, this office boy mixed his business in the perfect manner of an underdone lad dealing with matters too large for him, and throughout he displayed the pride and assurance of a god.

As Coleman crossed the large office his face still wore the stern expression which he invariably used to carry him unmolested through the ranks of the dismal band. As he was removing his London overcoat he addressed the imperturbable back of one of his staff, who had a desk against the opposite wall. " Has Hasskins sent in that drawing of the mine accident yet? " The man did not lift his head from his work-, but he answered at once: " No; not yet." Coleman was laying his hat on a chair. " Well, why hasn't he ? " he demanded. He glanced toward the door of the room in which the curly-headed scoundrel with the corncob pipe was still hurling paper balls at the man who was trying to invent the postures of dead mariners frozen in the rigging. The office boy came timidly from his post and informed Coleman of the waiting people. " All right," said the editor. He dropped into his chair and began to finger his letters, which had been neatly opened and placed in a little stack by a boy. Baker came in with the photograph of the miserable babe.

It was publicly believed that the Sunday staff of the Eclipse must have a kind of aesthetic delight in pictures of this kind, but Coleman's face betrayed no emotion as he looked at this specimen. He lit a fresh cigar, tilted his chair and surveyed it with a cold and stony stare. " Yes, that's all right," he said slowly. There seemed to be no affectionate relation between him and this picture. Evidently he was weighing its value as a morsel to be flung to a ravenous public, whose wolf-like appetite, could only satisfy itself upon mental entrails, abominations. As for himself, he seemed to be remote, exterior. It was a matter of the Eclipse business.

Suddenly Coleman became executive. " Better give it to Schooner and tell him to make a half-page—-or, no, send him in here and I'll tell him my idea. How's the article? Any good? Well, give it to Smith to rewrite."

An artist came from the other room and presented for inspection his drawing of the seamen dead in the rigging of the wreck, a company of grizzly and horrible figures, bony-fingered, shrunken and with awful eyes. " Hum," said Coleman, after a prolonged study, " that's all right. That's good, Jimmie. But you'd better work 'em up around the eyes a little more." The office boy was deploying in the distance, waiting for the correct moment to present some cards and names.

The artist was cheerfully taking away his corpses when Coleman hailed him. " Oh, Jim, let me see that thing again, will you? Now, how about this spar? This don't look right to me."

" It looks right to me," replied the artist, sulkily.

" But, see. It's going to take up half a page. Can't you change it somehow "

How am I going to change it?" said the other, glowering at Coleman. " That's the way it ought to be. How am I going to change it? That's the way it ought to be."

" No, it isn't at all," said Coleman. "You've got a spar sticking out of the main body of the drawing in a way that will spoil the look of the whole page."

The artist was a man of remarkable popular reputation and he was very stubborn and conceited of it, constantly making himself unbearable with covert, threats that if he was not delicately placated at all points, he would freight his genius over to the office of the great opposition journal.

" That's the way it ought to be," he repeated, in a tone at once sullen and superior. "The spar is all right. I can't rig spars on ships just to suit you."

" And I can't give up the whole paper to your accursed spars, either," said Coleman, with animation. " Don't you see you use about a third of a page with this spar sticking off into space? Now, you were always so clever, Jimmie, in adapting yourself to the page. Can't you shorten it, or cut it off, or something? Or, break it-that's the thing. Make it a broken spar dangling down. See? "

" Yes, I s'pose I could do that," said the artist, mollified by a thought of the ease with which he could make the change, and mollified, too, by the brazen tribute to a part of his cleverness.

" Well, do it, then," said the Sunday editor, turning abruptly away. The artist, with head high, walked majestically back to the other room. Whereat the curly-headed one immediately resumed the rain of paper balls upon him. The office boy came timidly to Coleman and suggested the presence of the people in the outer office. " Let them wait until I read my mail," said Coleman. He shuffled the pack of letters indifferently through his hands. Suddenly he came upon a little grey envelope. He opened it at once and scanned its contents with the speed of his craft. Afterward he laid it down before him on the desk and surveyed it with a cool and musing smile. "So?" he remarked. " That's the case, is it?"

He presently swung around in his chair, and for a time held the entire attention of the men at the various desks. He outlined to them again their various parts in the composition of the next great Sunday edition. In a few brisk sentences he set a complex machine in proper motion. His men no longer thrilled with admiration at the precision with which he grasped each obligation of the campaign toward a successful edition. They had grown to accept it as they accepted his hat or his London clothes. At this time his face was lit with something of the self-contained enthusiasm of a general.

Immediately afterward he arose and reached for his coat and hat.

The office boy, coming circuitously forward, presented him with some cards and also with a scrap of paper upon which was scrawled a long and semicoherent word. " What are these ? " grumbled Coleman.

"They are waiting outside," answered the boy, with trepidation. It was part of the law that the lion of the ante-room should cringe like a cold monkey, more or less, as soon as he was out of his private jungle. "Oh, Tallerman," cried the Sunday editor, "here's this Arctic man come to arrange about his illustration. I wish you'd go and talk it over with him." By chance he picked up the scrap of paper with its cryptic word. " Oh," he said, scowling at the office boy. "Pity you can't remember that fellow. If you can't remember faces any better than that you should be a detective. Get out now and tell him to go to the devil." The wilted slave turned at once, but Coleman hailed him. " Hold on. Come to think of it, I will see this idiot. Send him in," he commanded, grimly.

Coleman lapsed into a dream over the sheet of grey note paper. Presently, a middle-aged man, a palpable German, came hesitatingly into the room and bunted among the desks as unmanageably as a tempest-tossed scow. Finally he was impatiently towed in the right direction. He came and stood at Coleman's elbow and waited nervously for the engrossed man to raise his eyes. It was plain that this interview meant important things to him. Somehow on his commonplace countenance was to be found the expression of a dreamer, a fashioner of great and absurd projects, a fine, tender fool. He cast hopeful and reverent glances at the man who was deeply contemplative of the grey note. He evidently believed himself on the threshold of a triumph of some kind, and he awaited his fruition with a joy that was only made sharper by the usual human suspicion of coming events.

Coleman glanced up at last and saw his visitor.

" Oh, it's you, is it ? " he remarked icily, bending upon the German the stare of a tyrant. "So you've come again, have you? " He wheeled in his chair until he could fully display a contemptuous, merciless smile. "Now, Mr. What's-your-name, you've called here to see me about twenty times already and at last I am going to say something definite about your invention." His listener's face, which had worn for a moment a look of fright and bewilderment, gladdened swiftly to a gratitude that seemed the edge of an outburst of tears. " Yes," continued Coleman, " I am going to say something definite. I am going to say that it is the most imbecile bit of nonsense that has come within the range of my large newspaper experience. It is simply the aberration of a rather remarkable lunatic. It is no good; it is not worth the price of a cheese sandwich. I understand that its one feat has been to break your leg; if it ever goes off again, persuade it to break your neck. And now I want you to take this nursery rhyme of yours and get out. And don't ever come here again. Do You understand ? You understand, do you ?" He arose and bowed in courteous dismissal.

The German was regarding him with the surprise and horror of a youth shot mortally. He could not find his tongue for a moment. Ultimately he gasped : "But, Mister Editor "—Coleman interrupted him tigerishly. " You heard what I said? Get out." The man bowed his head and went slowly toward the door.

Coleman placed the little grey note in his breast pocket. He took his hat and top coat, and evading the dismal band by a shameless manoeuvre, passed through the halls to the entrance to the elevator shaft. He heard a movement behind him and saw that the German was also waiting for the elevator. Standing in the gloom of the corridor, Coleman felt the mournful owlish eyes of the German resting upon him. He took a case from his pocket and elaborately lit a cigarette. Suddenly there was a flash of light and a cage of bronze, gilt and steel dropped, magically from above. Coleman yelled: " Down!" A door flew open. Coleman, followed by the German, stepped upon the elevator. " Well, Johnnie," he said cheerfully to the lad who operated this machine, "is business good?" "Yes, sir, pretty good," answered the boy, grinning. The little cage sank swiftly; floor after floor seemed to be rising with marvellous speed; the whole building was winging straight into the sky. There were soaring lights, figures and the opalescent glow of ground glass doors marked with black inscriptions. Other lifts were springing heavenward. All the lofty corridors rang with cries. " Up! " Down! " " Down! " " Up! " The boy's hand grasped a lever and his machine obeyed his lightest movement with sometimes an unbalancing swiftness.

Coleman discoursed briskly to the youthful attendant. Once he turned and regarded with a quick stare of insolent annoyance the despairing countenance of the German whose eyes had never left him. When the elevator arrived at the ground floor, Coleman departed with the outraged air of a man who for a time had been compelled to occupy a cell in company with a harmless spectre.

He walked quickly away. Opposite a corner of the City Hall he was impelled to look behind him. Through the hordes of people with cable cars marching like panoplied elephants, he was able to distinguish the German, motionless and gazing after him. Coleman laughed. " That's a comic old boy," he said, to himself.

In the grill-room of a Broadway hotel he was obliged to wait some minutes for the fulfillment of his orders and he spent the time in reading and studying the little grey note. When his luncheon was served he ate with an expression of morose dignity.

CHAPTER IV.

MARJORY paused again at her father's door. After hesitating in the original way she entered the library. Her father almost represented an emblematic figure, seated upon a column of books. " Well," he cried. Then, seeing it was Marjory, he changed his tone. " Ah, under the circumstances, my dear, I admit your privilege of interrupting me at any hour of the day. You have important business with me." His manner was satanically indulgent.

The girl fingered a book. She turned the leaves in absolute semblance of a person reading. "Rufus Coleman called."

"Indeed," said the professor.

"And I've come to you, father, before seeing him."

The professor was silent for a time. " Well, Marjory," he said at last, "what do you want me to say?" He spoke very deliberately. " I am sure this is a singular situation. Here appears the man I formally forbid you to marry. I am sure I do not know what I am to say."

" I wish to see him," said the girl.

"You wish to see him?" enquired the professor. "You wish to see him " Marjory, I may as well tell you now that with all the books and plays I've read, I really don't know how the obdurate father should conduct himself. He is always pictured as an exceedingly dense gentleman with white whiskers, who does all the unintelligent things in the plot. You and I are going to play no drama, are we, Marjory? I admit that I have white whiskers, and I am an obdurate father. I am, as you well may say, a very obdurate father. You are not to marry Rufus Coleman. You understand the rest of the matter. He is here ; you want to see him. What will you say to him when you see him? "

" I will say that you refuse to let me marry him, father and-" She hesitated a moment before she lifted her eyes fully and formidably to her father's face. " And that I shall marry him anyhow."

The professor did not cavort when this statement came from his daughter. He nodded and then passed into a period of reflection. Finally he asked: "But when? That is the point. When?"

The girl made a sad gesture. "I don't know. I don't know.

Perhaps when you come to know Rufus better-"

" Know him better. Know that rapscallion better? Why, I know him much better than he knows himself. I know him too well. Do you think I am talking offhand about this affair? Do you think I am talking without proper information?"

Marjory made no reply.

"Well," said the professor, "you may see Coleman on condition that you inform him at once that I forbid your marriage to him. I don't understand at all how to manage these situations. I don't know what to do. I suppose I should go myself and-No, you can't see him, Majory."

Still the girl made no reply. Her head sank forward and she breathed a trifle heavily. "Marjory," cried the professor, it is impossible that you should think so much of this man." He arose and went to his daughter. " Marjory, many wise children have been guided by foolish fathers, but we both suspect that no foolish child has ever been guided by a wise father. Let us change it. I present myself to you as a wise father. Follow my wishes in this affair and you will be at least happier than if you marry this wretched Coleman."

She answered: " He is waiting for me."

The professor turned abruptly from her and dropped into his chair at the table. He resumed a grip on his pen. " Go," he said, wearily. " Go. But if you have a remnant of sense, remember what I have said to you. Go." He waved his hand in a dismissal that was slightly scornful. " I hoped you would have a minor conception of what you were doing. It seems a pity." Drooping in tears, the girl slowly left the room.

Coleman had an idea that he had occupied the chair for several months. He gazed about at the pictures and the odds and ends of a drawing-room in an attempt to take an interest in them. The great garlanded paper shade over the piano lamp consoled his impatience in a mild degree because he knew that Marjory had made it. He noted the clusters of cloth violets which she had pinned upon the yellow paper and he dreamed over the fact. He was able to endow this shade with certain qualities of sentiment that caused his stare to become almost a part of an intimacy, a communion. He looked as if he could have unburdened his soul to this shade over the piano lamp.

Upon the appearance of Marjory he sprang up and came forward rapidly. " Dearest," he murmured, stretching out both hands. She gave him one set of fingers with chilling convention. She said something which he understood to be " Good-afternoon." He started as if the woman before him had suddenly drawn a knife. " Marjory," he cried, "what is the matter?." They walked together toward a window. The girl looked at him in polite enquiry. " Why? " she said. " Do I seem strange? " There was a moment's silence while he gazed into her eyes, eyes full of innocence and tranquillity. At last she tapped her foot upon the floor in expression of mild impatience. " People do not like to be asked what is the matter when there is nothing the matter. What do you mean? "

Coleman's face had gradually hardened. " Well, what is wrong? " he demanded, abruptly. "What has happened? What is it, Marjory? "

She raised her glance in a perfect reality of wonder. "What is wrong? What has happened? How absurd! Why nothing, of course." She gazed out of the window. " Look," she added, brightly, the students are rolling somebody in a drift. Oh, the poor Man! "

Coleman, now wearing a bewildered air, made some pretense of being occupied with the scene. " Yes," he said, ironically. "Very interesting, indeed."

" Oh," said Marjory, suddenly, " I forgot to tell you. Father is going to take mother and me to Greece this winter with him and the class."

Coleman replied at once. " Ah, indeed? That will be jolly."

"Yes. Won't it be charming?"

" I don't doubt it," he replied. His composure May have displeased her, for she glanced at him furtively and in a way that denoted surprise, perhaps.

"Oh, of course," she said, in a glad voice. " It will be more fun. We expect to nave a fine time. There is such a nice lot of boys going Sometimes father chooses these dreadfully studious ones. But this time he acts as if he knew precisely how to make up a party."

He reached for her hand and grasped it vise-like. "Marjory," he breathed, passionately, " don't treat me so. Don't treat me-"

She wrenched her hand from him in regal indignation. " One or two rings make it uncomfortable for the hand that is grasped by an angry gentleman." She held her fingers and gazed as if she expected to find them mere debris. " I am sorry that you are not interested in the students rolling that man in the snow. It is the greatest scene our quiet life can afford."

He was regarding her as a judge faces a lying culprit. " I know," he said, after a pause. " Somebody has been telling you some stories. You have been hearing something about me."

" Some stories ? " she enquired. " Some stories about you? What do you mean? Do you mean that I remember stories I may happen to hear about people? "

There was another pause and then Coleman's face flared red.

He beat his hand violently upon a table. " Good God, Marjory!

Don't make a fool of me. Don't make this kind of a fool of me, at

any rate. Tell me what you mean. Explain-"

She laughed at him. " Explain? Really, your vocabulary is getting extensive, but it is dreadfully awkward to ask people to explain when there is nothing to explain."

He glanced at her, " I know as well as you do that your father is taking you to Greece in order to get rid of me."

" And do people have to go to Greece in order to get rid of you? " she asked, civilly. " I think you are getting excited."

" Marjory," he began, stormily. She raised her hand. " Hush," she said, "there is somebody coming." A bell had rung. A maid entered the room. " Mr. Coke," she said. Marjory nodded. In the interval of waiting, Coleman gave the girl a glance that mingled despair with rage and pride. Then Coke burst with half-tamed rapture into the room. " Oh, Miss Wainwright," he almost shouted, " I can't tell you how glad I am. I just heard to-day you were going. Imagine it. It will be more—oh, how are you Coleman, how are you " "

Marjory welcomed the new-comer with a cordiality that might not have thrilled Coleman with pleasure. They took chairs that formed a triangle and one side of it vibrated with talk. Coke and Marjory engaged in a tumultuous conversation concerning the prospective trip to Greece. The Sunday editor, as remote as if the apex of his angle was the top of a hill, could only study the girl's clear profile. The youthful voices of the two others rang like bells. He did not scowl at Coke; he merely looked at him as if be gently disdained his mental calibre. In fact all the talk seemed to tire him; it was childish; as for him, he apparently found this babble almost insupportable.

" And, just think of the camel rides we'll have," cried Coke.

" Camel rides," repeated Coleman, dejectedly. " My dear

Coke."

Finally he arose like an old man climbing from a sick bed. "Well, I am afraid I must go, Miss Wainwright." Then he said affectionately to Coke: " Good-bye, old boy. I hope you will have a good time."

Marjory walked with him to the door. He shook her hand in a friendly fashion. " Good-bye, Marjory,' he said. " Perhaps it may happen that I shan't see you again before you start for Greece and so I had best bid you God-speed—-or whatever the term is now. You will have a charming time; Greece must be a delightful place. Really, I envy you, Marjory. And now my dear child "-his voice grew brotherly, filled with the patronage of generous fraternal love, " although I may never see you again let me wish you fifty as happy years as this last one has been for me." He smiled frankly into her eyes; then dropping her hand, he went away.

Coke renewed his tempest of talk as Marjory turned toward him. But after a series of splendid eruptions, whose red fire illumined all of ancient and modem Greece, he too went away.

The professor was in his. library apparently absorbed in a book when a tottering pale-faced woman appeared to him and, in her course toward a couch in a corner of the room, described almost a semi-circle. She flung herself face downward. A thick strand of hair swept over her shoulder. " Oh, my heart is broken! My heart is broken! "

The professor arose, grizzled and thrice-old with pain. He went to the couch, but he found himself a handless, fetless man. " My poor child," he said. " My poor child." He remained listening stupidly to her convulsive sobbing. A ghastly kind of solemnity came upon the room.

Suddenly the girl lifted herself and swept the strand of hair away from her face. She looked at the professor with the wide- open dilated eyes of one who still sleeps. " Father," she said in a hollow voice, " he don't love me. He don't love me. He don't love me. at all. You were right, father." She began to laugh.

"Marjory," said the professor, trembling. "Be quiet, child. Be quiet."

" But," she said, " I thought he loved me—I was sure of it. But it don't-don't matter. I—I can't get over it. Women-women, the- but it don't matter."

" Marjory," said the professor. " Marjory, my poor daughter."

She did not heed his appeal, but continued in a dull whisper. " He was playing with me. He was—was-was flirting with me. He didn't care when I told him—I told him— I was going-going away." She turned her face wildly to the cushions again. Her young shoulders shook as if they might break. " Wo-men-women-they always——"

CHAPTER V.

By a strange mishap of management the train which bore Coleman back toward New York was fetched into an obscure side-track of some lonely region and there compelled to bide a change of fate. The engine wheezed and sneezed like a paused fat man. The lamps in the cars pervaded a stuffy odor of smoke and oil. Coleman examined his case and found only one cigar. Important brakemen proceeded rapidly along the aisles, and when they swung open the doors, a polar wind circled the legs of the passengers. " Well, now, what is all this for? " demanded Coleman, furiously. " I want to get back to New York."

The conductor replied with sarcasm, " Maybe you think I'm stuck on it " I ain't running the road. I'm running this train, and I run it according to orders." Amid the dismal comforts of the waiting cars, Coleman felt all the profound misery of the rebuffed true lover. He had been sentenced, he thought, to a penal servitude of the heart, as he watched the dusky, vague ribbons of smoke come from the lamps and felt to his knees the cold winds from the brakemen's busy flights. When the train started with a whistle and a jolt, he was elate as if in his abjection his beloved's hand had reached to him from the clouds.

When he had arrived in New York, a cab rattled him to an uptown hotel with speed. In the restaurant he first ordered a large bottle of champagne. The last of the wine he finished in sombre mood like an unbroken and defiant man who chews the straw that litters his prison house. During his dinner he was continually sending out messenger boys. He was arranging a poker party. Through a window he watched the beautiful moving life of upper Broadway at night, with its crowds and clanging cable cars and its electric signs, mammoth and glittering, like the jewels of a giantess.

Word was brought to him that the poker players were arriving. He arose joyfully, leaving his cheese. In the broad hall, occupied mainly by miscellaneous people and actors, all deep in leather chairs, he found some of his friends waiting. They trooped up stairs to Coleman's rooms, where as a preliminary, Coleman began to hurl books and papers from the table to the floor. A boy came with drinks. Most of the men, in order to prepare for the game, removed their coats and cuffs and drew up the sleeves of their shirts. The electric globes shed a blinding light upon the table. The sound of clinking chips arose; the elected banker spun the cards, careless and dexterous.

Later, during a pause of dealing, Coleman said:

" Billie, what kind of a lad is that young Coke up at Washurst?"

He addressed an old college friend.

" Oh, you mean the Sophomore Coke? " asked the friend.

" Seems a decent sort of a fellow. I don't know. Why? "

"Well, who is he? Where does he come from? What do you know about him? "

" He's one of those Ohio Cokes-regular thing— father millionaire-used to be a barber-good old boy -why? "

" Nothin'," said Coleman, looking at his cards. " I know the lad. I thought he was a good deal of an ass. I wondered who his people were."

" Oh, his people are all right-in one way. Father owns rolling mills. Do you raise it, Henry? Well, in order to make vice abhorrent to the young, I'm obliged to raise back."

" I'll see it," observed Coleman, slowly pushing forward two blue chips. Afterward he reached behind him and took another glass of wine.

To the others Coleman seemed to have something bitter upon his mind. He played poker quietly, steadfastly, and, without change of eye, following the mathematical religion of the game. Outside of the play he was savage, almost insupportable. " What's the matter with you, Rufus ? " said his old college friend. " Lost your job? Girl gone back on you? You're a hell of -a host. We don't get any. thing but insults and drinks."

Late at night Coleman began to lose steadily. In the meantime he drank glass after glass of wine. Finally he made reckless bets on a mediocre hand and an opponent followed him thoughtfully bet by bet, undaunted, calm, absolutely without emotion. Coleman lost; he hurled down his cards. " Nobody but a damned fool would have seen that last raise on anything less than a full hand."

" Steady. Come off. What's wrong with you, Rufus ? " cried his guests.

" You're not drunk, are you ? " said his old college friend, puritanically.

" 'Drunk' ?" repeated Coleman.

" Oh, say," cried a man, " let's play cards. What's all this gabbling? "

It was when a grey, dirty light of dawn evaded the thick curtains and fought on the floor with the feebled electric glow that Coleman, in the midst of play, lurched his chest heavily upon the table. Some chips rattled to the floor. " I'll call you," he murmured, sleepily.

" Well," replied a man, sternly, " three kings."

The other players with difficulty extracted five cards from beneath Coleman's pillowed head. " Not a pair! Come, come, this won't do. Oh, let's stop playing. This is the rottenest game I ever sat in. Let's go home. Why don't you put him. to bed, Billie?"

When Coleman awoke next morning, he looked back upon the poker game as something that had transpired in previous years. He dressed and went down to the grill-room. For his breakfast he ordered some eggs on toast and a pint of champagne. A privilege of liberty belonged to a certain Irish waiter, and this waiter looked at him, grinning. "Maybe you had a pretty lively time last night, Mr Coleman? "

" Yes, Pat," answered Coleman, " I did. It was all because of an unrequited affection, Patrick." The man stood near, a napkin over his arm. Coleman went on impressively. " The ways of the modern lover are strange. Now, I, Patrick, am a modern lover, and when, yesterday, the dagger of disappointment was driven deep into my heart, I immediately played poker as hard as I could and incidentally got loaded. This is the modern point of view. I understand on good authority that in old times lovers used to. languish. That is probably a lie, but at any rate we do not, in these times, languish to any great extent. We get drunk. Do you understand, Patrick? " The waiter was used to a harangue at Coleman's breakfast time. He placed his hand over his mouth and giggled. "Yessir."

" Of course," continued Coleman, thoughtfully. " It might be pointed out by uneducated persons that it is difficult to maintain a high standard of drunkenness for the adequate length of time, but in the series of experiments which I am about to make I am sure I can easily prove them to be in the wrong."

" I am sure, sir," said the waiter, " the young ladies would not like to be hearing you talk this way."

" Yes; no doubt, no doubt. The young ladies have still quite medieval ideas. They don't understand. They still prefer lovers to languish."

" At any rate, sir, I don't see that your heart is sure enough broken. You seem to take it very easy. "

" Broken! " cried Coleman. " Easy? Man, my heart is in fragments. Bring me another small bottle."

CHAPTER VI.

Six weeks later, Coleman went to the office of the proprietor of the Eclipse. Coleman was one of those smooth-shaven old-young men who wear upon some occasions a singular air of temperance and purity. At these times, his features lost their quality of worldly shrewdness and endless suspicion and bloomed as the face of some innocent boy. It then would be hard to tell that he had ever encountered even such a crime as a lie or a cigarette. As he walked into the proprietor's office he was a perfect semblance of a fine, inexperienced youth. People usually concluded this change was due to a Turkish bath or some other expedient of recuperation, but it was due probably to the power of a physical characteristic.

" Boss in ? " said Coleman.

" Yeh," said the secretary, jerking his thumb toward an inner door. In his private office, Sturgeon sat on the edge of the table dangling one leg and dreamily surveying the wall. As Coleman entered he looked up quickly. "Rufus," he cried, " you're just the man I wanted to see. I've got a scheme. A great scheme." He slid from the table and began to pace briskly to and fro, his hands deep in his trousers' pockets, his chin sunk in his collar, his light blue eyes afire with interest. " Now listen. This is immense. The Eclipse enlists a battalion of men to go to Cuba and fight the Spaniards under its own flag-the Eclipse flag. Collect trained officers from here and there-enlist every young devil we see-drill 'em—best rifles-loads of ammunition- provisions-staff of doctors and nurses -a couple of dynamite guns-everything complete best in the world. Now, isn't that great? What's the matter with that now? Eh? Eh? Isn't that great? It's great, isn't it? Eh? Why, my boy, we'll free-"

Coleman did not seem to ignite. " I have been arrested four or five times already on fool matters connected with the newspaper business," he observed, gloomily, " but I've never yet been hung. I think your scheme is a beauty."

Sturgeon paused in astonishment. " Why, what happens to be the matter with you? What are you kicking about? "

Coleman made a slow gesture. " I'm tired," he answered. " I need a vacation."

"Vacation!" cried Sturgeon. "Why don't you take one then? "

" That's what I've come to see you about. I've had a pretty heavy strain on me for three years now, and I want to get a little rest."

" Well, who in thunder has been keeping you from it? It hasn't been me."

" I know it hasn't been you, but, of course, I wanted the paper to go and I wanted to have my share in its success, but now that everything is all right I think I might go away for a time if you don't mind."

" Mind! " exclaimed Sturgeon falling into his chair and reaching for his check book. "Where do you want to go? How long do you want to be gone? How much money do you want ?"

" I don't want very much. And as for where I want to go, I thought I might like to go to Greece for a while."

Sturgeon had been writing a check. He poised his pen in the air and began to laugh. " That's a queer place to go for a rest. Why, the biggest war of modern times—a war that may involve all Europe-is likely to start there at any moment. You are not likely to get any rest in Greece."

" I know that," answered Coleman. " I know there is likely to be a war there. But I think that is exactly what would rest me. I would like to report the war."

"You are a queer bird," answered Sturgeon deeply fascinated with this new idea. He had apparently forgotten his vision of a Cuban volunteer battalion. " War correspondence is about the most original medium for a rest I ever heard of."

"Oh, it may seem funny, but really, any change will be good for me now. I've been whacking at this old Sunday edition until I'm sick of it, and some,. times I wish the Eclipse was in hell."

That's all right," laughed the proprietor of the Eclipse. " But I still don't see how you 'are going to get any vacation out of a war that will upset the whole of Europe. But that's your affair. If you want to become the chief correspondent in the field in case of any such war, why, of course, I would be glad to have you. I couldn't get anybody better. But I don't see where your vacation comes in."

" I'll take care of that," answered Coleman. " When I take a vacation I want to take it my own way, and I think this will be a vacation because it will be different -don't you see-different? "

" No, I don't see any sense in it, but if you think that is the way that suits you, why, go ahead. How much money do you want? "

" I don't want much. just enough to see me through nicely."

Sturgeon scribbled on his check book and then ripped a check from it. " Here's a thousand dollars. Will that do you to start with? "

" That's plenty."

"When do you want to start? "

" To-morrow."

"Oh," said Sturgeon. " You're in a hurry." This impetuous manner of exit from business seemed to appeal to him. " To-morrow," he repeated smiling. In reality he was some kind of a poet using his millions romantically, spending wildly on a sentiment that might be with beauty or without beauty, according to the momentary vacillation. The vaguely-defined desperation in Coleman's last announcement appeared to delight him. He grinned and placed the points of his fingers together stretching out his legs in a careful attitude of indifference which might even mean disapproval. " To-morrow," he murmured teasingly.

" By jiminy," exclaimed Coleman, ignoring the other man's mood, " I'm sick of the whole business. I've got out a Sunday paper once a week for three years and I feel absolutely incapable of getting out another edition. It would be all right if we were running on ordinary lines, but when each issue is more or less of an attempt to beat the previous issue, it becomes rather wearing, you know. If I can't get a vacation now I take one later in a lunatic asylum."

" Why, I'm not objecting to your having a vacation. I'm simply marvelling at the kind of vacation you want to take. And 'to-morrow,' too, eh? " " Well, it suits me," muttered Coleman, sulkily.

" Well, if it suits you, that's enough. Here's your check. Clear out now and don't let me see you again until you are thoroughly rested, even if it takes a year." He arose and stood smiling. He was mightily pleased with himself. He liked to perform in this way. He was almost seraphic as he thrust the check for a thousand dollars toward Coleman.

Then his manner changed abruptly. " Hold on a minute. I must think a little about this thing if you are going to manage the correspondence. Of course it will be a long and bloody war."

"You bet."

"The big chance is that all Europe will be dragged into it. Of course then you would have to come out of Greece and take up abetter position-say Vienna."

"No, I wouldn't care to do that," said Coleman positively. "I just want to take care of the Greek end of it."

" It will be an idiotic way to take a vacation," observed

Sturgeon.

" Well, it suits me," muttered Coleman again. " I tell you what it is-" he added suddenly. "I've got some private reasons- see? "

Sturgeon was radiant with joy. " Private reasons." He was charmed by the sombre pain in Coleman's eyes and his own ability to eject it. "Good. Go now and be blowed. I will cable final instruction to meet you in London. As soon as you get to Greece, cable me an account of the situation there and we will arrange our plans." He began to laugh. " Private reasons. Come out to dinner with me."

" I can't very well," said Coleman. " If I go tomorrow, I've got to pack-"

But here the real tyrant appeared, emerging suddenly from behind the curtain of sentiment, appearing like a red devil in a pantomine. " You can't ? " snapped Sturgeon. " Nonsense——"

CHAPTER VII.

SWEEPING out from between two remote, half-submerged dunes on which stood slender sentry light. houses, the steamer began to roll with a gentle insinuating motion. Passengers in their staterooms saw at rhythmical intervals the spray racing fleetly past the portholes. The waves grappled hurriedly at the sides of the great flying steamer and boiled discomfited astern in a turmoil of green and white. From the tops of the enormous funnels streamed level masses of smoke which were immediately torn to nothing by the headlong wind. Meanwhile as the steamer rushed into the northeast, men in caps and ulsters comfortably paraded the decks and stewards arranged deck chairs for the reception of various women who were coming from their cabins with rugs.

In the smoking room, old voyagers were settling down comfortably while new voyagers were regarding them with a diffident respect. Among the passengers Coleman found a number of people whom he knew, including a wholesale wine merchant, a Chicago railway magnate and a New York millionaire. They lived practically in the smoking room. Necessity drove them from time to time to the salon, or to their berths. Once indeed the millionaire was absent, from the group while penning a short note to his wife.

When the Irish coast was sighted Coleman came on deck to look at it. A tall young woman immediately halted in her walk until he had stepped up to her. " Well, of all ungallant men, Rufus Coleman, you are the star," she cried laughing and held out her hand.

" Awfully sorry, I'm sure," he murmured. " Been playing poker in the smoking room all voyage. Didn't have a look at the passenger list until just now. Why didn't you send me word?" These lies were told so modestly and sincerely that when the girl flashed her, brilliant eyes full upon their author there was a mixt of admiration in the indignation.

" Send you a card " I don't believe you can read, else you would have known I was to sail on this steamer. If I hadn't been ill until to-day you would have seen me in the salon. I open at the Folly Theatre next week. Dear ol' Lunnon, y' know."

" Of course, I knew you were going," said Coleman.

"But I thought you were to go later. What do you open in? "

" Fly by Night. Come walk along with me. See those two old ladies " They've been watching for me like hawks ever since we left New York. They expected me to flirt with every man on board. But I've fooled them. I've been just as g-o-o-d. I had to be."

As the pair moved toward the stern, enormous and radiant green waves were crashing futilely after the steamer. Ireland showed a dreary coast line to the north. A wretched man who had crossed the Atlantic eighty-four times was declaiming to a group of novices. A venerable banker, bundled in rugs, was asleep in his deck chair.

" Well, Nora," said Coleman, " I hope you make a hit in

London. You deserve it if anybody does. You've worked hard."

"Worked hard," cried the girl. "I should think so. Eight years ago I was in the rear row. Now I have the centre of the stage whenever I want it. I made Chalmers cut out that great scene in the second act between the queen and Rodolfo. The idea! Did he think I would stand that? And just because he was in love with Clara Trotwood, too."

Coleman was dreamy. " Remember when I was dramatic man for the Gazette and wrote the first notice? "

" Indeed, I do," answered the girl affectionately. " Indeed, I do, Rufus. Ah, that was a great lift. I believe that was the first thing that had an effect on old Oliver. Before that, he never would believe that I was any good. Give me your arm, Rufus. Let's parade before the two old women." Coleman glanced at her keenly. Her voice had trembled slightly. Her eyes were lustrous as if she were about to weep.

" Good heavens," he said. " You are the same old Nora Black. I thought you would be proud and 'aughty by this time."

" Not to my friends," she murmured., " Not to my friends. I'm always the same and I never forget. Rufus."

" Never forget what? " asked Coleman.

" If anybody does me a favour I never forget it as long as I live," she answered fervently.

" Oh, you mustn't be so sentimental, Nora. You remember that play you bought from little Ben Whipple, just because he had once sent you some flowers in the old days when you were poor and happened to bed sick. A sense of gratitude cost you over eight thousand dollars that time, didn't it? " Coleman laughed heartily.

" Oh, it wasn't the flowers at all," she interrupted seriously. " Of course Ben was always a nice boy, but then his play was worth a thousand dollars. That's all I gave him. I lost some more in trying to make it go. But it was too good. That was what was the matter. It was altogether too good for the public. I felt awfully sorry for poor little Ben."

"Too good?" sneered Coleman. "Too good? Too indifferently bad, you mean. My dear girl, you mustn't imagine that you know a good play. You don't, at all."

She paused abruptly and faced him. This regal, creature was looking at him so sternly that Coleman felt awed for a moment as if he, were in the presence of a great mind. " Do you mean to say that I'm not an artist ? " she asked.

Coleman remained cool. " I've never been decorated for informing people of their own affairs," he observed, " but I should say that you were about as much of an artist as I am."

Frowning slightly, she reflected upon this reply. Then, of a sudden, she laughed. " There is no use in being angry with you, Rufus. You always were a hopeless scamp. But," she added, childishly wistful, "have you ever seen Fly by Night? Don't you think my dance in the second act is artistic? "

" No," said Coleman, " I haven't seen Fly by Night yet, but of course I know that you are the most beautiful dancer on the stage. Everybody knows that."

It seemed that her hand tightened on his arm. Her face was radiant. " There," she exclaimed. " Now you are forgiven. You are a nice boy, Rufus-some- times."

When Miss Black went to her cabin, Coleman strolled into the smoking room. Every man there covertly or openly surveyed him. He dropped lazily into a chair at a table where the wine merchant, the Chicago railway king and the New York millionaire were playing cards. They made a noble pretense of not being aware of him. On the oil cloth top of the table the cards were snapped down, turn by turn.

Finally the wine merchant, without lifting his head to- address a particular person, said: " New conquest."

Hailing a steward Coleman asked for a brandy and soda.

The millionaire said: " He's a sly cuss, anyhow." The railway man grinned. After an elaborate silence the wine merchant asked: " Know Miss Black long, Rufus?" Coleman looked scornfully at his friends. " What's wrong with you there, fellows, anyhow?" The Chicago man answered airily. " Oh, nothin'. Nothin', whatever."

At dinner in the crowded salon, Coleman was aware that more than one passenger glanced first at Nora Black and then at him, as if connecting them in some train of thought, moved to it by the narrow horizon of shipboard and by a sense of the mystery that surrounds the lives of the beauties of the stage. Near the captain's right hand sat the glowing and splendid Nora, exhibiting under the gaze of the persistent eyes of many meanings, a practiced and profound composure that to the populace was terrfying dignity.

Strolling toward the smoking room after dinner, Coleman met the New York millionaire, who seemed agitated. He took Coleman fraternally by the arm. " Say, old man, introduce me, won't you? I'm crazy to know her."

"Do you mean Miss Black?" asked Coleman.

" Why, I don't know that I have a right. Of course, you know, she hasn't been meeting anybody aboard. I'll ask her, though- certainly."

" Thanks, old man, thanks. I'd be tickled to death. Come along and have a drink. When will you ask her? " " Why, I don't know when I'll see her. To-morrow, I suppose-"

They had not been long in the smoking room, however, when the deck steward came with a card to Coleman. Upon it was written: "Come for' a stroll?" Everybody, saw Coleman read this card and then look up and whisper to the deck steward. The deck steward bent his head and whispered discreetly in reply. There was an abrupt pause in the hum of conversation. The interest was acute.

Coleman leaned carelessly back in his chair, puffing at his cigar. He mingled calmly in a discussion of the comparative merits of certain trans-Atlantic lines. After a time he threw away his cigar and arose. Men nodded. "Didn't I tell you?" His studiously languid exit was made dramatic by the eagle-eyed attention of the smoking room.

On deck he found Nora pacing to and fro. "You didn't hurry yourself," she said, as he joined her. The lights of Queenstown were twinkling. A warm wind, wet with the moisture of rain- stricken sod, was coming from the land.

"Why," said Coleman, "we've got all these duffers very much excited."

"Well what do you care? " asked the girl. "You don't, care do you?"

"No, I don't care. Only it's rather absurd to be watched all the time." He said this precisely as if he abhorred being watched in this case. "Oh by the way," he added. Then he paused for a moment. "Aw—a friend of mine—not a bad fellow— he asked me for an introduction. Of course, I told him I'd ask you."

She made a contemptuous gesture. "Oh, another Willie. Tell him no. Tell him to go home to his family. Tell him to run away."

"He isn't a bad fellow. He—" said Coleman diffidently, "he would probably be at the theatre every night in a box."

"yes, and get drunk and throw a wine bottle on the stage instead of a bouquet. No," she declared positively, "I won't see him."

Coleman did not seem to be oppressed by this ultimatum.

"Oh, all right. I promised him—that was all."

"Besides, are you in a great hurry to get rid of me?"

"Rid of you? Nonsense."

They walked in the shadow. "How long are you going to be in London, Rufus?" asked Nora softly.

"Who? I? Oh, I'm going right off to Greece. First train. There's going to be a war, you know."

"A war? Why, who is going to fight? The Greeks and the—the—the what?"

"The Turks. I'm going right over there."

"Why, that's dreadful, Rufus," said the girl, mournfull

and shocked. "You might get hurt or something."

Presently she asked: "And aren't you going to be in

London any time at all?"

"Oh," he answered, puffing out his lips, "I may stop in London for three or four days on my way home. I'm not sure of it."

"And when will that be?"

"Oh, I can't tell. It may be in three or four months, or it may be a year from now. When the war stops."

There was a long silence as the walked up and down the swaying deck.

"Do you know," said Nora at last, "I like you, Rufus Coleman. I don't know any good reason for it either, unless it is because you are such a brute. Now, when I was asking you if you were to be in London you were perfectly detestable. You know I was anxious."

"I—detestable?" cried Coleman, feigning amazement.

"Why, what did I say?"

"It isn't so much what you said—" began Nora slowlly.

Then she suddenly changed her manner.

"Oh, well, don't let's talk about it any more. It's

too foolish. Only-you are a disagreeable person sometimes."

In the morning, as the vessel steamed up the Irish channel, Coleman was on deck, keeping furtive watch on the cabin stairs. After two hours of waiting, he scribbled a message on a card and sent it below. He received an answer that Miss Black had a headache, and felt too ill to come on deck. He went to the smoking room. The three card-players glanced up, grinning. "What's the matter?" asked the wine merchant. "You look angry." As a matter of fact, Coleman had purposely wreathed his features in a pleasant and satisfied expression, so he was for a moment furious at the wine merchant.

"Confound the girl," he thought to himself. "She has succeeded in making all these beggars laugh at me." He mused that if he had another chance he would show her how disagreeable or detestable or scampish he was under some circumstances. He reflected ruefully that the complacence with which he had accepted the comradeship of the belle of the voyage might have been somewhat overdone. Perhaps he had got a little out of proportion. He was annoyed at the stares of the other men in the smoking room, who seemed now to be reading his discomfiture. As for Nora Black he thought of her wistfully and angrily as a superb woman whose company was honour and joy, a payment for any sacrifices.

" What's the matter? " persisted the wine merchant. " You

look grumpy."

Coleman laughed. " Do I?"

At Liverpool, as the steamer was being slowly warped to the landing stage by some tugs, the passengers crowded the deck with their hand-bags. Adieus were falling as dead leaves fall from a great tree. The stewards were handling small hills of luggage marked with flaming red labels. The ship was firmly against the dock before Miss Black came from her cabin. Coleman was at the time gazing shoreward, but his three particular friends instantly nudged him. "What?" "There she is?" "Oh, Miss Black?" He composedly walked toward her. It was impossible to tell whether she saw him coming or whether it was accident, but at any rate she suddenly turned and moved toward the stern of the ship. Ten watchful gossips had noted Coleman's travel in her direction and more than half the passengers noted his defeat. He wheeled casually and returned to his three friends. They were colic-stricken with a coarse and yet silent merriment. Coleman was glad that the voyage was over.

After the polite business of an English custom house, the travellers passed out to the waiting train. A nimble little theatrical agent of some kind, sent from London, dashed forward to receive Miss Black. He had a first-class compartment engaged for her and he bundled her and her maid into it in an exuberance of enthusiasm and admiration.. Coleman passing moodily along the line of coaches heard Nora's voice hailing him.

" Rufus." There she was, framed in a carriage window, beautiful and smiling brightly. Every near. by person turned to contemplate this vision.

" Oh," said Coleman advancing, " I thought I was not going to get a chance to say good-bye to you." He held out his hand. " Good-bye."

She pouted. " Why, there's plenty of room in this compartment." Seeing that some forty people were transfixed in observation of her, she moved a short way back. " Come on in this compartment, Rufus," she said.

"Thanks. I prefer to smoke," said Coleman. He went off abruptly.

On the way to London, he brooded in his corner on the two divergent emotions he had experienced when refusing her invitation. At Euston Station in London, he was directing a porter, who had his luggage, when he heard Nora speak at his shoulder. " Well, Rufus, you sulky boy," she said, " I shall be at the Cecil. If you have time, come and see me."

“ Thanks, I’m sure, my dear Nora,” answered Coleman effusively. “But honestly, I’m off for Greece.”

A brougham was drawn up near them and the nimble little agent was waiting. The maid was directing the establishment of a mass of luggage on and in a four-wheeler cab. “ Well, put me into my carriage, anyhow,” said Nora. “ You will have time for that.”

Afterward she addressed him from the dark interior.

Now, Rufus, you must come to see me the minute you strike

London again- of She hesitated a moment and then smiling

gorgeously upon him, she said: “ Brute! “

CHAPTER VIII.

As soon as Coleman had planted his belongings in a hotel he was bowled in a hansom briskly along the smoky Strand, through a dark city whose walls dripped like the walls of a cave and whose passages were only illuminated by flaring yellow and red signs.

Walkley the London correspondent of the Eclipse, whirled from his chair with a shout of joy and relief -at sight of Coleman. " Cables," he cried. "Nothin' but cables! All the people in New York are writing cables to you. The wires groan with them. And we groan with them too. They come in here in bales. However, there is no reason why you should read them all. Many are similar in words and many more are similar in spirit. The sense of the whole thing is that you get to Greece quickly, taking with you immense sums of money and enormous powers over nations."

" Well, when does the row begin? "

" The most astute journalists in Europe have been predicting a general European smash-up every year since 1878," said Walkley, " and the prophets weep. The English are the only people who can pull off wars on schedule time, and they have to do it in odd corners of the globe. I fear the war business is getting tuckered. There is sorrow in the lodges of the lone wolves, the war correspondents. However, my boy, don't bury your face in your blanket. This Greek business looks very promising, very promising." He then began to proclaim trains and connections. " Dover, Calais, Paris, Brindisi, Corfu, Patras, Athens. That is your game. You are supposed to sky-rocket yourself over that route in the shortest possible time, but you would gain no time by starting before to-morrow, so you can cool your heels here in London until then. I wish I was going along."

Coleman returned to his hotel, a knight impatient and savage at being kept for a time out of the saddle. He went for a late supper to the grill room and as he was seated there alone, a party of four or five people came to occupy the table directly behind him. They talked a great deal even before they arrayed them. selves at the table, and he at once recognised the voice of Nora Black. She was queening it, apparently, over a little band of awed masculine worshippers.

Either by accident or for some curious reason, she took a chair back to back with Coleman's chair. Her sleeve of fragrant stuff almost touched his shoulder and he felt appealing to him seductively a perfume of orris root and violet. He was drinking bottled stout with his chop; be sat with a face of wood.

" Oh, the little lord? " Nora was crying to some slave. "Now, do you know, he won't do at all. He is too awfully charming. He sits and ruminates for fifteen minutes and then he pays me a lovely compliment. Then he ruminates for another fifteen minutes and cooks up another fine thing. It is too tiresome. Do you know what kind of man. I like? " she asked softly and confidentially. And here she sank back in her chair until. Coleman knew from the tingle that her head was but a few inches from his head. Her, sleeve touched him. He turned more wooden under the spell of the orris root and violet. Her courtiers thought it all a graceful pose, but Coleman believed otherwise. Her voice sank to the liquid, siren note of a succubus. " Do you know what kind of a man I like? Really like? I like a man that a woman can't bend in a thousand different ways in five minutes. He must have some steel in him. He obliges me to admire him the most when he remains stolid; stolid to me lures. Ah, that is the only kind of a man who cap ever break a heart among us women of the world. His stolidity is not real; no; it is mere art, but it is a highly finished art and often enough we can't cut through it. Really we can't. And, then we may actually come to—er—care for the man. Really we may. Isn't it funny?"

Alt the end Coleman arose and strolled out of the. room, smoking a cigarette. He did not betray, a sign. Before. the door clashed softly behind him, Nora laughed a little defiantly, perhaps a little loudly. It made every man in the grill-room perk up his ears. As for her courtiers, they were entranced. In her description of the conquering man, she had easily contrived that each one of them wondered if she might not mean him. Each man was perfectly sure that he had plenty of steel in his composition and that seemed to be a main point.

Coleman delayed for a time in the smoking room and then went to his own quarters. In reality he was Somewhat puzzled in his mind by a projection of the beauties of Nora Black upon his desire for Greece and Marjory, His thoughts formed a duality. Once he was on the point of sending his card to Nora Black's parlour, inasmuch as Greece was very distant and he could not start until the morrow. But he suspected that he was holding the interest of the actress because of his recent appearance of impregnable serenity in the presence of her fascinations. If he now sent his card, it was a form of surrender and he knew her to be one to take a merciless advantage. He would not make this tactical mistake. On the contrary he would go to bed and think of war,

In reality he found it easy to fasten his mind upon the prospective war. He regarded himself cynically in most affairs, but he could not be cynical of war, because had he - seen none of it. His rejuvenated imagination began to thrill to the roll of battle, through his thought passing all the lightning in the pictures of Detaille, de Neuville and Morot; lashed battery horse roaring over bridges; grand cuirassiers dashing headlong against stolid invincible red-faced lines of German infantry; furious and bloody grapplings in the streets of little villages of northeastern France. There was one thing at least of which he could still feel the spirit of a debutante. In this matter of war he was not, too, unlike a young girl embarking upon her first season of opera. Walkely, the next morning, saw this mood sitting quaintly upon Coleman and cackled with astonishment and glee. Coleman's usual manner did not return until he detected Walkely's appreciation of his state and then he snubbed him according to the ritual of the Sunday editor of the New York Eclipse. Parenthetically, it might be said that if Coleman now recalled Nora Black to his mind at all, it was only to think of her for a moment with ironical complacence. He had beaten her.

When the train drew out of the station, Coleman felt himself thrill. Was ever fate less perverse? War and love-war and Marjory-were in conjunction both in Greece-and he could tilt with one lance at both gods. It was a great fine game to play and no man was ever so blessed in vacations. He was smiling continually to himself and sometimes actually on the point of talking aloud. This was despite the presence in the compartment of two fellow passengers who preserved in their uncomfortably rigid, icy and uncompromising manners many of the more or less ridiculous traditions of the English first class carriage. Coleman's fine humour betrayed him once into addressing one of these passengers and the man responded simply with a wide look of incredulity, as if he discovered that he was travelling in the same compartment with a zebu. It turned Coleman suddenly to evil temper and he wanted to ask the man questions concerning his education and his present mental condition: and so until the train arrived at Dover, his ballooning soul was in danger of collapsing. On the packet crossing the channel, too, he almost returned to the usual Rufus Coleman since all the world was seasick and he could not get a cabin in which to hide himself from it. However he reaped much consolation by ordering a bottle of champagne and drinking it in sight of the people, which made them still more seasick. From Calais to Brindisi really nothing met his disapproval save the speed of the train, the conduct of some of the passengers, the quality of the food served, the manners of the guards, the temperature of the carriages, the prices charged and the length of the journey.

In time he passed as in a vision from wretched Brindisi to charming Corfu, from Corfu to the little war-bitten city of Patras and from Patras by rail at the speed of an ox-cart to Athens.

With a smile of grim content and surrounded in his carriage with all his beautiful brown luggage, he swept through the dusty streets of the Greek capital. Even as the vehicle arrived in a great terraced square in front of the yellow palace, Greek recruits in garments representing many trades and many characters were marching up cheering for Greece and the king. Officers stood upon the little iron chairs in front of the cafes; all the urchins came running and shouting; ladies waved their handkerchiefs from the balconies; the whole city was vivified with a leaping and joyous enthusiasm. The Athenians—as dragomen or otherwise-had preserved an ardor for their glorious traditions, and it was as if that in the white dust which lifted from the plaza and floated across the old-ivory face of the palace, there were the souls of the capable soldiers of the past. Coleman was almost intoxicated with it. It seemed to celebrate his own reasons, his reasons of love and ambition to conquer in love.

When the carriage arrived in front of the Hotel D'Angleterre, Coleman found the servants of the place with more than one eye upon the scene in the plaza, but they soon paid heed to the arrival of a gentleman with such an amount of beautiful leather luggage, all marked boldly with the initials "R. C." Coleman let them lead him and follow him and conduct him and use bad English upon him without noting either their words, their salaams or their work. His mind had quickly fixed upon the fact that here was the probable headquarters of the Wainwright party and, with the rush of his western race fleeting through his veins, he felt that he would choke and die if he did not learn of the Wainwrights in the first two minutes. It was a tragic venture to attempt to make the Levantine mind understand something off the course, that the new arrival's first thought was to establish a knowlege of the whereabouts of some of his friends rather than to swarm helter-skelter into that part of the hotel for which he was willing to pay rent. In fact he failed to thus impress them; failed in dark wrath, but, nevertheless, failed. At last he was simply forced to concede the travel of files of men up the broad, redcarpeted stair-case, each man being loaded with Coleman's luggage. The men in the hotel-bureau were then able to comprehend that the foreign gentleman might have something else on his mind. They raised their eyebrows languidly when he spoke of the Wainwright party in gentle surprise that he had not yet learned that they were gone some time. They were departed on some excursion. Where? Oh, really-it was almost laughable, indeed-they didn't know. Were they sure? Why, yes-it was almost laughable, indeed -they were quite sure. Where could the gentleman find out about them? Well, they-as they had explained-did not know, but-it was possible-the American minister might know. Where was he to be found? Oh, that was very simple. It was well known that the American minister had apartments in the hotel. Was he in? Ah, that they could not say. So Coleman, rejoicing at his final emancipation and with the grime of travel still upon him, burst in somewhat violently upon the secretary of the Hon. Thomas M. Gordner of Nebraska, the United States minister to Greece. From his desk the secretary arose from behind an accidental bulwark of books and govermental pamphets. " Yes, certainly. Mr. Gordner is in. If you would give me your card-"

Directly. Coleman was introduced into another room where a quiet man who was rolling a cigarette looked him frankly but carefully in the eye. "The Wainwrights," said the minister immediately after the question. "Why, I myself am immensely concerned about them at present. I'm afraid they've gotten themselves into trouble.'

" Really? " said Coleman.

" Yes. That little professor is ratherer—stubborn; Isn't he? He wanted to make an expedition to Nikopolis and I explained to him all the possibilities of war and begged him to at least not take his wife and daughter with him."

" Daughter," murmured Coleman, as if in his sleep.

"But that little old man had a head like a stone and only laughed at me. Of course those villainous young students were only too delighted at a prospect of war, but it was a stupid and absurd. thing for the man to take his wife and daughter there. They are up there now. I can't get a word from them or get a word to them."

Coleman had been choking. "Where is Nikopolis? " he asked.

The minister gazed suddenly in comprehension of the man before him. " Nikopolis is in Turkey," he answered gently.

Turkey at that time was believed to be a country of delay, corruption, turbulence and massacre. It meant everything. More than a half of the Christians of the world shuddered at the name of Turkey. Coleman's lips tightened and perhaps blanched, and his chin moved out strangely, once, twice, thrice. " How can I get to Nikopolis? " he said.

The minister smiled. " It would take you the better part of four days if you could get there, but as a matter of fact you can't get there at the present time. A Greek army and a Turkish army are looking at each other from the sides of the river at Arta-the river is there the frontier-and Nikopolis happens to be on the wrong side. You can't reach them. The forces at Arta will fight within three days. I know it. Of course I've notified our legation at Constantinople, but, with Turkish methods of communication, Nikopolis is about as far from Constantinople as New York is from Pekin."

Coleman arose. "They've run themselves into a nice mess," he said crossly. " Well, I'm a thousand times obliged to you, I'm sure."

The minister opened his eyes a trifle. You are not going to try to reach them, are you? "

" Yes," answered Coleman, abstractedly. " I'm going to have a try at it. Friends of mine, you know-"

At the bureau of the hotel, the correspondent found several cables awaiting him from the alert office of the New York Eclipse. One of them read: "State Department gives out bad plight of Wainwright party lost somewhere; find them. Eclipse." When Coleman perused the message he began to smile with seraphic bliss. Could fate have ever been less perverse.

Whereupon he whirled himself in Athens. And it was to the considerable astonishment of some Athenians. He discovered and instantly subsidised a young Englishman who, during his absence at the front, would act as correspondent for the Eclipse at the capital. He took unto himself a dragoman and then bought three horses and hired a groom at a speed that caused a little crowd at the horse dealer's place to come out upon the pavement and watch this surprising young man ride back toward his hotel. He had already driven his dragoman into a curious state of Oriental bewilderment and panic in which he could only lumber hastily and helplessly here and there, with his face in the meantime marked with agony. Coleman's own field equipment had been ordered by cable from New York to London, but it was necessary to buy much tinned meats, chocolate, coffee, candles, patent food, brandy, tobaccos, medicine and other things.

He went to bed that night feeling more placid. The train back to Patras was to start in the early morning, and he felt the satisfaction of a man who is at last about to start on his own great quest. Before he dropped off to slumber, he heard crowds cheering exultantly in the streets, and the cheering moved him as it had done in the morning. He felt that the celebration of the people was really an accompaniment to his primal reason, a reason of love and ambition to conquer in love-even as in the theatre, the music accompanies the heroin his progress. He arose once during the night to study a map of the Balkan peninsula and get nailed into his mind the exact position of Nikopolis. It was important.

CHAPTER IX.

COLEMAN'S dragoman aroused him in the blue before dawn. The correspondent arrayed himself in one of his new khaki suits- riding breeches and a tunic well marked with buttoned pockets- and accompanied by some of his beautiful brown luggage, they departed for the station.

The ride to Patras is a terror under ordinary circumstances. It begins in the early morning and ends in the twilight. To Coleman, having just come from Patras to Athens, this journey from Athens to Patras had all the exasperating elements of a forced recantation. Moreover, he had not come prepared to view with awe the ancient city of Corinth nor to view with admiration the limpid beauties of the gulf of that name with its olive grove shore. He was not stirred by Parnassus, a far-away snow-field high on the black shoulders of the mountains across the gulf. No; he wished to go to Nikopolis. He passed over the graves of an ancient race the gleam of whose mighty minds shot, hardly dimmed, through the clouding ages. No; he wished to go to Nikopolis. The train went at a snail's pace, and if Coleman bad an interest it was in the people who lined the route and cheered the soldiers on the train. In Coleman s compartment there was a greasy person who spoke a little English. He explained that he was a poet, a poet who now wrote of nothing but war. When a man is in pursuit of his love and success is known to be at least remote, it often relieves his strain if he is deeply bored from time to time.

The train was really obliged to arrive finally at Patras even if it was a tortoise, and when this happened, a hotel runner appeared, who lied for the benefit of the hotel in saying that there was no boat over to Mesalonghi that night. When, all too late, Coleman discovered the truth of the matter his wretched dragoman came in for a period of infamy and suffering. However, while strolling in the plaza at Patras, amid newsboys from every side, by rumour and truth, Coleman learned things to his advantage. A Greek fleet was bombarding Prevasa. Prevasa was near Nikopolis. The opposing armies at Arta were engaged, principally in an artillery duel. Arta was on the road from Nikopolis into Greece. Hearing this news in the sunlit square made him betray no weakness, but in the darkness of his room at the hotel, he seemed to behold Marjory encircled by insurmountable walls of flame. He could look out of his window into the black night of the north and feel every ounce of a hideous circumstance. It appalled him; here was no power of calling up a score of reporters and sending them scampering to accomplish everything. He even might as well have been without a tongue as far as it could serve him in goodly speech. He was alone, confronting the black ominous Turkish north behind which were the deadly flames; behind the flames was Marjory. It worked upon him until he felt obliged to call in his dragoman, and then, seated upon the edge of his bed and waving his pipe eloquently, he described the plight of some very dear friends who were cut off at Nikopolis in Epirus. Some of his talk was almost wistful in its wish for sympathy from his servant, but at the end he bade the dragoman understand that be, Coleman, was going to their rescue, and he defiantly asked the hireling if he was prepared to go with him. But he did not know the Greek nature. In two minutes the dragoman was weeping tears of enthusiasm, and, for these tears, Coleman was over-grateful, because he had not been told that any of the more crude forms of sentiment arouse the common Greek to the highest pitch, but sometimes, when it comes to what the Americans call a "show down," when he gets backed toward his last corner with a solitary privilege of dying for these sentiments, perhaps he does not always exhibit those talents which are supposed to be possessed by the bulldog. He often then, goes into the cafes and take's it out in oration, like any common Parisian.

In the morning A steamer carried them across the strait and landed them near Mesalonghi at the foot of the railroad that leads to Agrinion. At Agrinion Coleman at last began to feel that he was nearing his goal. There were plenty of soldiers in the town, who received with delight and applause this gentleman in the distinguished-looking khaki clothes with his revolver and his field glasses and his canteen and; his dragoman. The dragoman lied, of course, and vocifcrated that the gentleman in the distinguished-looking khaki clothes was an English soldier of reputation, who had, naturally, come to help the cross in its fight against, the crescent. He also said that his master had three superb horses coming from Athens in charge of a groom, and was undoubtedly going to join the cavalry. Whereupon the soldiers wished to embrace and kiss the gentleman in the distinguished-looking khaki clothes.

There was more or less of a scuffle. Coleman would have taken to kicking and punching, but he found that by a- series of elusive movements he could dodge the demonstrations of affection without losing his popularity. Escorted by the soldiers, citizens, children and dogs, he went to the diligence which was to take him and others the next stage of the journey. As the diligence proceeded, Coleman's mind suffered another little inroad of ill-fate as to the success of his expedition. In the first place it appeared foolish to expect that this diligence would ever arrive anywhere. Moreover, the accommodations were about equal to what one would endure if one undertook to sleep for a night in a tree. Then there was a devil-dog, a little black-and-tan terrier in a blanket gorgeous and belled, whose duty it was to stand on the top of the coach and bark incessantly to keep the driver fully aroused to the enormity of his occupation. To have this cur silenced either by strangulation or ordinary clubbing, Coleman struggled with his dragoman as Jacob struggled with the angel, but in the first place, the dragoman was a Greek whose tongue could go quite drunk, a Greek who became a slave to the heralding and establishment of one certain fact, or lie, and now he was engaged in describing to every village and to all the country side the prowess of the gentleman in the distinguished-looking khaki clothes. It was the general absurdity of this advance to the frontier and the fighting, to the crucial place where he was resolved to make an attempt to rescue his sweetheart ; it was this ridiculous aspect that caused to come to Coleman a premonition of failure. No knight ever went out to recover a lost love in such a diligence and with such a devil-dog, tinkling his little bells and yelping insanely to keep the driver awake. After night-fall they arrived at a town on the southern coast of the Gulf of Arta and the goaded dragoman was-thrust forth from the little inn into the street to find the first possible means of getting on to Arta. He returned at last to tremulously say that there was no single chance of starting for Arta that night. Where upon he was again thrust into the street with orders, strict orders. In due time, Coleman spread his rugs upon the floor of his little room and thought himself almost asleep,. when the dragoman entered with a really intelligent man who, for some reason, had agreed to consort with him in the business of getting the stranger off to Arta. They announced that there was a brigantine about to sail with a load of soldiers for a little port near Arta, and if Coleman hurried he could catch it, permission from an officer having already been obtained. He was up at once, and the dragoman and the unaccountably intelligent person hastily gathered his chattels. Stepping out into a black street and moving to the edge of black water and embarking in a black boat filled with soldiers whose rifles dimly shone, was as impressive to Coleman as if, really, it had been the first start. He had endured many starts, it was true, but the latest one always touched him as being conclusive.

There were no lights on the brigantine and the men swung precariously up her sides to the deck which was already occupied by a babbling multitude. The dragoman judiciously found a place for his master where during the night the latter had to move quickly everytime the tiller was shifted to starboard.

The craft raised her shadowy sails and swung slowly off into the deep gloom. Forward, some of the soldiers began to sing weird minor melodies. Coleman, enveloped in his rugs, -smoked three or four cigars. He was content and miserable, lying there, hearing these melodies which defined to him his own affairs.

At dawn they were at the little port. First, in the carmine and grey tints from a sleepy sun, they could see little mobs of soldiers working amid boxes of stores. And then from the back in some dun and green hills sounded a deep-throated thunder of artillery An officer gave Coleman and his dragoman positions in one of the first boats, but of course it could not be done without an almost endless amount of palaver. Eventually they landed with their traps. Coleman felt through the sole of his boot his foot upon the shore. He was within striking distance.

But here it was smitten into the head of Coleman's servant to turn into the most inefficient dragoman, probably in the entire East. Coleman discerned it immediately, before any blunder could tell him. He at first thought that it was the voices of the guns which had made a chilly inside for the man, but when he reflected upon the incompetency, or childish courier's falsity, at Patras and his discernible lack of sense from Agrinion onward, he felt that the fault was elemental in his nature. It was a mere basic inability to front novel situations which was somehow in the dragoman; he retreated from everything difficult in a smoke of gibberish and gesticulation. Coleman glared at him with the hatred that sometimes ensues when breed meets breed, but he saw that this man was indeed a golden link in his possible success. This man connected him with Greece and its language. If he destroyed him he delayed what was now his main desire in life. However, this truth did not prevent him from addressing the man in elegant speech.

The two little men who were induced to carry Coleman's luggage as far as the Greek camp were really procured by the correspondent himself, who pantomined vigourously and with unmistakable vividness. Followed by his dragoman and the two little men, he strode off along a road which led straight as a stick to where the guns were at intervals booming. Meanwhile the dragoman and the two little men talked, talked, talked.- Coleman was silent, puffing his cigar and reflecting upon the odd things which happen to chivalry in the modern age.

He knew of many men who would have been astonished if they could have seen into his mind at that time, and he knew of many more men who would have laughed if they had the same privilege of sight. He made no attempt to conceal from himself that the whole thing was romantic, romantic despite the little tinkling dog, the decrepit diligence, the palavering natives, the super-idiotic dragoman. It was fine, It was from another age and even the actors could not deface the purity of the picture. However it was true that upon the brigantine the previous night he had unaccountably wetted all his available matches. This was momentous, important, cruel truth, but Coleman, after all, was taking-as well as he could forgeta solemn and knightly joy of this adventure and there were as many portraits of his lady envisioning. before him as ever held the heart of an armour-encased young gentleman of medieval poetry. If he had been travelling in this region as an ordinary tourist, he would have been apparent mainly for his lofty impatience over trifles, but now there was in him a positive assertion of direction which was undoubtedly one of the reasons for the despair of the accomplished dragoman.

Before them the country slowly opened and opened, the straight white road always piercing it like a lanceshaft. Soon they could see black masses of men marking the green knolls. The artillery thundered loudly and now vibrated augustly through the air. Coleman quickened his pace, to the despair of the little men carrying the traps. They finally came up with one of these black bodies of men and found it to be composed of a considerable number of soldiers who were idly watching some hospital people bury a dead Turk. The dragoman at once dashed forward to peer through the throng and see the face of the corpse. Then he came and supplicated Coleman as if he were hawking him to look at a relic and Coleman moved by a strong, mysterious impulse, went forward to look at the poor little clay-coloured body. At that moment a snake ran out from a tuft of grass at his feet and wriggled wildly over the sod. The dragoman shrieked, of course, but one of the soldiers put his heel upon the head of the reptile and it flung itself into the agonising knot of death. Then the whole crowd powwowed, turning from the dead man to the dead snake. Coleman signaled his contingent and proceeded along the road.

This incident, this paragraph, had seemed a strange introduction to war. The snake, the dead man, the entire sketch, made him shudder of itself, but more than anything he felt an uncanny symbolism. It was no doubt a mere occurrence; nothing but an occurrence; but inasmuch as all the detail of this daily life associated itself with Marjory, he felt a different horror. He had thought of the little devil-dog and Marjory in an interwoven way. Supposing Marjory had been riding in the diligence with the devil-dog-a-top? What would she have said? Of her fund of expressions, a fund uncountable, which would she have innocently projected against the background of the Greek hills? Would it have smitten her nerves badly or would she have laughed? And supposing Marjory could have seen him in his new khaki clothes cursing his dragoman as he listened to the devil-dog?

And now he interwove his memory of Marjory with a dead man and with a snake in the throes of the end of life. They crossed, intersected, tangled, these two thoughts. He perceived it clearly; the incongruity of it. He academically reflected upon the mysteries of the human mind, this homeless machine which lives here and then there and often lives in two or three opposing places at the same instant. He decided that the incident of the snake and the dead man had no more meaning than the greater number of the things which happen to us in our daily lives. Nevertheless it bore upon him.

On a spread of plain they saw a force drawn up in a long line. It was a flagrant inky streak on the verdant prairie. From somewhere near it sounded the timed reverberations of guns. The brisk walk of the next ten minutes was actually exciting to Coleman. He could not but reflect that those guns were being fired with serious purpose at certain human bodies much like his own.

As they drew nearer they saw that the inky streak was composed of cavalry, the troopers standing at their bridles. The sunlight flicked, upon their bright weapons. Now the dragoman developed in one of his extraordinary directions. He announced forsooth that an intimate friend was a captain of cavalry in this command. Coleman at first thought. that this was some kind of mysterious lie, but when he arrived where they could hear the stamping of hoofs, the clank of weapons, and the murmur of men, behold, a most dashing young officer gave a shout of joy and he and the dragoman hurled themselves into a mad embrace. After this first ecstacy was over, the dragoman bethought him of his employer, and looking toward Coleman hastily explained him to the officer. The latter, it appeared, was very affable indeed. Much had happened. The Greeks and the Turks had been fighting over a shallow part of the river nearly opposite this point and the Greeks had driven back the Turks and succeeded in throwing a bridge of casks and planking across the stream. It was now the duty and the delight of this force of cavalry to cross the bridge and, passing, the little force of covering Greek infantry, to proceed into Turkey until they came in touch with the enemy.

Coleman's eyes dilated. Was ever fate less perverse? Partly in wretched French to the officer and partly in idiomatic English to the dragoman, he proclaimed his fiery desire to accompany the expedition. The officer immediately beamed upon him. In fact, he was delighted. The dragoman had naturally told him many falsehoods concerning Coleman, incidentally referring to himself more as a philanthropic guardian and, valuable friend of the correspondent than as, a plain, unvarnished. dragoman with an exceedingly good eye for the financial possibilities of his position.

Coleman wanted to ask his servant if there was any chance of the scout taking them near Nikopolis, but he delayed being informed upon this point until such time as he could find out, secretly, for himself. To ask the dragoman would be mere stupid questioning which would surely make the animal shy. He tried to be content that fate had given him this early opportunity of dealing with a Medieval situation with some show of proper form; that is to say, armed, a-horse- back, and in danger. Then he could feel that to the gods of the game he was not laughable, as when he rode to rescue his love in a diligence with a devil- dog yelping a-top.

With some flourish, the young captain presented him to the major who commanded the cavalry. This officer stood with his legs wide apart, eating the rind of a fresh lemon and talking betimes to some of his officers. The major also beamed upon Coleman when the captain explained that the gentleman in the distinguished-looking khaki clothes wished to accompany the expedition. He at once said that he would provide two troop horses for Coleman and the dragoman. Coleman thanked fate for his behaviour and his satisfaction was not without a vestige of surprise. At that time he judged it to be a remarkable amiability of individuals, but in later years he came to believe in certain laws which he deemed existent solely for the benefit of war correspondents. In the minds of governments, war offices and generals they have no function save one of disturbance, but Coleman deemed it proven that the common men, and many uncommon men, when they go away to the fighting ground, out of the sight, out of the hearing of the world known to them, and are eager to perform feats of war in this new place, they feel an absolute longing for a spectator. It is indeed the veritable coronation of this world. There is not too much vanity of the street in this desire of men to have some disinterested fellows perceive their deeds. It is merely that a man doing his best in the middle of a sea of war, longs to have people see him doing his best. This feeling is often notably serious if, in peace, a man has done his worst, or part of his worst. Coleman believed that, above everybody, young, proud and brave subalterns had this itch, but it existed, truly enough, from lieutenants to colonels. None wanted to conceal from his left hand that his right hand was performing a manly and valiant thing, although there might be times when an application of the principle would be immensely convenient. The war correspondent arises, then, to become a sort of a cheap telescope for the people at home; further still, there have been fights where the eyes of a solitary man were the eyes of the world; one spectator, whose business it was to transfer, according to his ability, his visual impressions to other minds.

Coleman and his servant were conducted to two saddled troop horses, and beside them, waited decently in the rear of the ranks. The uniform of the troopers was of plain, dark green cloth and they were well and sensibly equipped. The mounts, however, had in no way been picked; there were little horses and big horses, fat horses and thin horses. They looked the result of a wild conscription. Coleman noted the faces of the troopers, and they were calm enough save when a man betrayed himself by perhaps a disproportionate angry jerk at the bridle of his restive horse.

The major, artistically drooping his cloak from his left shoulder and tenderly and musingly fingering his long yellow moustache, rode slowly to the middle of the line and wheeled his horse to face his men. A bugle called attention, and then he addressed them in a loud and rapid speech, which did not seem to have an end. Coleman imagined that the major was paying tribute to the Greek tradition of the power of oratory. Again the trumpet rang out, and this parade front swung off into column formation. Then Coleman and the dragoman trotted at the tail of the squadron, restraining with difficulty their horses, who could not understand their new places in the procession, and worked feverishly to regain what they considered their positions in life.

The column jangled musically over the sod, passing between two hills on one of which a Greek light battery was posted. Its men climbed to the tops of their interenchments to witness the going of the cavalry. Then the column curved along over ditch and through hedge to the shallows of the river. Across this narrow stream was Turkey. Turkey, however, presented nothing to the eye but a muddy bank with fringes of trees back of it. It seemed to be a great plain with sparse collections of foliage marking it, whereas the Greek side, presented in the main a vista of high, gaunt rocks. Perhaps one of the first effects of war upon the mind, is a. new recognition and fear of the circumscribed ability of the eye, making all landscape seem inscrutable. The cavalry drew up in platoon formation on their own. bank of the stream and waited. If Coleman had known anything of war, he would have known, from appearances, that there was nothing in the immediate vicinity to, cause heart- jumping, but as a matter of truth he was deeply moved and wondered what was hidden, what was veiled by those trees. Moreover, the squadrons resembled art old picture of a body of horse awaiting Napoleon's order to charge. In the, meantime his mount fumed at the bit, plunging to get back to the ranks. The sky was, without a cloud, and the sun rays swept down upon them. Sometimes Coleman was on the verge of addressing the dragoman, according to his anxiety, but in the end he simply told him to go to the river and fill the can- teens.

At last an order came, and the first troop moved with muffled tumult across the bridge. Coleman and his dragoman followed the last troop. The horses scrambled up the muddy bank much as if they were merely breaking out of a pasture, but probably all the men felt a sudden tightening of their muscles. Coleman, in his excitement, felt, more than he saw, glossy horse flanks, green-clothed men chumping in their saddles, banging sabres and canteens, and carbines slanted in line.

There were some Greek infantry in a trench. They were heavily overcoated, despite the heat, and some were engaged in eating loaves of round, thick bread. They called out lustily as the cavalry passed them. The troopers smiled slowly, somewhat proudly in response.

Presently there was another halt and Coleman saw the major trotting busily here and there, while troop commanders rode out to meet him. Spreading groups of scouts and flankers moved off and disappeared. Their dashing young officer friend cantered past them with his troop at his heels. He waved a joyful good- bye. It was the doings of cavalry in actual service, horsemen fanning out in all forward directions. There were two troops held in reserve, and as they jangled ahead at a foot pace, Coleman and his dragoman followed them.

The dragoman was now moved to erect many reasons for an immediate return. It was plain that he had no stomach at all for this business, and that he wished himself safely back on the other side of the river. Coleman looked at him askance. When these men talked together Coleman might as well have been a polar bear for all he understood of it. When he saw the trepidation of his dragoman, he did not know what it foreboded. In this situation it was not for him to say that the dragoman's fears were founded on nothing. And ever the dragoman raised his reasons for a retreat. Coleman spoke to himself. "I am just a trifle rattled," he said to his heart, and after he had communed for a time upon the duty of steadiness, he addressed the dragoman in cool language. " Now, my persuasive friend, just quit all that, because business is business, and it may be rather annoying business, but you will have to go through with it." Long afterward, when ruminating over the feelings of that morning, he saw with some astonishment that there was not a single thing within sound or sight to cause a rational being any quaking. He was simply riding with some soldiers over a vast tree-dotted prairie.

Presently the commanding officer turned in his saddle and told the dragoman that he was going to ride forward with his orderly to where he could see the flanking parties and the scouts, and courteously, with the manner of a gentleman entertaining two guests, he asked if the civilians cared to accompany him. The dragoman would not have passed this question correctly on to Coleman if he had thought he could have avoided it, but, with both men regarding him, he considered that a lie probably meant instant detection. He spoke almost the truth, contenting himself with merely communicating to Coleman in a subtle way his sense that a ride forward with the commanding officer and his orderly would be depressing and dangerous occupation. But Coleman immediately accepted the invitation mainly because it was the invitation of the major, and in war it is a brave man who can refuse the invitation of a commanding officer. The little party of four trotted away from the reserves, curving in single file about the water-holes. In time they arrived at where the plain lacked trees and was one great green lake of grass; grass and scrubs. On this expanse they could see the Greek horsemen riding, mainly appearing as little black dots. Far to the left there was a squad said to be composed of only twenty troopers, but in the distance their black mass seemed to be a regiment.

As the officer and his guests advanced they came in view of what one may call the shore of the plain. The rise of ground was heavily clad with trees, and over the tops of them appeared the cupola and part of the walls of a large white house, and there were glimpses of huts near it as if a village was marked. The black specks seemed to be almost to it. The major galloped forward and the others followed at his pace. The house grew larger and larger and they came nearly to the advance scouts who they could now see were not quite close to the village. There had been a deception of the eye precisely as occurs at sea. Herds of unguarded sheep drifted over the plain and little ownerless horses, still cruelly hobbled, leaped painfully away, frightened, as if they understood that an anarchy had come upon them. The party rode until they were very nearly up with the scouts, and then from low down at the very edge of the plain there came a long rattling noise which endured as if some kind of grinding machine had been put in motion. Smoke arose, faintly marking the position of an intrenchment. Sometimes a swift spitting could be heard from the air over the party.

It was Coleman's fortune to think at first that the Turks were not firing in his direction, but as soon as he heard the weird voices in the air he knew that war was upon him. But it was plain that the range was almost excessive, plain even to his ignorance. The major looked at him and laughed; he found no difficulty in smiling in response. If this was war, it could be withstood somehow. He could not at this time understand what a mere trifle was the present incident. He felt upon his cheek a little breeze which was moving the grass-blades. He had tied his canteen in a wrong place on the saddle and every time the horse moved quickly the canteen banged the correspondent, to his annoyance and distress, forcibly on the knee. He had forgotten about his dragoman, but happening to look upon that faithful servitor, he saw him gone white with horror. A bullet at that moment twanged near his head and the slave to fear ducked in a spasm. Coleman called the orderly's attention and they both laughed discreetly. They made no pretension of being heroes, but they saw plainly that they were better than this man. Coleman said to him: " How far is it now to Nikopolis? " The dragoman replied only, with a look of agonized impatience.

But of course there was no going to Nikopolis that day. The officer had advanced his men as far as was intended by his superiors, and presently they were all recalled and trotted back to the bridge. They crossed it to their old camp.

An important part of Coleman's traps was back with his Athenian horses and their groom, but with his present equipment he could at least lie smoking on his blankets and watch the dragoman prepare food. But he reflected that for that day he had only attained the simple discovery that the approach to Nikopolis was surrounded with difficulties.

CHAPTER X.

The same afternoon Coleman and the dragoman rode up to Arta on their borrowed troop horses. The correspondent first went to the telegraph office and found there the usual number of despairing clerks. They were outraged when they found he was going to send messages and thought it preposterous that he insisted upon learning if there were any in the office for him. They had trouble enough with endless official communications without being hounded about private affairs by a confident young man in khaki. But Coleman at last unearthed six cablegrams which collective said that the Eclipse wondered why they did not hear from him, that Walkley had been relieved from duty in London and sent to join the army of the crown prince, that young Point, the artist, had been shipped to Greece, that if he, Coleman, succeeded in finding the Wainwright party the paper was prepared to make a tremendous uproar of a celebration over it and, finally, the paper wondered twice more why they did not hear from him.

When Coleman went forth to enquire if anybody knew of the whereabouts of the Wainwright party he thought first of his fellow correspondents. He found most of them in a cafe where was to be had about the only food in the soldier-laden town. It was a slothful den where even an ordinary boiled egg could be made unpalatable. Such a common matter as the salt men watched with greed and suspicion as if they were always about to grab it from each other. The proprietor, in a dirty shirt, could always be heard whining, evidently telling the world that he was being abused, but he had spirit enough remaining to charge three prices for everything with an almost Jewish fluency.

The correspondents consoled themselves largely upon black - bread and the native wines. Also there were certain little oiled fishes, and some green odds and ends for salads. The correspondents were practically all Englishmen. Some of them were veterans of journalism in the Sudan, in India, in South Africa; and there were others who knew as much of war as they could learn by sitting at a desk and editing the London stock reports. Some were on their own hook; some had horses and dragomen and some had neither the one nor the other; many knew how to write and a few had it yet to learn. The thing in common was a spirit of adventure which found pleasure in the extraordinary business of seeing how men kill each other.

They were talking of an artillery duel which had been fought the previous day between the Greek batteries above the town and the Turkish batteries across the river. Coleman took seat at one of the long tables, and the astute dragoman got somebody in the street to hold the horses in order that he might be present at any feasting.

One of the experienced correspondents was remarking that the fire of the Greek batteries in the engagement had been the finest artillery practice of the century. He spoke a little loudly, perhaps, in the wistful hope that some of the Greek officers would understand enough English to follow his meaning, for it is always good for a correspondent to admire the prowess on his own side of the battlefield. After a time Coleman spoke in a lull, and describing the supposed misfortunes of the Wainwright party, asked if anyone had news of them. The correspondents were surprised; they had none of them heard even of the existence of a Wainwright party. Also none of them seemed to care exceedingly. The conversation soon changed to a discussion of the probable result of the general Greek advance announced for the morrow.

Coleman silently commented that this remarkable appearance of indifference to the mishap of the Wainwrights, a little party, a single group, was a better definition of a real condition of war than that bit of long-range musketry of the morning. He took a certain despatch out of his pocket and again read it. " Find Wainwright party at all hazards; much talk here; success means red fire by ton. Eclipse." It was an important matter. He could imagine how the American people, vibrating for years to stories of the cruelty of the Turk, would tremble-indeed, was now trembling-while the newspapers howled out the dire possibilities. He saw all the kinds of people, from those who would read the Wainwright chapters from day to day as a sort of sensational novel, to those who would work up a gentle sympathy for the woe of others around the table in the evenings. He saw bar keepers and policemen taking a high gallery thrill out of this kind of romance. He saw even the emotion among American colleges over the tragedy of a professor and some students. It certainly was a big affair. Marjory of course was everything in one way, but that, to the world, was not a big affair. It was the romance of the Wainwright party in its simplicity that to the American world was arousing great sensation; one that in the old days would have made his heart leap like a colt.

Still, when batteries had fought each other savagely, and horse, foot and guns were now about to make a general advance, it was difficult, he could see, to stir men to think and feel out of the present zone of action; to adopt for a time in fact the thoughts and feelings of the other side of the world. It made Coleman dejected as he saw clearly that the task was wholly on his own shoulders.

Of course they were men who when at home manifested the most gentle and wide-reaching feelings; most of them could not by any possibility have slapped a kitten merely for the prank and yet all of them who had seen an unknown man shot through the head in battle had little more to think of it than if the man had been a rag-baby. Tender they might be; poets they might be; but they were all horned with a provisional, temporary, but absolutely essential callouse which was formed by their existence amid war with its quality of making them always think of the sights and sounds concealed in their own direct future.

They had been simply polite. " Yes ? " said one to Coleman. "How many people in the party? Are they all Americans? Oh, I suppose it will be quite right. Your minister in Constantinople will arrange that easily. Where did you say? At Nikopolis? Well, we conclude that the Turks will make no stand between here and Pentepigadia. In that case your Nikopolis will be uncovered unless the garrison at Prevasa intervenes. That garrison at Prevasa, by the way, may make a deal of trouble. Remember Plevna."

" Exactly how far is it to Nikopolis? " asked Coleman.

" Oh, I think it is about thirty kilometers," replied the

others. " There is a good miltary road as soon as you cross the

Louros river. I've got the map of the Austrian general staff.

Would you like to look at it?"

Coleman studied the map, speeding with his eye rapidly to and fro between Arta and Nikopolis. To him it was merely a brown lithograph of mystery, but he could study the distances.

He had received a cordial invitation from the com- mander of the cavalry to go with him for another ride into Turkey, and he inclined to believe that his project would be furthered if he stuck close to the cavalry. So he rode back to the cavalry camp and went peacefully to sleep on the sod. He awoke in the morning with chattering teeth to find his dragoman saying that the major had unaccountably withdrawn his loan of the two troop horses. Coleman of course immediately said to himself that the dragoman was lying a-gain in order to prevent another expedition into ominous Turkey, but after all if the commander, of the cavalry had suddenly turned the light of his favour from the correspondent it was only a proceeding consistent with the nature which Coleman now thought he was beginning to discern, a nature which can never think twice in the same place, a gageous mind which drifts, dissolves, combines, vanishes with the ability of an aerial thing until the man of the north feels that when he clutches it with full knowledge of his senses he is only the victim of his ardent imagination. It is the difference in standards, in creeds, which is the more luminous when men call out that they are all alike.

So Coleman and his dragoman loaded their traps and moved out to again invade Turkey. It was not yet clear daylight, but they felt that they might well start early since they were no longer mounted men.

On the way to the bridge, the dragoman, although he was curiously in love with his forty francs a day and his opportunities, ventured a stout protest, based apparently upon the fact that after all this foreigner, four days out from Athens was somewhat at his mercy. " Meester Coleman," he said, stopping suddenly, " I think we make no good if we go there. Much better we wait Arta for our horse. Much better. I think this no good. There is coming one big fight and I think much better we go stay Arta. Much better."

" Oh, come off," said Coleman. And in clear language he began to labour with the man. " Look here, now, if you think you are engaged in steering a bunch of wooden-headed guys about the Acropolis, my dear partner of my joys and sorrows, you are extremely mistaken. As a matter of fact you are now the dragoman of a war correspondent and you were engaged and are paid to be one. It becomes necessary that you make good. Make good, do you understand? I'm not out here to be buncoed by this sort of game." He continued indefinitely in this strain and at intervals he asked sharply Do you understand?

Perhaps the dragoman was dumbfounded that the laconic Coleman could on occasion talk so much, or perhaps he understood everything and was impressed by the argumentative power. At any rate he suddenly wilted. He made a gesture which was a protestation of martyrdom and picking up his burden proceeded on his way.

When they reached the bridge, they saw strong columns of Greek infantry, dead black in the dim light, crossing the stream and slowly deploying on the other shore. It was a bracing sight to the dragoman, who then went into one of his absurd babbling moods, in which he would have talked the head off any man who was not born in a country laved by the childish Mediterranean. Coleman could not understand what he said to the soldiers as they passed, but it was evidently all grandiose nonsense.

Two light batteries had precariously crossed the rickety bridge during the night, and now this force of several thousand infantry, with the two batteries, was moving out over the territory which the cavalry had reconnoitered on the previous day. The ground being familiar to Coleman, he no longer knew a tremour, and, regarding his dragoman, he saw that that invaluable servitor was also in better form. They marched until they found one of the light batteries unlimbered and aligned on the lake of grass about a mile from where parts of the white house appeared above the tree-tops. Here the dragoman talked with the captain of artillery, a tiny man on an immense horse, who for some unknown reason told him that this force was going to raid into Turkey and try to swing around the opposing army's right flank. He announced, as he showed his teeth in a smile, that it would be very, very dangerous work. The dragoman precipitated himself upon Coleman.

" This is much danger. The copten he tell me the trups go now in back of the Turks. It will be much danger. I think much better we go Arta wait for horse. Much better." Coleman, although be believed he despised the dragoman, could not help but be influenced by his fears. They were, so to speak, in a room with one window, and only the dragoman looked forth from the window, so if he said that what he saw outside frightened him, Coleman was perforce frightened also in a measure. But when the correspondent raised his eyes he saw the captain of the battery looking at him, his teeth still showing in a smile, as if his information, whether true or false, had been given to convince the foreigner that the Greeks were a very superior and brave people, notably one little officer of artillery. He had apparently assumed that Coleman would balk from venturing with such a force upon an excursion to trifle with the rear of a hard fighting Ottoman army. He exceedingly disliked that man, sitting up there on his tall horse and grinning like a cruel little ape with a secret. In truth, Coleman was taken back at the outlook, but he could no more refrain from instantly accepting this half-concealed challenge than he could have refrained from resenting an ordinary form of insult. His mind was not at peace, but the small vanities are very large. He was perfectly aware that he was, being misled into the thing by an odd pride, but anyhow, it easily might turn out to be a stroke upon the doors of Nikopolis. He nodded and smiled at the officer in grateful acknowledgment of his service.

The infantry was moving steadily a-field. Black blocks of men were trailing in column slowly over the plain. They were not unlike the backs of dominoes on a green baize table; they were so vivid, so startling. The correspondent and his servant followed them. Eventually they overtook two companies in command of a captain, who seemed immensely glad to have the strangers with him. As they marched, the captain spoke through the dragoman upon the virtues of his men, announcing with other news the fact that his first sergeant was the bravest man in the world.

A number of columns were moving across the plain parallel to their line of march, and the whole force seemed to have orders to halt when they reached a long ditch about four hundred yards from where the shore of the plain arose to the luxuriant groves with the cupola of the big white house sticking above them. The soldiers lay along the ditch, and the bravest man in the world spread his blanket on the ground for the captain, Coleman and himself. During a long pause Coleman tried to elucidate the question of why the Greek soldiers wore heavy overcoats, even in the bitter heat of midday, but he could only learn that the dews, when they came, were very destructive to the lungs, Further, he convinced himself anew that talking through an interpreter to the minds of other men was as satisfactory as looking at landscape through a stained glass window.

After a time there was, in front, a stir near where a curious hedge of dry brambles seemed to outline some sort of a garden patch. Many of the soldiers exclaimed and raised their guns. But there seemed to come a general understanding to the line that it was wrong to fire. Then presently into the open came a dirty brown figure, and Coleman could see through his glasses that its head was crowned with a dirty fez which had once been white. This indicated that the figure was that of one of the Christian peasants of Epirus. Obedient to the captain, the sergeant arose and waved invitation. The peasant wavered, changed his mind, was obviously terror-stricken, regained confidence and then began to advance circuitously toward the Greek lines. When he arrived within hailing dis- tance, the captain, the sergeant, Coleman's dragoman and many of the soldiers yelled human messages, and a moment later he was seen to be a poor, yellow-faced stripling with a body which seemed to have been first twisted by an ill-birth and afterward maimed by either labour or oppression, these being often identical in their effects.

His reception of the Greek soldiery was no less fervid than their welcome of him to their protection. He threw his grimy fez in the air and croaked out cheers, while tears wet his cheeks. When he had come upon the right side of the ditch he ran capering among them and the captain, the sergeant, the dragoman and a number of soldiers received wild embraces and kisses. He made a dash at Coleman, but Coleman was now wary in the game, and retired dexterously behind different groups with a finished appearance of not noting that the young man wished to greet him.

Behind the hedge of dry brambles there were more indications of life, and the peasant stood up and made beseeching gestures. Soon a whole flock of miserable people had come out to the Greeks, men, women and children, in crude and comic smocks, prancing here and there, uproariously embracing and kissing their deliverers. An old, tearful, toothless hag flung herself rapturously into the arms of the captain, and Coleman's brick-and-iron soul was moved to admiration at the way in which the officer administered a chaste salute upon the furrowed cheek. The dragoman told the correspondent that the Turks had run away from the village on up a valley toward Jannina. Everybody was proud and happy. A major of infantry came from the rear at this time and asked the captain in sharp tones who were the two strangers in civilian attire. When the captain had answered correctly the major was immediately mollified, and had it announced to the correspondent that his battalion was going to move immediately into the village, and that he would be delighted to have his company.

The major strode at the head of his men with the group of villagers singing and dancing about him and looking upon him as if he were a god. Coleman and the dragoman, at the officer's request, marched one on either side of him, and in this manner they entered the village. From all sorts of hedges and thickets, people came creeping out to pass into a delirium of joy. The major borrowed three little pack horses with rope-bridles, and thus mounted and followed by the clanking column, they rode on in triumph.

It was probably more of a true festival than most men experience even in the longest life time. The major with his Greek instinct of drama was a splendid personification of poetic quality; in fact he was himself almost a lyric. From time to time he glanced back at Coleman with eyes half dimmed with appreciation. The people gathered flowers, great blossoms of purple and corn colour. They sprinkled them over the three horsemen and flung them deliriously under the feet of the little nags. Being now mounted Coleman had no difficulty in avoiding the embraces of the peasants, but he felt to the tips of his toes an abandonment to a kind of pleasure with which he was not at all familiar. Riding thus amid cries of thanksgiving addressed at him equally with the others, he felt a burning virtue and quite lost his old self in an illusion of noble be. nignity. And there continued the fragrant hail of blossoms.

Miserable little huts straggled along the sides of the village street as if they were following at the heels of the great white house of the bey. The column proceeded northward, announcing laughingly to the glad villagers that they would never see another Turk. Before them on the road was here and there a fez from the head of a fled Turkish soldier and they lay like drops of blood from some wounded leviathan. Ultimately it grew cloudy. It even rained slightly. In the misty downfall the column of soldiers in blue was dim as if it were merely a long trail of low-hung smoke.

They came to the ruins of a church and there the major halted his battalion. Coleman worried at his dragoman to learn if the halt was only temporary. It was a long time before there was answer from the major, for he had drawn up his men in platoons and was addressing them in a speech as interminable as any that Coleman had heard in Greece. The officer waved his arms and roared out evidently the glories of patriotism and soldierly honour, the glories of their ancient people, and he may have included any subject in this wonderful speech, for the reason that he had plenty of time in which to do it. It was impossible to tell whether the oration was a good one or bad one, because the men stood in their loose platoons without discernible feelings as if to them this appeared merely as one of the inevitable consequences of a campaign, an established rule of warfare. Coleman ate black bread and chocolate tablets while the dragoman hovered near the major with the intention of pouncing upon him for information as soon as his lungs yielded to the strain upon them.

The dragoman at last returned with a very long verbal treatise from the major, who apparently had not been as exhausted after his speech to the men as one would think. The major had said that he had been ordered to halt here to form a junction with some of the troops coming direct from Arta, and that he expected that in the morning the army would be divided and one wing would chase the retreating Turks on toward Jannina, while the other wing would advance upon Prevasa because the enemy had a garrison there which had not retreated an inch, and, although it was cut off, it was necessary to send either a force to hold it in its place or a larger force to go through with the business of capturing it. Else there would be left in the rear of the left flank of a Greek advance upon Jannina a body of the enemy which at any moment might become active. The major said that his battalion would probably form part of the force to advance upon Prevasa. Nikopolis was on the road to Prevasa and only three miles away from it.

CHAPTER XI.

Coleman spent a long afternoon in the drizzle Enveloped in his macintosh he sat on a boulder in the lee of one of the old walls and moodily smoked cigars and listened to the ceaseless clatter of tongues. A ray of light penetrated the mind of the dragoman and he laboured assiduously with wet fuel until he had accomplished a tin mug of coffee. Bits of cinder floated in it, but Coleman rejoiced and was kind to the dragoman.

The night was of cruel monotony. Afflicted by the wind and the darkness, the correspondent sat with nerves keyed high waiting to hear the pickets open fire on a night attack. He was so unaccountably sure that there would be a tumult and panic of this kind at some time of the night that he prevented himself from getting a reasonable amount of rest. He could hear the soldiers breathing in sleep all about him. He wished to arouse them from this slumber which, to his ignorance, seemed stupid. The quality of mysterious menace in the great gloom and the silence would have caused him to pray if prayer would have transported him magically to New York and made him a young man with no coat playing billiards at his club.

The chill dawn came at last and with a fine elation which ever follows a dismal night in war; an elation which bounds in the bosom as soon as day has knocked the shackles from a trembling mind. Although Coleman had slept but a short time he was now as fresh as a total abstainer coming from the bath. He heard the creak of battery wheels; he saw crawling bodies of infantry moving in the dim light like ghostly processions. He felt a tremendous virility come with this new hope in the daylight. He again took satisfaction in his sentimental journey. It was a shining affair. He was on active service, an active service of the heart, and he' felt that he was a strong man ready to conquer difficulty even as the olden heroes conquered difficulty. He imagined himself in a way like them. He, too, had come out to fight for love with giants, dragons and witches. He had never known that he could be so pleased with that kind of a parallel.

The dragoman announced that the major had suddenly lent their horses to some other people, and after cursing this versatility of interest, he summoned his henchmen and they moved out on foot, following the sound of the creaking wheels. They came in time to a bridge, and on the side of this bridge was a hard military road which sprang away in two directions, north and west. Some troops were creeping out the westward way and the dragoman pointing at them said: " They going Prevasa. That is road to Nikopolis." Coleman grinned from ear to car and slapped his dragoman violently on the shoulder. For a moment he intended to hand the man a louis of reward, but he changed his mind.

Their traps were in the way of being heavy, but they minded little since the dragoman was now a victim of the influence of Coleman's enthusiasm. The road wound along the base of the mountain range, sheering around the abutments in wide white curves and then circling into glens where immense trees spread their shade over it. Some of the great trunks were oppressed with vines green as garlands, and these vines even ran like verdant foam over the rocks. Streams of translucent water showered down from the hills, and made pools in which every pebble, every leaf of a water plant shone with magic lustre, and if the bottom of a pool was only of clay, the clay glowed with sapphire light. The day was fair. The country was part of that land which turned the minds of its ancient poets toward a more tender dreaming, so that indeed their nymphs would die, one is sure, in the cold mythology of the north with its storms amid the gloom of pine forests. It was all wine to Coleman's spirit. It enlivened him to think of success with absolute surety. To be sure one of his boots began soon to rasp his toes, but he gave it no share of his attention. They passed at a much faster pace than the troops, and everywhere they met laughter and confidence and the cry. " On to Prevasa! "

At midday they were at the heels of the advance battalion, among its stragglers, taking its white dust into their throats and eyes. The dragoman was waning and he made a number of attempts to stay Coleman, but no one could have had influence upon Coleman's steady rush with his eyes always straight to the front as if thus to symbolize his steadiness of purpose. Rivulets of sweat marked the dust on his face, and two of his toes were now paining as if they were being burned off. He was obliged to concede a privilege of limping, but he would not stop.

At nightfall they halted with the outpost batallion of the infantry. All the cavalry had in the meantime come up and they saw their old friends. There was a village from which the Christian peasants came and cheered like a trained chorus. Soldiers were driving a great flock of fat sheep into a corral. They had belonged to a Turkish bey and they bleated as if they knew that they were now mere spoils of war. Coleman lay on the steps of the bey's house smoking with his head on his blanket roll. Camp fires glowed off in the fields. He was now about four miles from Nikopolis.

Within the house, the commander of the cavalry was writing dispatches. Officers clanked up and down the stairs. The dashing young captain came and said that there would be a general assault on Prevasa at the dawn of the next day. Afterward the dragoman descended upon the village and in some way wrenched a little grey horse from an inhabitant. Its pack saddle was on its back and it would very handily carry the traps. In this matter the dragoman did not consider his master; he considered his own sore back.

Coleman ate more bread and chocolate tablets and also some tinned sardines. He was content with the day's work. He did not see how he could have improved it. There was only one route by which the Wainwright party could avoid him, and that was by going to Prevasa and thence taking ship. But since Prevasa was blockaded by a Greek fleet, he conceived that event to be impossible. Hence, he had them hedged on this peninsula and they must be either at Nikopolis or Prevasa. He would probably know all early in the morning. He reflected that he was too tired to care if there might be a night attack and then wrapped in his blankets he went peacefully to sleep in the grass under a big tree with the crooning of some soldiers around their fire blending into his slumber.

And now, although the dragoman had performed a number of feats of incapacity, he achieved during the one hour of Coleman's sleeping a blunder which for real finish was simply a perfection of art. When Coleman, much later, extracted the full story, it appeared that ringing. events happened during that single hour of sleep. Ten minutes after he had lain down for a night of oblivion, the battalion of infantry, which had advanced a little beyond the village, was recalled and began a hurried night march back on the way it had so festively come. It was significant enough to appeal to almost any mind, but the dragoman was able to not understand it. He remained jabbering to some acquaintances among the troopers. Coleman had been asleep his hour when the dashing young captain perceived the dragoman, and completely horrified by his presence at that place, ran to him and whispered to him swiftly that the game was to flee, flee, flee. The wing of the army which had advanced northward upon Jannina had already been tumbled back by the Turks and all the other wing had been recalled to the Louros river and there was now nothing practically between him and his sleeping master and the enemy but a cavalry picket. The cavalry was immediately going to make a forced march to the rear. The stricken dragoman could even then see troopers getting into their saddles. He, rushed to, the, tree, and in. a panic simply bundled Coleman upon his feet before he was awake. He stuttered out his tale, and the dazed, correspondent heard it punctuated by the steady trample of the retiring cavalry. The dragoman saw a man's face then turn in a flash from an expression of luxurious drowsiness to an expression of utter malignancy. However, he was in too much of a hurry to be afraid of it; he ran off to the little grey horse and frenziedly but skilfully began to bind the traps upon the packsaddle. He appeared in a moment tugging at the halter. He could only say: "Come! Come! Come! Queek! Queek! " They slid hurriedly down a bank to the road and started to do again that which they had accomplished with considerable expenditure of physical power during the day. The hoof beats of the cavalry had already died away and the mountains shadowed them in lonely silence. They were the rear guard after the rear guard.

The dragoman muttered hastily his last dire rumours. Five hundred Circassian cavalry were coming. The mountains were now infested with the dread Albanian irregulars, Coleman had thought in his daylight tramp that he had appreciated the noble distances, but he found that he knew nothing of their nobility until he tried this night stumbling. And the hoofs of the little horse made on the hard road more noise than could be made by men beating with hammers upon brazen cylinders. The correspondent glanced continually up at the crags. From the other side he could sometimes hear the metallic clink of water deep down in a glen. For the first time in his life he seriously opened the flap of his holster and let his fingers remain on the handle of his revolver. From just in front of him he could hear the chattering of the dragoman's teeth which no attempt at more coolness could seem to prevent. In the meantime the casual manner of the little grey horse struck Coleman with maddening vividness. If the blank darkness was simply filled with ferocious Albanians, the horse did not care a button; he leisurely put his feet down with a resounding ring. Coleman whispered hastily to the dragoman. " If they rush us, jump down the bank, no matter how deep it is. That's our only chance. And try to keep together."

All they saw of the universe was, in front of them, a place faintly luminous near their feet, but fading in six yards to the darkness of a dungeon. This repre- sented the bright white road of the day time. It had no end. Coleman had thought that he could tell from the very feel of the air some of the landmarks of his daytime journey, but he had now no sense of location at all. He would not have denied that he was squirming on his belly like a worm through black mud. They went on and on. Visions of his past were sweeping through Coleman's mind precisely as they are said to sweep through the mind of a drowning person. But he had no regret for any bad deeds; he regretted merely distant hours of peace and protection. He was no longer a hero going to rescue his love. He was a slave making a gasping attempt to escape from the most incredible tyranny of circumstances. He half vowed to himself that if the God whom he had in no wise heeded, would permit him to crawl out of this slavery he would never again venture a yard toward a danger any greater than may be incurred from the police of a most proper metropolis. If his juvenile and uplifting thoughts of other days had reproached him he would simply have repeated and repeated: "Adventure be damned."

It became known to them that the horse had to be led. The debased creature was asserting its right to do as it had been trained, to follow its customs; it was asserting this right during a situation which required conduct superior to all training and custom. It was so grossly conventional that Coleman would have understood that demoniac form of anger which sometimes leads men to jab knives into warm bodies. Coleman from cowardice tried to induce the dragoman to go ahead leading the horse, and the dragoman from cowardice tried to induce Coleman to go ahead leading the horse. Coleman of course had to succumb. The dragoman was only good to walk behind and tearfully whisper maledictions as he prodded the flanks of their tranquil beast.

In the absolute black of the frequent forests, Coleman could not see his feet and he often felt like a man walking forward to fall at any moment down a thousand yards of chasm. He heard whispers; he saw skulking figures, and these frights turned out to be the voice of a little trickle of water or the effects of wind among the leaves, but they were replaced by the same terrors in slightly different forms.

Then the poignant thing interpolated. A volley crashed ahead of them some half of a mile away and another volley answered from a still nearer point. Swishing noises which the correspondent had heard in the air he now know to have been from the passing of bullets. He and the dragoman came stock still. They heard three other volleys sounding with the abrupt clamour of a hail of little stones upon a hollow surface. Coleman and the dragoman came close together and looked into the whites of each other's eyes. The ghastly horse at that moment stretched down his neck and began placidly to pluck the grass at the roadside. The two men were equally blank with fear and each seemed to seek in the other some newly rampant manhood upon which he could lean at this time. Behind them were the Turks. In front of them was a fight in the darkness. In front it was mathematic to suppose in fact were also the Turks. They were barred; enclosed; cut off. The end was come.

Even at that moment they heard from behind them the sound of slow, stealthy footsteps. They both wheeled instantly, choking with this additional terror. Coleman saw the dragoman move swiftly to the side of the road, ready to jump into whatever abyss happened to be there. Coleman still gripped the halter as if it were in truth a straw. The stealthy footsteps were much nearer. Then it was that an insanity came upon him as if fear had flamed up within him until it gave him all the magnificent desperation of a madman. He jerked the grey horse broadside to the approaching mystery, and grabbing out his revolver aimed it from the top of his improvised bulwark. He hailed the darkness.

"Halt. Who's there?" He had expected his voice to sound like a groan, but instead it happened to sound clear, stern, commanding, like the voice of a young sentry at an encampment of volunteers. He did not seem to have any privilege of selection as to the words. They were born of themselves.

He waited then, blanched and hopeless, for death to wing out of the darkness and strike him down. He heard a voice. The voice said: " Do you speak English? " For one or two seconds he could not even understand English, and then the great fact swelled up and within him. This voice with all its new quavers was still undoubtedly the voice of Prof. Harrison B.Wainwright of Washurst College

CHAPTER XII.

A CHANGE flashed over Coleman as if it had come from an electric storage. He had known the professor long, but he had never before heard a quaver in his voice, and it was this little quaver that seemed to impel him to supreme disregard of the dangers which he looked upon as being the final dangers. His own voice had not quavered.

When he spoke, he spoke in a low tone, it was the voice of the master of the situation. He could hear his dupes fluttering there in the darkness. " Yes," he said, " I speak English. There is some danger. Stay where you are and make no noise." He was as cool as an iced drink. To be sure the circumstances had in no wise changed as to his personal danger, but beyond the important fact that there were now others to endure it with him, he seemed able to forget it in a strange, unauthorized sense of victory. It came from the professor's quavers.

Meanwhile he had forgotten the dragoman, but he recalled him in time to bid him wait. Then, as well concealed as a monk hiding in his cowl, he tip-toed back into a group of people who knew him intimately.

He discerned two women mounted on little horses and about them were dim men. He could hear them breathing hard. " It is all right" he began smoothly. "You only need to be very careful—-"

Suddenly out of the blackness projected a half phosphorescent face. It was the face of the little professor. He stammered. " We-we-do you really speak English? " Coleman in his feeling of superb triumph could almost have laughed. His nerves were as steady as hemp, but he was in haste and his haste allowed him to administer rebuke to his old professor.

" Didn't you hear me ? " he hissed through his tightening lips. " They are fighting just ahead of us on the road and if you want to save yourselves don't waste time."

Another face loomed faintly like a mask painted in dark grey. It belonged to Coke, and it was a mask figured in profound stupefaction. The lips opened and tensely breathed out the name: " Coleman." Instantly the correspondent felt about him that kind of a tumult which tries to suppress itself. He knew that it was the most theatric moment of his life. He glanced quickly toward the two figures on horseback. He believed that one was making foolish gesticulation while the other sat rigid and silent. This latter one he knew to be Marjory. He was content that she did not move. Only a woman who was glad he had come but did not care for him would have moved. This applied directly to what he thought he knew of Marjory's nature.

There was confusion among the students, but Coleman suppressed it as in such situation might a centurion. " S-s-steady! " He seized the arm of the professor and drew him forcibly close. " The condition is this," he whispered rapidly. "We are in a fix with this fight on up the road. I was sent after you, but I can't get you into the Greek lines to-night. Mrs.Wainwright and Marjory must dismount and I and my man will take the horses on and hide them. All the rest of you must go up about a hundred feet into the woods and hide. When I come back, I'll hail you and you answer low." The professor was like pulp in his grasp. He choked out the word "Coleman" in agony and wonder, but he obeyed with a palpable gratitude. Coleman sprang to the side of the shadowy figure of Marjory. " Come," he said authoritatively. She laid in his palm a little icy cold hand and dropped from her horse. He had an impulse to cling to the small fingers, but he loosened them immediately, imparting to his manner, as well as the darkness per- mitted him, a kind of casual politeness as if he were too intent upon the business in hand. He bunched the crowd and pushed them into the wood. Then he and the dragoman took the horses a hundred yards onward and tethered them. No one would care if they were stolen; the great point was to get them where their noise would have no power of revealing the whole party. There had been no further firing.

After he had tied the little grey horse to a tree he unroped his luggage and carried the most of it back to the point where the others had left the road. He called out cautiously and received a sibilant answer. He and the dragoman bunted among the trees until they came to where a forlorn company was seated awaiting them lifting their faces like frogs out of a pond. His first question did not give them any assurance. He said at once: "Are any of you armed?" Unanimously they lowly breathed: "No." He searched them out one by one and finally sank down by the professor. He kept sort of a hypnotic handcuff upon the dragoman, because he foresaw that this man was really going to be the key to the best means of escape. To a large neutral party wandering between hostile lines there was technically no danger, but actually there was a great deal. Both armies had too many irregulars, lawless hillsmen come out to fight in their own way, and if they were encountered in the dead of night on such hazardous ground the Greek hillsmen with their white cross on a blue field would be precisely as dangerous as the blood-hungry Albanians. Coleman knew that the rational way was to reach the Greek lines, and he had no intention of reaching the Greek lines without a tongue, and the only tongue was in the mouth of the dragoman. He was correct in thinking that the professor's deep knowledge of the ancient language would give him small clue to the speech of the modern Greek.

As he settled himself by the professor the band of students, eight in number pushed their faces close.

He did not see any reason for speaking. There were thirty seconds of deep silence in which he felt that all were bending to hearken to his words of counsel The professor huskily broke the stillness. Well * * * what are we to do now? "

Coleman was decisive, indeed absolute. "We'll stay here until daylight unless you care to get shot."

" All right," answered the professor. He turned and made a useless remark to his flock. " Stay here."

Coleman asked civilly, " Have you had anything to eat?

Have you got anything to wrap around you? "

" We have absolutely nothing," answered the professor. " Our servants ran away and * * and then we left everything behind us * * and I've never been in such a position in my life."

Coleman moved softly in the darkness and unbuckled some of his traps.

On his knee he broke the hard cakes of bread and with his fingers he broke the little tablets of chocolate. These he distributed to his people. And at this time he felt fully the appreciation of the conduct of the eight American college students They had not yet said a word-with the exception of the bewildered exclamation from Coke. They all knew him well. In any circumstance of life which as far as he truly believed, they had yet encountered, they would have been privileged to accost him in every form of their remarkable vocabulary. They were as new to this game as, would have been eight newly-caught Apache Indians if such were set to run the elevators in the Tract Society Building. He could see their eyes gazing at him anxiously and he could hear their deep- drawn breaths. But they said no word. He knew that they were looking upon him as their leader, almost as their saviour, and he knew also that they were going to follow him without a murmur in the conviction that he knew ten-fold more than they knew. It occurred to him that his position was ludicrously false, but, anyhow, he was glad. Surely it would be a very easy thing to lead them to safety in the morning and he foresaw the credit which would come to him. He concluded that it was beneath his dignity as preserver to vouchsafe them many words. His business was to be the cold, masterful, enigmatic man. It might be said that these reflections were only half-thoughts in his mind. Meanwhile a section of his intellect was flying hither and thither, speculating upon the Circassian cavalry and the Albanian guerillas and even the Greek outposts.

He unbuckled his blanket roll and taking one blanket placed it about the shoulders of the shadow which was Mrs.Wainwright. The shadow protested incoherently,. but he muttered, "Oh that's all right." Then he took his other blanket and went to the shadow which was Marjory. It was something like putting a wrap about the shoulders of a statue. He was base enough to linger in the hopes that he could detect some slight trembling but as far as lie knew she was of stone. His macintosh he folded around the body of the professor amid quite senile protest, so senile that the professor seemed suddenly proven to him as an old, old man, a fact which had never occurred to Washurst or her children. Then he went to the dragoman and pre-empted half of his blankets, The dragoman grunted but Coleman It would not do to have this dragoman develop a luxurious temperament when eight American college students were, without speech, shivering in the cold night.

Coleman really begun to ruminate upon his glory, but he found that he could not do this well without Smoking, so he crept away some distance from this fireless, encampment, and bending his face to the ground at the foot of a tree he struck a match and lit a cigar. His return to the others would have been somewhat in the manner of coolness as displayed on the stage if he had not been prevented by the necessity of making no noise. He saw regarding him as before the dimly visible eyes of the eight students and Marjory and her father and mother. Then he whispered the conventional words. " Go to sleep if you can. You'll need your strength in the morning. I and this man here will keep watch." Three of the college students of course crawled up to him and each said: " I'll keep watch, old man." " No. We'll keep watch. You people try to sleep."

He deemed that it might be better to yield the dragoman his blanket, and So he got up and leaned against a tree, holding his hand to cover the brilliant point of his cigar. He knew perfectly well that none of them could sleep. But he stood there somewhat like a sentry without the attitude, but with all the effect of responsibility.

He had no doubt but what escape to civilisation would be easy, but anyhow his heroism should be preserved. He was the rescuer. His thoughts of Marjory were somewhat in a puzzle. The meeting had placed him in such a position that he had expected a lot of condescension on his own part. Instead she had exhibited about as much recognition of him as would a stone fountain on his grandfather's place in Connecticut. This in his opinion was not the way to greet the knight who had come to the rescue of his lady. He had not expected it so to happen. In fact from Athens to this place he had engaged himself with imagery of possible meetings. He was vexed, certainly, but, far beyond that, he knew a deeper adminiration for this girl. To him she represented the sex, and so the sex as embodied in her seemed a mystery to be feared. He wondered if safety came on the morrow he would not surrender to this feminine invulnerability. She had not done anything that he had expected of her and so inasmuch as he loved her he loved her more. It was bewitching. He half considered himself a fool. But at any rate he thought resentfully she should be thankful to him for having rendered her a great service. However, when he came to consider this proposition he knew that on a basis of absolute manly endeavour he had rendered her little or no service.

The night was long.

CHAPTER XIII.

COLEMAN suddenly found himself looking upon his pallid dragoman. He saw that he had been asleep crouched at the foot of the tree. Without any exchange of speech at all he knew there had been alarming noises. Then shots sounded from nearby. Some were from rifles aimed in that direction and some were from rifles opposed to them. This was distinguishable to the experienced man, but all that Coleman knew was that the conditions of danger were now triplicated. Unconsciously he stretched his hands in supplication over his charges. "Don't move! Don't move! And keep close to the ground!" All heeded him but Marjory. She still sat straight. He himself was on his feet, but he now knew the sound of bullets, and he knew that no bullets had spun through the trees. He could not see her distinctly, but it was known to him in some way that she was mutinous. He leaned toward her and spoke as harshly as possible. "Marjory, get down! " She wavered for a moment as if resolved to defy him. As he turned again to peer in the direction of the firing it went through his mind that she must love him very much indeed. He was assured of it. It must have been some small outpour between nervous pickets and eager hillsmen, for it ended in a moment. The party waited in abasement for what seemed to them a time, and the blue dawn began, to laggardly shift the night as they waited. The dawn itself seemed prodigiously long in arriving at anything like discernible landscape. When this was consummated, Coleman, in somewhat the manner of the father of a church, dealt bits of chocolate out to the others. He had already taken the precaution to confer with the dragoman, so he said: " Well, come ahead. We'll make a try for it." They arose at his bidding and followed him to the road. It was the same broad, white road, only that the white was in the dawning something like the grey of a veil. It took some courage to venture upon this thoroughfare, but Coleman stepped out-after looking quickly in both directions. The party tramped to where the horses had been left, and there they were found without change of a rope. Coleman rejoiced to see that his dragoman now followed him in the way of a good lieutenant. They both dashed in among the trees and had the horses out into the road in a twinkle. When Coleman turned to direct that utterly subservient, group he knew that his face was drawn from hardship and anxiety, but he saw everywhere the same style of face with the exception of the face of Marjory, who looked simply of lovely marble. He noted with a curious satisfaction, as if the thing was a tribute to himself, that his macintosh was over the professor's shoulder, that Marjory and her mother were each carrying a blanket, and that, the corps of students had dutifully brought all the traps which his dragoman had forgotten. It was grand.

He addressed them to say: " Now, approaching outposts is very dangerous business at this time in the morning. So my man, who can talk both Greek and Turkish, will go ahead forty yards, and I will follow somewhere between him and you. Try not to crowd forward."

He directed the ladies upon their horses and placed the professor upon the little grey nag. Then they took up their line of march. The dragoman had looked somewhat dubiously upon this plan of having him go forty yards in advance, but he had the utmost confidence in this new Coleman, whom yesterday he had not known. Besides, he himself was a very gallant man indeed, and it befitted him to take the post of danger before the eyes of all these foreigners. In his new position he was as proud and unreasonable as a rooster. He was continually turning his head to scowl back at them, when only the clank of hoofs was sounding. An impenetrable mist lay on the valley and the hill-tops were shrouded. As for the people, they were like mice. Coleman paid no attention to the Wainwright party, but walked steadily along near the dragoman.

Perhaps the whole thing was a trifle absurd, but to a great percentage, of the party it was terrible. For instance, those eight boys, fresh from a school, could in no wise gauge the dimensions. And if this was true of the students, it was more distinctly true of Marjory and her mother. As for the professor, he seemed Weighted to the earth by his love and his responsibility.

Suddenly the dragoman wheeled and made demoniac signs. Coleman half-turned to survey the main body, and then paid his attention swiftly to the front. The white road sped to the top of a hill where it seemed to make a rotund swing into oblivion. The top of the curve was framed in foliage, and therein was a horseman. He had his carbine slanted on his thigh, and his bridle-reins taut. Upon sight of them he immediately wheeled and galloped down the other slope and vanished.

The dragoman was throwing wild gestures into the air. As Coleman looked back at the Wainwright party he saw plainly that to an ordinary eye they might easily appear as a strong advance of troops. The peculiar light would emphasize such theory. The dragoman ran to him jubilantly, but he contained now a form of intelligence which caused him to whisper; " That was one Greek. That was one Greek-what do you call—sentree? "

Coleman addressed the others. He said: "It's all right. Come ahead. That was a Greek picket. There is only one trouble now, and that is to approach them easy-do you see-easy."

His obedient charges came forward at his word. When they arrived at the top of this rise they saw nothing. Coleman was very uncertain. He was not sure that this picket had not carried with him a general alarm, and in that case there would soon occur a certain amount of shooting. However, as far as he understood the business, there was no way but forward. Inasmuch as he did not indicate to the Wainwright party that he wished them to do differently, they followed on doggedly after him and the dragoman. He knew now that the dragoman's heart had for the tenth time turned to dog-biscuit, so he kept abreast of him. And soon together they walked into a cavalry outpost, commanded by no less a person than the dashing young captain, who came laughing out to meet them.

Suddenly losing all colour of war, the condition was now such as might occur in a drawing room. Coleman felt the importance of establishing highly conventional relations between the captain and the Wainwright party. To compass this he first seized his dragoman, and the dragoman, enlightened immediately, spun a series of lies which must have led the captain to believe that the entire heart of the American republic had been taken out of that western continent and transported to Greece. Coleman was proud of the captain, The latter immediately went and bowed in the manner of the French school and asked everybody to have a cup of coffee, although acceptation would have proved his ruin and disgrace. Coleman refused in the name of courtesy. He called his party forward, and now they proceeded merely as one crowd. Marjory had dismounted in the meantime.

The moment was come. Coleman felt it. The first rush was from the students. Immediately he was buried in a thrashing mob of them. "Good boy! Good boy! Great man! Oh, isn't he a peach? How did he do it? He came in strong at the finish ! Good boy, Coleman!" Through this mist of glowing youthful congratulatioin he saw the professor standing at the outskirts with direct formal thanks already moving on his lips, while near him his wife wept joyfully. Marjory was evidently enduring some inscrutable emotion.

After all, it did penetrate his mind that it was indecent to accept all this wild gratitude, but there was built within him no intention of positively declaring himself lacking in all credit, or at least, lacking in all credit in the way their praises defined it. In truth he had assisted them, but he had been at the time largely engaged in assisting himself, and their coming had been more of a boon to his loneliness than an addition to his care. However, he soon had no difficulty in making his conscience appropriate every line in these hymns sung in his honour. The students, curiously wise of men, thought his conduct quite perfect. " Oh, say, come off ! " he protested. " Why, I didn't do anything. You fellows are crazy. You would have gotten in all right by yourselves. Don't act like asses-"

As soon as the professor had opportunity he came to Coleman. He was a changed little man, and his extraordinary bewilderment showed in his face. It was the disillusion and amazement of a stubborn mind that had gone implacably in its one direction and found in the end that the direction was all wrong, and that really a certain mental machine had not been infallible. Coleman remembered what the American minister in Athens had described of his protests against the starting of the professor's party on this journey, and of the complete refusal of the professor to recognise any value in the advice. And here now was the consequent defeat. It was mirrored in the professor's astonished eyes. Coleman went directly to his dazed old teacher. " Well, you're out of it now, professor," he said warmly. " I congratulate you on your escape, sir." The professor looked at him, helpless to express himself, but the correspondent was at that time suddenly enveloped in the hysterical gratitude of Mrs. Wainwright, who hurled herself upon him with extravagant manifestations. Coleman played his part with skill. To both the professor and Mrs. Wainwright his manner was a combination of modestly filial affection and a pretentious disavowal of his having done anything at all. It seemed to charm everybody but Marjory. It irritated him to see that she was apparently incapable of acknowledging that he was a grand man.

He was actually compelled to go to her and offer congratulations upon her escape, as he had congratulated the professor. If his manner to her parents had been filial, his manner to her was parental. " Well, Marjory," he said kindly, "you have been in considerable danger. I suppose you're glad to be through with it." She at that time made no reply, but by her casual turn he knew that he was expected to walk along by her side. The others knew it, too, and the rest of the party left them free to walk side by side in the rear.

" This is a beautiful country here-abouts if one gets a good chance to see it," he remarked. Then he added: "But I suppose you had a view of it when you were going out to Nikopolis? "

She answered in muffled tones. "Yes, we thought it very beautiful."

Did you note those streams from the mountains " That seemed to me the purest water I'd ever seen, but I bet it would make one ill to drink it. There is, you know, a prominent German chemist who has almost proven that really pure water is practical poison to the human stomach."

"Yes ? " she said.

There was a period of silence, during which he was perfectly comfortable because he knew that she was ill at ease. If the silence was awkward, she was suffering from it. As for himself, he had no inclination to break it. His position was, as far as the entire Wainwright party was concerned, a place where he could afford to wait. She turned to him at last. "Of course, I know how much you have done for us, and I want you to feel that we all appreciate it deeply-deeply." There was discernible to the ear a certain note of desperation.

" Oh, not at all," he said generously. " Not at all. I didn't do anything. It was quite an accident. Don't let that trouble you for a moment."

"Well, of course you would say that," she said more steadily. " But I-we-we know how good and how-brave it was in you to come for us, and I—we must never forget it."

As a matter of fact," replied Coleman, with an appearance of ingenuous candor, " I was sent out here by the Eclipse to find you people, and of course I worked rather hard to reach you, but the final meeting was purely accidental and does not redound to my credit in the least."

As he had anticipated, Marjory shot him a little glance of disbelief. " Of course you would say that," she repeated with gloomy but flattering conviction.

" Oh, if I had been a great hero," he said smiling, "no doubt I would have kept up this same manner which now sets so well upon me, but I am telling you the truth when I say that I had no part in your rescue at all."

She became slightly indignant. " Oh, if you care to tell us constantly that you were of no service to us, I don't see what we can do but continue to declare that you were."

Suddenly he felt vulgar. He spoke to her this time with real meaning. " I beg of 'you never to mention it again. That will be the best way."

But to this she would not accede. "No, we will often want to speak of it."

He replied "How do you like Greece? Don't you think that some of these ruins are rather out of shape in the popular mind? Now, for my part, I would rather look at a good strong finish at a horserace than to see ten thousand Parthenons in a bunch."

She was immediately in the position of defending him from himself. "You would rather see no such thing. You shouldn't talk in that utterly trivial way. I like the Parthenon, of course, but I can't think of it now because my head. is too full of my escape from where I was so-so frightened."

Coleman grinned. " Were you really frightened?"

" Naturally," she answered. " I suppose I was more frightened for mother and father, but I was frightened enough for myself. It was not-not a nice thing."

"No, it wasn't," said Coleman. "I could hardly believe my senses, when the minister at Athens told me that, you all had ventured into such a trap, and there is no doubt but what you can be glad that you are well out of it."

She seemed to have some struggle with herself and then she deliberately said: "Thanks to you."

Coleman embarked on what he intended to make a series of high-minded protests. " Not at all-" but at that moment the dragoman whirled back from the van-guard with a great collection of the difficulties which had been gathering upon him. Coleman was obliged to resign Marjory and again take up the active leadership. He disposed of the dragoman's difficulties mainly by declaring that they were not difficulties at all. He had learned that this was the way to deal with dragomen. The fog had already lifted from the valley and, as they passed along the wooded mountain-side the fragrance of leaves and earth came to them. Ahead, along the hooded road, they could see the blue clad figures of Greek infantrymen. Finally they passed an encampment of a battalion whose line was at a right angle to the highway. A hundred yards in advance was the bridge across the Louros river. And there a battery of artillery was encamped. The dragoman became involved in all sorts of discussions with other Greeks, but Coleman stuck to his elbow and stifled all aimless oration. The Wainwright party waited for them in the rear in an observant but patient group.

Across a plain, the hills directly behind Arta loomed up showing the straight yellow scar of a modern entrenchment. To the north of Arta were some grey mountains with a dimly marked road winding to the summit. On one side of this road were two shadows. It took a moment for the eye to find these shadows, but when this was accomplished it was plain that they were men. The captain of the battery explained to the dragoman that he did not know that they were not also Turks. In which case the road to Arta was a dangerous path. It was no good news to Coleman. He waited a moment in order to gain composure and then walked back to the Wainwright party. They must have known at once from his peculiar gravity that all was not well. Five of the students and the professor immediately asked: "What is it?"

He had at first some old-fashioned idea of concealing the ill tidings from the ladies, but he perceived what flagrant nonsense this would be in circumstances in which all were fairly likely to incur equal dangers, and at any rate he did not see his way clear to allow their imagination to run riot over a situation which might not turn out to be too bad. He said slowly: " You see those mountains over there? Well, troops have been seen there and the captain of this battery thinks they are Turks. If they are Turks the road to Arta is distinctly-er-unsafe."

This new blow first affected the Wainwright party as being too much to endure. " They thought they had gone through enough. This was a general sentiment. Afterward the emotion took colour according to the individual character. One student laughed and said: " Well, I see our finish."

Another student piped out: " How do they know they are

Turks? What makes them think they are Turks "

Another student expressed himself with a sigh. "This is a long way from the Bowery."

The professor said nothing but looked annihilated; Mrs. Wainwright wept profoundly; Marjory looked expectantly toward Coleman.

As for the correspondent he was adamantine and reliable and stern, for he had not the slightest idea that those men on the distant hill were Turks at all.

CHAPTER XIV.

"OH," said a student, " this game ought to quit. I feel like thirty cents. We didn't come out here to be pursued about the country by these Turks. Why don't they stop it ?"

Coleman was remarking: "Really, the only sensible thing to do now is to have breakfast. There is no use in worrying ourselves silly over this thing until we've got to."

They spread the blankets on the ground and sat about a feast of bread, water cress and tinned beef. Coleman was the real host, but he contrived to make the professor appear as that honourable person. They ate, casting their eyes from time to time at the distant mountain with its two shadows. People began to fly down the road from Jannina, peasants hurriedly driving little flocks, women and children on donkeys and little horses which they clubbed unceasingly. One man rode at a gallop, shrieking and flailing his arms in the air. They were all Christian peasants of Turkey, but they were in flight now because they did not wish to be at home if the Turk was going to return and reap revenge for his mortification. The Wainwright party looked at Coleman in abrupt questioning.

"Oh, it's all right," he said, easily. "They are always taking on that way."

Suddenly the dragoman gave a shout and dashed up the road to the scene of a melee where a little ratfaced groom was vociferously defending three horses from some Greek officers, who as vociferously were stating their right to requisition them. Coleman ran after his dragoman. There was a sickening pow-wow, but in the end Coleman, straight and easy in the saddle, came cantering back on a superb open-mouthed snorting bay horse. He did not mind if the half-wild animal plunged crazily. It was part of his role. "They were trying to steal my horses," he explained. He leaped to the ground, and holding the horse by the bridle, he addressed his admiring companions. " The groom- the man who has charge of the horses -says that he thinks that the people on the mountain-side are Turks, but I don't see how that is possible. You see-" he pointed wisely-" that road leads directly south to Arta, and it is hardly possible that the Greek army would come over here and leave that approach to Arta utterly unguarded. It would be too foolish. They must have left some men to cover it, and that is certainly what those troops are. If you are all ready and willing, I don't see anything to do but make a good, stout-hearted dash for Arta. It would be no more dangerous than to sit here." The professor was at last able to make his formal speech. " Mr. Coleman," he said distinctly, "we place ourselves entirely in your hands." It was some. how pitiful. This man who, for years and years had reigned in a little college town almost as a monarch, passing judgment with the air of one who words the law, dealing criticism upon the universe as one to whom all things are plain, publicly disdaining defeat as one to whom all things are easy-this man was now veritably appealing to Coleman to save his wife, his daughter and himself, and really declared himself de. pendent for safety upon the ingenuity and courage of the correspondent.

The attitude of the students was utterly indifferent. They did not consider themselves helpless at all. they were evidently quite ready to withstand anything but they looked frankly up to Coleman as their intelligent leader. If they suffered any, their only expression of it was in the simple grim slang of their period.

" I wish I was at Coney Island."

" This is not so bad as trigonometry, but it's worse than playing billiards for the beers."

And Coke said privately to Coleman: " Say, what in hell are these two damn peoples fighting for, anyhow? "

When he saw that all opinions were in favour of following him loyally, Coleman was impelled to feel a responsibility. He was now no errant rescuer, but a properly elected leader of fellow beings in distress. While one of the students held his horse, he took the dragoman for another consultation with the captain of the battery. The officer was sitting on a large stone, with his eyes fixed into his field glasses. When again questioned he could give no satisfaction as to the identity of the troops on the distant mountain. He merely shrugged his shoulders and said that if they were Greeks it was very good, but if they were Turks it was very bad. He seemed more occupied in trying to impress the correspondent that it was a matter of soldierly indifference to himself. Coleman, after loathing him sufficiently in silence, returned to the others and said: " Well, we'll chance it."

They looked to him to arrange the caravan. Speaking to the men of the party he said: " Of course, any one of you is welcome to my horse if you can ride it, but-if you're not too tired-I think I had myself better ride, so that I can go ahead at times."

His manner was so fine as he said this that the students seemed fairly to worship him. Of course it had been most improbable that any of them could have ridden that volcanic animal even if one of them had tried it.

He saw Mrs. Wainwright and Marjory upon the backs of their two little natives, and hoisted the professor into the saddle of the groom's horse, leaving instructions with the servant to lead the animal always and carefully. He and the dragoman then mounted at the head of the procession, and amid curious questionings from the soldiery they crossed the bridge and started on the trail to Arta. The rear was brought up by the little grey horse with the luggage, led by one student and flogged by another.

Coleman, checking with difficulty the battling disposition of his horse, was very uneasy in his mind because the last words of the captain of the battery had made him feel that perhaps on this ride he would be placed in a position where only the best courage would count, and he did not see his way clear to feeling very confident about his conduct in such a case. Looking back upon the caravan, he saw it as a most unwieldy thing, not even capable of running away. He hurried it with sudden, sharp contemptuous phrases.

On the. march there incidentally flashed upon him a new truth. More than half of that student band were deeply in love with Marjory. Of course, when he had been distant from her he had had an eternal jealous reflection to that effect. It was natural that he should have thought of the intimate camping relations between Marjory and these young students with a great deal of bitterness, grinding his teeth when picturing their opportunities to make Marjory fall in love with some one of them. He had raged particularly about Coke, whose father had millions of dollars. But he had forgotten all these jealousies in the general splendour of his exploits. Now, when he saw the truth, it seemed. to bring him back to his common life and he saw himself suddenly as not being frantically superior in any way to those other young men. The more closely he looked at this last fact, the more convinced he was of its truth. He seemed to see that he had been improperely elated over his services to the Wainwrights, and that, in the end, the girl might fancy a man because the man had done her no service at all. He saw his proud position lower itself to be a pawn in the game. Looking back over the students, he wondered which one Marjory might love. This hideous Nikopolis had given eight men chance to win her. His scorn and his malice quite centered upon Coke, for he could never forget that the man's father had millions of dollars. The unfortunate Coke chose that moment to address him querulously: "Look here, Coleman, can't you tell us how far it is to Arta? "

"Coke," said Coleman, " I don't suppose you take me for a tourist agency, but if you can only try to distinguish between me and a map with the scale of miles printed in the lower left- hand corner, you will not contribute so much to the sufferings of the party which you now adorn."

The students within hearing guffawed and Coke retired, in confusion.

The march was not rapid. Coleman almost wore out his arms holding in check his impetuous horse. Often the caravan floundered through mud, while at the same time a hot, yellow dust came from the north.

They were perhaps half way to Arta when Coleman decided that a rest and luncheon were the things to be considered. He halted his troop then in the shade of some great trees, and privately he bade his dragoman prepare the best feast which could come out of those saddle-bags fresh from Athens. The result was rather gorgeous in the eyes of the poor wanderers. First of all there were three knives, three forks, three spoons, three tin cups and three tin plaies, which the entire party of twelve used on a most amiable socialistic principle. There were crisp, salty biscuits and olives, for which they speared in the bottle. There was potted turkey, and potted ham, and potted tongue, all tasting precisely alike. There were sardines and the ordinary tinned beef, disguised sometimes with onions, carrots and potatoes. Out of the saddle-bags came pepper and salt and even mustard. The dragoman made coffee over a little fire of sticks that blazed with a white light. The whole thing was prodigal, but any philanthropist would have approved of it if he could have seen the way in which the eight students laid into the spread. When there came a polite remonstrance-notably from Mrs. Wainwright-Coleman merely pointed to a large bundle strapped back of the groom's saddle. During the coffee he was considering how best to get the students one by one out of the sight of the Wainwrights where he could give them good drinks of whisky.

There was an agitation on the road toward Arta. Some people were coming on horses. He paid small heed until he heard a thump of pausing hoofs near him, and a musical voice say: "Rufus! "

He looked up quickly, and then all present saw his eyes really bulge. There on a fat and glossy horse sat Nora Black, dressed in probably one of the most correct riding habits which had ever been seen in the East. She was smiling a radiant smile, which held the eight students simpty spell-bound. They would have recognised her if it had not been for this apparitional coming in the wilds of southeastern Europe. Behind her were her people-some servants and an old lady on a very little pony. " Well, Rufus? " she said.

Coleman made the mistake of hesitating. For a fraction of a moment he had acted as if he were embarrassed, and was only going to nod and say: " How d'do ?"

He arose and came forward too late. She was looking at him with a menacing glance which meant difficulties for him if he was not skilful. Keen as an eagle, she swept her glance over the face and figure of Marjory. Without. further introduction, the girls seemed to understand that they were enemies.

Despite his feeling of awkwardness, Coleman's mind was mainly occupied by pure astonishment. "Nora Black? " he said, as if even then he could not believe his senses. " How in the world did you get down here?

She was not too amiable, evidently, over his reception, and she seemed to know perfectly that it was in her power to make him feel extremely unpleasant. " Oh, it's not so far," she answered. " I don't see where you come in to ask me what I'm doing here. What are you doing here? " She lifted her eyes and shot the half of a glance at Marjory. Into her last question she had interjected a spirit of ownership in which he saw future woe. It turned him cowardly. " Why, you know I was sent up here by the paper to rescue the Wainwright party, and I've got them. I'm taking them to Arta. But why are you here?"

" I am here," she said, giving him the most defiant of glances, " principally to look for you."

Even the horse she rode betrayed an intention of abiding upon that spot forever. She had made her communication with Coleman appear to the Wainwright party as a sort of tender reunion.

Coleman looked at her with a steely eye. "Nora, you can certainly be a devil when you choose."

" Why don't you present me to your friends? Mis,; Nora Black, special correspondent of the New York Daylighi, if you please. I belong to your opposition. I am your rival, Rufus, and I draw a bigger salary-see? Funny looking gang, that. Who is the old Johnnie in the white wig?"

"Er-where you goin'-you can't "-blundered Coleman miserably "Aw-the army is in retreat and you must go back to- don't you see?"

"Is it?" she asked. After a pause she added coolly: "Then I shall go back to Arta with you and your precious Wainwrights."

CHAPTER XV.

GIVING Coleman another glance of subtle menace Nora repeated: "Why don't you present me to your friends? " Coleman had been swiftly searching the whole world for a way clear of this unhappiness, but he knew at last that he could only die at his guns. " Why, certainly," he said quickly, " if you wish it." He sauntered easily back to the luncheon blanket. "This is Miss Black of the New York Daylight and she says that those people on the mountain are Greeks." The students were gaping at him, and Marjory and her father sat in the same silence. But to the relief of Coleman and to the high edification of the students, Mrs. Wainwright cried out: " Why, is she an American woman? " And seeing Coleman's nod of assent she rustled to her feet and advanced hastily upon the complacent horsewoman. " I'm delighted to see you. Who would think of seeing an American woman way over here. Have you been here long? Are you going on further? Oh, we've had such a dreadful time." Coleman remained long enough to hear Nora say: " Thank you very much, but I shan't dismount. I am going to ride back to Arta presently."

Then he heard Mrs. Wainwright cry: " Oh, are you indeed? Why we, too, are going at once to Arta. We can all go together." Coleman fled then to the bosom of the students, who all looked at him with eyes of cynical penetration. He cast a glance at Marjory more than fearing a glare which denoted an implacable resolution never to forgive this thing. On the contrary he had never seen her so content and serene. "You have allowed your coffee to get chilled," she said considerately. "Won't you have the man warm you some more?"

"Thanks, no," he answered with gratitude.

Nora, changing her mind, had dismounted and was coming with Mrs. Wainwright. That worthy lady had long had a fund of information and anecdote the sound of which neither her husband nor her daughter would endure for a moment. Of course the rascally students were out of the question.

Here, then, was really the first ear amiably and cheerfully open, and she was talking at what the students called her "thirty knot gait."

"Lost everything. Absolutely everything. Neither of us have even a brush and comb, or a cake of soap, or enough hairpins to hold up our hair. I'm going to take Marjory's away from her and let her braid her hair down her back. You can imagine how dreadful it is—-"

From time to time the cool voice of Nora sounded without effort through this clamour. " Oh, it will be no trouble at all. I have more than enough of everything. We can divide very nicely."

Coleman broke somewhat imperiously into this feminine chat. "Well, we must be moving, you know, " and his voice started the men into activity. When the traps were all packed again on the horse Coleman looked back surprised to see the three women engaged in the most friendly discussion. The combined parties now made a very respectable squadron. Coleman rode off at its head without glancing behind at all. He knew that they were following from the soft pounding of the horses hoofs on the sod and from the mellow hum of human voices.

For a long time he did not think to look upon himself as anything but a man much injured by circumstances. Among his friends he could count numbers who had lived long lives without having this peculiar class of misfortune come to them. In fact it was so unusual a misfortune that men of the world had not found it necessary to pass from mind to mind a perfec t formula for dealing with it. But he soon began to consider himself an extraordinarily lucky person inasmuch as Nora Black had come upon him with her saddle bags packed with inflammable substances, so to speak, and there had been as yet only enough fire to boil coffee for luncheon. He laughed tenderly when he thought of the innocence of Mrs. Wainwright, but his face and back flushed with heat when lie thought of the canniness of the eight American college students.

He heard a horse cantering up on his left side and looking he saw Nora Black. She was beaming with satisfaction and good nature. " Well, Rufus," she cried flippantly, " how goes it with the gallant rescuer? You've made a hit, my boy. You are the success of the season."

Coleman reflected upon the probable result of a direct appeal to Nora. He knew of course that such appeals were usually idle, but he did not consider Nora an ordinary person. His decision was to venture it. He drew his horse close to hers. " Nora," he said, " do you know that you are raising the very devil? "

She lifted her finely penciled eyebrows and looked at him with the baby-stare. " How ? " she enquired.

" You know well enough," he gritted out wrathfully.

"Raising the very devil?" she asked. " How do you mean?"

She was palpably interested for his answer. She waited for his

reply for an interval, and then she asked him outright. " Rufus

Coleman do you mean that I am not a respectable woman? "

In reality he had meant nothing of the kind, but this direct throttling of a great question stupefied him utterly, for he saw now that she' would probably never understand him in the least and that she would at any rate always pretend not to understand him and that the more he said the more harm he manufactured. She studied him over carefully and then wheeled her horse towards the rear with some parting remarks. " I suppose you should attend more strictly to your own affairs, Rufus. Instead of raising the devil I am lending hairpins. I have seen you insult people, but I have never seen you insult anyone quite for the whim of the thing. Go soak your head."

Not considering it advisable to then indulge in such immersion Coleman rode moodily onward. The hot dust continued to sting the cheeks of the travellers and in some places great clouds of dead leaves roared in circles about them. All of the Wainwright party were utterly fagged. Coleman felt his skin crackle and his throat seemed to be coated with the white dust. He worried his dragoman as to the distance to Arta until the dragoman lied to the point where he always declared that Arta was only off some hundreds of yards.

At their places in the procession Mrs. Wainwright and Marjory were animatedly talking to Nora and the old lady on the little pony. They had at first suffered great amazement at the voluntary presence of the old lady, but she was there really because she knew no better. Her colossal ignorance took the form, mainly, of a most obstreperous patriotism, and indeed she always acted in a foreign country as if she were the special commissioner of the President, or perhaps as a special commissioner could not act at all. She was very aggressive, and when any of the travelling arrangements in Europe did not suit her ideas she was won't to shrilly exclaim: "Well! New York is good enough for me." Nora, morbidly afraid that her ex- pense bill to the Daylight would not be large enough, had dragged her bodily off to Greece as her companion, friend and protection. At Arta they had heard of the grand success of the Greek army. The Turks had not stood for a moment before that gallant and terrible advance; no; they had scampered howling with fear into the north. Jannina would fall-well, Jannina would fall as soon as the Greeks arrived. There was no doubt of it. The correspondent and her friend, deluded and hurried by the light-hearted confidence of the Greeks in Arta, had hastened out then on a regular tourist's excursion to see Jannina after its capture. Nora concealed from her friend the fact that the editor of the Daylight particularly wished her to see a battle so that she might write an article on actual warfare from a woman's point of view. With her name as a queen of comic opera, such an article from her pen would be a burning, sensation.

Coleman had been the first to point out to Nora that instead of going on a picnic to Jannina, she had better run back to Arta. When the old lady heard that they had not been entirely safe, she was furious with Nora. "The idea!" she exclaimed to Mrs. Wainwright. "They might have caught us! They might have caught us! "

" Well," said Mrs. Wainwright. " I verily believe they would have caught us if it had not been for Mr. Coleman."

" Is he the gentleman on the fine horse?"

" Yes; that's him. Oh, he has been sim-plee splendid. I confess I was a little bit-er-surprised. He was in college under my husband. I don't know that we thought very great things of him, but if ever a man won golden opinions he has done so from us."

" Oh, that must be the Coleman who is such a great friend of

Nora's."

"Yes?" said Mrs. Wainwright insidiously. "Is he? I didn't know. Of course he knows so many people." Her mind had been suddenly illumined by the old lady and she thought extravagantly of the arrival of Nora upon the scene. She remained all sweetness to the old lady. "Did you know he was here? Did you expect to meet him? I seemed such a delightful coincidence." In truth she was being subterraneously clever.

" Oh, no; I don't think so. I didn't hear Nora mention it. Of course she would have told me. You know, our coming to Greece was such a surprise. Nora had an engagement in London at the Folly Theatre in Fly by Night, but the manager was insufferable, oh, insufferable. So, of course, Nora wouldn't stand it a minute, and then these newspaper people came along and asked her to go to Greece for them and she accepted. I am sure I never expected to find us-aw-fleeing from the Turks or I shouldn't have Come."

" Mrs. Wainwright was gasping. " You don't mean that she is— she is Nora Black, the actress."

" Of course she is," said the old lady jubilantly.

" Why, how strange," choked Mrs. Wainwrignt. Nothing she knew of Nora could account for her stupefaction and grief. What happened glaringly to her was the duplicity of man. Coleman was a ribald deceiver. He must have known and yet he had pretended throughout that the meeting was a pure accident She turned with a nervous impulse to sympathist with her daughter, but despite the lovely tranquillity of the girl's face there was something about her which forbade the mother to meddle. Anyhow Mrs. Wainwright was sorry that she had told nice things of Coleman's behaviour, so she said to the old lady: " Young men of these times get a false age so quickly. We have always thought it a great pity, about Mr. Coleman."

"Why, how so ? " asked the old lady.

"Oh, really nothing. Only, to us he seemed rather —er- prematurely experienced or something of that kind. The old lady did not catch the meaning of the phrase. She seemed surprised. " Why, I've never seen any full-grown person in this world who got experience any too quick for his own good."

At the tail of the procession there was talk between the two students who had in charge the little grey horse-one to lead and one to flog. " Billie," said one, " it now becomes necessary to lose this hobby into the hands of some of the other fellows. Whereby we will gain opportunity to pay homage to the great Nora. Why, you egregious thick-head, this is the chance of a life-time. I'm damned if I'm going to tow this beast of burden much further."

" You wouldn't stand a show," said Billie pessimistically. " Look at Coleman."

" That's all right. Do you mean to say that you prefer to continue towing pack horses in the presence of this queen of song and the dance just because you think Coleman can throw out his chest a little more than you. Not so. Think of your bright and sparkling youth. There's Coke and Pete Tounley near Marjory. We'll call 'em." Whereupon he set up a cry. " Say, you people, we're not getting a, salary for this. Supposin' you try for a time. It'll do you good." When the two addressed bad halted to await the arrival of the little grey horse, they took on glum expressions. " You look like poisoned pups," said the student who led the horse. " Too strong for light work. Grab onto the halter, now, Peter, and tow. We are going ahead to talk to Nora Black."

" Good time you'll have," answered Peter Tounley.

" Coleman is cuttin' up scandalous. You won't stand a show."

" What do you think of him ? " said Coke. " Seems curious, all 'round. Do you suppose he knew she would show up? It was nervy to—"

" Nervy to what? " asked Billie.

"Well," said Coke, " seems to me he is playing both ends against the middle. I don't know anything about Nora Black, but-"

The three other students expressed themselves with conviction and in chorus. " Coleman's all right."

" Well, anyhow," continued Coke, " I don't see my way free to admiring him introducing Nora Black to the Wainwrights."

" He didn't," said the others, still in chorus.

" Queer game," said Peter Tounley. " He seems to know her pretty well."

" Pretty damn well," said Billie.

"Anyhow he's a brick," said Peter Tounley. "We mustn't forget that. Lo, I begin to feel that our Rufus is a fly guy of many different kinds. Any play that he is in commands my respect. He won't be hit by a chimney in the daytime, for unto him has come much wisdom, I don't think I'll worry."

"Is he stuck on Nora Black, do you know?" asked Billie.

" One thing is plain," replied Coke. " She has got him somehow by the short hair and she intends him to holler murder. Anybody can see that."

" Well, he won't holler murder," said one of them with conviction. " I'll bet you he won't. He'll hammer the war-post and beat the tom-tom until he drops, but he won't holler murder."

" Old Mother Wainwright will be in his wool presently," quoth Peter Tounley musingly, " I could see it coming in her eye. Somebody has given his snap away, or something." " Aw, he had no snap," said Billie. " Couldn't you see how rattled he was? He would have given a lac if dear Nora hadn't turned up."

"Of course," the others assented. "He was rattled."

" Looks queer. And nasty," said Coke.

" Nora herself had an axe ready for him."

They began to laugh. " If she had had an umbrella she would have basted him over the head with it. Oh, my! He was green."

" Nevertheless," said Peter Tounley, " I refuse to worry over our Rufus.

When he can't take care of himself the rest of us want to hunt cover. He is a fly guy-"

Coleman in the meantime had become aware that the light of Mrs. Wainwright's countenance was turned from him. The party stopped at a well, and when he offered her a drink from his cup he thought she accepted it with scant thanks. Marjory was still gracious, always gracious, but this did not reassure him, because he felt there was much unfathomable deception in it. When he turned to seek consolation in the manner of the professor he found him as before, stunned with surprise, and the only idea he had was to be as tractable as a child.

When he returned to the head of the column, Nora again cantered forward to join him. " Well, me gay Lochinvar," she cried, " and has your disposition improved? "

" You are very fresh," he said.

She laughed loud enough to be heard the full length of the caravan. It was a beautiful laugh, but full of insolence and confidence. He flashed his eyes malignantly upon her, but then she only laughed more. She could see that he wished to strangle her. " What a disposition ! " she said. " What a disposition ! You are not. nearly so nice as your friends. Now, they are charming, but you-Rufus, I wish you would get that temper mended. Dear Rufus, do it to please me. You know you like to please me. Don't you now, dear? " He finally laughed. " Confound you, Nora. I would like to kill you."

But at his laugh she was all sunshine. It was as if she. had been trying to taunt him into good humour with her. "Aw, now, Rufus, don't be angry. I'll be good, Rufus. Really, I will. Listen. I want to tell you something. Do you know what I did? Well, you know, I never was cut out for this business, and, back there, when you told me about the Turks being near and all that sort of thing, I was frightened almost to death. Really, I was. So, when nobody was looking, I sneaked two or three little drinks out of my flask. Two or three little drinks-"

CHAPTER XVI.

" GOOD God!" said Coleman. "You don't Mean-"

Nora smiled rosily at him. " Oh, I'm all right," she answered. " Don't worry about your Aunt Nora, my precious boy. Not for a minute."

Coleman was horrified. " But you are not going to-you are not going to-"

"Not at all, me son. Not at all," she answered.

I'm not going to prance. I'm going to be as nice as pie, and just ride quietly along here with dear little Rufus. Only * * you know what I can do when I get started, so you had better be a very good boy. I might take it into my head to say some things, you know."

Bound hand and foot at his stake, he could not even chant his defiant torture song. It might precipitate— in fact, he was sure it would precipitate the grand smash. But to the very core of his soul, he for the time hated Nora Black. He did not dare to remind her that he would revenge himself; he dared only to dream of this revenge, but it fairly made his thoughts flame, and deep in his throat he was swearing an inflexible persecution of Nora Black. The old expression of his sex came to him, " Oh, if she were only a man ! " she had been a man, he would have fallen upon her tooth and nail. Her motives for all this impressed him not at all; she was simply a witch who bound him helpless with the power of her femininity, and made him eat cinders. He was so sure that his face betrayed him that he did not dare let her see it. " Well, what are you going to do about it ? " he asked, over his shoulder.

" 0-o-oh," she drawled, impudently. "Nothing." He could see that she was determined not to be confessed. " I may do this or I may do that. It all depends upon your behaviour, my dear Rufus."

As they rode on, he deliberated as to the best means of dealing with this condition. Suddenly he resolved to go with the whole tale direct to Marjory, and to this end he half wheeled his horse. He would reiterate that he loved her and then explain- explain! He groaned when he came to the word, and ceased formulation.

The cavalcade reached at last the bank of the Aracthus river, with its lemon groves and lush grass. A battery wheeled before them over the ancient bridge -a flight of short, broad cobbled steps up as far as the centre of the stream and a similar flight down to the other bank. The returning aplomb of the travellers was well illustrated by the professor, who, upon sighting this bridge, murmured: " Byzantine."

This was the first indication that he had still within him a power to resume the normal.

The steep and narrow street was crowded with soldiers; the smoky little coffee shops were a-babble with people discussing the news from the front. None seemed to heed the remarkable procession that wended its way to the cable office. Here Coleman resolutely took precedence. He knew that there was no good in expecting intelligence out of the chaotic clerks, but he managed to get upon the wires this message :

" Eclipse, New York: Got Wainwright party; all well. Coleman." The students had struggled to send messages to their people in America, but they had only succeeded in deepening the tragic boredom of the clerks.

When Coleman returned to the street he thought that he had seldom looked upon a more moving spectacle than the Wainwright party presented at that moment. Most of the students were seated in a row, dejectedly, upon the kerb. The professor and Mrs. Wainwright looked like two old pictures, which, after an existence in a considerate gloom, had been brought out in their tawdriness to the clear light. Hot white dust covered everybody, and from out the grimy faces the eyes blinked, red-fringed with sleeplessness. Desolation sat upon all, save Marjory. She possessed some marvellous power of looking always fresh. This quality had indeed impressed the old lady on the little pony until she had said to Nora Black: "That girl would look well anywhere." Nora Black had not been amiable in her reply.

Coleman called the professor and the dragoman for a durbar. The dragoman said: "Well, I can get one carriage, and we can go immediate-lee."

" Carriage be blowed! " said Coleman. " What these people need is rest, sleep. You must find a place at once. These people can't remain in the street." He spoke in anger, as if he had previously told the dragoman and the latter had been inattentive. The man immediately departed.

Coleman remarked that there was no course but to remain in the street until his dragoman had found them a habitation. It was a mournful waiting. The students sat on the kerb. Once they whispered to Coleman, suggesting a drink, but he told them that he knew only one cafe, the entrance of which would be in plain sight of the rest of the party. The ladies talked together in a group of four. Nora Black was bursting with the fact that her servant had hired rooms in Arta on their outcoming journey, and she wished Mrs. Wainwright and Marjory to come to them, at least for a time, but she dared not risk a refusal, and she felt something in Mrs. Wainwright's manner which led her to be certain that such would be the answer to her invitation. Coleman and the professor strolled slowly up and down the walk.

" Well, my work is over, sir," said Coleman. " My paper told me to find you, and, through no virtue of my own, I found you. I am very glad of it. I don't know of anything in my life that has given me greater pleasure."

The professor was himself again in so far as he had lost all manner of dependence. But still he could not yet be bumptious. " Mr. Coleman," he said, "I am placed under life-long obligation to you. * * * I am not thinking of myself so much. * * * My wife and daughter—-" His gratitude was so genuine that he could not finish its expression.

" Oh, don't speak of it," said Coleman. " I really didn't do anything at all."

The dragoman finally returned and led them all to a house which he had rented for gold. In the great, bare, upper chamber the students dropped wearily to the floor, while the woman of the house took the Wainwrights to a more secluded apartment., As the door closed on them, Coleman turned like a flash.

" Have a drink," he said. The students arose around him like the wave of a flood. "You bet." In the absence of changes of clothing, ordinary food, the possibility of a bath, and in the presence of great weariness and dust, Coleman's whisky seemed to them a glistening luxury. Afterward they laid down as if to sleep, but in reality they were too dirty and too fagged to sleep. They simply lay murmuring Peter Tounley even developed a small fever.

It was at this time that Coleman. suddenly discovered his acute interest in the progressive troubles of his affair of the heart had placed the business of his newspaper in the rear of his mind. The greater part of the next hour he spent in getting off to New York that dispatch which created so much excitement for him later. Afterward he was free to reflect moodily upon the ability of Nora Black to distress him. She, with her retinue, had disappeared toward her own rooms. At dusk he went into the street, and was edified to see Nora's dragoman dodging along in his wake. He thought that this was simply another manifestation of Nora's interest in his movements, and so he turned a corner, and there pausing, waited until the dragoman spun around directly into his arms. But it seemed that the man had a note to deliver, and this was only his Oriental way of doing it.

The note read: " Come and dine with me to-night." It was, not a request. It was peremptory. "All right," he said, scowling at the man.

He did not go at once, for he wished to reflect for a time and find if he could not evolve some weapons of his own. It seemed to him that all the others were liberally supplied with weapons.

A clear, cold night had come upon the earth when he signified to the lurking dragoman that he was in readiness to depart with him to Nora's abode. They passed finally into a dark court-yard, up a winding staircase, across an embowered balcony, and Coleman entered alone a room where there were lights.

His, feet were scarcely over the threshold before he had concluded that the tigress was now going to try some velvet purring. He noted that the arts of the stage had not been thought too cheaply obvious for use. Nora sat facing the door. A bit of yellow silk had been twisted about the crude shape of the lamp, and it made the play of light, amber-like, shadowy and yet perfectly clear, the light which women love. She was arrayed in a puzzling gown of that kind of Gre- cian silk which is so docile that one can pull yards of it through a ring. It was of the colour of new straw. Her chin was leaned pensively upon her palm and the light fell on a pearly rounded forearm. She was looking at him with a pair of famous eyes, azure, per- haps-certainly purple at times-and it may be, black at odd moments-a pair of eyes that had made many an honest man's heart jump if he thought they were looking at him. It was a vision, yes, but Coleman's cynical knowledge of drama overpowered his sense of its beauty. He broke out brutally, in the phrases of the American street. "Your dragoman is a rubber-neck. If he keeps darking me I will simply have to kick the stuffing out of him."

She was alone in the room. Her old lady had been instructed to have a headache and send apologies. She was not disturbed by Coleman's words. "Sit down, Rufus, and have a cigarette, and don't be cross, because I won't stand it."

He obeyed her glumly. She had placed his chair where not a charm of her could be lost upon an observant man. Evidently she did not purpose to allow him to irritate her away from her original plan. Purring was now her method, and none of his insolence could achieve a growl from the tigress. She arose, saying softly: "You look tired, almost ill, poor boy. I will give you some brandy. I have almost everything that I could think to make those Daylight people buy." With a sweep of her hand she indicated the astonishing opulence of the possessions in different parts of the room.

As she stood over him with the brandy there came through the smoke of his cigarette the perfume of orris-root and violet.

A servant began to arrange the little cold dinner on a camp table, and Coleman saw with an enthusiasm which he could not fully master, four quart bottles of a notable brand of champagne placed in a rank on the floor.

At dinner Nora was sisterly. She watched him, waited upon him, treated him to an affectionate intimacy for which he knew a thousand men who would have hated him. The champagne was cold.

Slowly he melted. By the time that the boy came with little cups of Turkish coffee he was at least amiable. Nora talked dreamily. " The dragoman says this room used to be part of the harem long ago." She shot him a watchful glance, as if she had expected the fact to affect him. "Seems curious, doesn't it? A harem. Fancy that." He smoked one cigar and then discarded tobacco, for the perfume of orris-root and violet was making him meditate. Nora talked on in a low voice. She knew that, through half-closed lids, he was looking at her in steady speculation. She knew that she was conquering, but no movement of hers betrayed an elation. With the most exquisite art she aided his contemplation, baring to him, for instance, the glories of a statuesque neck, doing it all with the manner of a splendid and fabulous virgin who knew not that there was such a thing as shame. Her stockings were of black silk.

Coleman presently answered her only in monosyllable, making small distinction between yes and no. He simply sat watching her with eyes in which there were two little covetous steel-coloured flames.

He was thinking, "To go to the devil-to go to the devil-to go to the devil with this girl is not a bad fate-not a bad fate-not a bad fate."

CHAPTER XVII.

" Come out on the balcony," cooed Nora. "There are some funny old storks on top of some chimneys near here and they clatter like mad all day and night."

They moved together out to the balcony, but Nora retreated with a little cry when she felt the coldness of the night. She said that she would get a cloak. Coleman was not unlike a man in a dream. He walked to the rail of the balcony where a great vine climbed toward the roof. He noted that it was dotted with. blossoms, which in the deep purple of the Oriental night were coloured in strange shades of maroon. This truth penetrated his abstraction until when Nora came she found him staring at them as if their colour was a revelation which affected him vitally. She moved to his side without sound and he first knew of her presence from the damning fragrance. She spoke just above her breath. "It's a beautiful evening." " Yes," he answered. She was at his shoulder. If he moved two inches he must come in contact. They remained in silence leaning upon the rail. Finally he began to mutter some commonplaces which meant nothing particularly, but into his tone as he mouthed them was the note of a forlorn and passionate lover. Then as if by accident he traversed the two inches and his shoulder was against the soft and yet firm shoulder of Nora Black. There was something in his throat at this time which changed his voice into a mere choking noise. She did not move. He could see her eyes glowing innocently out of the pallour which the darkness gave to her face. If he was touching her, she did not seem to know it.

"I am awfully tired," said Coleman, thickly. "I think I will go home and turn in."

" You must be, poor boy," said Nora tenderly.

"Wouldn't you like a little more of that champagne?"

" Well, I don't mind another glass."

She left him again and his galloping thought pounded to the old refrain.

" To go to the devil-to go to the devil-to go to the devil with this girl is not a bad fate-not a bad fate- not a bad fate." When she returned he drank his glass of champagne. Then he mumbled: " You must be cold. Let me put your cape around you better. It won't do to catch cold here, you know."

She made a sweet pretence of rendering herself to his care. " Oh, thanks * * * I am not really cold * * * There that's better."

Of course all his manipulation of the cloak had been a fervid caress, and although her acting up to this point had remained in the role of the splendid and fabulous virgin she now turned her liquid eyes to his with a look that expressed knowledge, triumph and delight. She was sure of her victory. And she said: "Sweetheart * * * don't you think I am as nice as Marjory ?" The impulse had been airily confident. It was as if the silken cords had been parted by the sweep of a sword. Coleman's face had instantly stiffened and he looked like a man suddenly recalled to the ways of light. It may easily have been that in a moment he would have lapsed again to his luxurious dreaming. But in his face the girl had read a fatal character to her blunder and her resentment against him took precedence of any other emotion. She wheeled abruptly from him and said with great contempt: " Rufus, you had better go home. You're tired and sleepy, and more or less drunk."

He knew that the grand tumble of all their little embowered incident could be neither stayed or mended. "Yes," he answered, sulkily, "I think so too." They shook hands huffily and he went away.

When he arrived among the students he found that they had appropriated everything of his which would conduce to their comfort. He was furious over it. But to his bitter speeches they replied in jibes.

"Rufus is himself again. Admire his angelic disposition. See him smile. Gentle soul."

A sleepy voice said from a comer: " I know what pinches him."

" What ? " asked several.

"He's been to see Nora and she flung him out bodily."

" Yes?" sneered Coleman. "At times I seem to see in you, Coke, the fermentation of some primeval form of sensation, as if it were possible for you to de- velop a mind in two or three thousand years, and then at other times you appear * * * much as you are now."

As soon as they had well measured Coleman's temper all of the students save Coke kept their mouths tightly closed. Coke either did not understand or his mood was too vindictive for silence. " Well, I know you got a throw-down all right," he muttered.

"And how would you know when I got a throw down? You pimply, milk-fed sophomore."

The others perked up their ears in mirthful appreciation of this language.

" Of course," continued Coleman, " no one would protest against your continued existence, Coke, unless you insist on recalling yourself violently to people's attention in this way. The mere fact of your living would not usually be offensive to people if you weren't eternally turning a sort of calcium light on your prehensile attributes." Coke was suddenly angry, angry much like a peasant, and his anger first evinced itself in a mere sputtering and spluttering. Finally he got out a rather long speech, full of grumbling noises, but he was understood by all to declare that his prehensile attributes had not led him to cart a notorious woman about the world with him. When they quickly looked at Coleman they saw that he was livid. " You-"

But, of course, there immediately arose all sorts of protesting cries from the seven non-combatants. Coleman, as he took two strides toward Coke's corner, looked fully able to break him across his knee, but for this Coke did not seem to care at all. He was on his feet with a challenge in his eye. Upon each cheek burned a sudden hectic spot. The others were clamouring, "Oh, say, this won't do. Quit it. Oh, we mustn't have a fight. He didn't mean it, Coleman." Peter Tounley pressed Coke to the wall saying: " You damned young jackass, be quiet."

They were in the midst of these. festivities when a door opened and disclosed the professor. He might. have been coming into the middle of a row in one of the corridors of the college at home only this time he carried a candle. His speech, however, was a Washurst speech: " Gentlemen, gentlemen, what does this mean? " All seemed to expect Coleman to make the answer. He was suddenly very cool. "Nothing, professor," he said, " only that this-only that Coke has insulted me. I suppose that it was only the irresponsibility of a boy, and I beg that you will not trouble over it."

" Mr. Coke," said the professor, indignantly, " what have you to say to this? " Evidently he could not clearly see Coke, and he peered around his candle at where the virtuous Peter Tounley was expostulating with the young man. The figures of all the excited group moving in the candle light caused vast and uncouth shadows to have conflicts in the end of the room.

Peter Tounley's task was not light, and beyond that he had the conviction that his struggle with Coke was making him also to appear as a rowdy. This conviction was proven to be true by a sudden thunder from the old professor, " Mr. Tounley, desist! "

In wrath he desisted and Coke flung himself forward. He paid less attention to the professor than if the latter had been a jack-rabbit. " You say I insulted you? he shouted crazily in Coleman's face.

"Well * * * I meant to, do you see? "

Coleman was glacial and lofty beyond everything.

"I am glad to have you admit the truth of what I have said."

Coke was, still suffocating with his peasant rage, which would not allow him to meet the clear, calm expressions of Coleman. "Yes * * * I insulted you * * * I insulted you because what I said was correct * * my prehensile attributes * * yes but I have never——"

He was interrupted by a chorus from the other students.

"Oh, no, that won't do. Don't say that. Don't repeat that, Coke."

Coleman remembered the weak bewilderment of the little professor in hours that had not long passed, and it was with something of an impersonal satisfac- tion that he said to himself: " The old boy's got his war-paint on again." The professor had stepped sharply up to Coke and looked at him with eyes that seemed to throw out flame and heat. There was a moment's pause, and then the old scholar spoke, bit- ing his words as if they were each a short section of steel wire. " Mr. Coke, your behaviour will end your college career abruptly and in gloom, I promise you. You have been drinking."

Coke, his head simply floating in a sea of universal defiance, at once blurted out: " Yes, sir."

"You have been drinking?" cried the professor, ferociously. "Retire to your-retire to your——retire—-" And then in a voice of thunder he shouted: "Retire."

Whereupon seven hoodlum students waited a decent moment, then shrieked with laughter. But the old professor would have none of their nonsense. He quelled them all with force and finish.

Coleman now spoke a few words." Professor, I can't tell you how sorry I am that I should be concerned in any such riot as this, and since we are doomed to be bound so closely into each other's society I offer myself without reservation as being willing to repair the damage as well as may be, done. I don t see how I can forget at once that Coke's conduct was insolently unwarranted, but * * * if he has anything to say of a nature that might heal the breach I would be willing to meet him in the openest manner." As he made these re- marks Coleman's dignity was something grand, and, Morever, there was now upon his face that curious look of temperance and purity which had been noted in New York as a singular physical characteristic. If he. was guilty of anything in this affair at all-in fact, if he had ever at any time been guilty of anything- no mark had come to stain that bloom of innocence. The professor nodded in the fullest appreciation and sympathy. " Of course * * * really there is no other sleeping place suppose it would be better-" Then he again attacked Coke. "Young man, you have chosen an unfortunate moment to fill us with a suspicion that you may not be a gentleman. For the time there is nothing to be done with you." He addressed the other students. " There is nothing for me to do, young gentleman, but to leave Mr. Coke in your care. Good-night, sirs. Good-night, Coleman." He left the room with his candle.

When Coke was bade to " Retire " he had, of course, simply retreated fuming to a corner of the room where he remained looking with yellow eyes like an animal from a cave. When the others were able to see through the haze of mental confusion they found that Coleman was with deliberation taking off his boots. " Afterward, when he removed his waist-coat, he took great care to wind his large gold watch.

The students, much subdued, lay again in their places, and when there was any talking it was of an extremely local nature, referring principally to the floor As being unsuitable for beds and also referring from time to time to a real or an alleged selfishness on the part of some one of the recumbent men. Soon there was only the sound of heavy breathing.

When the professor had returned to what he called the Wainwright part of the house he was greeted instantly with the question: "What was it?" His wife and daughter were up in alarm. "What was it " they repeated, wildly.

He was peevish. " Oh, nothing, nothing. But that young Coke is a regular ruffian. He had gotten him. self into some tremendous uproar with Coleman. When I arrived he seemed actually trying to assault him. Revolting! He had been drinking. Coleman's behaviour, I must say, was splendid. Recognised at once the delicacy of my position-he not being a student. If I had found him in the wrong it would have been simpler than finding him in the right. Confound that rascal of a Coke." Then, as he began a partial disrobing, he treated them to grunted scrap of information. " Coke was quite insane * * * I feared that I couldn't control him * * * Coleman was like ice * * * and as much as I have seen to admire in him during the last few days, this quiet beat it all. If he had not recognised my helplessness as far as he was concerned the whole thing might have been a most miserable business. He is a very fine young man." The dissenting voice to this last tribute was the voice of Mrs. Wainwright. She said: " Well, Coleman drinks, too-everybody knows that."

" I know," responded the professor, rather bashfully, but I am confident that he had not touched a drop. Marjory said nothing.

The earlier artillery battles had frightened most of the furniture out of the houses of Arta, and there was left in this room only a few old red cushions, and the Wainwrights were camping upon the floor. Marjory was enwrapped in Coleman's macintosh, and while the professor and his wife maintained some low talk of the recent incident she in silence had turned her cheek into the yellow velvet collar of the coat. She felt something against her bosom, and putting her hand carefully into the top pocket of the coat she found three cigars. These she took in the darkness and laid aside, telling herself to remember their position in the morning. She had no doubt that Coleman: would rejoice over them, before he could get back to, Athens where there were other good cigars.

CHAPTER XVIII.

THE ladies of the Wainwright party had not complained at all when deprived of even such civilised advantages as a shelter and a knife and fork and soap and water, but Mrs. Wainwright complained bitterly amid the half-civilisation of Arta. She could see here no excuse for the absence of several hundred things which she had always regarded as essential to life. She began at 8.30 A. M. to make both the professor and Marjory woeful with an endless dissertation upon the beds in the hotel at Athens. Of course she had not regarded them at the time as being exceptional beds * * * that was quite true, * * * but then one really never knew what one was really missing until one really missed it * * * She would never have thought that she would come to consider those Athenian beds as excellent * * * but experience is a great teacher * * * makes- one reflect upon the people who year in and year out have no beds at all, poor things. * * * Well, it made one glad if one did have a good bed, even if it was at the time on the other side of the world. If she ever reached it she did not know what could ever induce her to leave it again. * * * She would never be induced—-

"'Induced!'" snarled the professor. The word represented to him a practiced feminine misusage of truth, and at such his white warlock always arose. "" Induced!' Out of four American women I have seen lately, you seem to be the only one who would say that you had endured this thing because you had been 'induced' by others to come over here. How absurd!"

Mrs. Wainwright fixed her husband with a steely eye. She saw opportunity for a shattering retort. " You don't mean, Harrison, to include Marjory and I in the same breath with those two women? "

The professor saw no danger ahead for himself. He merely answered: " I had no thought either way. It did not seem important."

" Well, it is important," snapped Mrs. Wainwright.

" Do you know that you are speaking in the same breath of

Marjory and Nora Black, the actress? "

" No," said the professor. " Is that so? " He was astonished, but he was not aghast at all. "Do you mean to say that is Nora Black, the comic opera star?"

" That's exactly who she is," said Mrs. Wainwright, dramatically. " And I consider that-I consider that Rufus Coleman has done no less than-misled us."

This last declaration seemed to have no effect upon the professor's pure astonishment, but Marjory looked at her mother suddenly. However, she said no word, exhibiting again that strange and, inscrutable countenance which masked even the tiniest of her maidenly emotions.

Mrs. Wainwright was triumphant, and she immediately set about celebrating her victory. " Men never see those things," she said to her husband. " Men never see those things. You would have gone on forever without finding out that your-your- hospitality was, being abused by that Rufus Coleman."

The professor woke up." Hospitality ?" he said, indignantly. "Hospitality? I have not had any hospitality to be abused. Why don't you talk sense? It is not that, but-it might-" He hesitated and then spoke slowly. " It might be very awkward. Of course one never knows anything definite about such people, but I suppose * * * Anyhow, it was strange in Coleman to allow her to meet us. "

"It Was all a pre-arranged plan," announced the triumphant Mrs. Wainwright. " She came here on purpose to meet Rufus Coleman, and he knew it, and I should not wonder if they had not the exact spot picked out where they were going to meet."

"I can hardly believe that," said the professor, in distress.

"I can, hardly believe that. It does, not seem to me that

Coleman—"

" Oh yes. Your dear Rufus Coleman," cried Mrs.

Wainwright. " You think he is very fine now. But

I can remember when you didn't think—-"

And the parents turned together an abashed look at their daughter. The professor actually flushed with shame. It seemed to him that he had just committed an atrocity upon the heart of his child. The instinct of each of them was to go to her and console her in their arms. She noted it immediately, and seemed to fear it. She spoke in a clear and even voice. " I don't think, father, that you should distress me by supposing that I am concerned at all if Mr. Coleman cares to get Nora Black over here."

" Not at all," stuttered the professor. " I—-"

Mrs. Wainwright's consternation turned suddenly to, anger.

" He is a scapegrace. A rascal. A— a—"

" Oh," said Marjory, coolly, " I don't see why it isn't his own affair. He didn't really present her to you, mother, you remember? She seemed quite to force her way at first, and then you-you did the rest. It should be very easy to avoid her, now that we are out of the wilderness. And then it becomes a private matter of Mr. Coleman's. For my part, I rather liked her. I don't see such a dreadful calamity."

"Marjory!" screamed her mother. "How dreadful. Liked her!

Don't let me hear you say such shocking things."

" I fail to see anything shocking," answered Marjory, stolidly.

The professor was looking helplessly from his daughter to his wife, and from his wife to his daughter, like a man who was convinced that his troubles would never end. This new catastrophe created a different kind of difficulty, but he considered that the difficulties were as robust as had been the preceding ones. He put on his hat and went out of the room. He felt an impossibility of saying anything to Coleman, but he felt that he must look upon him. He must look upon this man and try to know from his manner the measure of guilt. And incidentally he longed for the machinery of a finished society which prevents its parts from clashing, prevents it with its great series of I law upon law, easily operative but relentless. Here he felt as a man flung into the jungle with his wife and daughter, where they could become the victims of any sort of savagery. His thought referred once more to what he considered the invaluable services of Coleman, and as he observed them in conjunction with the present accusation, he was simply dazed. It was then possible that one man could play two such divergent parts. He had not learned this at Washurst. But no; the world was not such a bed of putrefaction. He would not believe it; he would not believe it.

After adventures which require great nervous en. durance, it is only upon the second or third night that the common man sleeps hard. The students had expected to slumber like dogs on the first night after their trials. but none slept long, And few slept.

Coleman was the first man to arise. When he left the room the students were just beginning to blink. He took his dragoman among the shops and he bought there all the little odds and ends which might go to make up the best breakfast in Arta. If he had had news of certain talk he probably would not have been buying breakfast for eleven people. Instead, he would have been buying breakfast for one. During his absence the students arose and performed their frugal toilets. Considerable attention was paid to Coke by the others. " He made a monkey of you," said Peter Tounley with unction. " He twisted you until you looked like a wet, grey rag. You had better leave this wise guy alone."

It was not the night nor was it meditation that had taught Coke anything, but he seemed to have learned something from the mere lapse of time. In appearance he was subdued, but he managed to make a temporary jauntiness as he said: " Oh, I don't know."

" Well, you ought to know," said he who was called Billie. "You ought to know. You made an egregious snark of yourself. Indeed, you sometimes resembled a boojum. Anyhow, you were a plain chump. You exploded your face about something of which you knew nothing, and I'm damned if I believe you'd make even a good retriever."

"You're a half-bred water-spaniel," blurted Peter Tounley.

"And," he added, musingly, "that is a pretty low animal."

Coke was argumentative. "Why am I? " he asked, turning his head from side to side. " I don't see where I was so wrong."

" Oh, dances, balloons, picnics, parades and ascensions," they retorted, profanely. " You swam voluntarily into water that was too deep for you. Swim out. Get dry. Here's a towel."

Coke, smitten in the face with a wet cloth rolled into a ball, grabbed it and flung it futilely at a well-dodging companion " No," he cried, " I don't see it. Now look here. I don't see why we shouldn't all resent this Nora Black business."

One student said: "Well, what's the matter with Nora Black, anyhow ?"

Another student said, "I don't see how you've been issued any license to say things about Nora Black."

Another student said dubiously: " Well, he knows her well."

And then three or four spoke at once. " He was very badly rattled when she appeared upon the scene."

Peter Tounley asked: "Well, which of you people know anything wrong about Nora Black? "

There was a pause, and then Coke said: " Oh, of course-I don't know-but-"

He who was called Billie then addressed his com- panions. " It wouldn't be right to repeat any old lie about Nora Black, and by the same token it wouldn't be right to see old Mother Wainwright chummin' with her. There is no wisdom in going further than that. Old Mother Wainwright don't know that her fair companion of yesterday is the famous comic opera star. For my part, I believe that Coleman is simply afraid to tell her. I don't think he wished to see Nora Black yesterday any more than he wished to see the devil. The discussion, as I understand it concerned itself only with what Coleman had to do with the thing, and yesterday anybody could see that he was in a panic."

They heard a step on the stair, and directly Coleman entered, followed by his dragoman. They were laden with the raw material for breakfast. The correspondent looked keenly among the students, for it was plain that they had been talking of him. It, filled him with rage, and for a stifling moment he could not think why he failed to immediately decamp in chagrin and leave eleven orphans to whatever fate. their general incompetence might lead them. It struck him as a deep shame that even then he and his paid man were carrying in the breakfast. He wanted to fling it all on the floor and walk out. Then he remembered Marjory. She was the reason. She was the reason for everything.

But he could not repress certain, of his thoughts. "Say, you people," he said, icily, " you had better soon learn to hustle for yourselves. I may be a dragoman, and a butler, and a cook, and a housemaid, but I'm blowed if I'm a wet nurse." In reality, he had taken the most generous pleasure in working for the others before their eyes had even been opened from sleep, but it was now all turned to wormwood. It is certain that even this could not have deviated this executive man from labour and management. because these were his life. But he felt that he was about to walk out of the room, consigning them all to Hades. His glance of angry, reproach fastened itself mainly upon Peter Tounley, because he knew that of all, Peter was the most innocent.

Peter, Tounley was abashed by this glance. So you've brought us something to eat, old man. That is tremendously nice of you-we-appreciate it like everything."

Coleman was mollified by Peter's tone. Peter had had that emotion which is equivalent to a sense of guilt, although in reality he was speckless. Two or three of the other students bobbed up to a sense of the situation. They ran to Coleman, and with polite cries took his provisions from him. One dropped a bunch of lettuce on the floor, and others reproached him with scholastic curses. Coke was seated near the window, half militant, half conciliatory. It was impossible for him to keep up a manner of deadly enmity while Coleman was bringing in his breakfast. He would have much preferred that Coleman had not brought in his breakfast. He would have much preferred to have foregone breakfast altogether. He would have much preferred anything. There seemed to be a conspiracy of circumstance to put him in the wrong and make him appear as a ridiculous young peasant. He was the victim of a benefaction, and he hated Coleman harder now than at any previous time. He saw that if he stalked out and took his breakfast alone in a cafe, the others would consider him still more of an outsider. Coleman had expressed himself like a man of the world and a gentleman, and Coke was convinced that he was a superior man of the world and a superior gentleman, but that he simply had not had words to express his position at the proper time. Coleman was glib. Therefore, Coke had been the victim of an attitude as well as of a benefaction. And so he deeply hated Coleman.

The others were talking cheerfully. "What the deuce are these, Coleman? Sausages? Oh, my. And look at these burlesque fishes. Say, these Greeks don't care what they eat. Them thar things am sardines in the crude state. No? Great God, look at those things. Look. What? Yes, they are. Radishes. Greek synonym for radishes."

The professor entered. " Oh," he said apologetically, as if he were intruding in a boudoir. All his serious desire to probe Coleman to the bottom ended in embarrassment. Mayhap it was not a law of feeling, but it happened at any rate. " He had come in a puzzled frame of mind, even an accusative frame of mind, and almost immediately he found himself suffer. ing like a culprit before his judge. It is a phenomenon of what we call guilt and innocence.

" Coleman welcomed him cordially. " Well, professor, good-morning. I've rounded up some things that at least may be eaten."

" You are very good " very considerate, Mr. Coleman," answered the professor, hastily. " I'am sure we are much indebted to you." He had scanned the correspondent's face, land it had been so devoid of guile that he was fearful that his suspicion, a base suspicion, of this noble soul would be detected. " No, no, we can never thank you enough."

Some of the students began to caper with a sort of decorous hilarity before their teacher. " Look at the sausage, professor. Did you ever see such sausage " Isn't it salubrious " And see these other things, sir. Aren't they curious " I shouldn't wonder if they were alive. Turnips, sir? No, sir. I think they are Pharisees. I have seen a Pharisee look like a pelican, but I have never seen a Pharisee look like a turnip, so I think these turnips must be Pharisees, sir, Yes, they may be walrus. We're not sure. Anyhow, their angles are geometrically all wrong. Peter, look out." Some green stuff was flung across the room. The professor laughed; Coleman laughed. Despite Coke, dark-browed, sulking. and yet desirous of reinstating himself, the room had waxed warm with the old college feeling, the feeling of lads who seemed never to treat anything respectfully and yet at the same time managed to treat the real things with respect. The professor himself contributed to their wild carouse over the strange Greek viands. It was a vivacious moment common to this class in times of relaxation, and it was understood perfectly.

Coke arose. " I don't see that I have any friends here," he said, hoarsely, " and in consequence I don't see why I should remain here."

All looked at him. At the same moment Mrs. Wainwright and

Marjory entered the room.

CHAPTER XIX.

"Good-morning," said Mrs. Wainwright jovially to the students and then she stared at Coleman as if he were a sweep at a wedding.

" Good-morning," said Marjory.

Coleman and the students made reply. " Good-morning.

Good-morning. Good-morning. Good-morning—"

It was curious to see this greeting, this common phrase, this bit of old ware, this antique, come upon a dramatic scene and pulverise it. Nothing remained but a ridiculous dust. Coke, glowering, with his lips still trembling from heroic speech, was an angry clown, a pantaloon in rage. Nothing was to be done to keep him from looking like an ass. He, strode toward the door mumbling about a walk before breakfast.

Mrs. Wainwright beamed upon him. " Why, Mr. Coke, not before breakfast? You surely won't have time." It was grim punishment. He appeared to go blind, and he fairly staggered out of the door mumbling again, mumbling thanks or apologies or explanations. About the mouth of Coleman played a sinister smile. The professor cast. upon his wife a glance expressing weariness. It was as if he said " There you go again. You can't keep your foot out of it." She understood the glance, and so she asked blankly: "Why, What's the matter? Oh." Her belated mind grasped that it waw an aftermath of the quarrel of Coleman and Coke. Marjory looked as if she was distressed in the belief that her mother had been stupid. Coleman was outwardly serene. It was Peter Tounley who finally laughed a cheery, healthy laugh and they all looked at him with gratitude as if his sudden mirth had been a real statement or recon- ciliation and consequent peace.

The dragoman and others disported themselves until a breakfast was laid upon the floor. The adventurers squatted upon the floor. They made a large company. The professor and Coleman discussed the means of getting to Athens. Peter Tounley sat next to Marjory. " Peter," she said, privately, " what was all this trouble between Coleman and Coke? "

Peter answered blandly: " Oh, nothing at Nothing at all."

" Well, but—" she persisted, " what was the cause of it?"

He looked at her quaintly. He was not one of those in love with her, but be was interested in the affair. " Don't you know ? " he asked.

She understood from his manner that she had been some kind of an issue in the quarrel. " No," she answered, hastily. " I don't."

"Oh, I don't mean that," said Peter. "I only meant —I only meant—oh, well, it was nothing-really."

" It must have been about something," continued Marjory. She continued, because Peter had denied that she was concerned in it. " Whose fault? "

"I really don't know. It was all rather confusing," lied Peter, tranquilly.

Coleman and the professor decided to accept a plan of the correspondent's dragoman to start soon on the first stage of the journey to Athens. The dragoman had said that he had found two large carriages rentable.

Coke, the outcast, walked alone in the narrow streets. The flight of the crown prince's army from Larissa had just been announced in Arta, but Coke was probably the most woebegone object on the Greek peninsula.

He encountered a strange sight on the streets. A woman garbed in the style for walking of an afternoon on upper Broadway was approaching him through a mass of kilted mountaineers and soldiers in soiled overcoats. Of course he recognised Nora Black.

In his conviction that everybody in the world was at this time considering him a mere worm, he was sure that she would not heed him. Beyond that he had been presented to her notice in but a transient and cursory fashion. But contrary to his conviction, she turned a radiant smile upon him. " Oh," she said, brusquely, " you are one of the students. Good morning." In her manner was all the confidence of an old warrior, a veteran, who addresses the universe with assurance because of his past battles.

Coke grinned at this strange greeting. " Yes, Miss Black," he answered, " I am one of the students."

She did not seem to quite know how to formulate her next speech. " Er-I suppose you're going to Athens at once " You must be glad after your horrid experiences."

" I believe they are going to start for Athens today," said

Coke.

Nora was all attention. "'They ?'" she repeated.

"Aren't you going with them? "

" Well," he said, " * * Well—"

She saw of course that there had been some kind of trouble. She laughed. " You look as if somebody had kicked you down stairs," she said, candidly. She at once assumed an intimate manner toward him which was like a temporary motherhood. " Come, walk with me and tell me all about it." There was in her tone a most artistic suggestion that whatever had happened she was on his side. He was not loath. The street was full of soldiers whose tongues clattered so loudly that the two foreigners might have been wandering in a great cave of the winds. " Well, what was the row about ? " asked Nora. " And who was in it? "

It would have been no solace to Coke to pour out his tale even if it had been a story that he could have told Nora. He was not stopped by the fact that he had gotten himself in the quarrel because he had insulted the name of the girt at his side. He did not think of it at that time. The whole thing was now extremely vague in outline to him and he only had a dull feeling of misery and loneliness. He wanted her to cheer him.

Nora laughed again. " Why, you're a regular little kid. Do you mean to say you've come out here sulking alone because of some nursery quarrel? " He was ruffled by her manner. It did not contain the cheering he required. " Oh,

I don't know that I'm such a regular little kid," he said, sullenly. " The quarrel was not a nursery quarrel."

"Why don't you challenge him to a duel? " asked Nora, suddenly. She was watching him closely.

" Who?" said Coke.

" Coleman, you stupid," answered Nora.

They stared at each other, Coke paying her first the tribute of astonishment and then the tribute of admiration. "Why, how did you guess that?" he demanded.

" Oh," said Nora., " I've known Rufus Coleman for years, and he is always rowing with people."

"That is just it," cried Coke eagerly. "That is just it. I fairly hate the man. Almost all of the other fellows will stand his abuse, but it riles me, I tell you. I think he is a beast. And, of course, if you seriously meant what you said about challenging him to a duel—I mean if there is any sense in that sort of thing-I would challenge Coleman. I swear I would. I think he's a great bluffer, anyhow. Shouldn't wonder if he would back out. Really, I shouldn't.

Nora smiled humourously at a house on her side of the narrow way. "I wouldn't wonder if he did either " she answered. After a time she said " Well, do you mean to say that you have definitely shaken them? Aren't you going back to Athens with them or anything? "

" I-I don't see how I can," he said, morosely.

" Oh," she said. She reflected for a time. At last she turned to him archly and asked: "Some words over a lady?"

Coke looked at her blankly. He suddenly remembered the horrible facts. " No-no-not over a lady."

" My dear boy, you are a liar," said Nora, freely. "You are a little unskilful liar. It was some words over a lady, and the lady's name is Marjory Wainwright."

Coke felt as though he had suddenly been let out of a cell, but he continued a mechanical denial. "No, no * * It wasn't truly * * upon my word * * "

"Nonsense," said Nora. " I know better. Don't you think you can fool me, you little cub. I know you're in love with Marjory Wainwright, and you think Coleman is your rival. What a blockhead you are. Can't you understand that people see these things?"

" Well-" stammered Coke.

"Nonsense," said Nora again. "Don't try to fool me, you may as well understand that it's useless. I am too wise."

" Well-" stammered Coke.

" Go ahead," urged Nora. " Tell me about it. Have it out."

He began with great importance and solemnity. "Now, to tell you the truth * * that is why I hate him * * I hate him like anything. * * I can't see why everybody admires him so. I don't see anything to him myself. I don't believe he's got any more principle than a wolf. I wouldn't trust him with two dollars. Why, I know stories about him that would make your hair curl. When I think of a girl like Marjory— "

His speech had become a torrent. But here Nora raised her hand. " Oh! Oh! Oh! That will do. That will do. Don't lose your senses. I don't see why this girl Marjory is any too good. She is no chicken, I'll bet. Don't let yourself get fooled with that sort of thing."

Coke was unaware of his incautious expressions. He floundered on. while Nora looked at him as if she wanted to wring his neck. " No-she's too fine and too good-for him or anybody like him-she's too fine and too good-"

" Aw, rats," interrupted Nora, furiously. "You make me tired."

Coke had a wooden-headed conviction that he must make Nora understand Marjory's infinite superiority to all others of her sex, and so he passed into a pariegyric, each word of which was a hot coal to the girl addressed. Nothing would stop him, apparently. He even made the most stupid repetitions. Nora finally stamped her foot formidably. "Will you stop? Will you stop ? " she said through her clenched teeth. " Do you think I want to listen to your everlasting twaddle about her? Why, she's-she's no better than other people, you ignorant little mamma's boy. She's no better than other people, you swab! "

Coke looked at her with the eyes of a fish. He did not understand. "But she is better than other people," he persisted.

Nora seemed to decide suddenly that there would be no accomplishment in flying desperately against this rock-walled conviction. " Oh, well," she said, with marvellous good nature, " perhaps you are right, numbskull. But, look here; do you think she cares for him?"

In his heart, his jealous heart, he believed that Marjory loved Coleman, but he reiterated eternally to himself that it was not true. As for speaking it to, another, that was out of the question. " No," he said, stoutly, " she doesn't care a snap for him." If he had admitted it, it would have seemed to him that. he was somehow advancing Coleman's chances.

"'Oh, she doesn't, eh ?" said Nora enigmatically.

"She doesn't?" He studied her face with an abrupt, miserable suspicion, but he repeated doggedly: " No, she doesn't."

"Ahem," replied Nora. " Why, she's set her cap for him all right. She's after him for certain. It's as plain as day. Can't you see that, stupidity ?"

"No," he said hoarsely.

"You are a fool," said Nora. " It isn't Coleman that's after her. It is she that is after Coleman."

Coke was mulish. " No such thing. Coleman's crazy about her. Everybody has known it ever since he was in college. You ask any of the other fellows."

Nora was now very serious, almost doleful. She remained still for a time, casting at Coke little glances of hatred. " I don't see my way clear to ask any of the other fellows," she said at last, with considerable bitterness. " I'm not in the habit of conducting such enquiries."

Coke felt now that he disliked her, and he read plainly her dislike of him. If they were the two villains of the play, they were not having fun together at all. Each had some kind of a deep knowledge that their aspirations, far from colliding, were of such character that the success of one would mean at least assistance to the other, but neither could see how to confess if. Pethapt it was from shame, perhaps it was because Nora thought Coke to have little wit ; perhaps it was because Coke thought Nora to have little conscience. Their talk was mainly rudderless. From time to time Nora had an inspiration to come boldly at the point, but this inspiration was commonly defeated by, some extraordinary manifestation of Coke's incapacity. To her mind, then, it seemed like a proposition to ally herself to a butcher-boy in a matter purely sentimental. She Wondered indignantly how she was going to conspire With this lad, who puffed out his infantile cheeks in order to conceitedly demonstrate that he did not understand the game at all. She hated Marjory for it. Evidently it was only the weaklings who fell in love with that girl. Coleman was an exception, but then, Coleman was misled, by extraordinary artifices. She meditated for a moment if she should tell Coke to go home and not bother her. What at last decided the question was his unhappiness. Shd clung to this unhappiness for its value as it stood alone, and because its reason for existence was related to her own unhappiness. " You Say you are not going back to Athens with your party. I don't suppose you're going to stay here. I'm going back to Athens to-day. I came up here to see a battle, but it doesn't seem that there are to be any more battles., The fighting will now all be on the other side of the mountains." Apparent she had learned in some haphazard way that the Greek peninsula was divided by a spine of almost inaccessible mountains, and the war was thus split into two simultaneous campaigns. The Arta campaign was known to be ended. "If you want to go back to Athens without consorting with your friends, you had better go back with me. I can take you in my carriage as far as the beginning of the railroad. Don't you worry. You've got money enough, haven't you? The pro- fessor isn't keeping your money ?"

"Yes," he said slowly, "I've got money enough." He was apparently dubious over the proposal. In their abstracted walk they had arrived in front of the house occupied by Coleman and the Wainwright party. Two carriages, forlorn in dusty age, stood be- fore the door. Men were carrying out new leather luggage and flinging it into the traps amid a great deal of talk which seemed to refer to nothing. Nora and Coke stood looking at the scene without either thinking of the importance of running away, when out tumbled seven students, followed immediately but in more decorous fashion by the Wainwrights and Coleman.

Some student set up a whoop. " Oh, there he is.

There's Coke. Hey, Coke, where you been? Here

he is, professor."

For a moment after the hoodlum had subsided, the

two camps stared at each other in silence.

CHAPTER XX.

NORA and Coke were an odd looking pair at the time. They stood indeed as if rooted to the spot, staring vacuously, like two villagers, at the surprising travellers. It was not an eternity before the practiced girl of the stage recovered her poise, but to the end of the incident the green youth looked like a culprit and a fool. Mrs. Wainwright's glower of offensive incredulity was a masterpiece. Marjory nodded pleasantly; the professor nodded. The seven students clambered boisterously into the forward carriage making it clang with noise like a rook's nest. They shouted to Coke. " Come on; all aboard; come on, Coke; - we're off. Hey, there, Cokey, hurry up." The professor, as soon as he had seated himself on the forward seat of' the second carriage, turned in Coke's general direction and asked formally: " Mr. Coke, you are coming with us? " He felt seemingly much in doubt as to the propriety of abandoning the headstrong young man, and this doubt was not at all decreased by Coke's appearance with Nora Black. As far as he could tell, any assertion of authority on his part would end only in a scene in which Coke would probably insult him with some gross violation of collegiate conduct. As at first the young man made no reply, the professor after waiting spoke again. "You understand, Mr. Coke, that if you separate yourself from the party you encounter my strongest disapproval, and if I did not feel responsible to the college and your father for your safe journey to New York I-I don't know but what I would have you ex- pelled by cable if that were possible."

Although Coke had been silent, and Nora Black had had the appearance of being silent, in reality she had lowered her chin and whispered sideways and swiftly. She had said: " Now, here's your time. Decide quickly, and don't look such a wooden Indian." Coke pulled himself together with a visible effort, and spoke to the professor from an inspiration in which he had no faith. " I understand my duties to you, sir, perfectly. I also understand my duty to the college. But I fail to see where either of these obligations require me to accept the introduction of objectionable people into the party. If I owe a duty to the college and to you, I don't owe any to Coleman, and, as I understand it,

Coleman was not in the original plan of this expedition. If such had been the case, I would not have been here. I can't tell what the college may see fit to do, but as for my father I have no doubt of how he will view it."

The first one to be electrified by the speech was Coke himself. He saw with a kind of sub-conscious amazement this volley of bird-shot take effect upon the face of the old professor. The face of Marjory flushed crimson as if her mind had sprung to a fear that if Coke could develop ability in this singular fashion he might succeed in humiliating her father in the street in the presence of the seven students, her mother, Coleman and-herself. She had felt the bird- shot sting her father.

When Coke had launched forth, Coleman with his legs stretched far apart had just struck a match on the wall of the house and was about to light a cigar. His groom was leading up his horse. He saw the value of Coke's argument more appreciatively and sooner perhaps than did Coke. The match dropped from his fingers, and in the white sunshine and still air it burnt on the pavement orange coloured and with langour. Coleman held his cigar with all five fingers-in a manner out of all the laws of smoking. He turned toward Coke. There was danger in the moment, but then in a flash it came upon him that his role was not of squabbling with Coke, far less of punching him. On the contrary, he was to act the part of a cool and instructed man who refused to be waylaid into foolishness by the outcries of this pouting youngster and who placed himself in complete deference to the wishes of the professor. Before the professor had time to embark upon any reply to Coke, Coleman was at the side of the carriage and, with a fine assumption of distress, was saying: "Professor, I could very easily ride back to Agrinion alone. It would be all right. I don't want to-"

To his surprise the professor waved at him to be silent as if he were a mere child. The old man's face was set with the resolution of exactly what he was going to say to Coke. He began in measured tone, speaking with feeling, but with no trace of anger.

" Mr. Coke, it has probably escaped your attention that Mr. Coleman, at what I consider a great deal of peril to himself, came out to rescue this party-you and others-and although he studiously disclaims all merit in his finding us and bringing us in, I do not regard it in that way, and I am surprised that any member of this party should conduct himself in this manner toward a man who has been most devotedly and generously at our service." It was at this time that the professor raised himself and shook his finger at Coke, his voice now ringing with scorn. In such moments words came to him and formed themselves into sentences almost too rapidly for him to speak them. " You are one of the most remarkable products of our civilisation which I have yet come upon. What do you mean, sir? Where are your senses? Do you think that all this pulling and pucking is manhood? I will tell you what I will do with you. I thought I brought out eight students to Greece, but when I find that I brought out, seven students and—er—an—ourang-outang—don't get angry, sir—I don't care for your anger—I say when I discover this I am naturally puzzled for a moment. I will leave you to the judgment of your peers. Young gentlemen! " Of the seven heads of the forward carriage none had to be turned. All had been turned since the beginning of the talk. If the professor's speech had been delivered in one of the class-rooms of Washurst they would have glowed with delight over the butchery of Coke, but they felt its portentous aspect. Butchery here in Greece thousands of miles from home presented to them more of the emphasis of downright death and destruction. The professor called out " Young gentlemen, I have done all that I can do without using force, which, much to my regret, is impracticable. If you will persuade your fellow student to accompany you I think our consciences will be the better for not having left a weak minded brother alone among the by-paths." The valuable aggregation of intelligence and refine- ment which decorated the interior of the first carriage did not hesitate over answering this appeal. In fact, his fellow students had worried among themselves over Coke, and their desire to see him come out of his troubles in fair condition was intensified by the fact that they had lately concentrated much thought upon him. There was a somewhat comic pretense of speaking so that only Coke could hear. Their chorus was law sung. " Oh, cheese it, Coke. Let up on your-self, you blind ass. Wait till you get to Athens and then go and act like a monkey. All this is no good-"

The advice which came from the carriage was all in one direction, and there was so much of it that the hum of voices sounded like a wind blowing through a forest.

Coke spun suddenly and said something to Nora Black. Nora laughed rather loudly, and then the two turned squarely and the Wainwright party contemplated what were surely at that time the two most insolent backs in the world.

The professor looked as if he might be going to have a fit. Mrs. Wainwright lifted her eyes toward heaven, and flinging out her trembling hands, cried: " Oh, what an outrage. What an outrage! That minx-" The concensus of opinion in the first carriage was perfectly expressed by Peter Tounley, who with a deep drawn breath, said: " Well, I'm damned! " Marjory had moaned and lowered her head as from a sense of complete personal shame. Coleman lit his cigar and mounted his horse. " Well, I suppose there is nothing for it but to be off, professor? " His tone was full of regret, with sort of poetic regret. For a moment the professor looked at him blankly, and then gradually recovered part of his usual manner. " Yes," he said sadly, " there is nothing for it but to go on." At a word from the dragoman, the two impatient drivers spoke gutturally to their horses and the car- riages whirled out of Arta. Coleman, his dragoman and the groom trotted in the dust from the wheels of the Wainwright carriage. The correspondent always found his reflective faculties improved by the constant pounding of a horse on the trot, and he was not sorry to have now a period for reflection, as well as this artificial stimulant. As he viewed the game he had in his hand about all the cards that were valuable. In fact, he considered that the only ace against him was Mrs. Wainwright. He had always regarded her as a stupid person, concealing herself behind a mass of trivialities which were all conventional, but he thought now that the more stupid she was and the more conventional in her triviality the more she approached to being the very ace of trumps itself. She was just the sort of a card that would come upon the table mid the neat play of experts and by some inexplicable arrangement of circumstance, lose a whole game for the wrong man. After Mrs. Wainwright he worried over the students. He believed them to be reasonable enough; in fact, he honoured them distinctly in regard to their powers of reason, but he knew that people generally hated a row. It, put them off their balance, made them sweat over a lot of pros and cons, and prevented them from thinking for a time at least only of themselves. Then they came to resent the principals in a row. Of course the principal, who was thought to be in the wrong, was the most resented, but Coleman be- lieved that, after all, people always came to resent the other principal, or at least be impatient and suspicious of him. If he was a correct person, why was he in a row at all? The principal who had been in the right often brought this impatience and suspicion upon himself, no doubt, by never letting the matter end, continuing to yawp about his virtuous suffering, and not allowing people to return to the steady contemplation of their own affairs. As a precautionary measure he decided to say nothing at all about the late trouble, unless some one addressed him upon it. Even then he would be serenely laconic. He felt that he must be popular with the seven students. In the first place, it was nice that in the presence of Marjory they should like him, and in the second place he feared to displease them as a body because he believed that he had some dignity. Hoodlums are seldom dangerous to other hoodlums, but if they catch pomposity alone in the field, pomposity is their prey. They tear him to mere bloody ribbons, amid heartless shrieks. When Coleman put himself on the same basis with the students, he could cope with them easily, but he did not want the wild pack after him when Marjory could see the chase. And so be rea- soned that his best attitude was to be one of rather taciturn serenity.

On the hard military road the hoofs of the horses made such clatter that it was practically impossible to hold talk between the carriages and the horsemen without all parties bellowing. The professor, how- ever, strove to overcome the difficulties. He was apparently undergoing a great amiability toward Coleman. Frequently he turned with a bright face, and pointing to some object in the landscape, obviously tried to convey something entertaining to Coleman's mind. Coleman could see his lips mouth the words. He always nodded cheerily in answer and yelled.

The road ultimately became that straight lance-handle which Coleman-it seemed as if many years had passed-had traversed with his dragoman and the funny little carriers. He was fixing in his mind a possible story to the Wainwrights about the snake and his first dead Turk. But suddenly the carriages left this road and began a circuit of the Gulf of Arta, winding about an endless series of promontories. The journey developed into an excess of dust whirling from a road, which half circled the waist of cape after cape. All dramatics were lost in the rumble of wheels and in the click of hoofs. They passed a little soldier leading a prisoner by a string. They passed more frightened peasants, who seemed resolved to flee down into the very boots of Greece. And people looked at them with scowls, envying them their speed. At the little town from which Coleman embarked at one stage of the upward journey, they found crowds in the streets. There was no longer any laughter, any confidence, any vim. All the spirit of the visible Greek nation seemed to have been knocked out of it in two blows. But still they talked and never ceased talking. Coleman noticed that the most curious changes had come upon them since his journey to the frontier. They no longer approved of foreigners. They seemed to blame the travellers for something which had transpired in the past few days. It was not that they really blamed the travellers for the nation's calamity: It was simply that their minds were half stunned by the news of defeats, and, not thinking for a moment to blame themselves, or even not thinking to attribute the defeats to mere numbers and skill, they were savagely eager to fasten it upon something near enough at hand for the operation of vengeance.

Coleman perceived that the dragoman, all his former plumage gone, was whining and snivelling as he argued to a dark-browed crowd that was running beside the cavalcade. The groom, who always had been a miraculously laconic man, was suddenly launched forth garrulously. The, drivers, from their high seats, palavered like mad men, driving with oat hand and gesturing with the other, explaining evidently their own great innocence.

Coleman saw that there was trouble, but he only sat more stiffly in his saddle. The eternal gabble moved him to despise the situation. At any rate, the travellers would soon be out of this town and on to a more sensible region.

However he saw the driver of the first carriage sud- denly pull up boforg a little blackened coffee shop and inn. The dragman spurred forward and began wild expostulation. The second carriage pulled close behind the other. The crowd, murmuring like a Roman mob in Nero's time, closed around them.

CHAPTER XXI.

COLEMAN pushed his horse coolly through to the dragoman;s side. " What is it ? " he demanded. The dragoman was broken-voiced. " These peoples, they say you are Germans, all Germans, and they are angry," he wailed. " I can do nossing-nossing."

" Well, tell these men to drive on," said Coleman, "tell them they must drive on."

" They will not drive on," wailed the dragoman, still more loudly. " I can do nossing. They say here is place for feed the horse. It is the custom and they will note drive on."

" Make them drive on."

" They will note," shrieked the agonised servitor. Coleman looked from the men waving their arms and chattering on the box-seats to the men of the crowd who also waved their arms and chattered. In this throng far to the rear of the fighting armies there did not seem to be a single man who was not ablebodied, who had not been free to enlist as a soldier. They were of that scurvy behind-the-rear-guard which every nation has in degree proportionate to its worth. The manhood of Greece had gone to the frontier, leaving at home this rabble of talkers, most of whom were armed with rifles for mere pretention. Coleman loathed them to the end of his soul. He thought them a lot of infants who would like to prove their courage upon eleven innocent travellers, all but unarmed, and in this fact he was quick to see a great danger to the Wainwright party. One could deal with soldiers; soldiers would have been ashamed to bait helpless people ; but this rabble-

The fighting blood of the correspondent began to boil, and he really longed for the privilege to run amuck through the multitude. But a look at the Wainwrights kept him in his senses. The professor had turned pale as a dead man. He sat very stiff and still while his wife clung to him, hysterically beseeching him to do something, do something, although what he was to do she could not have even imagined.

Coleman took the dilemma by its beard. He dismounted from his horse into the depths of the crowd and addressed the Wainwrights. " I suppose we had better go into this place and have some coffee while the men feed their horses. There is no use in trying to make them go on." His manner was fairly casual, but they looked at him in glazed horror. " It is the only thing to do. This crowd is not nearly so bad as they think they are. But we've got to look as if we felt confident." He himself had no confidence with this angry buzz in his ears, but be felt certain that the only correct move was to get everybody as quickly as possible within the shelter of the inn. It might not be much of a shelter for them, but it was better than the carriages in the street.

The professor and Mrs. Wainwright seemed to be considering their carriage as a castle, and they looked as if their terror had made them physically incapable of leaving it. Coleman stood waiting. Behind him the clapper-tongued crowd was moving ominously. Marjory arose and stepped calmly down to him. He thrilled to the end of every nerve. It was as if she had said: " I don't think there is great danger, but if there is great danger, why * * here I am * ready * with you." It conceded everything, admitted everything. It was a surrender without a blush, and it was only possible in the shadow of the crisis when they did not know what the next moments might contain for them. As he took her hand and she stepped past him he whispered swiftly and fiercely in her ear, " I love you." She did not look up, but he felt that in this quick incident they had claimed each other, accepted each other with a far deeper meaning and understanding than could be possible in a mere drawing-room. She laid her hand on his arm, and with the strength of four men he twisted his horse into the making of furious prancing side-steps toward the door of the inn, clanking side- steps which mowed a wide lane through the crowd for Marjory, his Marjory. He was as haughty as a new German lieutenant, and although he held the fuming horse with only his left hand, he seemed perfectly capable of hurling the animal over a house without calling into service the arm which was devoted to Marjory.

It was not an exhibition of coolness such as wins applause on the stage when the hero placidly lights a cigarette before the mob which is clamouring for his death. It was, on the contrary, an exhibition of downright classic disdain, a disdain which with the highest arrogance declared itself in every glance of his eye into the faces about him. " Very good * * attack me if you like * * there is nothing to prevent it * * you mongrels." Every step of his progress was made a renewed insult to them. The very air was charged with what this lone man was thinking of this threatening crowd.

His audacity was invincible. They actually made way for it as quickly as children would flee from a ghost. The horse, dancing; with ringing steps, with his glistening neck arched toward the iron hand at his bit, this powerful, quivering animal was a regular engine of destruction, and they gave room until Coleman halted him -at an exclamation from Marjory.

" My mother and father." But they were coming close behind and Coleman resumed this contemptuous journey to the door of the inn. The groom, with his new-born tongue, was clattering there to the populace. Coleman gave him the horse and passed after the Wainwrights into the public room of the inn. He was smiling. What simpletons!

A new actor suddenly appeared in the person of the keeper of the inn. He too had a rifle and a prodigious belt of cartridges, but it was plain at once that he had elected to be a friend of the worried travellers. A large part of the crowd were thinking it necessary to enter the inn and pow-wow more. But the innkeeper stayed at the door with the dragoman, and together they vociferously held back the tide. The spirit of the mob had subsided to a more reasonable feeling. They no longer wished to tear the strangers limb from limb on the suspicion that they were Germans. They now were frantic to talk as if some inexorable law had kept them silent for ten years and this was the very moment of their release. Whereas, their simul- taneous and interpolating orations had throughout made noise much like a coal-breaker. Coleman led the Wainwrights to a table in a far part of the room. They took chairs as if he had com- manded them. " What an outrage," he said jubilantly. " The apes." He was keeping more than half an eye upon the door, because he knew that the quick coming of the students was important.

Then suddenly the storm broke in wrath. Something had happened in the street. The jabbering crowd at the door had turned and were hurrying upon some central tumult. The dragoman screamed to Coleman. Coleman jumped and grabbed the dragoman. " Tell this man to take them somewhere up stairs," he cried, indicating the Wainwrights with a sweep of his arm. The innkeeper seemed to understand sooner than the dragoman, and he nodded eagerly. The professor was crying: "What is it, Mr. Coleman? What is it? " An instant later, the correspondent was out in the street, buffeting toward a scuffle. Of course it was the students. It appeared, afterward, that those seven young men, with their feelings much ruffled, had been making the best of their way toward the door of the inn, when a large man in the crowd, during a speech which was surely most offensive, had laid an arresting hand on the shoulder of Peter Tounley. Whereupon the excellent Peter Tounley had hit the large man on the jaw in such a swift and skilful manner that the large man had gone spinning through a group of his countrymen to the hard earth, where he lay holding his face together and howling. Instantly, of course, there had been a riot. It might well be said that even then the affair could have ended in a lot of talking, but in the first place the students did not talk modern Greek, and in the second place they were now past all thought of talking. They regarded this affair seriously as a fight, and now that they at last were in it, they were in it for every pint of blood in their bodies. Such a pack of famished wolves had never before been let loose upon men armed with Gras rifles.

They all had been expecting the row, and when Peter Tounley had found it expedient to knock over the man, they had counted it a signal: their arms immediately begun to swing out as if they had been wound up. It was at this time that Coleman swam brutally through the Greeks and joined his countrymen. He was more frightened than any of those novices. When he saw Peter Tounley overthrow a dreadful looking brigand whose belt was full of knives, and who -crashed to the ground amid a clang of cartridges, he was appalled by the utter simplicity with which the lads were treating the crisis. It was to them no com- mon scrimmage at Washurst, of course, but it flashed through Coleman's mind that they had not the slightegt sense of the size of the thing. He expected every instant to see the flash of knives or to hear the deafening intonation of a rifle fired against his ear. It seemed to him miraculous that the tragedy was so long delayed.

In the meantime he was in the affray. He jilted one man under the chin with his elbow in a way that reeled him off from Peter Tounley's back; a little person in thecked clothes he smote between the eyes; he recieved a gun-butt emphatically on the aide of the neck; he felt hands tearing at him; he kicked the pins out from under three men in rapid succession. He was always yelling. " Try to get to the inn, boys, try to get to the inn. Look out, Peter. Take care for his knife, Peter—" Suddenly he whipped a rifle out of the hands of a man and swung it, whistling. He had gone stark mad with the others.

The boy Billy, drunk from some blows and bleeding, was already. staggering toward the inn over the clearage which the wild Coleman made with the clubbed rifle. Tho others follewed as well as they might while beating off a discouraged enemy. The remarkable innkeeper had barred his windows with strong wood shutters. He held the door by the crack for them, and they stumbled one by on through the portal. Coleman did not know why they were not all dead, nor did he understand the intrepid and generous behaviour of the innkeeper, but at any rate he felt that the fighting was suspended, and he wanted to see Marjory. The innkeeper was, doing a great pantomime in the middle of the darkened room, pointing to the outer door and then aiming his rifle at it to explain his intention of defending them at all costs. Some of the students moved to a billiard table and spread them- selves wearily upon it. Others sank down where they stood. Outside the crowd was beginning to roar. Coleman's groom crept out from under the little Coffee bar and comically saluted his master. The dragoman was not present. Coleman felt that he must see Marjory, and he made signs to the innkeeper. The latter understood quickly, and motioned that Coleman should follow him. They passed together through a dark hall and up a darker stairway, where after Coleman stepped out into a sun-lit room, saying loudly: "Oh, it's all right. It's all over. Don't worry."

Three wild people were instantly upon him. " Oh, what was it? What did happen? Is anybody hurt? Oh, tell us, quick!" It seemed at the time that it was an avalanche of three of them, and it was not until later that he recognised that Mrs. Wainwright had tumbled the largest number of questions upon him. As for Marjory, she had said nothing until the time when she cried: "

Oh-he is bleeding-he is bleeding. Oh, come, quick!" She fairly dragged him out of one room into another room, where there was a jug of water. She wet her handkerchief and softly smote his wounds. "Bruises," she said, piteously, tearfully. " Bruises. Oh, dear! How they must hurt you.' The handkerchief was soon stained crimson.

When Coleman spoke his voice quavered. " It isn't anything. Really, it isn't anything." He had not known of these wonderful wounds, but he almost choked in the joy of Marjory's ministry and her half coherent exclamations. This proud and beautiful girl, this superlative creature, was reddening her handkerchief with his blood, and no word of his could have prevented her from thus attending him. He could hear the professor and Mrs. Wainwright fussing near him, trying to be of use. He would have liked to have been able to order them out of the room. Marjory's cool fingers on his face and neck had conjured within him a vision at an intimacy that was even sweeter than anything which he had imagined, and he longed to pour out to her the bubbling, impassioned speech which came to his lips. But, always doddering behind him, were the two old people, strenuous to be of help to him.

Suddenly a door opened and a youth appeared, simply red with blood. It was Peter Tounley. His first remark was cheerful. "Well, I don't suppose those people will be any too quick to look for more trouble."

Coleman felt a swift pang because he had forgotten to announce the dilapidated state of all the students. He had been so submerged by Marjory's tenderness that all else had been drowned from his mind. His heart beat quickly as he waited for Marjory to leave him and rush to Peter Tounley.

But she did nothing of the sort. " Oh, Peter," she cried in distress, and then she turned back to Coleman. It was the professor and Mrs. Wainwright who, at last finding a field for their kindly ambitions, flung them. selves upon Tounley and carried him off to another place. Peter was removed, crying: " Oh, now, look

here, professor, I'm not dying or anything of the sort Coleman and Marjory were left alone. He suddenly and forcibly took one of her hands and the blood stained hankerchief dropped to the floor.

CHAPTER XXII.

From below they could hear the thunder of weapons and fits upon the door of the inn amid a great clamour of. tongues. Sometimes there arose the argumtntative howl of the innkeeper. Above this roar, Coleman's quick words sounded in Marjory's ear.

" I've got to go. I've got to go back to the boys, but

-I love you."

" Yes go, go," she whispered hastily. " You should be there, but-come back."

He held her close to him. " But you are mine, remember," he said fiercely and sternly. " You are mine-forever-As I am yours-remember." Her eyes half closed. She made intensely solemn answer. "Yes." He released her and vphs gone. In the glooming coffee room of the inn he found the students, the dragoman, the groom and the innkeeper armed with a motley collection of weapons which ranged from the rifle of the innkeeper to the table leg in the hands of PeterTounley. The last named young student of archeology was in a position of temporary leadefship and holding a great pow-bow with the innkeeper through the medium of peircing outcries by the dragoman. Coleman had not yet undestood why none of them had been either stabbed or shot in the fight in the steeet, but it seemed to him now that affairs were leading toward a crisis of tragedy. He thought of the possibilities of having the dragoman go to an upper window and harangue the people, but he saw no chance of success in such a plan. He saw that the crowd would merely howl at the dragoman while the dragoman howled at the crowd. He then asked if there was any other exit from the inn by which they could secretly escape. He learned that the door into the coffee room was the only door which pierced the four great walls. All he could then do was to find out from the innkeeper how much of a siege the place could stand, and to this the innkeeper answered volubly and with smiles that this hostelry would easily endure until the mercurial temper of the crowd had darted off in a new direction. It may be curious to note here that all of Peter Tounley's impassioned communication with the innkeeper had been devoted to an endeavour to learn what in the devil was the matter with these people, as a man about to be bitten by poisonous snakes should, first of all, furiously insist upon learning their exact species before deciding upon either his route, if he intended to run away, or his weapon if he intended to fight them.

The innkeeper was evidently convinced that this house would withstand the rage of the populace, and he was such an unaccountably gallant little chap that Coleman trusted entirely to his word. His only fear or suspicion was an occasional one as to the purity of the dragoman's translation.

Suddenly there was half a silence on the mob without the door. It is inconceivable that it could become altogether silent, but it was as near to a rational stillness of tongues as it was able. Then there was a loud knocking by a single fist and a new voice began to spin Greek, a voice that was somewhat like the rattle of pebbles in a tin box. Then a startling voice called out in English. " Are you in there, Rufus? "

Answers came from every English speaking person in the room in one great outburst. "Yes."

" Well, let us in," called Nora Black. " It is all right. We've got an officer with us."

" Open the door," said Coleman with speed. The little innkeeper labouriously unfastened the great bars, and when the door finally opened there appeared on the threshold Nora Black with Coke and an officer of infantry, Nora's little old companion, and Nora's dragoman.

" We saw your carriage in the street," cried the queen of comic opera as she swept into the room. She was beaming with delight. " What is all the row, anyway? O-o-oh, look at that student's nose. Who hit him? And look at Rufus. What have you boys been doing?"

Her little Greek officer of infantry had stopped the mob from flowing into the room. Coleman looked toward the door at times with some anxiety.

Nora, noting it, waved her hand in careless reassurance; " Oh, it's, all right. Don't worry about them any more. He is perfectly devoted to me. He would die there on the threshold if I told him it would please me. Speaks splendid French. I found him limping along the road and gave him a lift. And now do hurry up and tell me exactly what happened." They all told what had happened, while Nora and Coke listened agape. Coke, by the way, had quite floated back to his old position with the students. It had been easy in the stress of excitement and wonder. Nobody had any titne to think of the excessively remote incidents of the early morning. All minor interests were lost in the marvel of the present situation.

"Who landed you in the eye, Billie?" asked the awed Coke. " That was a bad one." " Oh, I don't know," said Billie. " You really couldn't tell who hit you, you know. It was a football rush. They had guns and knives, but they didn't use 'em. I don't know why Jinks! I'm getting pretty stiff. My face feels as if it were made of tin. Did they give you people a row, too? "

" No; only talk. That little officer managed them. Out-talked them, I suppose. Hear him buzz, now." The Wainwrights came down stairs. Nora Black went confidently forward to meet them. "You've added one more to your list of rescuers," She cried, with her glowing, triumphant smile. "Miss Black of the New York Daylight-at your service. How in the world do you manage to get yourselves into such dreadful Scrapes? You are the most remarkable people. You need a guardian. Why, you might have all been killed. How exciting it must seem to be regularly of your party." She had shaken cordiaily one of Mrs. Wainwright's hands without that lady indicating assent to the proceeding but Mrs. Wainwright had not felt repulsion. In fact she had had no emotion springing directly from it. Here again the marvel of the situation came to deny Mrs. Wainwright the right to resume a state of mind which had been so painfully interesting to her a few hours earlier.

The professor, Coleman and all the students were talking together. Coke had addressed Coleman civilly and Coleman had made a civil reply. Peace was upon them.

Nora slipped her arm lovingly through Marjbry's arm. "That Rufus! Oh, that Rufus," she cried joyously. " I'll give him a good scolding as soon as I see him alone. I might have foreseen that he would get you all into trouble. The old stupid! "

Marjory did not appear to resent anything. " Oh, I don't think it was Mr. Coleman's fault at ail," she an- swered calmly. "I think it was more the fault of Peter Tounley, poor boy."

" Well, I'd be glad to believe it, I'd be glad to believe it," said Nora. "I want Rufus to keep out of that sort of thing, but he is so hot-headed and foolish." If she had pointed out her proprietary stamp on Coleman's cheek she could not have conveyed what she wanted with more clearness.

" Oh," said the impassive Marjory, " I don't think you need have any doubt as to whose fault it was, if there were any of our boys at fault. Mr. Coleman was inside when the fighting commenced, and only ran out to help the boys. He had just brought us safely through the mob, and, far from being hot-headed and foolish, he was utterly cool in manner, impressively cool, I thought. I am glad to be able to reassure you on these points, for I see that they worry you."

".Yes, they do worry me," said Nora, densely. They worry me night and day when he is away from me."

" Oh," responded Marjory, " I have never thought of Mr. Coleman as a man that one would worry about much. We consider him very self-reliant, able to take care of himself under almost any conditions, but then, of course, we do not know him at all in the way that you know him. I should think that you would find that he came off rather better than you expected from most of his difficulties. But then, of course, as. I said, you know him so much better than we do." Her easy indifference was a tacit dismissal of Coleman as a topic.

Nora, now thoroughly alert, glanced keenly into the other girl's face, but it was inscrutable. The actress had intended to go careering through a whole circle of daring illusions to an intimacy with,Coleman, but here, before she had really developed her attack, Marjory, with a few conventional and indifferent sentences, almost expressive of boredom, had made the subject of

Coleman impossible. An effect was left upon Nora's mind that Marjory had been extremely polite in listening to much nervous talk about a person in whom she had no interest.

The actress was dazed. She did not know how it had all been done. Where was the head of this thing? And where Was the tail? A fog had mysteriously come upon all her brilliant prospects of seeing Marjory Wainwright suffer, and this fog was the product of a kind of magic with which she was not familiar. She could not think how to fight it. After being simply dubious throughout a long pause, she in the end went into a great rage. She glared furiously at Marjory, dropped her arm as if it had burned her and moved down upon Coleman. She must have reflected that at any rate she could make him wriggle. When she was come near to him, she called out: "Rufus!" In her tone was all the old insolent statement of ownership. Coleman might have been a poodle. She knew how to call his same in a way that was anything less than a public scandal. On this occasion everybody looked at him and then went silent, as people awaiting the startling denouement of a drama. " Rufus! " She was baring his shoulder to show the fieur-de-lis of the criminal. The students gaped.

Coleman's temper was, if one may be allowed to speak in that way, broken loose inside of him. He could hardly beeathe; he felt that his body was about to explode into a thousand fragments. He simply snarled out " What? " Almost at once he saw that she had at last goaded him into making a serious tactical mistake. It must be admitted that it is only when the relations between a man and a woman are the relations of wedlock, or at least an intimate resemblance to it, that the man snarls out " What? " to the woman. Mere lovers say " I beg your pardon? " It is only Cupid's finished product that spits like a cat. Nora Black had called him like a wife, and he had answered like a husband. For his cause, his manner could not possibly have been worse. He saw the professor stare at him in surprise and alarm, and felt the excitement of the eight students. These latter were diabolic in the celerity with which they picked out meanings. It was as plain to them as if Nora Black had said: " He is my property."

Coleman would have given his nose to have been able to recall that single reverberating word. But he saw that the scene was spelling downfall for him, and he went still more blind and desperate of it. His despair made him burn to make matters Worse. He did not want to improve anything at all. " What?" he demanded. " What do ye' want?"

Nora was sweetly reproachful. " I left my jacket in the carriage, and I want you to get it for me."

" Well, get it for yourself, do you see? Get it for yourself."

Now it is plainly to be seen that no one of the people listening there had ever heard a man speak thus to a woman who was not his wife. Whenever they had heard that form of spirited repartee it had come from the lips of a husband. Coleman's rude speech was to their ears a flat announcement of an extraordinary intimacy between Nora Black and the correspondent. Any other interpretation would not have occurred to them. It was so palpable that it greatly distressed them with its arrogance and boldness. The professor had blushed. The very milkiest word in his mind at the time was the word vulgarity.

Nora Black had won a great battle. It was her Agincourt. She had beaten the clever Coleman in a way that had left little of him but rags. However, she could have lost it all again if she had shown her feeling of elation. At Coleman's rudeness her manner indicated a mixture of sadness and embarrassment. Her suffering was so plain to the eye that Peter Tounley was instantly moved. " Can't I get your jacket for you, Miss Black? " he asked hastily, and at her grateful nod he was off at once.

Coleman was resolved to improve nothing. His overthrow seemed to him to be so complete that he could not in any way mend it without a sacrifice of his dearest prides. He turned away from them all and walked to an isolated corner of the room. He would abide no longer with them. He had been made an outcast by Nora Black, and he intended to be an outcast. There was no sense in attempting to stem this extraordinary deluge. It was better to acquiesce. Then suddenly he was angry with Marjory. He did not exactly see why he was angry at Marjory, but he was angry at her nevertheless. He thought of how he could revenge himself upon her. He decided to take horse with his groom and dragoman and proceed forthwith on the road, leaving the jumble as it stood. This would pain Marjory, anyhow, he hoped. She would feel it deeply, he hoped. Acting upon this plan, he went to the professor. Well, of course you are all right now, professor, and if you don't mind, I would like to leave you-go on ahead. I've got a considerable pressure of business on my mind, and I think I should hurry on to Athens, if you don't mind."

The professor did not seem to know what to say. " Of course, if you wish it-sorry, I'm sure-of course it is as you please-but you have been such a power in our favour-it seems too bad to lose you-but-if you wish it-if you insist-"

" Oh, yes, I quite insist," said Coleman, calmly. "I quite insist. Make your mind easy on that score, professor. I insist."

"Well, Mr. Coleman," stammered the old man. " Well, it seems a great pity to lose you-you have been such a power in our favour-"

"Oh, you are now only eight hours from the rail- way. It is very easy. You would not need my as- sistance, even if it were a benefit!

" But-" said the professor.

Coleman's dragoman came to him then and said: "There is one man here who says you made to take one rifle in the fight and was break his head. He was say he wants sunthing for you was break his head. He says hurt."

"How much does he want?" asked Coleman, im- patiently.

The dragoman wrestled then evidently with a desire to protect this mine from outside fingers. "I-I think two gold piece plenty." "Take them," said Coleman. It seemed to him preposterous that this idiot with a broken head should interpolate upon his tragedy. " Afterward you and the groom get the three horses and we will start for Athens at once."

"For Athens? At once? " said Marjory's voice in his ear.

CHAPTER XXIII

"Om," said Coleman, " I was thinking of starting."

"Why? " asked Marjory, unconcernedly.

Coleman shot her a quick glance. " I believe my period of usefulness is quite ended," he said. with just a small betrayal of bitter feeling.

" It is certainly true that you have had a remark- able period of usefulness to us," said Marjory with a slow smile, "but if it is ended, you should not run away from us."

Coleman looked at her to see what she could mean. From many women, these words would have been equal, under the circumstances, to a command to stay, but he felt that none might know what impulses moved the mind behind that beautiful mask. In his misery he thought to hurt her into an expression of feeling by a rough speech. " I'm so in love with Nora Black, you know, that I have to be very careful of myself."

" Oh," said Marjory, never thought of that. I should think you would have to be careful of yourself." She did not seem moved in any way. Coleman despaired of finding her weak spot. She was a'damantine, this girl. He searched his mind for something to say which would be still more gross than his last outbreak, but when he felt that he was about to hit upon it, the professor interrupted with an agitated speech to Marjory. "You had better go to your mother, my child, and see that you are all ready to leave here as soon as the carriages come up."

"We have absolutely nothing to make ready," said Marjory, laughing. " But I'll go and see if mother needs anything before we start that I can get for her." She went away without bidding good-bye to Coleman. The sole maddening impression to him was that the matter of his going had not been of sufficient importance to remain longer than a moment upon her mind. At the same time he decided that he would go, irretrievably go.

Even then the dragoman entered the room. " We will pack everything -upon the horse?"

" Everything-yes."

Peter Tounley came afterward. " You are not going to bolt? "

" Yes, I'm off," answered Coleman recovering him- self for Peter's benefit. " See you in Athens, probably."

Presently the dragoman announced the readiness of the horses. Coleman shook hands with the students and the Professor amid cries of surprise and polite regret. "What? Going, oldman? Really? What for? Oh, wait for us. We're off in a few minutes. Sorry as the devil, old boy, to' see you go." He accepted their protestations with a somewhat sour face. He knew perfectly well that they were thinking of his departure as something that related to Nora Black. At the last, he bowed to the ladies as a collection. Marjory's answering bow was affable; the bow of Mrs. Wainwright spoke a resentment for some- thing; and Nora's bow was triumphant mockery. As he swung into the saddle an idea struck him with over whelming force. The idea was that he was a fool. He was a colossal imbecile. He touched the spur to his horse and the animal leaped superbly, making the Greeks hasten for safety in all directions. He was off ; he could no more return to retract his devious idiocy than he could make his horse fly to Athens. What was done was done. He could not mend it. And he felt like a man that had broken his own heart; perversely, childishly, stupidly broken his own heart. He was sure that Marjory was lost to him. No man could be degraded so publicly and resent it so crudely and still retain a Marjory. In his abasement from his defeat at the hands of Nora Black he had performed every imaginable block-headish act and had finally climaxed it all by a departure which left the tongue of Nora to speak unmolested into the ear of Marjory. Nora's victory had been a serious blow to his fortunes, but it had not been so serious as his own subsequent folly. He had generously muddled his own affairs until he could read nothing out of them but despair.

He was in the mood for hatred. He hated many people. Nora Black was the principal item, but he did not hesitate to detest the professor, Mrs. Wain- wright, Coke and all the students. As for Marjory, he would revenge himself upon her. She had done nothing that he defined clearly but, at any rate, he would take revenge for it. As much as was possible, he would make her suffer. He would convince her that he was a tremendous and inexorable person. But it came upon his mind that he was powerless in all ways. If he hated many people they probably would not be even interested in his emotion and, as for his revenge upon Marjory, it was beyond his strength. He was nothing but the complaining victim of Nora Black and himself.

He felt that he would never again see Marjory, and while feeling it he began to plan his attitude when next they met. He would be very cold and reserved. At Agrinion he found that there would be no train until the next daybreak. The dragoman was excessively annoyed over it, but Coleman did not scold at all. As a matter of fact his heart had given a great joyus bound. He could not now prevent his being overtaken. They were only a few leagues away, and while he was waiting for the train they would easily cover the distance. If anybody expressed surprise at seeing him he could exhibit the logical reasons. If there had been a train starting at once he would have taken it. His pride would have put up with no subterfuge. If the Wainwrights overtook him it was because he could not help it. But he was delighted that he could not help it. There had been an inter- position by some specially beneficent fate. He felt like whistling. He spent the early half of the night in blissful smoke, striding the room which the dragoman had found for him. His head was full of plans and detached impressive scenes in which he figured before Marjory. The simple fact that there was no train away from Agrinion until the next daybreak had wrought a stupendous change in his outlook. He unhesitatingly considered it an omen of a good future. He was up before the darkness even contained presage of coming light, but near the railway station was a little hut where coffee was being served to several prospective travellers who had come even earlier to the rendezvous. There was no evidence of the Wainwrights.

Coleman sat in the hut and listened for the rumble of wheels. He was suddenly appalled that the Wainwrights were going to miss the train. Perhaps they had decided against travelling during the night. Perbaps this thing, and perhaps that thing. The morning was very cold. Closely muffled in his cloak, he went to the door and stared at where the road was whiten- ing out of night. At the station stood a little spectral train, and the engine at intervals emitted a long, piercing scream which informed the echoing land that, in all probability, it was going to start after a time for the south. The Greeks in the coffee room were, of course, talking.

At last Coleman did hear the sound of hoofs and wheels. The three carriages swept up in grand procession. The first was laden with students; in the second was the professor, the Greek officer, Nora Black's old lady and other persons, all looking marvellously unimportant and shelved. It was the third carriage at which Coleman stared. At first be thought the dim light deceived his vision, but in a moment he knew that his first leaping conception of the arrangement of the people in this vehicle had been perfectly correct. Nora Black and Mrs. Wainwright sat side by side on the back seat, while facing them were Coke and Marjory.

They looked cold but intimate.

The oddity of the grouping stupefied Coleman. It was anarchy, naked and unashamed. He could not imagine how such changes could have been consummated in the short time he had been away from them, but he laid it all to some startling necromancy on the part of Nora Black, some wondrous play which had captured them all because of its surpassing skill and because they were, in the main, rather gullible people. He was wrong. The magic had been wrought by the unaided foolishness of Mrs. Wainwfight. As soon as Nora Black had succeeded in creating an effect of intimacy and dependence between herself and Coleman, the professor had flatly stated to his wife that the presence of Nora Black in the party, in the inn, in the world, was a thiag that did not meet his approval in any way. She should be abolished. As for Coleman, he would not defend him. He preferred not to talk to him. It made him sad. Coleman at least had been very indiscreet, very indiscreet. It was a great pity. But as for this blatant woman, the sooner they rid themselves of her, the sooner he would feel that all the world was not evil.

Whereupon Mrs. Wainwright had changed front with the speed of light and attacked with horse, foot and guns. She failed to see, she had declared, where this poor, lone girt was in great fault. Of course it was probable that she had listened to this snaky. tongued Rufus Coleman, but that was ever the mistake that women made. Oh, certainly ; the professor would like to let Rufus Coleman off scot-free. That was the way with men. They defended each other in all cases. If wrong were done it was the woman who suffered. Now, since this poor girl was alone far off here in Greece, Mrs. Wainwright announced that she had such full sense of her duty to her sex that her conscience would not allow her to scorn and desert a sister, even if that sister was, approximately, the victim of a creature like Rufus Coleman. Perhaps the poor thing loved this wretched man, although it was hard to imagine any woman giving her heart to such. a monster.

The professor had then asked with considerable spirit for the proofs upon which Mrs. Wainwright named Coleman a monster, and had made a wry face over her completely conventional reply. He had told her categorically his opinion of her erudition in such matters.

But Mrs. Wainwright was not to be deterred from an exciting espousal of the cause of her sex. Upon the instant that the professor strenuously opposed her she became an apostle, an enlightened, uplifted apostle to the world on the wrongs of her sex. She had come down with this thing as if it were a disease. Nothing could stop her. Her husband, her daughter, all influences in other directions, had been overturned with a roar, and the first thing fully clear to the professor's mind had been that his wife was riding affably in the carriage with Nora Black. Coleman aroused when he heard one of the students cry out: " Why, there is Rufus Coleman's dragoman. He must be here." A moment later they thronged upon him. " Hi, old man, caught you again! Where did you break to? Glad to catch you, old boy. How are you making it? Where's your horse?"

" Sent the horses on to, Athens," said Coleman. He had not yet recovered his composure, and he was glad to find available this commonplace return to their exuberant greetings and questions. " Sent them on to Athens with the groom."

In the mean time the engine of the little train was screaming to heaven that its intention of starting was most serious. The diligencia careered to the station platform and unburdened. Coleman had had his dragoman place his luggage in a little first-class carriage and he defiantly entered it and closed the door. He had a sudden return to the old sense of downfall, and with it came the original rebellious desires. However, he hoped that somebody would intrude upon him. It was Peter Tounley. The student flung open the door and then yelled to the distance : " Here's an empty one." He clattered into the compartment. " Hello, Coleman! Didn't know you were in here! " At his heels came Nora Black, Coke and Marjory. " Oh! " they said, when they saw the occupant of the carriage. " Oh ! " Coleman was furious. He could have distributed some of his traps in a way to create more room, but he did not move.

CHAPTER XXIV.

THERE was a demonstration of the unequalled facilities of a European railway carriage for rendering unpleasant things almost intolerable. These people could find no way to alleviate the poignancy of their position. Coleman did not know where to look. Every personal mannerism becomes accentuated in a European railway carriage. If you glance at a man, your glance defines itself as a stare. If you carefully look at nothing, you create for yourself a resemblance to all wooden-headed things. A newspaper is, then, in the nature of a preservative, and Coleman longed for a newspaper.

It was this abominable railway carriage which exacted the first display of agitation from Marjory. She flushed rosily, and her eyes wavered over the cornpartment. Nora Black laughed in a way that was a shock to the nerves. Coke seemed very angry, indeed, and Peter Tounley was in pitiful distress. Everything was acutely, painfully vivid, bald, painted as glaringly as a grocer's new wagon. It fulfilled those traditions which the artists deplore when they use their pet phrase on a picture, "It hurts." The damnable power of accentuation of the European railway carriage seemed, to Coleman's amazed mind, to be redoubled and redoubled.

It was Peter Tounley who seemed to be in the greatest agony. He looked at the correspondent beseechingly and said: "It's a very cold morning, Coleman." This was an actual appeal in the name of humanity.

Coleman came squarely. to the front and even grinned a little at poor Peter Tounley's misery. "Yes, it is a cold morning, Peter. I should say it to one of the coldest mornings in my recollection."

Peter Tounley had not intended a typical American emphasis on the polar conditions which obtained in the compartment at this time, but Coleman had given the word this meaning. Spontaneously every body smiled, and at once the tension was relieved. But of course the satanic powers of the railway carriage could not be altogether set at naught. Of course it fell to the lot of

Coke to get the seat directly in front of Coleman, and thus, face to face, they were doomed to stare at each other.

Peter Tounley was inspired to begin conventional babble, in which he took great care to make an appear. ance of talking to all in the carriage. " Funny thing I never knew these mornings in Greece were so cold. I thought the climate here was quite tropical. It must have been inconvenient in the ancient times, when, I am told, people didn't wear near so many- er-clothes. Really, I don't see how they stood it. For my part, I would like nothing so much as a buffalo robe. I suppose when those great sculptors were doing their masterpieces, they had to wear gloves. Ever think of that? Funny, isn't it? Aren't you cold, Marjory? I am. jingo! Imagine the Spartans in ulsters, going out to meet an enemy in cape-overcoats, and being desired by their mothers to return with their ulsters or wrapped in them."

It was rather hard work for Peter Tounley. Both Marjory and Coleman tried to display an interest in his labours, and they laughed not at what he said, but because they believed it assisted him. The little train, meanwhile, wandered up a great green slope, and the day rapidly coloured the land.

At first Nora Black did not display a militant mood, but as time passed Coleman saw clearly that she was considering the advisability of a new attack. She had Coleman and Marjory in conjunction and where they were unable to escape from her. The opportunities were great. To Coleman, she seemed to be gloating over the possibilities of making more mischief. She was looking at him speculatively, as if considering the best place to hit him first. Presently she drawled : " Rufus, I wish you would fix my rug about me a little better." Coleman saw that this was a beginning. Peter Tounley sprang to his feet with speed and en- thusiasm. " Oh, let me do it for you." He had her well muffled in the rug before she could protest, even if a protest had been rational. The young man had no idea of defending Coleman. He had no knowledge of the necessity for it. It had been merely the exercise of his habit of amiability, his chronic desire to see everybody comfortable. His passion in this direction was well known in Washurst, where the students had borrowed a phrase from the photographers in order to describe him fully in a nickname. They called him " Look-pleasant Tounley." This did not in any way antagonise his perfect willingness to fight on occasions with a singular desperation, which usually has a small stool in every mind where good nature has a throne.

" Oh, thank you very much, Mr. Tounley," said Nora Black, without gratitude. " Rufus is always so lax in these matters."

"I don't know how you know it," said Coleman boldly, and he looked her fearlessly in the eye. The battle had begun.

" Oh," responded Nora, airily, " I have had opportunity enough to know it, I should think, by this time."

" No," said Coleman, " since I have never paid you particular and direct attention, you cannot possibly know what I am lax in and what I am not lax in. I would be obliged to be of service at any time, Nora, but surely you do not consider that you have a right to my services superior to any other right."

Nora Black simply went mad, but fortunately part of her madness was in the form of speechlessness. Otherwise there might have been heard something approaching to billingsgate.

Marjory and Peter Tounley turned first hot and then cold, and looked as if they wanted to fly away; and even Coke, penned helplessly in with this unpleasant incident, seemed to have a sudden attack of distress. The only frigid person was Coleman. He had made his declaration of independence, and he saw with glee that the victory was complete. Nora Black might storm and rage, but he had announced his position in an unconventional blunt way which nobody in the carriage could fail to understand. He felt somewhat like smiling with confidence and defiance in Nora's face, but he still had the fear for Marjory.

Unexpectedly, the fight was all out of Nora Black. She had the fury of a woman scorned, but evidently she had perceived that all was over and lost. The remainder of her wrath dispensed itself in glares which Coleman withstood with great composure.

A strained silence fell upon the group which lasted until they arrived at the little port of Mesalonghi, whence they were to take ship for Patras.

Coleman found himself wondering why he had not gone flatly at the great question at a much earlier period, indeed at the first moment when the great question began to make life exciting for him. He thought that if he had charged Nora's guns in the beginning they would have turned out to be the same incapable artillery. Instead of that he had run away and continued to run away until he was actually cornered and made to fight, and his easy victory had defined him as a person who had, earlier, indulged in much stupidity and cowardice. Everything had worked out so simply, his terrors had been dispelled so easily, that he probably was led to overestimate his success. And it occurred suddenly to him. He foresaw a fine occasion to talk privately to Marjory when all had boarded the steamer for Patras and he resolved to make use of it. This he believed would end the strife and conclusively laurel him.

The train finally drew up on a little stone pier and some boatmen began to scream like gulls. The steamer lay at anchor in the placid blue cove. The embarkation was chaotic in the Oriental fashion and there was the customary misery which was only relieved when the travellers had set foot on the deck of the steamer. Coleman did not devote any premature attention to finding Marjory, but when the steamer was fairly out on the calm waters of the Gulf of Corinth, he saw her pacing to and fro with Peter Tounley. At first he lurked in the distance waiting for an opportunity, but ultimately he decided to make his own opportunity. He approached them. "Marjory,would you let me speak to you alone for a few moments? You won't mind, will you, Peter? "

" Oh, no, certainly not," said Peter Tounley.

"Of course. It is not some dreadful revelation, is it? " said Marjory, bantering him coolly.

" No," answered Coleman, abstractedly. He was thinking of what he was going to say. Peter Tounley vanished around the corner of a deck-house and Marjory and Coleman began to pace to and fro even as Marjory and Peter Tounley had done. Coleman had thought to speak his mind frankly and once for all, and on the train he had invented many clear expressions of his feeling. It did not appear that he had forgotten them. It seemed, more, that they had become entangled in his mind in such a way that he could not unravel the end of his discourse.

In the pause, Marjory began to speak in admiration of the scenery. " I never imagined that Greece was so full of mountains. One reads so much of the Attic Plains, but aren't these mountains royal? They look so rugged and cold, whereas the bay is absolutely as blue as the old descriptions of a summer sea."

" I wanted to speak to you about Nora Black," said

Coleman.

"Nora Black? Why?" said Marjory, lifting her eye- brows.

You know well enough," said Coleman, in a head. long fashion. " You must know, you must have seen it. She knows I care for you and she wants to stop it. And she has no right to-to interfere. She is a fiend, a perfect fiend. She is trying to make you feel that I care for her."

" And don't you care for her ? " asked Marjory.

"No," said Coleman, vehemently. " I don't care for her at all."

" Very well," answered Marjory, simply. " I believe you." She managed to give the words the effect of a mere announcement that she believed him and it was in no way plain that she was glad or that she esteemed the matter as being of consequence.

He scowled at her in dark resentment. " You mean by that, I suppose, that you don't believe me? "

" Oh," answered Marjory, wearily, " I believe you.

I said so. Don't talk about it any more."

"Then," said Coleman, slowly, " you mean that you do not care whether I'm telling the truth or not?"

" Why, of course I care," she said. " Lying is not nice."

He did not know, apparently, exactly how to deal with her manner, which was actually so pliable that-it was marble, if one may speak in that way. He looked ruefully at the sea. He had expected a far easier time. " Well-" he began.

" Really," interrupted Marjory, " this is something which I do not care to discuss. I would rather you would not speak to me at all about it. It seems too -too-bad. I can readily give you my word that I believe you, but I would prefer you not to try to talk to me about it or-anything of that sort. Mother!"

Mrs. Wainwright was hovering anxiously in the vicinity, and she now bore down rapidly upon the pair. "You are very nearly to Patras," she said reproachfully to her daughter, as if the fact had some fault of Marjory's concealed in it. She in no way ac- knowledged the presence of Coleman.

" Oh, are we ? " cried Marjory.

"Yes," said Mrs. Wainwright. " We are."

She stood waiting as if she expected Marjory to in- stantly quit Coleman. The girl wavered a moment and then followed her mother. " Good-bye." she said. "I hope we may see you again in Athens." It was a command to him to travel alone with his servant on the long railway journey from Patras to Athens. It was a dismissal of a casual acquaintance given so graciously that it stung him to the depths of his pride. He bowed his adieu and his thanks. When the yelling boatmen came again, he and his man proceeded to the shore in an early boat without looking in any way after the welfare of the others.

At the train, the party split into three sections.

Coleman and his man had one compartment, Nora

Black and her squad had another, and the Wainwrights

and students occupied two more.

The little officer was still in tow of Nora Black. He was very enthusiastic. In French she directed him to remain silent, but he did not appear to understand. " You tell him," she then said to her dragoman, " to sit in a corner and not to speak until I tell him to, or I won't have him in here." She seemed anxious to unburden herself to the old lady companion. " Do you know," she said, " that girl has a nerve like steel. I tried to break it there in that inn, but I couldn't budge her. If I am going to have her beaten I must prove myself to be a very, very artful person."

" Why did you try to break her nerve ? " asked the old lady, yawning. "Why do you want to have her beaten? "

" Because I do, old stupid," answered Nora. " You should have heard the things I said to her."

"About what?"

" About Coleman. Can't you understand anything at all?"

" And why should you say anything about Coleman to her?" queried the old lady, still hopelessly befogged.

" Because," cried Nora, darting a look of wrath at her companion, " I want to prevent that marriage." She had been betrayed into this avowal by the singularly opaque mind of the old lady. The latter at once sat erect. - " Oh, ho," she said, as if a ray of light had been let into her head. " Oh, ho. So that's it, is it? "

"Yes, that's it, rejoined Nora, shortly.

The old lady was amazed into a long period of meditation. At last she spoke depressingly. " Well, how are you going to prevent it? Those things can't be done in these days at all. If they care for each other-"

Nora burst out furiously. "Don't venture opinions until you know what you are talking about, please. They don't care for each other, do you see? She cares for him, but he don't give a snap of his fingers for her."

" But," cried the bewildered lady, " if he don't care for her, there will be nothing to prevent. If he don't care for her, he won't ask her to marry him, and so there won't be anything to prevent."

Nora made a broad gesture of impatience. " Oh, can't you get anything through your head? Haven't you seen that the girl has been the only young woman in that whole party lost up there in the mountains, and that naturally more than half of the men still think they are in love with her? That's what it is. Can't you see? It always happens that way. Then Coleman comes along and makes a fool of himself with the others."

The old lady spoke up brightly as if at last feeling able to contribute something intelligent to the talk. " Oh, then, he does care for her."

Nora's eyes looked as if their glance might shrivel the old lady's hair. "Don't I keep telling you that it is no such thing? Can't you understand? It is all glamour! Fascination! Way up there in the wilderness! Only one even passable woman in sight."

" I don't say that I am so very keen," said the old lady, somewhat offended, "but I fail to see where I could improve when first you tell me he don't care for her, and then you tell me that he does care for her."

" Glamour,' ' Fascination,'" quoted Nora. " Don't you understand the meaning of the words ? "

" Well," asked the other, didn't he know her, then, before he came over here ?"

Nora was silent for a time, while a gloom upon her face deepened. It had struck her that the theories for which she protested so energetically might not be of such great value. Spoken aloud, they had a sudden new flimsiness. Perhaps she had reiterated to herself that Coleman was the victim of glamour only because she wished it to be true. One theory, however, re- mained unshaken. Marjory was an artful rninx, with no truth in her.

She presently felt the necessity of replying to the question of her companion. " Oh," she said, care- lessly, " I suppose they were acquainted-in a way."

The old lady was giving the best of her mind to the subject. " If that's the case-" she observed, musingly, " if that's the case, you can't tell what is between 'em."

The talk had so slackened that Nora's unfortunate Greek admirer felt that here was a good opportunity to present himself again to the notice of the actress. The means was a smile and a French sentence, but his reception would have frightened a man in armour. His face blanched with horror at the storm, he had invoked, and he dropped limply back as if some one had shot him. "You tell this little snipe to let me alone! " cried Nora, to the dragoman. " If he dares to come around me with any more of those Parisian dude speeches, I-I don't know what I'll do! I won't have it, I say." The impression upon the dragoman was hardly less in effect. He looked with bulging eyes at Nora, and then began to stammer at the officer. The latter's voice could sometimes be heard in awed whispers for the more elaborate explanation of some detail of the tragedy. Afterward, he remained meek and silent in his corner, barely more than a shadow, like the proverbial husband of imperious beauty.

"Well," said the old lady, after a long and thoughtful pause, " I don't know, I'm sure, but it seems to me that if Rufus Coleman really cares for that girl, there isn't much use in trying to stop him from getting her. He isn't that kind of a man."

" For heaven's sake, will you stop assuming that he does care for her ? " demanded Nora, breathlessly.

"And I don't see," continued the old lady, "what you want to prevent him for, anyhow."

CHAPTER XXV.

" I FEEL in this radiant atmosphere that there could be no such thing as war-men striving together in black and passionate hatred." The professor's words were for the benefit of his wife and daughter. ,He was viewing the sky-blue waters of the Gulf of Corinth with its background of mountains that in the sunshine were touched here and there with a copperish glare. The train was slowly sweeping along the southern shore. " It is strange to think of those men fighting up there in the north. And it is strange to think that we ourselves are but just returning from it."

" I cannot begin to realise it yet," said Mrs. Wain- wright, in a high voice.

" Quite so," responded the professor, reflectively.

"I do not suppose any of us will realise it fully for some time. It is altogether too odd, too very odd."

"To think of it!" cried Mrs. WainWright. "To think of it! Supposing those dreadful Albanians or those awful men from the Greek mountains had caught us! Why, years from now I'll wake up in the night and think of it! "

The professor mused. " Strange that we cannot feel it strongly now. My logic tells me to be aghast that we ever got into such a place, but my nerves at present refuse to thrill. I am very much afraid that this singular apathy of ours has led us to be unjust to poor Coleman." Here Mrs. Wainwright objected. " Poor Coleman! I don't see why you call him poor Coleman.

" Well," answered the professor, slowly, " I am in doubt about our behaviour. It-"

" Oh," cried the wife, gleefully," in doubt about our behaviour! I'm in doubt about his behaviour."

" So, then, you do have a doubt. of his behaviour?" " Oh, no," responded Mrs. Wainwright, hastily, " not about its badness. What I meant to say was that in the face of his outrageous conduct with that- that woman, it is curious that you should worry about our behaviour. It surprises me, Harrison."

The professor was wagging his head sadly. " I don't know I don't know It seems hard to judge * * I hesitate to-"

Mrs. Wainwright treated this attitude with disdain.

" It is not hard to judge," she scoffed, " and I fail to

see why you have any reason for hesitation at all.

Here he brings this woman— "

The professor got angry. "Nonsense! Nonsense! I do not believe that he brought her. If I ever saw a spectacle of a woman bringing herself, it was then. You keep chanting that thing like an outright parrot."

"Well," retorted Mrs. Wainwright, bridling, "I suppose you imagine that you understand such things, Men usually think that, but I want to tell you that you seem to me utterly blind."

" Blind or not, do stop the everlasting reiteration of that sentence."

Mrs. Wainwright passed into an offended silence, and the professor, also silent, looked with a gradually dwindling indignation at the scenery.

Night was suggested in the sky before the train was near to Athens. " My trunks," sighed Mrs. Wainwright. " How glad I will be to get back to my trunks! Oh, the dust! Oh, the misery! Do find out when we will get there, Harrison. Maybe the train is late."

But, at last, they arrived in Athens, amid a darkness which was confusing, and, after no more than the common amount of trouble, they procured carriages and were taken to the hotel. Mrs. Wainwright's impulses now dominated the others in the family. She had one passion after another. The majority of the servants in the hotel pretended that they spoke English, but, in three minutes, she drove them distracted with the abundance and violence of her requests. It came to pass that in the excitement the old couple quite forgot Marjory. It was not until Mrs. Wainwright, then feeling splendidly, was dressed for dinner, that she thought to open Marjory's door and go to render a usual motherly supervision of the girl's toilet.

There was no light: there did not seem to be any- body in the room. " Marjory ! " called the mother, in alarm. She listened for a moment and then ran hastily out again. " Harrison ! " she cried. " I can't find Marjory!" The professor had been tying his cravat. He let the loose ends fly. "What?" he ejaculated, opening his mouth wide. Then they both rushed into Marjory's room. "Marjory!" beseeched the old man in a voice which would have invoked the grave.

The answer was from the bed. "Yes?" It was low, weary, tearful. It was not like Marjory. It was dangerously the voice of a hcart-broken woman. They hurried forward with outcries. "Why, Marjory! Are you ill, child? How long have you been lying in the dark? Why didn't you call us? Are you ill?"

" No," answered this changed voice, " I am not ill.

I only thought I'd rest for a time. Don't bother."

The professor hastily lit the gas and then father and mother turned hurriedly to the bed. In the first of the illumination they saw that tears were flowing unchecked down Marjory's face.

The effect.of this grief upon the professor was, in part, an effect of fear. He seemed afraid to touch it, to go near it. He could, evidently, only remain in the outskirts, a horrified spectator. The mother, how. ever, flung her arms about her daughter. " Oh, Marjory! " She, too, was weeping.

The girl turned her face to the pillow and held out a hand of protest. " Don't, mother! Don't !"

"Oh, Marjory! Oh, Marjory!"

" Don't, mother. Please go away. Please go away. Don't speak at all, I beg of you."

" Oh, Marjory! Oh, Marjory!"

" Don't." The girl lifted a face which appalled them. It had something entirely new in it. " Please go away, mother. I will speak to father, but I won't -I can't-I can't be pitied."

Mrs. Wainwright looked at her husband. " Yes," said the old man, trembling. "Go! " She threw up her hands in a sorrowing gesture that was not without its suggestion that her exclusion would be a mistake. She left the room.

The professor dropped on his knees at the bedside and took one of Marjory's hands. His voice dropped to its tenderest note. "Well, my Marjory?"

She had turned her face again to the pillow. At last she answered in muffled tones, " You know." Thereafter came a long silence full of sharpened pain. It was Marjory who spoke first. "I have saved my pride, daddy, but-I have-lost-everything —else." Even her sudden resumption of the old epithet of her childhood was an additional misery to the old man. He still said no word. He knelt, gripping her fingers and staring at the wall.

" Yes, I have lost~everything-else."

The father gave a low groan. He was thinking deeply, bitterly. Since one was only a human being, how was one going to protect beloved hearts assailed with sinister fury from the inexplicable zenith? In this tragedy he felt as helpless as an old grey ape. He did not see a possible weapon with which he could defend his child from the calamity which was upon her. There was no wall, no shield which could turn this sorrow from the heart of his child. If one of his hands loss could have spared her, there would have been a sacrifice of his hand, but he was potent for nothing. He could only groan and stare at the wall. He reviewed the past half in fear that he would suddenly come upon his error which was now the cause of Marjory's tears. He dwelt long upon the fact that in Washurst he had refused his consent to Marjory's marriage with Coleman, but even now he could not say that his judgment was not correct. It was simply that the doom of woman's woe was upon Marjory, this ancient woe of the silent tongue and the governed will, and he could only kneel at the bedside and stare at the wall.

Marjory raised her voice in a laugh. " Did I betray myself? Did I become the maiden all forlorn? Did I giggle to show people that I did not care? No-I did not-I did not. And it was such a long time, daddy! Oh, such a long time! I thought we would never get here. I thought I would never get where I could be alone like this, where I could-cry-if I wanted to. I am not much of - a crier, am I, daddy? But this time-this-time-"

She suddenly drew herself over near to her father and looked at him. " Oh, daddy, I want to tell you one thing. just one simple little thing." She waited then, and while she waited her father's head went lower and lower. " Of course, you know-I told you once. I love him! I love him! Yes, probably he is a rascal, but, do you know, I don't think I would mind if he was a-an assassin. This morning I sent him away, but, daddy, he didn't want to go at all. I know he didn't. This Nora Black is nothing to him. I know she is not. I am sure of it. Yes-I am sure of it. * * * I never expected to talk this way to any living creature, but-you are so good, daddy. Dear old daddy—-"

She ceased, for she saw that her father was praying.

The sight brought to her a new outburst of sobbing, for her sorrow now had dignity and solemnity from the bowed white head of her old father, and she felt that her heart was dying amid the pomp of the church. It was the last rites being performed at the death-bed. Into her ears came some imagining of the low melan. choly chant of monks in a gloom.

Finally her father arose. He kissed her on the brow. " Try to sleep, dear," he said. He turned out the gas and left the room. His thought was full of chastened emotion.

But if his thought was full of chastened emotion, it received some degree of shock when he arrived in the presence of Mrs. Wainwright. " Well, what is all this about ? " she demanded, irascibly. " Do you mean to say that Marjory is breaking her heart over that man Coleman? It is all your fault-" She was apparently still ruffled over her exclusion.

When the professor interrupted her he did not speak with his accustomed spirit, but from something novel in his manner she recognised a danger signal. " Please do not burst out at it in that way."

"Then it Is true?" she asked. Her voice was a mere awed whisper.

" It is true," answered the professor.

"Well," she said, after reflection, "I knew it. I alway's knew it. If you hadn't been so blind! You turned like a weather-cock in your opinions of Coleman. You never could keep your opinion about him for more than an hour. Nobody could imagine what you might think next. And now you see the result of it! I warned you! I told you what this Coleman was, and if Marjory is suffering now, you have only yourself to blame for it. I warned you! "

" If it is my fault," said the professor, drearily, " I hope God may forgive me, for here is a great wrong to my daughter."

Well, if you had done as I told you-" she began.

Here the professor revolted. " Oh, now, do not be- gin on that," he snarled, peevishly. Do not begin on that."

" Anyhow," said Mrs. Wainwright, it is time that we should be going down to dinner. Is Marjory com- ing? "

" No, she is not," answered the professor, " and I do not know as I shall go myself."

" But you must go. Think how it would look! All the students down there dining without us, and cutting up capers! You must come."

" Yes," he said, dubiously, " but who will look after

Marjory? "

" She wants to be left alone," announced Mrs. Wainwright, as if she was the particular herald of this news. " She wants to be left alone."

" Well, I suppose we may as well go down." Before they went, the professor tiptoed into his daughter's room. In the darkness he could only see her waxen face on the pillow, and her two eyes gazing fixedly at the ceiling. He did not speak, but immediately withdrew, closing the door noiselessly behind him.

CHAPTER XXVI.

IF the professor and Mrs. Wainwright had descended sooner to a lower floor of the hotel, they would have found reigning there a form of anarchy. The students were in a smoking room which was also an entrance hall to the dining room, and because there was in the middle of this apartment a fountain containing gold fish, they had been moved to license and sin. They had all been tubbed and polished and brushed and dressed until they were exuberantly beyond themselves. The proprietor of the hotel brought in his dignity and showed it to them, but they minded it no more than if he had been only a common man. He drew himself to his height and looked gravely at them and they jovially said: " Hello, Whiskers." American college students are notorious in their country for their inclination to scoff at robed and crowned authority, and, far from being awed by the dignity of the hotel-keeper, they were delighted with it. It was something with which to sport. With immeasurable impudence, they copied his attitude, and, standing before him, made comic speeches, always alluding with blinding vividness to his beard. His exit disappointed them. He had not remained long under fire. They felt that they could have interested themselves with him an entire evening. " Come back, Whiskers! Oh, come back! " Out in the main hall he made a gesture of despair to some of his gaping minions and then fled to seclusion.

A formidable majority then decided that Coke was a gold fish, and that therefore his proper place was in the fountain. They carried him to it while he struggled madly. This quiet room with its crimson rugs and gilded mirrors seemed suddenly to have become an important apartment in hell. There being as yet no traffic in the dining room, the waiters were all at liberty to come to the open doors, where they stood as men turned to stone. To them, it was no less than incendiarism.

Coke, standing with one foot on the floor and the other on the bottom of the shallow fountain, blas- phemed his comrades in a low tone, but with inten- tion. He was certainly desirous of lifting his foot out of the water, but it seemed that all movement to that end would have to wait until he had successfully ex- pressed his opinions. In the meantime, there was heard slow footsteps and the rustle of skirts, and then some people entered the smoking room on their way to dine. Coke took his foot hastily out of the fountain.

The faces of the men of the arriving party went blank, and they turned their cold and pebbly eyes straight to the front, while the ladies, after little expressions of alarm, looked As if they wanted to run. In fact, the whole crowd rather bolted from this ex- traordinary scene.

" There, now," said Coke bitterly to his companions.

"You see? We looked like little schoolboys-"

" Oh, never mind, old man," said Peter Tounley.

"We'll forgive you, although you did embarrass us.

But, above everything, don't drip. Whatever you do,

don't drip."

The students took this question of dripping and played upon it until they would have made quite insane anybody but another student. They worked it into all manner of forms, and hacked and haggled at Coke until he was driven to his room to seek other apparel. " Be sure and change both legs," they told him. " Remember you can't change one leg without changing both legs."

After Coke's departure, the United States minister entered the room, and instantly they were subdued. It was not his lofty station-that affected them. There are probably few stations that would have at all af- fected them. They became subdued because they un- feignedly liked the United States minister. They, were suddenly a group of well-bred, correctly attired young men who had not put Coke's foot in the fountain. Nor had they desecrated the majesty of the hotelkeeper.

"Well, I am delighted," said the minister, laughing as he shook hands with them all. " I was not sure I would ever see you again. You are not to be trusted, and, good boys as you are, I'll be glad to see you once and forever over the boundary of my jurisdiction. Leave Greece, you vagabonds. However, I am truly delighted to see you all safe."

" Thank you, sir," they said.

" How in the world did you get out of it? You must be remarkable chaps. I thought you were in a hopeless position. I wired and cabled everywhere I could, but I could find out nothing."

" A correspondent," said Peter Tounley. " I don't know if you have met him. His name is Coleman. He found us."

" Coleman ? " asked the minister, quickly.

" Yes, sir. He found us and brought us out safely."

" Well, glory be to Coleman," exclaimed the min- ister, after a long sigh of surprise. " Glory be to Cole- man! I never thought he could do it."

The students were alert immediately. "Why, did you know about it, sir? Did he tell you he was coming after us? "

"Of course. He came tome here in Athens. and asked where you were. I told him you were in a peck of trouble. He acted quietly and somewhat queerly,. and said that he would try to look you up. He said you were friends of his. I warned him against trying it. Yes, I said it was impossible, I had no idea that he would really carry the thing out. But didn't he tell you anything about this himself?"

" No, sir ' " answered Peter Tounley. " He never said much about it. I think he usually contended that it was mainly an accident."

" It was no accident," said the minister, sharply. "When a man starts out to do a thing and does it, you can't say it is an accident."

" I didn't say so, sir," said Peter Tounley diffidently.

" Quite true, quite true! You didn't, but-this

Coleman must be a man! "

" We think so, sir," said be who was called Billie.

" He certainly brought us through in style."

" But how did he manage it? " cried the minister, keenly interested. " How did he do it? "

" It is hard to say, sir. But he did it. He met us in the dead of night out near Nikopolis-"

"Near Nikopolis?"

"Yes, sir. And he hid us in a forest while a fight was going on, and then in the morning he brought us inside the Greek lines. Oh, there is a lot to tell-"

Whereupon they told it, or as much as they could of it. In the end, the minister said: " Well, where are the professor and Mrs. Wainwright? I want you all to dine with me to-night. I am dining in the public room, but you won't mind that after Epirus." " They should be down now, sir," answered a Student.

People were now coming rapidly to dinner and presently the professor and Mrs. Wainwright appeared. The old man looked haggard and white. He accepted the minister's warm greeting with a strained pathetic smile. " Thank you. We are glad to return safely."

Once at dinner the minister launched immediately into the subject of Coleman. " He must be altogether a most remarkable man. When he told me, very quietly, that he was going to try to rescue you, I frankly warned him against any such attempt. I thought he would merely add one more to a party of suffering people. But the. boys tell- me that he did actually rescue you."

"Yes, he did," said the professor. " It was a very gallant performance, and we are very grateful."

"Of course," spoke Mrs. Wainwright, "we might have rescued ourselves. We were on the right road, and all we had to do was to keep going on."

" Yes, but I understand-" said the minister. " I understand he took you into a wood to protect you from that fight, and generally protected you from all, kinds of trouble. It seems wonderful to me, not so much because it was done as because it was done by the man who, some time ago, calmy announced to me that he was going to do it. Extraordinary."

"Of course," said Mrs. Wainwright. " Oh, of course."

"And where is he now? " asked the minister suddenly.

"Has he now left you to the mercies of civilization? "

There was a moment's curious stillness, and then Mrs. Wainwright used that high voice which-the students believed-could only come to her when she was about to say something peculiarly destructive to the sensibilities. " Oh, of course, Mr. Coleman rendered us a great service, but in his private character he is not a man whom we exactly care to associate with."

" Indeed," said the minister staring. Then he hastily addressed the students. " Well, isn't this a comic war? Did you ever imagine war could be like this? " The professor remained looking at his wife with an air of stupefaction, as if she had opened up to him visions of imbecility of which he had not even dreamed. The students loyally began to chatter at the minister. " Yes, sir, it is a queer war. After all their bragging, it is funny to hear that they are running away with such agility. We thought, of course, of the old Greek wars."

Later, the minister asked them all to his rooms for coffee and cigarettes, but the professor and Mrs. Wainwright apologetically retired to their own quarters. The minister and the students made clouds of smoke, through which sang the eloquent descriptions of late adventures.

The minister had spent days of listening to questions from the State Department at Washington as to the whereabouts of the Wainwright party. "I suppose you know that you,are very prominent people in, the United States just now? Your pictures must have been in all the papers, and there must have been columns printed about you. My life here was made almost insupportable by your friends, who consist, I should think, of about half the population of the country. Of course they laid regular siege to the department. I am angry at Coleman for only one thing. When he cabled the news of your rescue to his news. paper from Arta, he should have also wired me, if only to relieve my failing mind. My first news of your escape was from Washington-think of that."

"Coleman had us all on his hands at Arta," said

Peter Tounley. " He was a fairly busy man."

" I suppose so," said the minister. " By the way," he asked bluntly, "what is wrong with him? What did Mrs. Wainwright mean? "

They were silent for a time, but it seemed plain to him that it was not evidence that his question had demoralised them. They seemed to be deliberating upon the form of answer. Ultimately Peter Tounley coughed behind his hand. " You see, sir," he began, " there is-well, there is a woman in the case. Not that anybody would care to speak of it excepting to you. But that is what is the cause of things, and then, you see, Mrs. Wainwright is-well-" He hesitated a moment and then completed his sentence in the ingenuous profanity of his age and condition. " She is rather an extraordinary old bird."

" But who is the woman?

"Why, it is Nora Blaick, the actress." "Oh," cried the minister, enlightened. " Her Why, I saw her here. She was very beautiful, but she seemed harmless enough. She was somewhat-er- confident, perhaps, but she did not alarm me. She called upon me, and I confess I-why, she seemed charming." " She's sweet on little Rufus. That's the point," said an oracular voice.

" Oh," cried the host, suddenly. " I remember. She asked me where he was. She said she had heard he was in Greece, and I told her he had gone knight- erranting off after you people. I remember now. I suppose she posted after him up to Arta, eh? "

" That's it. And so she asked you where he was?

" Yes."

" Why, that old flamingo-Mrs. Wainwright insists that it was a rendezvous."

Every one exchanged glances and laughed a little. " And did you see any actual fighting ? " asked the minister.

" No. We only beard it-"

Afterward, as they were trooping up to their rooms, Peter Tounley spoke musingly. " Well, it looks to me now as if Old Mother Wainwright was just a bad-minded old hen."

" Oh, I don't know. How is one going to tell what the truth is? "

" At any rate, we are sure now that Coleman had nothing to do with Nora's debut in Epirus."

They had talked much of Coleman, but in their tones there always had been a note of indifference or carelessness. This matter, which to some people was as vital and fundamental as existence, remained to others who knew of it only a harmless detail of life, with no terrible powers, and its significance had faded greatly when had ended the close associat.ions of the late adventure.

After dinner the professor had gone directly to his daughter's room. Apparently she had not moved. He knelt by the bedside again and took one of her hands. She was not weeping. She looked at him and smiled through the darkness. " Daddy, I would like to die," she said. " I think-yes-I would like to die."

For a long time the old man was silent, but he arose at last with a definite abruptness and said hoarsely " Wait! "

Mrs. Wainwright was standing before her mirror with her elbows thrust out at angles above her head, while her fingers moved in a disarrangement of 'her hair. In the glass she saw a reflection of her husband coming from Marjory's room, and his face was set with some kind of alarming purpose. She turned to watch him actually, but he walked toward the door into the corridor and did not in any wise heed her.

" Harrison! " she called. " Where are you going? "

He turned a troubled face upon her, and, as if she had hailed him in his sleep, he vacantly said: "What? "

"Where are you going?" she demanded with increasing trepidation.

He dropped heavily into a chair. "Going?" he repeated.

She was angry. "Yes! Going? Where are you going? "

"I am going-" he answered, "I am going to see Rufus Coleman."

Mrs. Wainwright gave voice to a muffled scream.

" Not about Marjory? "

"Yes," he said, "about Marjory."

It was now Mrs. Wainwright's turn to look at her husband with an air of stupefaction as if he had opened up to her visions of imbecility of which she had not even dreamed. " About Marjory!" she gurgled. Then suddenly her wrath flamed out. "Well, upon my word, Harrison Wainwright, you are, of all men in the world, the most silly and stupid. You are absolutely beyond belief. Of all projects! And what do you think Marjory would have to say of it if she knew it? I suppose you think she would like it? Why, I tell you she would keep her right hand in the fire until it was burned off before she would allow you to do such a thing."

" She must never know it," responded the professor, in dull misery.

" Then think of yourself! Think of the shame of it! The shame of it! "

The professor raised his eyes for an ironical glance at his wife. " Oh I have thought of the shame of it!"

" And you'll accomplish nothing," cried Mrs. Wain- wright. " You'll accomplish nothing. He'll only laugh at you."

" If he laughs at me, he will laugh at nothing but a poor, weak, unworldly old man. It is my duty to go."

Mrs. Wainwright opened her mouth as if she was about to shriek. After choking a moment she said: " Your duty? Your duty to go and bend the knee to that man? Yourduty?"

"'It is my duty to go,"' he repeated humbly. "If I can find even one chance for my daughter's happi- ness in a personal sacrifice. He can do no more than he can do no more than make me a little sadder."

His wife evidently understood his humility as a tribute to her arguments and a clear indication that she had fatally undermined his original intention. " Oh, he would have made you sadder," she quoth grimly. "No fear! Why, it was the most insane idea I ever heard of."

The professor arose wearily. " Well, I must be going to this work. It is a thing to have ended quickly." There was something almost biblical in his manner.

" Harrison! " burst out his wife in amazed lamenta- tion. You are not really going to do it? Not really!"

" I am going to do it," he answered.

" Well, there! " ejaculated Mrs. Wainwright to the heavens. She was, so to speak, prostrate. " Well, there! "

As the professor passed out of the door she cried beseechingly but futilely after him. " Harrison." In a mechanical way she turned then back to the mirror and resumed the disarrangement of her hair. She ad- dressed her image. " Well, of all stupid creatures under the sun, men are the very worst! " And her image said this to her even as she informed it, and afterward they stared at each other in a profound and tragic reception and acceptance of this great truth. Presently she began to consider the advisability of going to Marjdry with the whole story. Really, Harrison must not be allowed to go on blundering until the whole world heard that Marjory was trying to break her heart over that common scamp of a Coleman. It seemed to be about time for her, Mrs. Wainwright, to come into the situation and mend matters.

CHAPTER XXVII.

WHEN the professor arrived before Coleman's door, he paused a moment and looked at it. Previously, he could not have imagined that a simple door would ever so affect him. Every line of it seemed to express cold superiority and disdain. It was only the door of a former student, one of his old boys, whom, as the need arrived, he had whipped with his satire in the class rooms at Washurst until the mental blood had come, and all without a conception of his ultimately arriving before the door of this boy in the attitude of a supplicant. He would not say it; Coleman probably would not say it; but-they would both know it. A single thought of it, made him feel like running away. He would never dare to knock on that door. It would be too monstrous. And even as he decided that he was afraid to knock, he knocked.

Coleman's voice said; "Come in." The professor opened the door. The correspondent, without a coat, was seated at a paper-littered table. Near his elbow, upon another table, was a tray from which he had evidently dined and also a brandy bottle with several recumbent bottles of soda. Although he had so lately arrived at the hotel he had contrived to diffuse his traps over the room in an organised disarray which represented a long and careless occupation if it did not represent t'le scene of a scuffle. His pipe was in his mouth.

After a first murmur of surprise, he arose and reached in some haste for his coat. " Come in, professor, come in," he cried, wriggling deeper into his jacket as he held out his hand. He had laid aside his pipe and had also been very successful in flinging a newspaper so that it hid the brandy and soda. This act was a feat of deference to the professor's well known principles.

"Won't you sit down, sir ? " said Coleman cordially. His quick glance of surprise had been immediately suppressed and his manner was now as if the pro- fessor's call was a common matter.

" Thank you, Mr. Coleman, I-yes, I will sit down,". replied the old man. His hand shook as he laid it on the back of the chair and steadied himself down into it. " Thank you!" -

Coleman looked at him with a great deal of ex- pectation.

" Mr. Coleman ! "

"Yes, sir."

" I—"

He halted then and passed his hand over his face. His eyes did not seem to rest once upon Coleman, but they occupied themselves in furtive and frightened glances over the room. Coleman could make neither head nor tail of the affair. He would not have believed any man's statement that the professor could act in such an extraordinary fashion. " Yes, sir," he said again suggestively. The simple strategy resulted in a silence that was actually awkward. Coleman, despite his bewilderment, hastened into a preserving gossip. " I've had a great many cables waiting for me for heaven knows- how long and others have been arriving in flocks to-night. You have no idea of the row in America, professor. Why, everybody must have gone wild over the lost sheep. My paper has cabled some things that are evidently for you. For instance, here is one that says a new puzzle-game called Find the Wainwright Party has had a big success. Think of that, would you." Coleman grinned at the professor. " Find the Wainwright Party, a new puzzle-game."

The professor had seemed grateful for Coleman's tangent off into matters of a light vein. " Yes?" he said, almost eagerly. " Are they selling a game really called that?"

" Yes, really," replied Coleman. " And of course you know that-er-well, all the Sunday papers would of course have big illustrated articles-full pages-with your photographs and general private histories pertaining mostly to things which are none of their business." " Yes, I suppose they would do that," admitted the professor. " But I dare say it may not be as bad as you suggest."

" Very like not," said Coleman. " I put it to you forcibly so that in the future the blow will not be too cruel. They are often a weird lot."

" Perhaps they can't find anything very bad about us."

" Oh, no. And besides the whole episode will probably be forgotten by the time you return to the United States."

They talked on in this way slowly, strainedly, until they each found that the situation would soon become insupportable. The professor had come for a distinct purpose and Coleman knew it; they could not sit there lying at each other forever. Yet when he saw the pain deepening in the professor's eyes, the correspondent again ordered up his trivialities. " Funny thing. My paper has been congratulating me, you know, sir, in a wholesale fashion, and I think-I feel sure-that they have been exploiting my name all over the country as the Heroic Rescuer. There is no sense in trying to stop them, because they don't care whether it is true or not true. All they want is the privilege of howling out that their correspondent rescued you, and they would take that privilege without in any ways worrying if I refused my consent. You see, sir? I wouldn't like you to feel that I was such a strident idiot as I doubtless am appearing now before the public."

" No," said the professor absently. It was plain that he had been a very slack listener. " I-Mr. Coleman-" he began.

"Yes, sir," answered Coleman promptly and gently.

It was obviously only a recognition of the futility of further dallying that was driving the old man on- ward. He knew, of course, that if he was resolved to take this step, a longer delay would simply make it harder for him. The correspondent, leaning forward, was watching him almost breathlessly.

" Mr. Coleman, I understand-or at least I am led to believe-that you-at one time, proposed marriage to my daughter? "

The faltering words did not sound as if either man had aught to do with them. They were an expression by the tragic muse herself. Coleman's jaw fell and he looked glassily at the professor. He said: "Yes!" But already his blood was leaping as his mind flashed everywhere in speculation.

" I refused my consent to that marriage," said the old man more easily. " I do not know if the matter has remained important to you, but at any rate, I-I retract my refusal."

Suddenly the blank expression left Coleman's face and he smiled with sudden intelligence, as if informa- tion of what the professor had been saying had just reached him. In this smile there was a sudden betrayal, too, of something keen and bitter which had lain hidden in the man's mind. He arose and made a step towards the professor and held out his hand. "Sir, I thank you from the bottom of my heart!" And they both seemed to note with surprise that Coleman's voice had broken.

The professor had arisen to receive Coleman's hand.

His nerve was now of iron and he was very formal.

" I judge from your tone that I have not made a mis-

take-something which I feared."

Coleman did not seem to mind the professor's formality. " Don't fear anything. Won't you sit down again? Will you have a cigar. * * No, I couldn't tell you how glad I am. How glad I am. I feel like a fool. It—"

But the professor fixed him with an Arctic eye and bluntly said: " You love her? "

The question steadied Coleman at once. He looked undauntedly straight into the professor's face. He simply said: " I love her! "

" You love her ? " repeated the professor.

" I love her," repeated Coleman.

After some seconds of pregnant silence, the professor arose. " Well, if she cares to give her life to you I will allow it, but I must say that I do not consider you nearly good enough. Good-night." He smiled faintly as he held out his hand.

" Good-night, sir," said Coleman. " And I can't tell, you, now-"

Mrs. Wainwright, in her room was languishing in a chair and applying to her brow a handkerch-ief wet with cologne water. She, kept her feverish glarice upon the door. Remembering well the manner of her husband when he went out she could hardly identify him when he came in. Serenity, composure, even self-satisfaction, was written upon him. He, paid no attention to her, but going to a chair sat down with a groan of contentment.

" Well ? " cried Mrs. Wainwright, starting up.

"Well? "

" Well-what ? " he asked.

She waved her hand impatiently. " Harrison, don't be absurd. You know perfectly well what I mean. It is a pity you couldn't think of the anxiety I have been in." She was going to weep.

"Oh, I'll tell you after awhile," he said stretching out his legs with the complacency of a rich merchant after a successful day.

"No! Tell me now," she implored him. "Can't you see I've worried myself nearly to death?" She was not going to weep, she was going to wax angry.

"Well, to tell the truth," said the professor with considerable pomposity, " I've arranged it. Didn't think I could do it at first, but it turned out "

"I Arranged it,"' wailed Mrs. Wainwright. " Arranged what? "

It here seemed to strike the professor suddenly that he was not such a flaming example for diplomatists as he might have imagined. " Arranged," he stammered. " Arranged ."

" Arranged what? "

" Why, I fixed-I fixed it up."

" Fixed what up? "

"It-it-" began the professor. Then he swelled with indignation. " Why, can't you understand anything at all? I-I fixed it."

" Fixed what? "

" Fixed it. Fixed it with Coleman."

" Fixed what with Coleman?

The professor's wrath now took control of him. "Thunder and lightenin' ! You seem to jump at the conclusion that I've made some horrible mistake. For goodness' sake, give me credit for a particle of sense."

" What did you do? " she asked in a sepulchral voice.

" Well," said the professor, in a burning defiance, " I'll tell you what I did. I went to Coleman and told him that once-as he of course knew-I had re- fused his marriage with my daughter, but that now—-"

" Grrr," said Mrs. Wainwright.

" But that now-" continued the professor,

" I retracted that refusal."

" Mercy on us! " cried Mrs. Wainwright, throwing herself back in the chair. " Mercy on us! What fools men are!"

" Now, wait a minute-"

But Mrs. Wainwright began to croon: " Oh, if

Marjory should hear of this! Oh, if she should hear

of it! just let her. Hear-"

" But she must not," cried the professor, tigerishly. just you dare! " And the woman saw before her a man whose eyes were lit with a flame which almost expressed a temporary hatred.

The professor had left Coleman so abruptly that the correspondent found himself murmuring half. coherent gratitude to the closed door of his room. Amazement soon began to be mastered by exultation. He flung himself upon the brandy and soda and nego- tiated a strong glass. Pacing. the room with nervous steps, he caught a vision of himself in a tall mirror. He halted before it. " Well, well," he said. " Rufus, you're a grand man. There is not your equal anywhere. You are a great, bold, strong player, fit to sit down to a game with the -best."

A moment later it struck him that he had appropriated too much. If the professor had paid him a visit and made a wonderful announcement, he, Coleman, had not been the engine of it. And then he enunciated clearly something in his mind which, even in a vague form, had been responsible for much of his early elation. Marjory herself had compassed this thing. With shame he rejected a first wild and preposterous idea that she had sent her father to him. He reflected that a man who for an instant could conceive such a thing was a natural-born idiot. With an equal feeling, he rejected also an idea that she could have known anything of her father's purpose. If she had known of his purpose, there would have been no visit.

What, then, was the cause? Coleman soon decided that the professor had witnessed some demonstration of Marjory's emotion which had been sufficiently severe in its character to force him to the extraordinary visit. But then this also was wild and preposterous. That coldly beautiful goddess would not have given a demonstration of emotion over Rufus Coleman sufficiently alarming to have forced her father on such an errand. That was impossible. No, he was wrong; Marjory even indirectly, could not be connected with the visit. As he arrived at this decision, the enthusiasm passed out of him and he wore a doleful, monkish face.

"Well, what, then, was the cause?" After eliminating Marjory from the discussion waging in his mind, he found it hard to hit upon anything rational. The only remaining theory was to the effect that the professor, having a very high sense of the correspond. ent's help in the escape of the Wainwright party, had decided that the only way to express his gratitude was to revoke a certain decision which he now could see had been unfair. The retort to this theory seemed to be that if the professor had had such a fine conception of the services rendered by Coleman, he had had ample time to display his appreciation on the road to Arta and on the road down from Arta. There was no necessity for his waiting until their arrival in Athens. It was impossible to concede that the professor's emotion could be anew one; if he had it now, he must have had it in far stronger measure directly after he had been hauled out of danger.

So, it may be seen that after Coleman had eliminated Marjory from the discussion that was waging in his mind, he had practically succeeded in eliminating the professor as well. This, he thought, mournfully, was eliminating with a vengeance. If he dissolved all the factors he could hardly proceed.

The mind of a lover moves in a circle, or at least on a more circular course than other minds, some of which at times even seem to move almost in a straight line. Presently, Coleman was at the point where he bad started, and he did not pause until he reached that theory which asserted that the professor had been inspired to his visit by some sight or knowledge of Marjory in distress. Of course, Coleman was wistfully desirous of proving to himself the truth of this theory.

The palpable agitation of the professor during the interview seemed to support it. If he had come on a mere journey of conscience, he would have hardly appeared as a white and trembling old, man. But then, said Coleman, he himself probably exaggerated this idea of the professor's appearance. It might have been that he was only sour and distressed over the performance of a very disagreeable duty.

The correspondent paced his room and smoked. Sometimes he halted at the little table where was the brandy and soda. He thought so hard that sometimes it seemed that Marjory had been to him to propose marriage, and at other times it seemed that there had been no visit from any one at all.

A desire to talk to somebody was upon him. He strolled down stairs and into the smoking and reading rooms, hoping to see a man he knew, even if it were Coke. But the only occupants were two strangers, furiously debating the war. Passing the minister's room, Coleman saw that there was a light within, and he could not forbear knocking. He was bidden to enter, and opened the door upon the minister, care- fully reading his Spectator fresh from London. He looked up and seemed very glad. "How are you?" he cried. "I was tremendously anxious to see you, do you know! I looked for you to dine with me to-night, but you were not down?" "No; I had a great deal of work."

" Over the Wainwright affair? By the way, I want you to accept my personal thanks for that work. In a week more I would have gone demented and spent the rest of my life in some kind of a cage, shaking the bars and howling out State Department messages about the Wainwrights. You see, in my territory there are no missionaries to get into trouble, and I was living a life of undisturbed and innocent calm, ridiculing the sentiments of men from Smyrna and other interesting towns who maintained that the diplomatic service was exciting. However, when the Wainwright party got lost, my life at once became active. I was all but helpless, too; which was the worst of it. I suppose Terry at Constantinople must have got grandly stirred up, also. Pity he can't see you to thank you for saving him from probably going mad. By the way," he added, while looking keenly at Coleman, " the Wainwrights don't seem to be smothering you with gratitude? "

" Oh, as much as I deserve-sometimes more," answered Coleman. " My exploit was more or less of a fake, you know. I was between the lines by accident, or through the efforts of that blockhead of a dragoman. I didn't intend it. And then, in the night, when we were waiting in the road because of a fight, they almost bunked into us. That's all."

"They tell it better," said the minister, severely.

" Especially the youngsters."

"Those kids got into a high old fight at a town up there beyond Agrinion. Tell you about that, did they? I thought not. Clever kids. You have noted that there are signs of a few bruises and scratches?" " Yes, but I didn't ask-" " Well, they are from the fight. It seems the people took us for Germans, and there was an awful palaver, which ended in a proper and handsome shindig. It raised the town, I tell you."

The minister sighed in mock despair. " Take these people home, will you? Or at any rate, conduct them out of the field of my responsibility. Now, they would like Italy immensely, I am sure."

Coleman laughed, and they smoked for a time.

" That's a charming girl-Miss Wainwright," said the minister, musingly. "And what a beauty! It does my exiled eyes good to see her. I suppose all those youngsters are madly in love with her? I don't see how they could help it."

" Yes," said Coleman, glumly. " More than half of them."

The minister seemed struck with a sudden thought.

" You ought to try to win that splendid prize yourself.

The rescuer! Perseus! What more fitting? "

Coleman answered calmly: "Well * * * I think

I'll take your advice."

CHAPTER XXVIII.

THE next morning Coleman awoke with a sign of a resolute decision on his face, as if it had been a development of his sleep. He would see Marjory as soon as possible, see her despite any barbed-wire entanglements which might be placed in the way by her mother, whom he regarded as his strenuous enemy. And he would ask Marjory's hand in the presence of all Athens if it became necessary.

He sat a long time at his breakfast in order to see the Wainwrights enter the dining room, and as he was about to surrender to the will of time, they came in, the professor placid and self-satisfied, Mrs. Wainwright worried and injured and Marjory cool, beautiful, serene. If there had been any kind of a storm there was no trace of it on the white brow of the girl. Coleman studied her closely but furtively while his mind spun around his circle of speculation. Finally he noted the waiter who was observing him with a pained air as if it was on the tip of his tongue to ask this guest if he was going to remain at breakfast forever. Coleman passed out to the reading room where upon the table a multitude of great red guide books were crushing the fragile magazines of London and Paris. On the walls were various depressing maps with the name of a tourist agency luridly upon them, and there were also some pictures of hotels with their rates-in francs-printed beneath. The room was cold, dark, empty, with the trail of the tourist upon it.

Coleman went to the picture of a hotel in Corfu and stared at it precisely as if he was interested. He was standing before it when he heard Marjory's voice just without the door. "All right! I'll wait." He did not move for the reason that the hunter moves not when the unsuspecting deer approaches his hiding place. She entered rather quickly and was well toward the centre of the room before she perceived Coleman. " Oh," she said and stopped. Then she spoke the immortal sentence, a sentence which, curiously enough is common to the drama, to the novel, and to life. " I thought no one was here." She looked as if she was going to retreat, but it would have been hard to make such retreat graceful, and probably for this reason she stood her ground.

Coleman immediately moved to a point between her and the door. "You are not going to run away from me, Marjory Wainwright," he cried, angrily. " You at least owe it to me to tell me definitely that you don't love me-that you can't love me-"

She did not face him with all of her old spirit, but she faced him, and in her answer there was the old Marjory. " A most common question. Do you ask all your feminine acquaintances that? "

"I mean-" he said. "I mean that I love you and-"

"Yesterday-no. To-day-yes. To-morrow-who knows. Really, you ought to take some steps to know your own mind."

" Know my own mind," he retorted in a burst of in- dignation. "You mean you ought to take steps to know your own mind."

" My own mind! You-" Then she halted in acute confusion and all her face went pink. She had been far quicker than the man to define the scene. She lowered her head. Let me past, please-"

But Coleman sturdily blocked the way and even took one of her struggling hands. "Marjory-" And then his brain must have roared with a thousand quick sentences for they came tumbling out, one over the other. * * Her resistance to the grip of his fingers grew somewhat feeble. Once she raised her eyes in a quick glance at him. * * Then suddenly she wilted. She surrendered, she confessed without words. " Oh, Marjory, thank God, thank God-" Peter Tounley made a dramatic entrance on the gallop. He stopped, petrified. "Whoo!" he cried. "My stars! " He turned and fled. But Coleman called after him in a low voice, intense with agitation.

" Come back here, you young scoundrel! Come back here I "

Peter returned, looking very sheepish. " I hadn't the slightest idea you-"

" Never mind that now. But look here, if you tell a single soul-particularly those other young scoundrels-I'll break-"

" I won't, Coleman. Honest, I won't." He was far more embarrassed than Coleman and almost equally so with Marjory. He was like a horse tugging at a tether. "I won't, Coleman! Honest!"

" Well, all right, then." Peter escaped.

The professor and his wife were in their sitting room writing letters. The cablegrams had all been answered, but as the professor intended to prolong his journey homeward into a month of Paris and London, there remained the arduous duty of telling their friends at length exactly what had happened. There was considerable of the lore of olden Greece in the professor's descriptions of their escape, and in those of Mrs. Wainwright there was much about the lack of hair-pins and soap.

Their heads were lowered over their writing when the door into the corridor opened and shut quickly, and upon looking up they saw in the room a radiant girl, a new Marjory. She dropped to her knees by her father's chair and reached her arms to his neck. " Oh, daddy! I'm happy I I'm so happy! "

" Why-what-" began the professor stupidly.

" Oh, I am so happy, daddy!

Of course he could not be long in making his conclusion. The one who could give such joy to Marjory was the one who, last night, gave her such grief. The professor was only a moment in understanding. He laid his hand tenderly upon her head " Bless my soul," he murmured. "And so-and so-he-"

At the personal pronoun, Mrs. Wainwright lum- bered frantically to her feet. " What ? " she shouted. Coleman? "

" Yes," answered Marjory. " Coleman." As she spoke the name her eyes were shot with soft yet tropic flashes of light.

Mrs. Wainwright dropped suddenly back into her chair. "Well-of-all-things!" The professor was stroking his daughter's hair and although for a time after Mrs. Wainwright's outbreak there was little said, the old man and the girl seemed in gentle communion, she making him feel her happiness, he making her feel his appreciation. Providentially Mrs. Wainwright had been so stunned by the first blow that she was evidently rendered incapable of speech.

" And are you sure you will be happy with him? asked her father gently.

" All my life long," she answered.

" I am glad! I am glad! " said the father, but even as he spoke a great sadness came to blend with his joy. The hour when he was to give this beautiful and beloved life into the keeping of another had been heralded by the god of the sexes, the ruthless god that devotes itself to the tearing of children from the parental arms and casting them amid the mysteries of an irretrievable wedlock. The thought filled him with solemnity.

But in the dewy eyes of the girl there was no question.

The world to her was a land of glowing promise.

" I am glad," repeated the professor.

The girl arose from her knees. " I must go away and-think all about it," she said, smiling. When the door of her room closed upon her, the mother arose in majesty.

" Harrison Wainwright," she declaimed, "you are not going to allow this monstrous thing! "

The professor was aroused from a reverie by these words. "What monstrous thing ? " he growled.

" Why, this between Coleman and Marjory."

" Yes," he answered boldly.

" Harrison! That man who-"

The professor crashed his hand down on the table.

"Mary! I will not hear another word of it! "

" Well," said Mrs. Wainwright, sullen and ominous, " time will tell! Time will tell!"

When Coleman bad turned from the fleeing Peter Tounley again to

Marjory, he found her making the preliminary movements of a flight. "What's the matter? " he demanded anxiously.

" Oh, it's too dreadful"

" Nonsense," lie retorted stoutly. " Only Peter

Tounley! He don't count. What of that? "

' Oh, dear! " She pressed her palm to a burning cheek. She gave him a star-like, beseeching glance. Let me go now-please."

" Well," he answered, somewhat affronted, " if you like—"

At the door she turned to look at him, and this glance expressed in its elusive way a score of things which she had not yet been able to speak. It explained that she was loth to leave him, that she asked forgiveness for leaving him, that even for a short absence she wished to take his image in her eyes, that he must not bully her, that there was something now in her heart which frightened her, that she loved him, that she was happy—-

When she had gone, Coleman went to the rooms of the American minister. A Greek was there who talked wildly as he waved his cigarette. Coleman waited in well-concealed impatience for the dvapora- tion of this man. Once the minister, regarding the correspondent hurriedly, interpolated a comment. " You look very cheerful? "

" Yes," answered Coleman, " I've been taking your advice."

" Oh, ho ! " said the minister.

The Greek with the cigarette jawed endlessly. Coleman began to marvel at the enduring good man- ners of the minister, who continued to nod and nod in polite appreciation of the Greek's harangue, which, Coleman firmly believed, had no point of interest whatever. But at last the man, after an effusive farewell, went his way.

" Now," said the minister, wheeling in his chair tell me all about it."

Coleman arose, and thrusting his hands deep in his trousers' pockets, began to pace the room with long strides. He, said nothing, but kept his eyes on the floor.

" Can I have a drink ? " he asked, abruptly pausing.

" What would you like? " asked the minister, benevolently, as he touched the bell.

" A brandy and soda. I'd like it very much. You see," he said, as he resumed his walk, " I have no kind of right to burden you with my affairs, but, to tell the truth, if I don't get this news off my mind and into somebody's ear, I'll die. It's this-I asked Marjory Wainwright to marry me, and-she accepted, and- that's all."

" Well, I am very glad," cried the minister, arising and giving his hand. "And as for burdening me with your affairs, no one has a better right, you know, since you released me from the persecution of Washington and the friends of the Wainwrights. May good luck follow you both forever. You, in my opinion, are a very, very fortunate man. And, for her part she has not done too badly."

Seeing that it was important that Coleman should have his spirits pacified in part, the minister continued: " Now, I have got to write an official letter, so you just walk up and down here and use up this surplus steam. Else you'll explode."

But Coleman was not to be detained. Now that he had informed the minister, he must rush off some. where, anywhere, and do-he knew not what.

All right," said the minister, laughing. " You have a wilder head than I thought. But look here," he called, as Coleman was making for the door. " Am I to keep this news a secret? "

Coleman with his hand on the knob, turned im. pressively. He spoke with deliberation. " As far as I am concerned, I would be glad to see a man paint it in red letters, eight feet high, on the front of the king's palace."

The minister, left alone, wrote steadily and did not even look up when Peter Tounley and two others entered, in response to his cry of permission.

How ever, he presently found time to speak over his shoulder to them. "Hear the news?"

"No, sir," they answered.

" Well, be good boys, now, and read the papers and look at pictures until I finish this letter. Then I will tell you."

They surveyed him keenly. They evidently judged that the news was worth hearing, but, obediently, they said nothing. Ultimately the minister affixed a rapid signature to the letter, and turning, looked at the students with a smile. " Haven't heard the news, eh ?"

"No, Sir."

"Well, Marjory Wainwright is engaged to marry

Coleman."

The minister was amazed to see the effect of this announcement upon the three students. He had expected the crows and cackles of rather absurd merriment with which unbearded youth often greets, such news. But there was no crow or cackle. One young man blushed scarlet and looked guiltily at the floor. With a great effort he muttered: " She is too good for him." Another student had turned ghastly pate and was staring. It was Peter Tounley who relieved the minister's mind, for upon that young man's face was a broad jack-o-lantern grin, and the minister saw that, at any rate, he had not made a complete massacre.

Peter Tounley said triumphantly: "I knew it! "

The minister was anxious over the havoc he had wrought with the two other students, but slowly the colour abated in one face and grew in the other. To give them opportunity, the minister talked busily to Peter Tounley. "And how did you know it, you young scamp ?"

Peter was jubilant. " Oh, -I knew it! I knew it I

I am very clever."

The student who had blushed now addressed the minister in a slightly strained voice. " Are you positive that it is true, Mr. Gordner?,"

" I had it on the best authority," replied the minister gravely.

The student who had turned pale said: " Oh, it's true, of course."

" Well," said crudely the one who had blushed, she's a great sight too good for Coleman or anybody like him. That's all I've got to say."

" Oh, Coleman is a good fellow," said Peter Tounley,

reproachfully. " You've no right to say that-exactly.

You don't know where you'd. be now if it were not for

Coleman."

The, response was, first, an angry gesture. " Oh, don't keep everlasting rubbing that in. For heaven's sake, let up. - Supposing I don't. know where I'd be now if,it were not for Rufus Coleman? What of it? For the rest of my life have I got to—"

The minister saw. that this was the embittered speech of a really defeated youth, so, to save scenes, he gently ejected the trio. " There, there, now! Run along home like good boys. I'll be busy until luncheon. And I -dare say you won't find Coleman such a bad chap."'

In the corridor, one of the students said offensively to Peter Tounley: " Say, how in hell did you find out all this so early? "

Peter's reply was amiable in tone. " You are a damned bleating little kid and you made a holy show of yourself before Mr. Gordner. There's where you stand. Didn't you see that he turned us out because he didn't know but what you were going to blubber or something. - you are a sucking pig, and if you want to know how I find out things go ask the Delphic Oracle, you blind ass."

" You better look out or you may get a punch in the eye!,"

"You take one punch in the general direction of my eye, me son," said -Peter cheerfully, " and I'll distribute your remains, over this hotel in a way that will cause your, friends years of trouble to collect you. Instead of anticipating an attack upon my eye, you had much better be engaged in improving your mind, which is at present not a fit machine to cope with exciting situations. There's Coke! Hello, Coke, hear the news? Well, Marjory Wainwright and Rufus Coleman, are engaged.. Straight? Certainly ! Go ask the minister."

Coke did not take Peter's word. "Is that so ? " he asked the others.

" So the minister told us," they answered, and then these two, who seemed so unhappy, watched Coke's face to see if they could not find surprised misery there. But Coke coolly said: " Well, then, I suppose it's true."

It soon became evident that the students did not care for each other's society. Peter Tounley was probably an exception, but the others seemed to long for quiet corners. They were distrusting each other, and, in a boyish way, they were even capable of maligant things. Their excuses for separation were badly made.

"I-I think I'll go for a walk."

" I'm going up stairs to read."

" Well, so long, old man.' " So long." There was

no heart to it.

Peter Tounley went to Coleman's door, where he knocked with noisy hilarity. " Come in I " The correspondent apparently had just come from the street, for his hat was on his head and a light top-coat was on his back. He was searching hurriedly through some, papers. " Hello, you young devil What are you doing here?

Peter's entrance was a somewhat elaborate comedy which Coleman watched in icy silence. Peter after a long,and impudent pantomime halted abruptly and fixing Coleman with his eye demanded: "Well?"

"Well-what?." said Coleman, bristling a trifle.

" Is it true ?"

" Is what true ?"

" Is it true? " Peter was extremely solemn. " Say, me bucko," said Coleman suddenly, " if you've. come up here to twist the beard of the patriarch, don't you think you are running a chance? "

"All right. I'll be good," said Peter, and he sat on the bed. " But-is it true?

" Is what true? "

" What the whole hotel is saying."

] "I haven't heard the hotel making any remarks lately. Been talking to the other buildings, I sup- pose."

"Well, I want to tell you that everybody knows that you and Marjory have done gone and got yourselves engaged," said Peter bluntly.

"And well? " asked Coleman imperturbably.

" Oh, nothing," replied Peter, waving his hand.

" Only-I thought it might interest you."

Coleman was silent for some time. He fingered his papers. At last he burst out joyously. "And so they know it already, do they? Well-damn them-let them know it. But you didn't tell them yourself? "

" I ! " quoth Peter wrathfully. " No! The minister told us."

Then Coleman was again silent for a time and Peter Tounley sat on the. bed reflectively looking at the ceiling. " Funny thing, Marjory 'way over here in Greece, and then you happening over here the way you did."

" It isn't funny at all."

" Why isn't it? "

" Because," said Coleman impressively,, " that is why I came to Greece. It was all planned. See?"

"Whirroo," exclaimed Peter. "This here is magic."

" No magic at all." Coleman displayed some complacence. " No magic at all. just pure, plain— whatever you choose to call it."

" Holy smoke," said Peter, admiring the situation. "Why, this is plum romance, Coleman. I'm blowed if it isn't."

Coleman was grinning with delight. He took a fresh cigar and his bright eyes looked at Peter through the smoke., "Seems like it, don't it? Yes. Regular romance. Have a drink, my boy, just to celebrate my good luck. And be patient if I talk a great deal of my-my-future. My head spins with it." He arose to pace the room flinging out bis arms in a great gesture. " God! When I think yesterday was not like to-day I wonder how I stood it." There was a knock at the door and a waiter left a note in Coleman's hand

"Dear Ruf us:-We are going for a drive this afternoon at three, and mother wishes you to come, if you. care to. I too wish it, if you care to. Yours, " MARJORY."

With a radiant face, Coleman gave the note a little crackling flourish in the air. " Oh, you don't know what life is, kid."

" S-steady the Blues," said Peter Tounley seriously.

You'll lose your head if you don't watch out."

" Not I" cried Coleman with irritation. " But a man must turn loose some times, mustn't he?"

When the four, students had separated in the corri- dor, Coke had posted at once to Nora Black's sitting room. His entrance was somewhat precipitate, but he cooled down almost at once, for he reflected that he was not bearing good news. He ended by perching in awkward fashion on the brink of his chair and fumbling his hat uneasily. Nora floated to him in a cloud of a white dressing gown. She gave him a plump hand. "Well, youngman? "she said, with a glowing smile. She took a chair, and the stuff of her gown fell in curves over the arms of it.,

Coke looked hot and bothered, as if he could have more than half wanted to retract his visit. " I-aw- we haven't seen much of you lately," he began, sparing. He had expected to tell his news at once.

No," said Nora, languidly. " I have been resting after that horrible journey-that horrible journey. Dear, dear! Nothing,will ever induce me to leave London, New York and Paris. I am at home there. But here I Why, it is worse than living in Brooklyn. And that journey into the wilds! No. no; not for me! "

" I suppose we'll all be glad to get home," said

Coke, aimlessly.

At the moment a waiter entered the room and began to lay the table for luncheon. He kept open the door to the corridor, and he had the luncheon at a point just outside the door. His excursions to the trays were flying ones, so that, as far as Coke's purpose was concerned, the waiter was always in the room. Moreover, Coke was obliged, naturally, to depart at once. He had bungled everything.

As he arose he whispered hastily: " Does this waiter understand English? "

"Yes," answered Nora. "Why?"

"Because I have something to tell you-important."

"What is it? " whispered Nora, eagerly.

He leaned toward her and replied: " Marjory

Wainwright and Coleman are engaged."

To his unfeigned astonishment, Nora Black burst into peals of silvery laughter, " Oh, indeed? And so this is your tragic story, poor, innocent lambkin? And what did you expect? That I would faint?" -

" I thought-I don't know-" murmured Coke in confusion.

Nora became suddenly business-like. " But how do you know? Are you sure? Who told you? Anyhow, stay to luncheon. Do-like a good boy. Oh, you must."

Coke dropped again into his chair. He studied her in some wonder. " I thought you'd be surprised," he said, ingenuously.

" Oh, you did, did you? Well, you see I'm not.

And now tell me all about it."

"There's really nothing to tell but the plain fact.

Some of the boys dropped in at the minister's

rooms a little while ago, and, he told them of it.

That's all."

Well, how did he know?

"I am sure I can't tell you. Got it first hand, I suppose. He likes Coleman, and Coleman is always hanging up there."

" Oh, perhaps Coleman was lying," said Nora easily. Then suddenly her face brightened and she spoke with animation. " Oh, I haven't told you how my little Greek officer has turned out. Have I? No? Well, it is simply lovely. Do you know, he belongs to one of the best families in Athens? He does. And they're rich-rich as can be. My courier tells me that the marble palace where they live is enough to blind you, and that if titles hadn't gone out of style-or something-here in Greece, my little officer would be a prince! Think of that! The courier didn't know it until we got to Athens, and the little officer-the prince-gave me his card, of course. One of the oldest, noblest and richest families in Greece. Think of that! There I thought he was only a bothersome little officer who came in handy at times, and there he turns out to be a prince. I could hardly keep myself from rushing right off to find him and apologise to him for the way I treated him. It was awful! And-" added the fair Nora, pensively, "if he does meet me in Paris, I'll make him wear that title down to a shred, you can bet. What's the good of having a title unless you make it work?"

CHAPTER XXIX.

COKE did not stay to luncheon with Nora Black. He went away saying to himself either that girl don't care a straw for Coleman or she has got a heart absolutely of flint, or she is the greatest actress on earth or-there is some other reason."

At his departure, Nora turned and called into an adjoining room. " Maude I " The voice of her companion and friend answered her peevishly. " What ?"

"Don't bother me. I'm reading."

" Well, anyhow, luncheon is ready, so you will have to stir your precious self," responded Nora. " You're lazy."

" I don't want any luncheon. Don't bother me.

I've got a headache."

" Well, if you don't come out, you'll miss the news.

That's all I've got to say."

There was a rustle in the adjoining room, and immediately the companion appeared, seeming much annoyed but curious. " Well, what is it ? "

" Rufus Coleman is engaged to be married to that

Wainwright girl, after all."

" Well I declare! " ejaculated the little old lady. " Well I declare." She meditated for a moment, and then continued in a tone of satisfaction. " I told you that you couldn't stop that man Coleman if he had really made up his mind to-"

" You're a fool," said Nora, pleasantly.

" Why? " said the old lady.

Because you are. Don't talk to me about it. I

want to think of Marco."

" 'Marco,'" quoted the old lady startled.

"The prince. The prince. Can't you understand?

I mean the prince."

" ' Marco!'" again quoted the old lady, under her breath.

" Yes, 'Marco,'" cried Nora, belligerently. " 'Marco,' Do you object to the name? What's the matter with you, anyhow?"

" Well," rejoined the other, nodding her head wisely, "he may be a prince, but I've always heard that these continental titles are no good in comparison to the English titles."

"Yes, but who told you so, eh? " demanded Nora, noisily. She herself answered the question. " The English! "

" Anyhow, that little marquis who tagged after you in London is a much bigger man in every way, I'll bet, than this little prince of yours."

" But-good heavens-he didn't mean it. Why, he was only one of the regular rounders. But Marco, he is serious I He means it. He'd go through fire and water for me and be glad of the chance."

" Well," proclaimed the old lady, " if you are not the strangest woman in the world, I'd like to know! Here I thought-"

"What did you think?" demanded Nora, suspisciously.

" I thought that Coleman—-"

"Bosh!" interrupted, the graceful Nora. "I tell you what, Maude; you'd better try to think as little as possible. It will suit your style of beauty better. And above all, don't think of my affairs. I myself am taking pains not to think of them. It's easier."

Mrs. Wainwright, with no spirit of intention what. ever, had sit about readjusting her opinions. It is certain that she was unconscious of any evolution. If some one had said to her that she was surrendering to the inevitable, she would have been immediately on her guard, and would have opposed forever all suggestions of a match between Marjory and Coleman. On the other hand, if some one had said to her that her daughter was going to marry a human serpent, and that there were people in Athens who would be glad to explain his treacherous character, she would have haughtily scorned the tale-bearing and would have gone with more haste into the professor's way of thinking. In fact, she was in process of undermining herself., and the work could have been. retarded or advanced by any irresponsible, gossipy tongue.

The professor, from the depths of his experience with her, arranged a course of conduct. " If I just leave her to herself she will come around all right, but if I go 'striking while the iron is hot,' or any of those things, I'll bungle it surely."

As they were making ready to go down to luncheon, Mrs. Wainwright made her speech which first indicated a changing mind. " Well, what will be, will be," she murmured with a prolonged sigh of resignation. " What will be, will be. Girls are very headstrong in these days, and there is nothing much to be done with them. They go their own roads. It wasn't so in my girlhood. - We were obliged to pay attention to our mothers wishes."

" I did not notice that you paid much attention to your mother's wishes when you married me," remarked the professor. " In fact, I thought-"

" That was another thing," retorted Mrs. Wainwright with severity. " You were a steady young man who had taken the highest honours all through your college course, and my mother's sole objection was that we were too hasty. She thought we -ought to wait until you had a penny to bless yourself with, and I can see now where she was quite right." " Well, you married me, anyhow," said the professor, victoriously.

Mrs. Wainwright allowed her husband's retort to pass over her thoughtful mood. " They say * * they say Rufus Coleman makes as much as fifteen thousand dollars a year. That's more than three times your income * * I don't know. * * It all depends on whether they try to save or not. His manner of life is, no doubt, very luxurious. I don't suppose he knows how to economise at all. That kind of a man usually doesn't. And then, in the newspaper world positions are so very precarious. Men may have valuable positions one minute and be penniless in the street the next minute. It isn't as if he had any real income, and of course he has no real ability. If he was suddenly thrown out of his position, goodness knows what would become of him. Still still fifteen thousand dollars a year is a big income while it lasts. I suppose he is very extravagant. That kind of a man usually is. And I wouldn't be surprised if he was heavily in debt; very heavily in debt. Still * * if Marjory has set her heart there is nothing to be done, I suppose. It wouldn't have happened if you had been as wise as you thought you were. * * I suppose he thinks I have been very rude to him. Well, some times I wasn't nearly so rude as I felt like being. Feeling as I did, I could hardly be very amiable. * * Of course this drive this afternoon was all your affair and Marjory's. But, of course, I shall be nice to him."

" And what of all this Nora Black business? " asked the professor, with, a display of valour, but really with much trepidation.

" She is a hussy," responded Mrs. Wainwright with energy. " Her conversation in the carriage on the way down to Agrinion sickened me! "

" I really believe that her plan was simply to break everything off between Marjory and Coleman," said the professor, " and I don't believe she had any-grounds for all that appearance of owning Coleman and the rest of it."

" Of course she didn't" assented Mrs. Wainwright.

The vicious thing! "

" On the other hand," said the professor, " there

might be some truth in it."

" I don't think so," said Mrs. Wainwright seriously.

I don't believe a word of it."

“ You do not mean to say that you think Coleman a model man ? “ demanded the professor.

“Not at all! Not at all!” she hastily answered.

“ But * * one doesn’t look for model men these days.”

“’Who told you he made fifteen thousand a year? asked the professor.

“It was Peter Tounley this morning. We were talking upstairs after breakfast, and he remarked that he if could make fifteen thousand, a year: like Coleman, he’d-I’ve forgotten what-some fanciful thing.”

“ I doubt if it is true,” muttered the old man wagging his head.

“Of course it’s true,” said his wife emphatically.

“ Peter Tounley says everybody knows it.”

Well * anyhow * money is not everything.”

But it’s a. great deal, you know well enough. You know you are always speaking of poverty as an evil, as a grand resultant, a collaboration of many lesser evils. Well, then?

“ But,” began the professor meekly, when I say that I mean-”

“ Well, money is money and poverty is poverty,” interrupted his wife. “ You don’t have to be very learned to know that.”

“I do not say that Coleman has not a very nice thing of it, but I must say it is hard to think of his getting any such sum, as you mention.”

“ Isn’t he known as the most brilliant journalist in

New York?” she demanded harshly.

“ Y-yes, as long as it lasts, but then one never knows when he will be out in the street penniless. Of course he has no particular ability which would be marketable if he suddenly lost his present employment. Of course it is not as if he was a really talented young man. He might not be able to make his way at all in any new direction.”

" I don't know about that," said Mrs. Wainwright in reflective protestation. " I don't know about that. I think he would."

" I thought you said a moment ago-" The professor spoke with an air of puzzled hesitancy. "I thought you said a moment ago that he wouldn't succeed in anything but journalism."

Mrs. Wainwright swam over the situation with a fine tranquility. " Well-I-I," she answered musingly, "if I did say that, I didn't mean it exactly."

" No, I suppose not," spoke the professor, and de- spite the necessity for caution he could not keep out of his voice a faint note of annoyance.

" Of course," continued the wife, " Rufus Coleman is known everywhere as a brilliant man, a very brilliant man, and he even might do well in-in politics or something of that sort."

" I have a very poor opinion of that kind of a mind which does well in American politics," said the pro- fessor, speaking as a collegian, " but I suppose there may be something in it."

" Well, at any rate," decided Mrs. Wainwright.

" At any rate-"

At that moment, Marjory attired for luncheon and the drive entered from her room, and Mrs. Wainwright checked the expression of her important conclusion. Neither father or mother had ever seen her so glowing with triumphant beauty, a beauty which would carry the mind of a spectator far above physical appreciation into that realm of poetry where creatures of light move and are beautiful because they cannot know pain or a burden. It carried tears to the old father's eyes. He took her hands. " Don't be too happy, my child, don't be too happy," he admonished her tremulously. " It makes me afraid-it makes me afraid."

CHAPTER XXX

IT seems strange that the one who was the most hilarious over the engagement of Marjory and Cole- man should be Coleman's dragoman who was indeed in a state bordering on transport. It is not known how he learned the glad tidings, but it is certain that he learned them before luncheon. He told all the visible employes of the hotel and allowed them to know that the betrothal really had been his handi-work He had arranged it. He did not make quite clear how he had performed this feat, but at least he was perfectly frank in acknowledging it.

When some of the students came down to luncheon, they saw him but could not decide what ailed him. He was in the main corridor of the hotel, grinning from ear to ear, and when he perceived the students he made signs to intimate that they possessed in com- mon a joyous secret. " What's the matter with that idiot?" asked Coke morosely. " Looks as if his wheels were going around too fast." Peter Tounley walked close to him and scanned him imperturbably, but with care. " What's up, Phidias? " The man made no articulate reply. He continued to grin and gesture. "Pain in oo tummy? Mother dead? Caught the cholera? Found out that you've swallowed a pair of hammered brass and irons in your beer? Say, who are you, anyhow? " But he could not shake this invincible glee, so he went away.

The dragoman's rapture reached its zenith when Coleman lent him to the professor and he was commissioned to bring a carriage for four people to the door at three o'clock. He himself was to sit on the box and tell the driver what was required of him. He dashed off, his hat in his hand, his hair flying, puffing, important beyond everything, and apparently babbling his mission to half the people he met on the street. In most countries he would have landed speedily in jail, but among a people who exist on a basis of'jibbering, his violent gabble aroused no suspicions as to his sanity. However, he stirred several livery stables to their depths and set men running here and there wildly and for the most part futiltiy.

At fifteen minutes to three o'clock, a carriage with its horses on a gallop tore around the corner and up to the front of the hotel, where it halted with the pomp and excitement of a fire engine. The dragoman jumped down from his seat beside the driver and scrambled hurriedly into the hotel, in the gloom of which he met a serene stillness which was punctuated only by the leisurely tinkle of silver and glass in the dining room. For a moment the dragoman seemed really astounded out of speech. Then he plunged into the manager's room. Was it conceivable that Monsieur Coleman was still at luncheon? Yes; in fact, it was true. But the carriage, was at the door! The carriage was at the door! The manager, undisturbed, asked for what hour Monsieur Coleman had been pleased to order a carriage. Three o'clock ! Three o'clock? The manager pointed calmly at the clock. Very well. It was now only thirteen minutes of three o'clock. Monsieur Coleman doubtless would appear at three. Until that hour the manager would not disturb Monsieur Coleman. The dragoman clutched both his hands in his hair and cast a look of agony to the ceiling. Great God! Had he accomplished the herculean task of getting a carriage for four people to the door of the hotel in time for a drive at three o'clock, only to meet with this stoniness, this inhumanity? Ah, it was unendurable? He begged the manager; he implored him. But at every word. the manager seemed to grow more indifferent, more callous. He pointed with a wooden finger at the clock-face. In reality, it is thus, that Greek meets Greek.

Professor Wainwright and Coleman strolled together out of the dining room. The dragoman rushed ecstatically upon the correspondent. " Oh, Meester Coleman! The carge is ready !"

"Well, all right," said Coleman, knocking ashes from his cigar. "Don't be in a hurry. I suppose we'll be ready, presently." The man was in despair.

The departure of the Wainwrights and Coleman on this ordinary drive was of a somewhat dramatic and public nature, No one seemed to know how to prevent its being so. In the first place, the attendants thronged out en masse for a reason which was plain at the time only to Coleman's dragoman. And, rather in the background, lurked the interested students. The professor was surprised and nervous. Coleman was rigid and angry. Marjory was flushed and some what hurried, and Mrs. Wainwright was as proud as an old turkey-hen.

As the carriage rolled away, Peter Tounley turned to his companions and said: " Now, that's official! That is the official announcement! Did you see Old Mother Wainwright? Oh, my eye, wasn't she puffed up ! Say, what in hell do you suppose all these jay hawking bell-boys poured out to the kerb for? Go back to your cages, my good people-"

As soon as the carriage wheeled into another street, its occupants exchanged easier smiles, and they must have confessed in some subtle way of glances that now at last they were upon their own mission, a mission undefined but earnest to them all. Coleman had a glad feeling of being let into the family, or becoming one of them

The professor looked sideways at him and smiled gently. " You know, I thought of driving you to some ruins, but Marjory would not have it. She flatly objected to any more ruins. So I thought we would drive down to New Phalerum." Coleman nodded and smiled as if he were immensely pleased, but of course New Phalerum was to him no more nor-less than Vladivostok or Khartoum. Neither place nor distance had interest for him. They swept along a shaded avenue where the dust lay thick on the leaves; they passed cafes where crowds were angrily shouting over the news in the little papers; they passed a hospital before which wounded men, white with bandages, were taking the sun; then came soon to the and valley flanked by gaunt naked mountains, which would lead them to the sea. Sometimes to accentuate the dry nakedness of this valley, there would be a patch of grass upon which poppies burned crimson spots. The dust writhed out from under the wheels of the carriage; in the distance the sea appeared, a blue half-disc set between shoulders of barren land. It would be common to say that Coleman was oblivious to all about him but Marjory. On the contrary, the parched land, the isolated flame of poppies, the cool air from the sea, all were keenly known to him, and they had developed an extraordinary power of blending sympathetically into his mood. Meanwhile the professor talked a great deal. And as a somewhat exhilarating detail, Coleman perceived that Ms. Wainwright was beaming upon him.

At New Phalerum-a small collection of pale square villas-they left the carriage and strolled, by the sea. The waves were snarling together like wolves amid the honeycomb rocks and from where the blue plane sprang level to the horizon, came a strong cold breeze, the kind of a breeze which moves an exulting man or a parson to take off his hat and let his locks flutter and tug back from his brow.

The professor and Mrs. Wainwright were left to themselves.

Marjory and Coleman did not speak for a time. It might have been that they did not quite know where to make a beginning. At last Marjory asked: "What has become of your splendid horse?"

"Oh, I've told the dragoman to have him sold as soon as he arrives," said Coleman absently.

" Oh. I'm sorry * * I liked that horse."

"Why? "

"Oh, because-"

"Well, he was a fine-" Then he, too, interrupted himself, for he saw plainly that they had not come to this place to talk about a horse. Thereat he made speech of matters which at least did not afford as many opportunities for coherency as would the horse. Marjory, it can't be true * * * Is it true, dearest * * I can hardly believe it. -I-"

" Oh, I know I'm not nearly good enough for you."

" Good enough for me, dear?

" They all told me so, and they were right ! Why, even the American minister said it. Everybody thinks it."

"Why, aren 't they wretches To think of them saying such a thing! As if-as if anybody could be too—"

" Do you know-" She paused and looked at him with a certain timid challenge. " I don't know why I feel it, but-sometimes I feel that I've been I've been flung at your head."

He opened his mouth in astonishment. " Flung at my head!

She held up her finger. "And if I thought you could ever believe it! "

" Is a girl flung at a man's head when her father carries her thousands of miles away and the man follows her all these miles, and at last-"

" Her eyes were shining. "And you really came to

Greece-on purpose to-to-"

" Confess you knew it all the time! Confess!" The answer was muffled. " Well, sometimes I thought you did, and at other times I thought you- didn't."

In a secluded cove, in which the sea-maids once had played, no doubt, Marjory and Coleman sat in silence. He was below her, and if he looked at her he had to turn his glance obliquely upward. She was staring at the sea with woman's mystic gaze, a gaze which men at once reverence and fear since it seems to look into the deep, simple heart of nature, and men begin to feel that their petty wisdoms are futile to control these strange spirits, as wayward as nature and as pure as nature, wild as the play of waves, sometimes as unalterable as the mountain amid the winds; and to measure them, man must perforce use a mathematical formula.

He wished that she would lay her hand upon his hair. He would be happy then. If she would only, of her own will, touch his hair lightly with her fingers-if she would do it with an unconscious air it would be even better. It would show him that she was thinking of him, even when she did not know she was thinking of him.

Perhaps he dared lay his head softly against her knee.

Did he dare?

As his head touched her knee, she did not move. She seemed to be still gazing at the sea. Presently idly caressing fingers played in his hair near the forehead. He looked up suddenly lifting his arms. He breathed out a cry which was laden with a kind of diffident ferocity. " I haven't kissed you yet-"

MAGGIE

Chapter I

A very little boy stood upon a heap of gravel for the honor of Rum Alley. He was throwing stones at howling urchins from Devil's Row who were circling madly about the heap and pelting at him.

His infantile countenance was livid with fury. His small body was writhing in the delivery of great, crimson oaths.

"Run, Jimmie, run! Dey'll get yehs," screamed a retreating Rum Alley child.

"Naw," responded Jimmie with a valiant roar, "dese micks can't make me run."

Howls of renewed wrath went up from Devil's Row throats. Tattered gamins on the right made a furious assault on the gravel heap. On their small, convulsed faces there shone the grins of true assassins. As they charged, they threw stones and cursed in shrill chorus.

The little champion of Rum Alley stumbled precipitately down the other side. His coat had been torn to shreds in a scuffle, and his hat was gone. He had bruises on twenty parts of his body, and blood was dripping from a cut in his head. His wan features wore a look of a tiny, insane demon.

On the ground, children from Devil's Row closed in on their antagonist. He crooked his left arm defensively about his head and fought with cursing fury. The little boys ran to and fro, dodging, hurling stones and swearing in barbaric trebles.

From a window of an apartment house that upreared its form from amid squat, ignorant stables, there leaned a curious woman. Some laborers, unloading a scow at a dock at the river, paused for a moment and regarded the fight. The engineer of a passive tugboat hung lazily to a railing and watched. Over on the Island, a worm of yellow convicts came from the shadow of a building and crawled slowly along the river's bank.

A stone had smashed into Jimmie's mouth. Blood was bubbling over his chin and down upon his ragged shirt. Tears made furrows on his dirt-stained cheeks. His thin legs had begun to tremble and turn weak, causing his small body to reel. His roaring curses of the first part of the fight had changed to a blasphemous chatter.

In the yells of the whirling mob of Devil's Row children there were notes of joy like songs of triumphant savagery. The little boys seemed to leer gloatingly at the blood upon the other child's face.

Down the avenue came boastfully sauntering a lad of sixteen years, although the chronic sneer of an ideal manhood already sat upon his lips. His hat was tipped with an air of challenge over his eye. Between his teeth, a cigar stump was tilted at the angle of defiance. He walked with a certain swing of the shoulders which appalled the timid. He glanced over into the vacant lot in which the little raving boys from Devil's Row seethed about the shrieking and tearful child from Rum Alley.

"Gee!" he murmured with interest. "A scrap. Gee!"

He strode over to the cursing circle, swinging his shoulders in a manner which denoted that he held victory in his fists. He approached at the back of one of the most deeply engaged of the Devil's Row children.

"Ah, what deh hell," he said, and smote the deeply-engaged one on the back of the head. The little boy fell to the ground and gave a hoarse, tremendous howl. He scrambled to his feet, and perceiving, evidently, the size of his assailant, ran quickly off, shouting alarms. The entire Devil's Row party followed him. They came to a stand a short distance away and yelled taunting oaths at the boy with the chronic sneer. The latter, momentarily, paid no attention to them.

"What deh hell, Jimmie?" he asked of the small champion.

Jimmie wiped his blood-wet features with his sleeve.

"Well, it was dis way, Pete, see! I was goin' teh lick dat Riley kid and dey all pitched on me."

Some Rum Alley children now came forward. The party stood for a moment exchanging vainglorious remarks with Devil's Row. A few stones were thrown at long distances, and words of challenge passed between small warriors. Then the Rum Alley contingent turned slowly in the direction of their home street. They began to give, each to each, distorted versions of the fight. Causes of retreat in particular cases were magnified. Blows dealt in the fight were enlarged to catapultian power, and stones thrown were alleged to have hurtled with infinite accuracy. Valor grew strong again, and the little boys began to swear with great spirit.

"Ah, we blokies kin lick deh hull damn Row," said a child, swaggering.

Little Jimmie was striving to stanch the flow of blood from his cut lips. Scowling, he turned upon the speaker.

"Ah, where deh hell was yeh when I was doin' all deh fightin?" he demanded. "Youse kids makes me tired."

"Ah, go ahn," replied the other argumentatively.

Jimmie replied with heavy contempt. "Ah, youse can't fight, Blue Billie! I kin lick yeh wid one han'."

"Ah, go ahn," replied Billie again.

"Ah," said Jimmie threateningly.

"Ah," said the other in the same tone.

They struck at each other, clinched, and rolled over on the cobble stones.

"Smash 'im, Jimmie, kick deh damn guts out of 'im," yelled Pete, the lad with the chronic sneer, in tones of delight.

The small combatants pounded and kicked, scratched and tore. They began to weep and their curses struggled in their throats with sobs. The other little boys clasped their hands and wriggled their legs in excitement. They formed a bobbing circle about the pair.

A tiny spectator was suddenly agitated.

"Cheese it, Jimmie, cheese it! Here comes yer fader," he yelled.

The circle of little boys instantly parted. They drew away and waited in ecstatic awe for that which was about to happen. The two little boys fighting in the modes of four thousand years ago, did not hear the warning.

Up the avenue there plodded slowly a man with sullen eyes. He was carrying a dinner pail and smoking an apple-wood pipe.

As he neared the spot where the little boys strove, he regarded them listlessly. But suddenly he roared an oath and advanced upon the rolling fighters.

"Here, you Jim, git up, now, while I belt yer life out, you damned disorderly brat."

He began to kick into the chaotic mass on the ground. The boy Billie felt a heavy boot strike his head. He made a furious effort and disentangled himself from Jimmie. He tottered away, damning.

Jimmie arose painfully from the ground and confronting his father, began to curse him. His parent kicked him. "Come home, now," he cried, "an' stop yer jawin', er I'll lam the everlasting head off yehs."

They departed. The man paced placidly along with the apple-wood emblem of serenity between his teeth. The boy followed a dozen feet in the rear. He swore luridly, for he felt that it was degradation for one who aimed to be some vague soldier, or a man of blood with a sort of sublime license, to be taken home by a father.

Chapter II

Eventually they entered into a dark region where, from a careening building, a dozen gruesome doorways gave up loads of babies to the street and the gutter. A wind of early autumn raised yellow dust from cobbles and swirled it against an hundred windows. Long streamers of garments fluttered from fire-escapes. In all unhandy places there were buckets, brooms, rags and bottles. In the street infants played or fought with other infants or sat stupidly in the way of vehicles. Formidable women, with uncombed hair and disordered dress, gossiped while leaning on railings, or screamed in frantic quarrels. Withered persons, in curious postures of submission to something, sat smoking pipes in obscure corners. A thousand odors of cooking food came forth to the street. The building quivered and creaked from the weight of humanity stamping about in its bowels.

A small ragged girl dragged a red, bawling infant along the crowded ways. He was hanging back, baby-like, bracing his wrinkled, bare legs.

The little girl cried out: "Ah, Tommie, come ahn. Dere's Jimmie and fader. Don't be a-pullin' me back."

She jerked the baby's arm impatiently. He fell on his face, roaring. With a second jerk she pulled him to his feet, and they went on. With the obstinacy of his order, he protested against being dragged in a chosen direction. He made heroic endeavors to keep on his legs, denounce his sister and consume a bit of orange peeling which he chewed between the times of his infantile orations.

As the sullen-eyed man, followed by the blood-covered boy, drew near, the little girl burst into reproachful cries. "Ah, Jimmie, youse bin fightin' agin."

The urchin swelled disdainfully.

"Ah, what deh hell, Mag. See?"

The little girl upbraided him, "Youse allus fightin', Jimmie, an' yeh knows it puts mudder out when yehs come home half dead, an' it's like we'll all get a poundin'."

She began to weep. The babe threw back his head and roared at his prospects.

"Ah, what deh hell!" cried Jimmie. "Shut up er I'll smack yer mout'. See?"

As his sister continued her lamentations, he suddenly swore and struck her. The little girl reeled and, recovering herself, burst into tears and quaveringly cursed him. As she slowly retreated her brother advanced dealing her cuffs. The father heard and turned about.

"Stop that, Jim, d'yeh hear? Leave yer sister alone on the street. It's like I can never beat any sense into yer damned wooden head."

The urchin raised his voice in defiance to his parent and continued his attacks. The babe bawled tremendously, protesting with great violence. During his sister's hasty manoeuvres, he was dragged by the arm.

Finally the procession plunged into one of the gruesome doorways. They crawled up dark stairways and along cold, gloomy halls. At last the father pushed open a door and they entered a lighted room in which a large woman was rampant.

She stopped in a career from a seething stove to a pan-covered table. As the father and children filed in she peered at them.

"Eh, what? Been fightin' agin, by Gawd!" She threw herself upon Jimmie. The urchin tried to dart behind the others and in the scuffle the babe, Tommie, was knocked down. He protested with his usual vehemence, because they had bruised his tender shins against a table leg.

The mother's massive shoulders heaved with anger. Grasping the urchin by the neck and shoulder she shook him until he rattled. She dragged him to an unholy sink, and, soaking a rag in water, began to scrub his lacerated face with it. Jimmie screamed in pain and tried to twist his shoulders out of the clasp of the huge arms.

The babe sat on the floor watching the scene, his face in contortions like that of a woman at a tragedy. The father, with a newly-ladened pipe in his mouth, crouched on a backless chair near the stove. Jimmie's cries annoyed him. He turned about and bellowed at his wife:

"Let the damned kid alone for a minute, will yeh, Mary? Yer allus poundin' 'im. When I come nights I can't git no rest 'cause yer allus poundin' a kid. Let up, d'yeh hear? Don't be allus poundin' a kid."

The woman's operations on the urchin instantly increased in violence. At last she tossed him to a corner where he limply lay cursing and weeping.

The wife put her immense hands on her hips and with a chieftain-like stride approached her husband.

"Ho," she said, with a great grunt of contempt. "An' what in the devil are you stickin' your nose for?"

The babe crawled under the table and, turning, peered out cautiously. The ragged girl retreated and the urchin in the corner drew his legs carefully beneath him.

The man puffed his pipe calmly and put his great mudded boots on the back part of the stove.

"Go teh hell," he murmured, tranquilly.

The woman screamed and shook her fists before her husband's eyes. The rough yellow of her face and neck flared suddenly crimson. She began to howl.

He puffed imperturbably at his pipe for a time, but finally arose and began to look out at the window into the darkening chaos of back yards.

"You've been drinkin', Mary," he said. "You'd better let up on the bot', ol' woman, or you'll git done."

"You're a liar. I ain't had a drop," she roared in reply.

They had a lurid altercation, in which they damned each other's souls with frequence.

The babe was staring out from under the table, his small face working in his excitement.

The ragged girl went stealthily over to the corner where the urchin lay.

"Are yehs hurted much, Jimmie?" she whispered timidly.

"Not a damn bit! See?" growled the little boy.

"Will I wash deh blood?"

"Naw!"

"Will I—"

"When I catch dat Riley kid I'll break 'is face! Dat's right! See?"

He turned his face to the wall as if resolved to grimly bide his time.

In the quarrel between husband and wife, the woman was victor. The man grabbed his hat and rushed from the room, apparently determined upon a vengeful drunk. She followed to the door and thundered at him as he made his way down stairs.

She returned and stirred up the room until her children were bobbing about like bubbles.

"Git outa deh way," she persistently bawled, waving feet with their dishevelled shoes near the heads of her children. She shrouded herself, puffing and snorting, in a cloud of steam at the stove, and eventually extracted a frying-pan full of potatoes that hissed.

She flourished it. "Come teh yer suppers, now," she cried with sudden exasperation. "Hurry up, now, er I'll help yeh!"

The children scrambled hastily. With prodigious clatter they arranged themselves at table. The babe sat with his feet dangling high from a precarious infant chair and gorged his small stomach. Jimmie forced, with feverish rapidity, the grease-enveloped pieces between his wounded lips. Maggie, with side glances of fear of interruption, ate like a small pursued tigress.

The mother sat blinking at them. She delivered reproaches, swallowed potatoes and drank from a yellow-brown bottle. After a time her mood changed and she wept as she carried little Tommie into another room and laid him to sleep with his fists doubled in an old quilt of faded red and green grandeur. Then she came and moaned by the stove. She rocked to and fro upon a chair, shedding tears and crooning miserably to the two children about their "poor mother" and "yer fader, damn 'is soul."

The little girl plodded between the table and the chair with a dish-pan on it. She tottered on her small legs beneath burdens of dishes.

Jimmie sat nursing his various wounds. He cast furtive glances at his mother. His practised eye perceived her gradually emerge from a muddled mist of sentiment until her brain burned in drunken heat. He sat breathless.

Maggie broke a plate.

The mother started to her feet as if propelled.

"Good Gawd," she howled. Her eyes glittered on her child with sudden hatred. The fervent red of her face turned almost to purple. The little boy ran to the halls, shrieking like a monk in an earthquake.

He floundered about in darkness until he found the stairs. He stumbled, panic-stricken, to the next floor. An old woman opened a door. A light behind her threw a flare on the urchin's quivering face.

"Eh, Gawd, child, what is it dis time? Is yer fader beatin' yer mudder, or yer mudder beatin' yer fader?"

Chapter III

Jimmie and the old woman listened long in the hall. Above the muffled roar of conversation, the dismal wailings of babies at night, the thumping of feet in unseen corridors and rooms, mingled with the sound of varied hoarse shoutings in the street and the rattling of wheels over cobbles, they heard the screams of the child and the roars of the mother die away to a feeble moaning and a subdued bass muttering.

The old woman was a gnarled and leathery personage who could don, at will, an expression of great virtue. She possessed a small music-box capable of one tune, and a collection of "God bless yehs" pitched in assorted keys of fervency. Each day she took a position upon the stones of Fifth Avenue, where she crooked her legs under her and crouched immovable and hideous, like an idol. She received daily a small sum in pennies. It was contributed, for the most part, by persons who did not make their homes in that vicinity.

Once, when a lady had dropped her purse on the sidewalk, the gnarled woman had grabbed it and smuggled it with great dexterity beneath her cloak. When she was arrested she had cursed the lady into a partial swoon, and with her aged limbs, twisted from rheumatism, had almost kicked the stomach out of a huge policeman whose conduct upon that occasion she referred to when she said: "The police, damn 'em."

"Eh, Jimmie, it's cursed shame," she said. "Go, now, like a dear an' buy me a can, an' if yer mudder raises 'ell all night yehs can sleep here."

Jimmie took a tendered tin-pail and seven pennies and departed. He passed into the side door of a saloon and went to the bar. Straining up on his toes he raised the pail and pennies as high as his arms would let him. He saw two hands thrust down and take them. Directly the same hands let down the filled pail and he left.

In front of the gruesome doorway he met a lurching figure. It was his father, swaying about on uncertain legs.

"Give me deh can. See?" said the man, threateningly.

"Ah, come off! I got dis can fer dat ol' woman an' it 'ud be dirt teh swipe it. See?" cried Jimmie.

The father wrenched the pail from the urchin. He grasped it in both hands and lifted it to his mouth. He glued his lips to the under edge and tilted his head. His hairy throat swelled until it seemed to grow near his chin. There was a tremendous gulping movement and the beer was gone.

The man caught his breath and laughed. He hit his son on the head with the empty pail. As it rolled clanging into the street, Jimmie began to scream and kicked repeatedly at his father's shins.

"Look at deh dirt what yeh done me," he yelled. "Deh ol' woman 'ill be raisin' hell."

He retreated to the middle of the street, but the man did not pursue. He staggered toward the door.

"I'll club hell outa yeh when I ketch yeh," he shouted, and disappeared.

During the evening he had been standing against a bar drinking whiskies and declaring to all comers, confidentially: "My home reg'lar livin' hell! Damndes' place! Reg'lar hell! Why do I come an' drin' whisk' here thish way? 'Cause home reg'lar livin' hell!"

Jimmie waited a long time in the street and then crept warily up through the building. He passed with great caution the door of the gnarled woman, and finally stopped outside his home and listened.

He could hear his mother moving heavily about among the furniture of the room. She was chanting in a mournful voice, occasionally interjecting bursts of volcanic wrath at the father, who, Jimmie judged, had sunk down on the floor or in a corner.

"Why deh blazes don' chere try teh keep Jim from fightin'? I'll break her jaw," she suddenly bellowed.

The man mumbled with drunken indifference. "Ah, wha' deh hell. W'a's odds? Wha' makes kick?"

"Because he tears 'is clothes, yeh damn fool," cried the woman in supreme wrath.

The husband seemed to become aroused. "Go teh hell," he thundered fiercely in reply. There was a crash against the door and something broke into clattering fragments. Jimmie partially suppressed a howl and darted down the stairway. Below he paused and listened. He heard howls and curses, groans and shrieks, confusingly in chorus as if a battle were raging. With all was the crash of splintering furniture. The eyes of the urchin glared in fear that one of them would discover him.

Curious faces appeared in doorways, and whispered comments passed to and fro. "Ol' Johnson's raisin' hell agin."

Jimmie stood until the noises ceased and the other inhabitants of the tenement had all yawned and shut their doors. Then he crawled upstairs with the caution of an invader of a panther den. Sounds of labored breathing came through the broken door-panels. He pushed the door open and entered, quaking.

A glow from the fire threw red hues over the bare floor, the cracked and soiled plastering, and the overturned and broken furniture.

In the middle of the floor lay his mother asleep. In one corner of the room his father's limp body hung across the seat of a chair.

The urchin stole forward. He began to shiver in dread of awakening his parents. His mother's great chest was heaving painfully. Jimmie paused and looked down at her. Her face was inflamed and swollen from drinking. Her yellow brows shaded eyelids that had brown blue. Her tangled hair tossed in waves over her forehead. Her mouth was set in the same lines of vindictive hatred that it had, perhaps, borne during the fight. Her bare, red arms were thrown out above her head in positions of exhaustion, something, mayhap, like those of a sated villain.

The urchin bended over his mother. He was fearful lest she should open her eyes, and the dread within him was so strong, that he could not forbear to stare, but hung as if fascinated over the woman's grim face.

Suddenly her eyes opened. The urchin found himself looking straight into that expression, which, it would seem, had the power to change his blood to salt. He howled piercingly and fell backward.

The woman floundered for a moment, tossed her arms about her head as if in combat, and again began to snore.

Jimmie crawled back in the shadows and waited. A noise in the next room had followed his cry at the discovery that his mother was awake. He grovelled in the gloom, the eyes from out his drawn face riveted upon the intervening door.

He heard it creak, and then the sound of a small voice came to him. "Jimmie! Jimmie! Are yehs dere?" it whispered. The urchin started. The thin, white face of his sister looked at him from the door-way of the other room. She crept to him across the floor.

The father had not moved, but lay in the same death-like sleep. The mother writhed in uneasy slumber, her chest wheezing as if she were in the agonies of strangulation. Out at the window a florid moon was peering over dark roofs, and in the distance the waters of a river glimmered pallidly.

The small frame of the ragged girl was quivering. Her features were haggard from weeping, and her eyes gleamed from fear. She grasped the urchin's arm in her little trembling hands and they huddled in a corner. The eyes of both were drawn, by some force, to stare at the woman's face, for they thought she need only to awake and all fiends would come from below.

They crouched until the ghost-mists of dawn appeared at the window, drawing close to the panes, and looking in at the prostrate, heaving body of the mother.

Chapter IV

The babe, Tommie, died. He went away in a white, insignificant coffin, his small waxen hand clutching a flower that the girl, Maggie, had stolen from an Italian.

She and Jimmie lived.

The inexperienced fibres of the boy's eyes were hardened at an early age. He became a young man of leather. He lived some red years without laboring. During that time his sneer became chronic. He studied human nature in the gutter, and found it no worse than he thought he had reason to believe it. He never conceived a respect for the world, because he had begun with no idols that it had smashed.

He clad his soul in armor by means of happening hilariously in at a mission church where a man composed his sermons of "yous." While they got warm at the stove, he told his hearers just where he calculated they stood with the Lord. Many of the sinners were impatient over the pictured depths of their degradation. They were waiting for soup-tickets.

A reader of words of wind-demons might have been able to see the portions of a dialogue pass to and fro between the exhorter and his hearers.

"You are damned," said the preacher. And the reader of sounds might have seen the reply go forth from the ragged people: "Where's our soup?"

Jimmie and a companion sat in a rear seat and commented upon the things that didn't concern them, with all the freedom of English gentlemen. When they grew thirsty and went out their minds confused the speaker with Christ.

Momentarily, Jimmie was sullen with thoughts of a hopeless altitude where grew fruit. His companion said that if he should ever meet God he would ask for a million dollars and a bottle of beer.

Jimmie's occupation for a long time was to stand on streetcorners and watch the world go by, dreaming blood-red dreams at the passing of pretty women. He menaced mankind at the intersections of streets.

On the corners he was in life and of life. The world was going on and he was there to perceive it.

He maintained a belligerent attitude toward all well-dressed men. To him fine raiment was allied to weakness, and all good coats covered faint hearts. He and his order were kings, to a certain extent, over the men of untarnished clothes, because these latter dreaded, perhaps, to be either killed or laughed at.

Above all things he despised obvious Christians and ciphers with the chrysanthemums of aristocracy in their button-holes. He considered himself above both of these classes. He was afraid of neither the devil nor the leader of society.

When he had a dollar in his pocket his satisfaction with existence was the greatest thing in the world. So, eventually, he felt obliged to work. His father died and his mother's years were divided up into periods of thirty days.

He became a truck driver. He was given the charge of a painstaking pair of horses and a large rattling truck. He invaded the turmoil and tumble of the down-town streets and learned to breathe maledictory defiance at the police who occasionally used to climb up, drag him from his perch and beat him.

In the lower part of the city he daily involved himself in hideous tangles. If he and his team chanced to be in the rear he preserved a demeanor of serenity, crossing his legs and bursting forth into yells when foot passengers took dangerous dives beneath the noses of his champing horses. He smoked his pipe calmly for he knew that his pay was marching on.

If in the front and the key-truck of chaos, he entered terrifically into the quarrel that was raging to and fro among the drivers on their high seats, and sometimes roared oaths and violently got himself arrested.

After a time his sneer grew so that it turned its glare upon all things. He became so sharp that he believed in nothing. To him the police were always actuated by malignant impulses and the rest of the world was composed, for the most part, of despicable creatures who were all trying to take advantage of him and with whom, in defense, he was obliged to quarrel on all possible occasions. He himself occupied a down-trodden position that had a private but distinct element of grandeur in its isolation.

The most complete cases of aggravated idiocy were, to his mind, rampant upon the front platforms of all the street cars. At first his tongue strove with these beings, but he eventually was superior. He became immured like an African cow. In him grew a majestic contempt for those strings of street cars that followed him like intent bugs.

He fell into the habit, when starting on a long journey, of fixing his eye on a high and distant object, commanding his horses to begin, and then going into a sort of a trance of observation. Multitudes of drivers might howl in his rear, and passengers might load him with opprobrium, he would not awaken until some blue policeman turned red and began to frenziedly tear bridles and beat the soft noses of the responsible horses.

When he paused to contemplate the attitude of the police toward himself and his fellows, he believed that they were the only men in the city who had no rights. When driving about, he felt that he was held liable by the police for anything that might occur in the streets, and was the common prey of all energetic officials. In revenge, he resolved never to move out of the way of anything, until formidable circumstances, or a much larger man than himself forced him to it.

Foot-passengers were mere pestering flies with an insane disregard for their legs and his convenience. He could not conceive their maniacal desires to cross the streets. Their madness smote him with eternal amazement. He was continually storming at them from his throne. He sat aloft and denounced their frantic leaps, plunges, dives and straddles.

When they would thrust at, or parry, the noses of his champing horses, making them swing their heads and move their feet, disturbing a solid dreamy repose, he swore at the men as fools, for he himself could perceive that Providence had caused it clearly to be written, that he and his team had the unalienable right to stand in the proper path of the sun chariot, and if they so minded, obstruct its mission or take a wheel off.

And, perhaps, if the god-driver had an ungovernable desire to step down, put up his flame-colored fists and manfully dispute the right of way, he would have probably been immediately opposed by a scowling mortal with two sets of very hard knuckles.

It is possible, perhaps, that this young man would have derided, in an axle-wide alley, the approach of a flying ferry boat. Yet he achieved a respect for a fire engine. As one charged toward his truck, he would drive fearfully upon a sidewalk, threatening untold people with annihilation. When an engine would strike a mass of blocked trucks, splitting it into fragments, as a blow annihilates a cake of ice, Jimmie's team could usually be observed high and safe, with whole wheels, on the sidewalk. The fearful coming of the engine could break up the most intricate muddle of heavy vehicles at which the police had been swearing for the half of an hour.

A fire engine was enshrined in his heart as an appalling thing that he loved with a distant dog-like devotion. They had been known to overturn street-cars. Those leaping horses, striking sparks from the cobbles in their forward lunge, were creatures to be ineffably admired. The clang of the gong pierced his breast like a noise of remembered war.

When Jimmie was a little boy, he began to be arrested. Before he reached a great age, he had a fair record.

He developed too great a tendency to climb down from his truck and fight with other drivers. He had been in quite a number of miscellaneous fights, and in some general barroom rows that had become known to the police. Once he had been arrested for assaulting a Chinaman. Two women in different parts of the city, and entirely unknown to each other, caused him considerable annoyance by breaking forth, simultaneously, at fateful intervals, into wailings about marriage and support and infants.

Nevertheless, he had, on a certain star-lit evening, said wonderingly and quite reverently: "Deh moon looks like hell, don't it?"

Chapter V

The girl, Maggie, blossomed in a mud puddle. She grew to be a most rare and wonderful production of a tenement district, a pretty girl.

None of the dirt of Rum Alley seemed to be in her veins. The philosophers up-stairs, down-stairs and on the same floor, puzzled over it.

When a child, playing and fighting with gamins in the street, dirt disguised her. Attired in tatters and grime, she went unseen.

There came a time, however, when the young men of the vicinity said: "Dat Johnson goil is a puty good looker." About this period her brother remarked to her: "Mag, I'll tell yeh dis! See? Yeh've edder got teh go teh hell or go teh work!" Whereupon she went to work, having the feminine aversion of going to hell.

By a chance, she got a position in an establishment where they made collars and cuffs. She received a stool and a machine in a room where sat twenty girls of various shades of yellow discontent. She perched on the stool and treadled at her machine all day, turning out collars, the name of whose brand could be noted for its irrelevancy to anything in connection with collars. At night she returned home to her mother.

Jimmie grew large enough to take the vague position of head of the family. As incumbent of that office, he stumbled up-stairs late at night, as his father had done before him. He reeled about the room, swearing at his relations, or went to sleep on the floor.

The mother had gradually arisen to that degree of fame that she could bandy words with her acquaintances among the police-justices. Court-officials called her by her first name. When she appeared they pursued a course which had been theirs for months. They invariably grinned and cried out: "Hello, Mary, you here again?" Her grey head wagged in many a court. She always besieged the bench with voluble excuses, explanations, apologies and prayers. Her flaming face and rolling eyes were a sort of familiar sight on the island. She measured time by means of sprees, and was eternally swollen and dishevelled.

One day the young man, Pete, who as a lad had smitten the Devil's Row urchin in the back of the head and put to flight the antagonists of his friend, Jimmie, strutted upon the scene. He met Jimmie one day on the street, promised to take him to a boxing match in Williamsburg, and called for him in the evening.

Maggie observed Pete.

He sat on a table in the Johnson home and dangled his checked legs with an enticing nonchalance. His hair was curled down over his forehead in an oiled bang. His rather pugged nose seemed to revolt from contact with a bristling moustache of short, wire-like hairs. His blue double-breasted coat, edged with black braid, buttoned close to a red puff tie, and his patent-leather shoes looked like murder-fitted weapons.

His mannerisms stamped him as a man who had a correct sense of his personal superiority. There was valor and contempt for circumstances in the glance of his eye. He waved his hands like a man of the world, who dismisses religion and philosophy, and says "Fudge." He had certainly seen everything and with each curl of his lip, he declared that it amounted to nothing. Maggie thought he must be a very elegant and graceful bartender.

He was telling tales to Jimmie.

Maggie watched him furtively, with half-closed eyes, lit with a vague interest.

"Hully gee! Dey makes me tired," he said. "Mos' e'ry day some farmer comes in an' tries teh run deh shop. See? But dey gits t'rowed right out! I jolt dem right out in deh street before dey knows where dey is! See?"

"Sure," said Jimmie.

"Dere was a mug come in deh place deh odder day wid an idear he wus goin' teh own deh place! Hully gee, he wus goin' teh own deh place! I see he had a still on an' I didn' wanna giv 'im no stuff, so I says: 'Git deh hell outa here an' don' make no trouble,' I says like dat! See? 'Git deh hell outa here an' don' make no trouble'; like dat. 'Git deh hell outa here,' I says. See?"

Jimmie nodded understandingly. Over his features played an eager desire to state the amount of his valor in a similar crisis, but the narrator proceeded.

"Well, deh blokie he says: 'T'hell wid it! I ain' lookin' for no scrap,' he says (See?), 'but' he says, 'I'm 'spectable cit'zen an' I wanna drink an' purtydamnsoon, too.' See? 'Deh hell,' I says. Like dat! 'Deh hell,' I says. See? 'Don' make no trouble,' I says. Like dat. 'Don' make no trouble.' See? Den deh mug he squared off an' said he was fine as silk wid his dukes (See?) an' he wanned a drink damnquick. Dat's what he said. See?"

"Sure," repeated Jimmie.

Pete continued. "Say, I jes' jumped deh bar an' deh way I plunked dat blokie was great. See? Dat's right! In deh jaw! See? Hully gee, he t'rowed a spittoon true deh front windee. Say, I taut I'd drop dead. But deh boss, he comes in after an' he says, 'Pete, yehs done jes' right! Yeh've gota keep order an' it's all right.' See? 'It's all right,' he says. Dat's what he said."

The two held a technical discussion.

"Dat bloke was a dandy," said Pete, in conclusion, "but he hadn' oughta made no trouble. Dat's what I says teh dem: 'Don' come in here an' make no trouble,' I says, like dat. 'Don' make no trouble.' See?"

As Jimmie and his friend exchanged tales descriptive of their prowess, Maggie leaned back in the shadow. Her eyes dwelt wonderingly and rather wistfully upon Pete's face. The broken furniture, grimey walls, and general disorder and dirt of her home of a sudden appeared before her and began to take a potential aspect. Pete's aristocratic person looked as if it might soil. She looked keenly at him, occasionally, wondering if he was feeling contempt. But Pete seemed to be enveloped in reminiscence.

"Hully gee," said he, "dose mugs can't phase me. Dey knows I kin wipe up deh street wid any t'ree of dem."

When he said, "Ah, what deh hell," his voice was burdened with disdain for the inevitable and contempt for anything that fate might compel him to endure.

Maggie perceived that here was the beau ideal of a man. Her dim thoughts were often searching for far away lands where, as God says, the little hills sing together in the morning. Under the trees of her dream-gardens there had always walked a lover.

Chapter VI

Pete took note of Maggie.

"Say, Mag, I'm stuck on yer shape. It's outa sight," he said, parenthetically, with an affable grin.

As he became aware that she was listening closely, he grew still more eloquent in his descriptions of various happenings in his career. It appeared that he was invincible in fights.

"Why," he said, referring to a man with whom he had had a misunderstanding, "dat mug scrapped like a damn dago. Dat's right. He was dead easy. See? He tau't he was a scrapper. But he foun' out diff'ent! Hully gee."

He walked to and fro in the small room, which seemed then to grow even smaller and unfit to hold his dignity, the attribute of a supreme warrior. That swing of the shoulders that had frozen the timid when he was but a lad had increased with his growth and education at the ratio of ten to one. It, combined with the sneer upon his mouth, told mankind that there was nothing in space which could appall him. Maggie marvelled at him and surrounded him with greatness. She vaguely tried to calculate the altitude of the pinnacle from which he must have looked down upon her.

"I met a chump deh odder day way up in deh city," he said. "I was goin' teh see a frien' of mine. When I was a-crossin' deh street deh chump runned plump inteh me, an' den he turns aroun' an' says, 'Yer insolen' ruffin,' he says, like dat. 'Oh, gee,' I says, 'oh, gee, go teh hell and git off deh eart',' I says, like dat. See? 'Go teh hell an' git off deh eart',' like dat. Den deh blokie he got wild. He says I was a contempt'ble scoun'el, er somet'ing like dat, an' he says I was doom' teh everlastin' pe'dition an' all like dat. 'Gee,' I says, 'gee! Deh hell I am,' I says. 'Deh hell I am,' like dat. An' den I slugged 'im. See?"

With Jimmie in his company, Pete departed in a sort of a blaze of glory from the Johnson home. Maggie, leaning from the window, watched him as he walked down the street.

Here was a formidable man who disdained the strength of a world full of fists. Here was one who had contempt for brass-clothed power; one whose knuckles could defiantly ring against the granite of law. He was a knight.

The two men went from under the glimmering street-lamp and passed into shadows.

Turning, Maggie contemplated the dark, dust-stained walls, and the scant and crude furniture of her home. A clock, in a splintered and battered oblong box of varnished wood, she suddenly regarded as an abomination. She noted that it ticked raspingly. The almost vanished flowers in the carpet-pattern, she conceived to be newly hideous. Some faint attempts she had made with blue ribbon, to freshen the appearance of a dingy curtain, she now saw to be piteous.

She wondered what Pete dined on.

She reflected upon the collar and cuff factory. It began to appear to her mind as a dreary place of endless grinding. Pete's elegant occupation brought him, no doubt, into contact with people who had money and manners. It was probable that he had a large acquaintance of pretty girls. He must have great sums of money to spend.

To her the earth was composed of hardships and insults. She felt instant admiration for a man who openly defied it. She thought that if the grim angel of death should clutch his heart, Pete would shrug his shoulders and say: "Oh, ev'ryt'ing goes."

She anticipated that he would come again shortly. She spent some of her week's pay in the purchase of flowered cretonne for a lambrequin. She made it with infinite care and hung it to the slightly-careening mantel, over the stove, in the kitchen. She studied it with painful anxiety from different points in the room. She wanted it to look well on Sunday night when, perhaps, Jimmie's friend would come. On Sunday night, however, Pete did not appear.

Afterward the girl looked at it with a sense of humiliation. She was now convinced that Pete was superior to admiration for lambrequins.

A few evenings later Pete entered with fascinating innovations in his apparel. As she had seen him twice and he had different suits on each time, Maggie had a dim impression that his wardrobe was prodigiously extensive.

"Say, Mag," he said, "put on yer bes' duds Friday night an' I'll take yehs teh deh show. See?"

He spent a few moments in flourishing his clothes and then vanished, without having glanced at the lambrequin.

Over the eternal collars and cuffs in the factory Maggie spent the most of three days in making imaginary sketches of Pete and his daily environment. She imagined some half dozen women in love with him and thought he must lean dangerously toward an indefinite one, whom she pictured with great charms of person, but with an altogether contemptible disposition.

She thought he must live in a blare of pleasure. He had friends, and people who were afraid of him.

She saw the golden glitter of the place where Pete was to take her. An entertainment of many hues and many melodies where she was afraid she might appear small and mouse-colored.

Her mother drank whiskey all Friday morning. With lurid face and tossing hair she cursed and destroyed furniture all Friday afternoon. When Maggie came home at half-past six her mother lay asleep amidst the wreck of chairs and a table. Fragments of various household utensils were scattered about the floor. She had vented some phase of drunken fury upon the lambrequin. It lay in a bedraggled heap in the corner.

"Hah," she snorted, sitting up suddenly, "where deh hell yeh been? Why deh hell don' yeh come home earlier? Been loafin' 'round deh streets. Yer gettin' teh be a reg'lar devil."

When Pete arrived Maggie, in a worn black dress, was waiting for him in the midst of a floor strewn with wreckage. The curtain at the window had been pulled by a heavy hand and hung by one tack, dangling to and fro in the draft through the cracks at the sash. The knots of blue ribbons appeared like violated flowers. The fire in the stove had gone out. The displaced lids and open doors showed heaps of sullen grey ashes. The remnants of a meal, ghastly, like dead flesh, lay in a corner. Maggie's red mother, stretched on the floor, blasphemed and gave her daughter a bad name.

Chapter VII

An orchestra of yellow silk women and bald-headed men on an elevated stage near the centre of a great green-hued hall, played a popular waltz. The place was crowded with people grouped about little tables. A battalion of waiters slid among the throng, carrying trays of beer glasses and making change from the inexhaustible vaults of their trousers pockets. Little boys, in the costumes of French chefs, paraded up and down the irregular aisles vending fancy cakes. There was a low rumble of conversation and a subdued clinking of glasses. Clouds of tobacco smoke rolled and wavered high in air about the dull gilt of the chandeliers.

The vast crowd had an air throughout of having just quitted labor. Men with calloused hands and attired in garments that showed the wear of an endless trudge for a living, smoked their pipes contentedly and spent five, ten, or perhaps fifteen cents for beer. There was a mere sprinkling of kid-gloved men who smoked cigars purchased elsewhere. The great body of the crowd was composed of people who showed that all day they strove with their hands. Quiet Germans, with maybe their wives and two or three children, sat listening to the music, with the expressions of happy cows. An occasional party of sailors from a war-ship, their faces pictures of sturdy health, spent the earlier hours of the evening at the small round tables. Very infrequent tipsy men, swollen with the value of their opinions, engaged their companions in earnest and confidential conversation. In the balcony, and here and there below, shone the impassive faces of women. The nationalities of the Bowery beamed upon the stage from all directions.

Pete aggressively walked up a side aisle and took seats with Maggie at a table beneath the balcony.

"Two beehs!"

Leaning back he regarded with eyes of superiority the scene before them. This attitude affected Maggie strongly. A man who could regard such a sight with indifference must be accustomed to very great things.

It was obvious that Pete had been to this place many times before, and was very familiar with it. A knowledge of this fact made Maggie feel little and new.

He was extremely gracious and attentive. He displayed the consideration of a cultured gentleman who knew what was due.

“Say, what deh hell? Bring deh lady a big glass! What deh hell use is dat pony?”

“Don’t be fresh, now,” said the waiter, with some warmth, as he departed.

“Ah, git off deh eart’,” said Pete, after the other’s retreating form.

Maggie perceived that Pete brought forth all his elegance and all his knowledge of high-class customs for her benefit. Her heart warmed as she reflected upon his condescension.

The orchestra of yellow silk women and bald-headed men gave vent to a few bars of anticipatory music and a girl, in a pink dress with short skirts, galloped upon the stage. She smiled upon the throng as if in acknowledgment of a warm welcome, and began to walk to and fro, making profuse gesticulations and singing, in brazen soprano tones, a song, the words of which were inaudible. When she broke into the swift rattling measures of a chorus some half-tipsy men near the stage joined in the rollicking refrain and glasses were pounded rhythmically upon the tables. People leaned forward to watch her and to try to catch the words of the song. When she vanished there were long rollings of applause.

Obedient to more anticipatory bars, she reappeared amidst the half-suppressed cheering of the tipsy men. The orchestra plunged into dance music and the laces of the dancer fluttered and flew in the glare of gas jets. She divulged the fact that she was attired in some half dozen skirts. It was patent that any one of them would have proved adequate for the purpose for which skirts are intended. An occasional man bent forward, intent upon the pink stockings. Maggie wondered at the splendor of the costume and lost herself in calculations of the cost of the silks and laces.

The dancer's smile of stereotyped enthusiasm was turned for ten minutes upon the faces of her audience. In the finale she fell into some of those grotesque attitudes which were at the time popular among the dancers in the theatres up-town, giving to the Bowery public the phantasies of the aristocratic theatre-going public, at reduced rates.

"Say, Pete," said Maggie, leaning forward, "dis is great."

"Sure," said Pete, with proper complacence.

A ventriloquist followed the dancer. He held two fantastic dolls on his knees. He made them sing mournful ditties and say funny things about geography and Ireland.

"Do dose little men talk?" asked Maggie.

"Naw," said Pete, "it's some damn fake. See?"

Two girls, on the bills as sisters, came forth and sang a duet that is heard occasionally at concerts given under church auspices. They supplemented it with a dance which of course can never be seen at concerts given under church auspices.

After the duettists had retired, a woman of debatable age sang a negro melody. The chorus necessitated some grotesque waddlings supposed to be an imitation of a plantation darkey, under the influence, probably, of music and the moon. The audience was just enthusiastic enough over it to have her return and sing a sorrowful lay, whose lines told of a mother's love and a sweetheart who waited and a young man who was lost at sea under the most harrowing circumstances. From the faces of a score or so in the crowd, the self-contained look faded. Many heads were bent forward with eagerness and sympathy. As the last distressing sentiment of the piece was brought forth, it was greeted by that kind of applause which rings as sincere.

As a final effort, the singer rendered some verses which described a vision of Britain being annihilated by America, and Ireland bursting her bonds. A carefully prepared crisis was reached in the last line of the last verse, where the singer threw out her arms and cried, "The star-spangled banner." Instantly a great cheer swelled from the throats of the assemblage of the masses. There was a heavy rumble of booted feet thumping the floor. Eyes gleamed with sudden fire, and calloused hands waved frantically in the air.

After a few moments' rest, the orchestra played crashingly, and a small fat man burst out upon the stage. He began to roar a song and stamp back and forth before the foot-lights, wildly waving a glossy silk hat and throwing leers, or smiles, broadcast. He made his face into fantastic grimaces until he looked like a pictured devil on a Japanese kite. The crowd laughed gleefully. His short, fat legs were never still a moment. He shouted and roared and bobbed his shock of red wig until the audience broke out in excited applause.

Pete did not pay much attention to the progress of events upon the stage. He was drinking beer and watching Maggie.

Her cheeks were blushing with excitement and her eyes were glistening. She drew deep breaths of pleasure. No thoughts of the atmosphere of the collar and cuff factory came to her.

When the orchestra crashed finally, they jostled their way to the sidewalk with the crowd. Pete took Maggie's arm and pushed a way for her, offering to fight with a man or two.

They reached Maggie's home at a late hour and stood for a moment in front of the gruesome doorway.

"Say, Mag," said Pete, "give us a kiss for takin' yeh teh deh show, will yer?"

Maggie laughed, as if startled, and drew away from him.

"Naw, Pete," she said, "dat wasn't in it."

"Ah, what deh hell?" urged Pete.

The girl retreated nervously.

"Ah, what deh hell?" repeated he.

Maggie darted into the hall, and up the stairs. She turned and smiled at him, then disappeared.

Pete walked slowly down the street. He had something of an astonished expression upon his features. He paused under a lamp-post and breathed a low breath of surprise.

"Gawd," he said, "I wonner if I've been played fer a duffer."

Chapter VIII

As thoughts of Pete came to Maggie's mind, she began to have an intense dislike for all of her dresses.

"What deh hell ails yeh? What makes yeh be allus fixin' and fussin'? Good Gawd," her mother would frequently roar at her.

She began to note, with more interest, the well-dressed women she met on the avenues. She envied elegance and soft palms. She craved those adornments of person which she saw every day on the street, conceiving them to be allies of vast importance to women.

Studying faces, she thought many of the women and girls she chanced to meet, smiled with serenity as though forever cherished and watched over by those they loved.

The air in the collar and cuff establishment strangled her. She knew she was gradually and surely shrivelling in the hot, stuffy room. The begrimed windows rattled incessantly from the passing of elevated trains. The place was filled with a whirl of noises and odors.

She wondered as she regarded some of the grizzled women in the room, mere mechanical contrivances sewing seams and grinding out, with heads bended over their work, tales of imagined or real girlhood happiness, past drunks, the baby at home, and unpaid wages. She speculated how long her youth would endure. She began to see the bloom upon her cheeks as valuable.

She imagined herself, in an exasperating future, as a scrawny woman with an eternal grievance. Too, she thought Pete to be a very fastidious person concerning the appearance of women.

She felt she would love to see somebody entangle their fingers in the oily beard of the fat foreigner who owned the establishment. He was a detestable creature. He wore white socks with low shoes.

He sat all day delivering orations, in the depths of a cushioned chair. His pocketbook deprived them of the power to retort.

"What een hell do you sink I pie fife dolla a week for? Play? No, py damn!" Maggie was anxious for a friend to whom she could talk about Pete. She would have liked to discuss his admirable mannerisms with a reliable mutual friend. At home, she found her mother often drunk and always raving. It seems that the world had treated this woman very badly, and she took a deep revenge upon such portions of it as came within her reach. She broke furniture as if she were at last getting her rights. She swelled with virtuous indignation as she carried the lighter articles of household use, one by one under the shadows of the three gilt balls, where Hebrews chained them with chains of interest.

Jimmie came when he was obliged to by circumstances over which he had no control. His well-trained legs brought him staggering home and put him to bed some nights when he would rather have gone elsewhere.

Swaggering Pete loomed like a golden sun to Maggie. He took her to a dime museum where rows of meek freaks astonished her. She contemplated their deformities with awe and thought them a sort of chosen tribe.

"What een hell do you sink I pie fife dolla a week for? Play? No, py damn!" Maggie was anxious for a friend to whom she could talk about Pete. She would have liked to discuss his admirable mannerisms with a reliable mutual friend. At home, she found her mother often drunk and always raving. It seems that the world had treated this woman very badly, and she took a deep revenge upon such portions of it as came within her reach. She broke furniture as if she were at last getting her rights. She swelled with virtuous indignation as she carried the lighter articles of household use, one by one under the shadows of the three gilt balls, where Hebrews chained them with chains of interest.

Jimmie came when he was obliged to by circumstances over which he had no control. His well-trained legs brought him staggering home and put him to bed some nights when he would rather have gone elsewhere.

Swaggering Pete loomed like a golden sun to Maggie. He took her to a dime museum where rows of meek freaks astonished her. She contemplated their deformities with awe and thought them a sort of chosen tribe.

Pete, raking his brains for amusement, discovered the Central Park Menagerie and the Museum of Arts. Sunday afternoons would sometimes find them at these places. Pete did not appear to be particularly interested in what he saw. He stood around looking heavy, while Maggie giggled in glee.

Once at the Menagerie he went into a trance of admiration before the spectacle of a very small monkey threatening to thrash a cageful because one of them had pulled his tail and he had not wheeled about quickly enough to discover who did it. Ever after Pete knew that monkey by sight and winked at him, trying to induce hime to fight with other and larger monkeys. At the Museum, Maggie said, "Dis is outa sight."

"Oh hell," said Pete, "wait 'till next summer an' I'll take yehs to a picnic."

While the girl wandered in the vaulted rooms, Pete occupied himself in returning stony stare for stony stare, the appalling scrutiny of the watch-dogs of the treasures. Occasionally he would remark in loud tones: "Dat jay has got glass eyes," and sentences of the sort.

When he tired of this amusement he would go to the mummies and moralize over them.

Usually he submitted with silent dignity to all which he had to go through, but, at times, he was goaded into comment.

"What deh hell," he demanded once. "Look at all dese little jugs! Hundred jugs in a row! Ten rows in a case an' 'bout a t'ousand cases! What deh blazes use is dem?"

Evenings during the week he took her to see plays in which the brain-clutching heroine was rescued from the palatial home of her guardian, who is cruelly after her bonds, by the hero with the beautiful sentiments. The latter spent most of his time out at soak in pale-green snow storms, busy with a nickel-plated revolver, rescuing aged strangers from villains.

Maggie lost herself in sympathy with the wanderers swooning in snow storms beneath happy-hued church windows. And a choir within singing "Joy to the World." To Maggie and the rest of the audience this was transcendental realism. Joy always within, and they, like the actor, inevitably without. Viewing it, they hugged themselves in ecstatic pity of their imagined or real condition.

The girl thought the arrogance and granite-heartedness of the magnate of the play was very accurately drawn. She echoed the maledictions that the occupants of the gallery showered on this individual when his lines compelled him to expose his extreme selfishness.

Shady persons in the audience revolted from the pictured villainy of the drama. With untiring zeal they hissed vice and applauded virtue. Unmistakably bad men evinced an apparently sincere admiration for virtue.

The loud gallery was overwhelmingly with the unfortunate and the oppressed. They encouraged the struggling hero with cries, and jeered the villain, hooting and calling attention to his whiskers. When anybody died in the pale-green snow storms, the gallery mourned. They sought out the painted misery and hugged it as akin.

In the hero's erratic march from poverty in the first act, to wealth and triumph in the final one, in which he forgives all the enemies that he has left, he was assisted by the gallery, which applauded his generous and noble sentiments and confounded the speeches of his opponents by making irrelevant but very sharp remarks. Those actors who were cursed with villainy parts were confronted at every turn by the gallery. If one of them rendered lines containing the most subtile distinctions between right and wrong, the gallery was immediately aware if the actor meant wickedness, and denounced him accordingly.

The last act was a triumph for the hero, poor and of the masses, the representative of the audience, over the villain and the rich man, his pockets stuffed with bonds, his heart packed with tyrannical purposes, imperturbable amid suffering.

Maggie always departed with raised spirits from the showing places of the melodrama. She rejoiced at the way in which the poor and virtuous eventually surmounted the wealthy and wicked. The theatre made her think. She wondered if the culture and refinement she had seen imitated, perhaps grotesquely, by the heroine on the stage, could be acquired by a girl who lived in a tenement house and worked in a shirt factory.

Chapter IX

A group of urchins were intent upon the side door of a saloon. Expectancy gleamed from their eyes. They were twisting their fingers in excitement.

"Here she comes," yelled one of them suddenly.

The group of urchins burst instantly asunder and its individual fragments were spread in a wide, respectable half circle about the point of interest. The saloon door opened with a crash, and the figure of a woman appeared upon the threshold. Her grey hair fell in knotted masses about her shoulders. Her face was crimsoned and wet with perspiration. Her eyes had a rolling glare.

"Not a damn cent more of me money will yehs ever get, not a damn cent. I spent me money here fer t'ree years an' now yehs tells me yeh'll sell me no more stuff! T'hell wid yeh, Johnnie Murckre! 'Disturbance'? Disturbance be damned! T'hell wid yeh, Johnnie—"

The door received a kick of exasperation from within and the woman lurched heavily out on the sidewalk.

The gamins in the half-circle became violently agitated. They began to dance about and hoot and yell and jeer. Wide dirty grins spread over each face.

The woman made a furious dash at a particularly outrageous cluster of little boys. They laughed delightedly and scampered off a short distance, calling out over their shoulders to her. She stood tottering on the curb-stone and thundered at them.

"Yeh devil's kids," she howled, shaking red fists. The little boys whooped in glee. As she started up the street they fell in behind and marched uproariously. Occasionally she wheeled about and made charges on them. They ran nimbly out of reach and taunted her.

In the frame of a gruesome doorway she stood for a moment cursing them. Her hair straggled, giving her crimson features a look of insanity. Her great fists quivered as she shook them madly in the air.

The urchins made terrific noises until she turned and disappeared. Then they filed quietly in the way they had come.

The woman floundered about in the lower hall of the tenement house and finally stumbled up the stairs. On an upper hall a door was opened and a collection of heads peered curiously out, watching her. With a wrathful snort the woman confronted the door, but it was slammed hastily in her face and the key was turned.

She stood for a few minutes, delivering a frenzied challenge at the panels.

"Come out in deh hall, Mary Murphy, damn yeh, if yehs want a row. Come ahn, yeh overgrown terrier, come ahn."

She began to kick the door with her great feet. She shrilly defied the universe to appear and do battle. Her cursing trebles brought heads from all doors save the one she threatened. Her eyes glared in every direction. The air was full of her tossing fists.

"Come ahn, deh hull damn gang of yehs, come ahn," she roared at the spectators. An oath or two, cat-calls, jeers and bits of facetious advice were given in reply. Missiles clattered about her feet.

"What deh hell's deh matter wid yeh?" said a voice in the gathered gloom, and Jimmie came forward. He carried a tin dinner-pail in his hand and under his arm a brown truckman's apron done in a bundle. "What deh hell's wrong?" he demanded.

"Come out, all of yehs, come out," his mother was howling. "Come ahn an' I'll stamp her damn brains under me feet."

"Shet yer face, an' come home, yeh damned old fool," roared Jimmie at her. She strided up to him and twirled her fingers in his face. Her eyes were darting flames of unreasoning rage and her frame trembled with eagerness for a fight.

"T'hell wid yehs! An' who deh hell are yehs? I ain't givin' a snap of me fingers fer yehs," she bawled at him. She turned her huge back in tremendous disdain and climbed the stairs to the next floor.

Jimmie followed, cursing blackly. At the top of the flight he seized his mother's arm and started to drag her toward the door of their room.

"Come home, damn yeh," he gritted between his teeth.

"Take yer hands off me! Take yer hands off me," shrieked his mother.

She raised her arm and whirled her great fist at her son's face. Jimmie dodged his head and the blow struck him in the back of the neck. "Damn yeh," gritted he again. He threw out his left hand and writhed his fingers about her middle arm. The mother and the son began to sway and struggle like gladiators.

"Whoop!" said the Rum Alley tenement house. The hall filled with interested spectators.

"Hi, ol' lady, dat was a dandy!"

"T'ree to one on deh red!"

"Ah, stop yer damn scrappin'!"

The door of the Johnson home opened and Maggie looked out. Jimmie made a supreme cursing effort and hurled his mother into the room. He quickly followed and closed the door. The Rum Alley tenement swore disappointedly and retired.

The mother slowly gathered herself up from the floor. Her eyes glittered menacingly upon her children.

"Here, now," said Jimmie, "we've had enough of dis. Sit down, an' don' make no trouble."

He grasped her arm, and twisting it, forced her into a creaking chair.

"Keep yer hands off me," roared his mother again.

"Damn yer ol' hide," yelled Jimmie, madly. Maggie shrieked and ran into the other room. To her there came the sound of a storm of crashes and curses. There was a great final thump and Jimmie's voice cried: "Dere, damn yeh, stay still." Maggie opened the door now, and went warily out. "Oh, Jimmie."

He was leaning against the wall and swearing. Blood stood upon bruises on his knotty fore-arms where they had scraped against the floor or the walls in the scuffle. The mother lay screeching on the floor, the tears running down her furrowed face.

Maggie, standing in the middle of the room, gazed about her. The usual upheaval of the tables and chairs had taken place. Crockery was strewn broadcast in fragments. The stove had been disturbed on its legs, and now leaned idiotically to one side. A pail had been upset and water spread in all directions.

The door opened and Pete appeared. He shrugged his shoulders. "Oh, Gawd," he observed.

He walked over to Maggie and whispered in her ear. "Ah, what deh hell, Mag? Come ahn and we'll have a hell of a time."

The mother in the corner upreared her head and shook her tangled locks.

"Teh hell wid him and you," she said, glowering at her daughter in the gloom. Her eyes seemed to burn balefully. "Yeh've gone teh deh devil, Mag Johnson, yehs knows yehs have gone teh deh devil. Yer a disgrace teh yer people, damn yeh. An' now, git out an' go ahn wid dat doe-faced jude of yours. Go teh hell wid him, damn yeh, an' a good riddance. Go teh hell an' see how yeh likes it."

Maggie gazed long at her mother.

"Go teh hell now, an' see how yeh likes it. Git out. I won't have sech as yehs in me house! Get out, d'yeh hear! Damn yeh, git out!"

The girl began to tremble.

At this instant Pete came forward. "Oh, what deh hell, Mag, see," whispered he softly in her ear. "Dis all blows over. See? Deh ol' woman 'ill be all right in deh mornin'. Come ahn out wid me! We'll have a hell of a time."

The woman on the floor cursed. Jimmie was intent upon his bruised fore-arms. The girl cast a glance about the room filled with a chaotic mass of debris, and at the red, writhing body of her mother.

"Go teh hell an' good riddance."

She went.

Chapter X

Jimmie had an idea it wasn't common courtesy for a friend to come to one's home and ruin one's sister. But he was not sure how much Pete knew about the rules of politeness.

The following night he returned home from work at rather a late hour in the evening. In passing through the halls he came upon the gnarled and leathery old woman who possessed the music box. She was grinning in the dim light that drifted through dust-stained panes. She beckoned to him with a smudged forefinger.

"Ah, Jimmie, what do yehs t'ink I got onto las' night. It was deh funnies' t'ing I ever saw," she cried, coming close to him and leering. She was trembling with eagerness to tell her tale. "I was by me door las' night when yer sister and her jude feller came in late, oh, very late. An' she, the dear, she was a-cryin' as if her heart would break, she was. It was deh funnies' t'ing I ever saw. An' right out here by me door she asked him did he love her, did he. An' she was a-cryin' as if her heart would break, poor t'ing. An' him, I could see by deh way what he said it dat she had been askin' orften, he says: 'Oh, hell, yes,' he says, says he, 'Oh, hell, yes.'"

Storm-clouds swept over Jimmie's face, but he turned from the leathery old woman and plodded on up-stairs.

"Oh, hell, yes," called she after him. She laughed a laugh that was like a prophetic croak. "'Oh, hell, yes,' he says, says he, 'Oh, hell, yes.'"

There was no one in at home. The rooms showed that attempts had been made at tidying them. Parts of the wreckage of the day before had been repaired by an unskilful hand. A chair or two and the table, stood uncertainly upon legs. The floor had been newly swept. Too, the blue ribbons had been restored to the curtains, and the lambrequin, with its immense sheaves of yellow wheat and red roses of equal size, had been returned, in a worn and sorry state, to its position at the mantel. Maggie's jacket and hat were gone from the nail behind the door.

Jimmie walked to the window and began to look through the blurred glass. It occurred to him to vaguely wonder, for an instant, if some of the women of his acquaintance had brothers.

Suddenly, however, he began to swear.

"But he was me frien'! I brought 'im here! Dat's deh hell of it!"

He fumed about the room, his anger gradually rising to the furious pitch.

"I'll kill deh jay! Dat's what I'll do! I'll kill deh jay!"

He clutched his hat and sprang toward the door. But it opened and his mother's great form blocked the passage.

"What deh hell's deh matter wid yeh?" exclaimed she, coming into the rooms.

Jimmie gave vent to a sardonic curse and then laughed heavily.

"Well, Maggie's gone teh deh devil! Dat's what! See?"

"Eh?" said his mother.

"Maggie's gone teh deh devil! Are yehs deaf?" roared Jimmie, impatiently.

"Deh hell she has," murmured the mother, astounded.

Jimmie grunted, and then began to stare out at the window. His mother sat down in a chair, but a moment later sprang erect and delivered a maddened whirl of oaths. Her son turned to look at her as she reeled and swayed in the middle of the room, her fierce face convulsed with passion, her blotched arms raised high in imprecation.

"May Gawd curse her forever," she shrieked. "May she eat nothin' but stones and deh dirt in deh street. May she sleep in deh gutter an' never see deh sun shine agin. Deh damn—"

"Here, now," said her son. "Take a drop on yourself."

The mother raised lamenting eyes to the ceiling.

"She's deh devil's own chil', Jimmie," she whispered. "Ah, who would t'ink such a bad girl could grow up in our fambly, Jimmie, me son. Many deh hour I've spent in talk wid dat girl an' tol' her if she ever went on deh streets I'd see her damned. An' after all her bringin' up an' what I tol' her and talked wid her, she goes teh deh bad, like a duck teh water."

The tears rolled down her furrowed face. Her hands trembled.

"An' den when dat Sadie MacMallister next door to us was sent teh deh devil by dat feller what worked in deh soap-factory, didn't I tell our Mag dat if she—"

"Ah, dat's annuder story," interrupted the brother. "Of course, dat Sadie was nice an' all dat—but—see—it ain't dessame as if—well, Maggie was diff'ent—see—she was diff'ent."

He was trying to formulate a theory that he had always unconsciously held, that all sisters, excepting his own, could advisedly be ruined.

He suddenly broke out again. "I'll go t'ump hell outa deh mug what did her deh harm. I'll kill 'im! He t'inks he kin scrap, but when he gits me a-chasin' 'im he'll fin' out where he's wrong, deh damned duffer. I'll wipe up deh street wid 'im."

In a fury he plunged out of the doorway. As he vanished the mother raised her head and lifted both hands, entreating.

"May Gawd curse her forever," she cried.

In the darkness of the hallway Jimmie discerned a knot of women talking volubly. When he strode by they paid no attention to him.

"She allus was a bold thing," he heard one of them cry in an eager voice. "Dere wasn't a feller come teh deh house but she'd try teh mash 'im. My Annie says deh shameless t'ing tried teh ketch her feller, her own feller, what we useter know his fader."

"I could a' tol' yehs dis two years ago," said a woman, in a key of triumph. "Yessir, it was over two years ago dat I says teh my ol' man, I says, 'Dat Johnson girl ain't straight,' I says. 'Oh, hell,' he says. 'Oh, hell.' 'Dat's all right,' I says, 'but I know what I knows,' I says, 'an' it 'ill come out later. You wait an' see,' I says, 'you see.'"

"Anybody what had eyes could see dat dere was somethin' wrong wid dat girl. I didn't like her actions."

On the street Jimmie met a friend. "What deh hell?" asked the latter.

Jimmie explained. "An' I'll t'ump 'im till he can't stand."

"Oh, what deh hell," said the friend. "What's deh use! Yeh'll git pulled in! Everybody 'ill be onto it! An' ten plunks! Gee!"

Jimmie was determined. "He t'inks he kin scrap, but he'll fin' out diff'ent."

"Gee," remonstrated the friend. "What deh hell?"

Chapter XI

On a corner a glass-fronted building shed a yellow glare upon the pavements. The open mouth of a saloon called seductively to passengers to enter and annihilate sorrow or create rage.

The interior of the place was papered in olive and bronze tints of imitation leather. A shining bar of counterfeit massiveness extended down the side of the room. Behind it a great mahogany-appearing sideboard reached the ceiling. Upon its shelves rested pyramids of shimmering glasses that were never disturbed. Mirrors set in the face of the sideboard multiplied them. Lemons, oranges and paper napkins, arranged with mathematical precision, sat among the glasses. Many-hued decanters of liquor perched at regular intervals on the lower shelves. A nickel-plated cash register occupied a position in the exact centre of the general effect. The elementary senses of it all seemed to be opulence and geometrical accuracy.

Across from the bar a smaller counter held a collection of plates upon which swarmed frayed fragments of crackers, slices of boiled ham, dishevelled bits of cheese, and pickles swimming in vinegar. An odor of grasping, begrimed hands and munching mouths pervaded.

Pete, in a white jacket, was behind the bar bending expectantly toward a quiet stranger. "A beeh," said the man. Pete drew a foam-topped glassful and set it dripping upon the bar.

At this moment the light bamboo doors at the entrance swung open and crashed against the siding. Jimmie and a companion entered. They swaggered unsteadily but belligerently toward the bar and looked at Pete with bleared and blinking eyes.

"Gin," said Jimmie.

"Gin," said the companion.

Pete slid a bottle and two glasses along the bar. He bended his head sideways as he assiduously polished away with a napkin at the gleaming wood. He had a look of watchfulness upon his features.

Jimmie and his companion kept their eyes upon the bartender and conversed loudly in tones of contempt.

"He's a dindy masher, ain't he, by Gawd?" laughed Jimmie.

"Oh, hell, yes," said the companion, sneering widely. "He's great, he is. Git onto deh mug on deh blokie. Dat's enough to make a feller turn handsprings in 'is sleep."

The quiet stranger moved himself and his glass a trifle further away and maintained an attitude of oblivion.

"Gee! ain't he hot stuff!"

"Git onto his shape! Great Gawd!"

"Hey," cried Jimmie, in tones of command. Pete came along slowly, with a sullen dropping of the under lip.

"Well," he growled, "what's eatin' yehs?"

"Gin," said Jimmie.

"Gin," said the companion.

As Pete confronted them with the bottle and the glasses, they laughed in his face. Jimmie's companion, evidently overcome with merriment, pointed a grimy forefinger in Pete's direction.

"Say, Jimmie," demanded he, "what deh hell is dat behind deh bar?"

"Damned if I knows," replied Jimmie. They laughed loudly. Pete put down a bottle with a bang and turned a formidable face toward them. He disclosed his teeth and his shoulders heaved restlessly.

"You fellers can't guy me," he said. "Drink yer stuff an' git out an' don' make no trouble."

Instantly the laughter faded from the faces of the two men and expressions of offended dignity immediately came.

"Who deh hell has said anyt'ing teh you," cried they in the same breath.

The quiet stranger looked at the door calculatingly.

"Ah, come off," said Pete to the two men. "Don't pick me up for no jay. Drink yer rum an' git out an' don' make no trouble."

"Oh, deh hell," airily cried Jimmie.

"Oh, deh hell," airily repeated his companion.

"We goes when we git ready! See!" continued Jimmie.

"Well," said Pete in a threatening voice, "don' make no trouble."

Jimmie suddenly leaned forward with his head on one side. He snarled like a wild animal.

"Well, what if we does? See?" said he.

Dark blood flushed into Pete's face, and he shot a lurid glance at Jimmie.

"Well, den we'll see whose deh bes' man, you or me," he said.

The quiet stranger moved modestly toward the door.

Jimmie began to swell with valor.

"Don' pick me up fer no tenderfoot. When yeh tackles me yeh tackles one of deh bes' men in deh city. See? I'm a scrapper, I am. Ain't dat right, Billie?"

"Sure, Mike," responded his companion in tones of conviction.

"Oh, hell," said Pete, easily. "Go fall on yerself."

The two men again began to laugh.

"What deh hell is dat talkin'?" cried the companion.

"Damned if I knows," replied Jimmie with exaggerated contempt.

Pete made a furious gesture. "Git outa here now, an' don' make no trouble. See? Youse fellers er lookin' fer a scrap an' it's damn likely yeh'll fin' one if yeh keeps on shootin' off yer mout's. I know yehs! See? I kin lick better men dan yehs ever saw in yer lifes. Dat's right! See? Don' pick me up fer no stuff er yeh might be jolted out in deh street before yeh knows where yeh is. When I comes from behind dis bar, I t'rows yehs bote inteh deh street. See?"

"Oh, hell," cried the two men in chorus.

The glare of a panther came into Pete's eyes. "Dat's what I said! Unnerstan'?"

He came through a passage at the end of the bar and swelled down upon the two men. They stepped promptly forward and crowded close to him.

They bristled like three roosters. They moved their heads pugnaciously and kept their shoulders braced. The nervous muscles about each mouth twitched with a forced smile of mockery.

"Well, what deh hell yer goin' teh do?" gritted Jimmie.

Pete stepped warily back, waving his hands before him to keep the men from coming too near.

"Well, what deh hell yer goin' teh do?" repeated Jimmie's ally. They kept close to him, taunting and leering. They strove to make him attempt the initial blow.

"Keep back, now! Don' crowd me," ominously said Pete.

Again they chorused in contempt. "Oh, hell!"

In a small, tossing group, the three men edged for positions like frigates contemplating battle.

"Well, why deh hell don' yeh try teh t'row us out?" cried Jimmie and his ally with copious sneers.

The bravery of bull-dogs sat upon the faces of the men. Their clenched fists moved like eager weapons.

The allied two jostled the bartender's elbows, glaring at him with feverish eyes and forcing him toward the wall.

Suddenly Pete swore redly. The flash of action gleamed from his eyes. He threw back his arm and aimed a tremendous, lightning-like blow at Jimmie's face. His foot swung a step forward and the weight of his body was behind his fist. Jimmie ducked his head, Bowery-like, with the quickness of a cat. The fierce, answering blows of him and his ally crushed on Pete's bowed head.

The quiet stranger vanished.

The arms of the combatants whirled in the air like flails. The faces of the men, at first flushed to flame-colored anger, now began to fade to the pallor of warriors in the blood and heat of a battle. Their lips curled back and stretched tightly over the gums in ghoul-like grins. Through their white, gripped teeth struggled hoarse whisperings of oaths. Their eyes glittered with murderous fire.

Each head was huddled between its owner's shoulders, and arms were swinging with marvelous rapidity. Feet scraped to and fro with a loud scratching sound upon the sanded floor. Blows left crimson blotches upon pale skin. The curses of the first quarter minute of the fight died away. The breaths of the fighters came wheezingly from their lips and the three chests were straining and heaving. Pete at intervals gave vent to low, labored hisses, that sounded like a desire to kill. Jimmie's ally gibbered at times like a wounded maniac. Jimmie was silent, fighting with the face of a sacrificial priest. The rage of fear shone in all their eyes and their blood-colored fists swirled.

At a tottering moment a blow from Pete's hand struck the ally and he crashed to the floor. He wriggled instantly to his feet and grasping the quiet stranger's beer glass from the bar, hurled it at Pete's head.

High on the wall it burst like a bomb, shivering fragments flying in all directions. Then missiles came to every man's hand. The place had heretofore appeared free of things to throw, but suddenly glass and bottles went singing through the air. They were thrown point blank at bobbing heads. The pyramid of shimmering glasses, that had never been disturbed, changed to cascades as heavy bottles were flung into them. Mirrors splintered to nothing.

The three frothing creatures on the floor buried themselves in a frenzy for blood. There followed in the wake of missiles and fists some unknown prayers, perhaps for death.

The quiet stranger had sprawled very pyrotechnically out on the sidewalk. A laugh ran up and down the avenue for the half of a block.

"Dey've trowed a bloke inteh deh street."

People heard the sound of breaking glass and shuffling feet within the saloon and came running. A small group, bending down to look under the bamboo doors, watching the fall of glass, and three pairs of violent legs, changed in a moment to a crowd.

A policeman came charging down the sidewalk and bounced through the doors into the saloon. The crowd bended and surged in absorbing anxiety to see.

Jimmie caught first sight of the on-coming interruption. On his feet he had the same regard for a policeman that, when on his truck, he had for a fire engine. He howled and ran for the side door.

The officer made a terrific advance, club in hand. One comprehensive sweep of the long night stick threw the ally to the floor and forced Pete to a corner. With his disengaged hand he made a furious effort at Jimmie's coat-tails. Then he regained his balance and paused.

"Well, well, you are a pair of pictures. What in hell yeh been up to?"

Jimmie, with his face drenched in blood, escaped up a side street, pursued a short distance by some of the more law-loving, or excited individuals of the crowd.

Later, from a corner safely dark, he saw the policeman, the ally and the bartender emerge from the saloon. Pete locked the doors and then followed up the avenue in the rear of the crowd-encompassed policeman and his charge.

On first thoughts Jimmie, with his heart throbbing at battle heat, started to go desperately to the rescue of his friend, but he halted.

"Ah, what deh hell?" he demanded of himself.

Chapter XII

In a hall of irregular shape sat Pete and Maggie drinking beer. A submissive orchestra dictated to by a spectacled man with frowsy hair and a dress suit, industriously followed the bobs of his head and the waves of his baton. A ballad singer, in a dress of flaming scarlet, sang in the inevitable voice of brass. When she vanished, men seated at the tables near the front applauded loudly, pounding the polished wood with their beer glasses. She returned attired in less gown, and sang again. She received another enthusiastic encore. She reappeared in still less gown and danced. The deafening rumble of glasses and clapping of hands that followed her exit indicated an overwhelming desire to have her come on for the fourth time, but the curiosity of the audience was not gratified.

Maggie was pale. From her eyes had been plucked all look of self-reliance. She leaned with a dependent air toward her companion. She was timid, as if fearing his anger or displeasure. She seemed to beseech tenderness of him.

Pete's air of distinguished valor had grown upon him until it threatened stupendous dimensions. He was infinitely gracious to the girl. It was apparent to her that his condescension was a marvel.

He could appear to strut even while sitting still and he showed that he was a lion of lordly characteristics by the air with which he spat.

With Maggie gazing at him wonderingly, he took pride in commanding the waiters who were, however, indifferent or deaf.

"Hi, you, git a russle on yehs! What deh hell yehs lookin' at? Two more beehs, d'yeh hear?"

He leaned back and critically regarded the person of a girl with a straw-colored wig who upon the stage was flinging her heels in somewhat awkward imitation of a well-known danseuse.

At times Maggie told Pete long confidential tales of her former home life, dwelling upon the escapades of the other members of the family and the difficulties she had to combat in order to obtain a degree of comfort. He responded in tones of philanthropy. He pressed her arm with an air of reassuring proprietorship.

"Dey was damn jays," he said, denouncing the mother and brother.

The sound of the music which, by the efforts of the frowsy-headed leader, drifted to her ears through the smoke-filled atmosphere, made the girl dream. She thought of her former Rum Alley environment and turned to regard Pete's strong protecting fists. She thought of the collar and cuff manufactory and the eternal moan of the proprietor: "What een hell do you sink I pie fife dolla a week for? Play? No, py damn." She contemplated Pete's man-subduing eyes and noted that wealth and prosperity was indicated by his clothes. She imagined a future, rose-tinted, because of its distance from all that she previously had experienced.

As to the present she perceived only vague reasons to be miserable. Her life was Pete's and she considered him worthy of the charge. She would be disturbed by no particular apprehensions, so long as Pete adored her as he now said he did. She did not feel like a bad woman. To her knowledge she had never seen any better.

At times men at other tables regarded the girl furtively. Pete, aware of it, nodded at her and grinned. He felt proud.

"Mag, yer a bloomin' good-looker," he remarked, studying her face through the haze. The men made Maggie fear, but she blushed at Pete's words as it became apparent to her that she was the apple of his eye.

Grey-headed men, wonderfully pathetic in their dissipation, stared at her through clouds. Smooth-cheeked boys, some of them with faces of stone and mouths of sin, not nearly so pathetic as the grey heads, tried to find the girl's eyes in the smoke wreaths. Maggie considered she was not what they thought her. She confined her glances to Pete and the stage.

The orchestra played negro melodies and a versatile drummer pounded, whacked, clattered and scratched on a dozen machines to make noise.

Those glances of the men, shot at Maggie from under half-closed lids, made her tremble. She thought them all to be worse men than Pete.

"Come, let's go," she said.

As they went out Maggie perceived two women seated at a table with some men. They were painted and their cheeks had lost their roundness. As she passed them the girl, with a shrinking movement, drew back her skirts.

Chapter XIII

Jimmie did not return home for a number of days after the fight with Pete in the saloon. When he did, he approached with extreme caution.

He found his mother raving. Maggie had not returned home. The parent continually wondered how her daughter could come to such a pass. She had never considered Maggie as a pearl dropped unstained into Rum Alley from Heaven, but she could not conceive how it was possible for her daughter to fall so low as to bring disgrace upon her family. She was terrific in denunciation of the girl's wickedness.

The fact that the neighbors talked of it, maddened her. When women came in, and in the course of their conversation casually asked, "Where's Maggie dese days?" the mother shook her fuzzy head at them and appalled them with curses. Cunning hints inviting confidence she rebuffed with violence.

"An' wid all deh bringin' up she had, how could she?" moaningly she asked of her son. "Wid all deh talkin' wid her I did an' deh t'ings I tol' her to remember? When a girl is bringed up deh way I bringed up Maggie, how kin she go teh deh devil?"

Jimmie was transfixed by these questions. He could not conceive how under the circumstances his mother's daughter and his sister could have been so wicked.

His mother took a drink from a squdgy bottle that sat on the table. She continued her lament.

"She had a bad heart, dat girl did, Jimmie. She was wicked teh deh heart an' we never knowed it."

Jimmie nodded, admitting the fact.

"We lived in deh same house wid her an' I brought her up an' we never knowed how bad she was."

Jimmie nodded again.

"Wid a home like dis an' a mudder like me, she went teh deh bad," cried the mother, raising her eyes.

One day, Jimmie came home, sat down in a chair and began to wriggle about with a new and strange nervousness. At last he spoke shamefacedly.

"Well, look-a-here, dis t'ing queers us! See? We're queered! An' maybe it 'ud be better if I—well, I t'ink I kin look 'er up an'—maybe it 'ud be better if I fetched her home an'—"

The mother started from her chair and broke forth into a storm of passionate anger.

"What! Let 'er come an' sleep under deh same roof wid her mudder agin! Oh, yes, I will, won't I? Sure? Shame on yehs, Jimmie Johnson, for sayin' such a t'ing teh yer own mudder—teh yer own mudder! Little did I t'ink when yehs was a babby playin' about me feet dat ye'd grow up teh say sech a t'ing teh yer mudder—yer own mudder. I never taut—"

Sobs choked her and interrupted her reproaches.

"Dere ain't nottin' teh raise sech hell about," said Jimmie. "I on'y says it 'ud be better if we keep dis t'ing dark, see? It queers us! See?"

His mother laughed a laugh that seemed to ring through the city and be echoed and re-echoed by countless other laughs. "Oh, yes, I will, won't I! Sure!"

"Well, yeh must take me fer a damn fool," said Jimmie, indignant at his mother for mocking him. "I didn't say we'd make 'er inteh a little tin angel, ner nottin', but deh way it is now she can queer us! Don' che see?"

"Aye, she'll git tired of deh life atter a while an' den she'll wanna be a-comin' home, won' she, deh beast! I'll let 'er in den, won' I?"

"Well, I didn' mean none of dis prod'gal bus'ness anyway," explained Jimmie.

"It wasn't no prod'gal dauter, yeh damn fool," said the mother. "It was prod'gal son, anyhow."

"I know dat," said Jimmie.

For a time they sat in silence. The mother's eyes gloated on a scene her imagination could call before her. Her lips were set in a vindictive smile.

"Aye, she'll cry, won' she, an' carry on, an' tell how Pete, or some odder feller, beats 'er an' she'll say she's sorry an' all dat an' she ain't happy, she ain't, an' she wants to come home agin, she does."

With grim humor, the mother imitated the possible wailing notes of the daughter's voice.

"Den I'll take 'er in, won't I, deh beast. She kin cry 'er two eyes out on deh stones of deh street before I'll dirty deh place wid her. She abused an' ill-treated her own mudder—her own mudder what loved her an' she'll never git anodder chance dis side of hell."

Jimmie thought he had a great idea of women's frailty, but he could not understand why any of his kin should be victims.

"Damn her," he fervidly said.

Again he wondered vaguely if some of the women of his acquaintance had brothers. Nevertheless, his mind did not for an instant confuse himself with those brothers nor his sister with theirs. After the mother had, with great difficulty, suppressed the neighbors, she went among them and proclaimed her grief. "May Gawd forgive dat girl," was her continual cry. To attentive ears she recited the whole length and breadth of her woes.

"I bringed 'er up deh way a dauter oughta be bringed up an' dis is how she served me! She went teh deh devil deh first chance she got! May Gawd forgive her."

When arrested for drunkenness she used the story of her daughter's downfall with telling effect upon the police justices. Finally one of them said to her, peering down over his spectacles: "Mary, the records of this and other courts show that you are the mother of forty-two daughters who have been ruined. The case is unparalleled in the annals of this court, and this court thinks—"

The mother went through life shedding large tears of sorrow. Her red face was a picture of agony.

Of course Jimmie publicly damned his sister that he might appear on a higher social plane. But, arguing with himself, stumbling about in ways that he knew not, he, once, almost came to a conclusion that his sister would have been more firmly good had she better known why. However, he felt that he could not hold such a view. He threw it hastily aside.

Chapter XIV

In a hilarious hall there were twenty-eight tables and twenty-eight women and a crowd of smoking men. Valiant noise was made on a stage at the end of the hall by an orchestra composed of men who looked as if they had just happened in. Soiled waiters ran to and fro, swooping down like hawks on the unwary in the throng; clattering along the aisles with trays covered with glasses; stumbling over women's skirts and charging two prices for everything but beer, all with a swiftness that blurred the view of the cocoanut palms and dusty monstrosities painted upon the walls of the room. A bouncer, with an immense load of business upon his hands, plunged about in the crowd, dragging bashful strangers to prominent chairs, ordering waiters here and there and quarreling furiously with men who wanted to sing with the orchestra.

The usual smoke cloud was present, but so dense that heads and arms seemed entangled in it. The rumble of conversation was replaced by a roar. Plenteous oaths heaved through the air. The room rang with the shrill voices of women bubbling o'er with drink-laughter. The chief element in the music of the orchestra was speed. The musicians played in intent fury. A woman was singing and smiling upon the stage, but no one took notice of her. The rate at which the piano, cornet and violins were going, seemed to impart wildness to the half-drunken crowd. Beer glasses were emptied at a gulp and conversation became a rapid chatter. The smoke eddied and swirled like a shadowy river hurrying toward some unseen falls. Pete and Maggie entered the hall and took chairs at a table near the door. The woman who was seated there made an attempt to occupy Pete's attention and, failing, went away.

Three weeks had passed since the girl had left home. The air of spaniel-like dependence had been magnified and showed its direct effect in the peculiar off-handedness and ease of Pete's ways toward her.

She followed Pete's eyes with hers, anticipating with smiles gracious looks from him.

A woman of brilliance and audacity, accompanied by a mere boy, came into the place and took seats near them.

At once Pete sprang to his feet, his face beaming with glad surprise.

"By Gawd, there's Nellie," he cried.

He went over to the table and held out an eager hand to the woman.

"Why, hello, Pete, me boy, how are you," said she, giving him her fingers.

Maggie took instant note of the woman. She perceived that her black dress fitted her to perfection. Her linen collar and cuffs were spotless. Tan gloves were stretched over her well-shaped hands. A hat of a prevailing fashion perched jauntily upon her dark hair. She wore no jewelry and was painted with no apparent paint. She looked clear-eyed through the stares of the men.

"Sit down, and call your lady-friend over," she said cordially to Pete. At his beckoning Maggie came and sat between Pete and the mere boy.

"I thought yeh were gone away fer good," began Pete, at once. "When did yeh git back? How did dat Buff'lo bus'ness turn out?"

The woman shrugged her shoulders. "Well, he didn't have as many stamps as he tried to make out, so I shook him, that's all."

"Well, I'm glad teh see yehs back in deh city," said Pete, with awkward gallantry.

He and the woman entered into a long conversation, exchanging reminiscences of days together. Maggie sat still, unable to formulate an intelligent sentence upon the conversation and painfully aware of it.

She saw Pete's eyes sparkle as he gazed upon the handsome stranger. He listened smilingly to all she said. The woman was familiar with all his affairs, asked him about mutual friends, and knew the amount of his salary.

She paid no attention to Maggie, looking toward her once or twice and apparently seeing the wall beyond.

The mere boy was sulky. In the beginning he had welcomed with acclamations the additions.

"Let's all have a drink! What'll you take, Nell? And you, Miss what's-your-name. Have a drink, Mr. ——-, you, I mean."

He had shown a sprightly desire to do the talking for the company and tell all about his family. In a loud voice he declaimed on various topics. He assumed a patronizing air toward Pete. As Maggie was silent, he paid no attention to her. He made a great show of lavishing wealth upon the woman of brilliance and audacity.

"Do keep still, Freddie! You gibber like an ape, dear," said the woman to him. She turned away and devoted her attention to Pete.

"We'll have many a good time together again, eh?"

"Sure, Mike," said Pete, enthusiastic at once.

"Say," whispered she, leaning forward, "let's go over to Billie's and have a heluva time."

"Well, it's dis way! See?" said Pete. "I got dis lady frien' here."

"Oh, t'hell with her," argued the woman.

Pete appeared disturbed.

"All right," said she, nodding her head at him. "All right for you! We'll see the next time you ask me to go anywheres with you."

Pete squirmed.

"Say," he said, beseechingly, "come wid me a minit an' I'll tell yer why."

The woman waved her hand.

"Oh, that's all right, you needn't explain, you know. You wouldn't come merely because you wouldn't come, that's all there is of it."

To Pete's visible distress she turned to the mere boy, bringing him speedily from a terrific rage. He had been debating whether it would be the part of a man to pick a quarrel with Pete, or would he be justified in striking him savagely with his beer glass without warning. But he recovered himself when the woman turned to renew her smilings. He beamed upon her with an expression that was somewhat tipsy and inexpressibly tender.

"Say, shake that Bowery jay," requested he, in a loud whisper.

"Freddie, you are so droll," she replied.

Pete reached forward and touched the woman on the arm.

"Come out a minit while I tells yeh why I can't go wid yer. Yer doin' me dirt, Nell! I never taut ye'd do me dirt, Nell. Come on, will yer?" He spoke in tones of injury.

"Why, I don't see why I should be interested in your explanations," said the woman, with a coldness that seemed to reduce Pete to a pulp.

His eyes pleaded with her. "Come out a minit while I tells yeh."

The woman nodded slightly at Maggie and the mere boy, "'Scuse me."

The mere boy interrupted his loving smile and turned a shrivelling glare upon Pete. His boyish countenance flushed and he spoke, in a whine, to the woman:

"Oh, I say, Nellie, this ain't a square deal, you know. You aren't goin' to leave me and go off with that duffer, are you? I should think—"

"Why, you dear boy, of course I'm not," cried the woman, affectionately. She bended over and whispered in his ear. He smiled again and settled in his chair as if resolved to wait patiently.

As the woman walked down between the rows of tables, Pete was at her shoulder talking earnestly, apparently in explanation. The woman waved her hands with studied airs of indifference. The doors swung behind them, leaving Maggie and the mere boy seated at the table.

Maggie was dazed. She could dimly perceive that something stupendous had happened. She wondered why Pete saw fit to remonstrate with the woman, pleading for forgiveness with his eyes. She thought she noted an air of submission about her leonine Pete. She was astounded.

The mere boy occupied himself with cock-tails and a cigar. He was tranquilly silent for half an hour. Then he bestirred himself and spoke.

"Well," he said, sighing, "I knew this was the way it would be." There was another stillness. The mere boy seemed to be musing.

"She was pulling m'leg. That's the whole amount of it," he said, suddenly. "It's a bloomin' shame the way that girl does. Why, I've spent over two dollars in drinks to-night. And she goes off with that plug-ugly who looks as if he had been hit in the face with a coin-die. I call it rocky treatment for a fellah like me. Here, waiter, bring me a cock-tail and make it damned strong."

Maggie made no reply. She was watching the doors. "It's a mean piece of business," complained the mere boy. He explained to her how amazing it was that anybody should treat him in such a manner. "But I'll get square with her, you bet. She won't get far ahead of yours truly, you know," he added, winking. "I'll tell her plainly that it was bloomin' mean business. And she won't come it over me with any of her 'now-Freddie-dears.' She thinks my name is Freddie, you know, but of course it ain't. I always tell these people some name like that, because if they got onto your right name they might use it sometime. Understand? Oh, they don't fool me much."

Maggie was paying no attention, being intent upon the doors. The mere boy relapsed into a period of gloom, during which he exterminated a number of cock-tails with a determined air, as if replying defiantly to fate. He occasionally broke forth into sentences composed of invectives joined together in a long string.

The girl was still staring at the doors. After a time the mere boy began to see cobwebs just in front of his nose. He spurred himself into being agreeable and insisted upon her having a charlotte-russe and a glass of beer.

"They's gone," he remarked, "they's gone." He looked at her through the smoke wreaths. "Shay, lil' girl, we mightish well make bes' of it. You ain't such bad-lookin' girl, y'know. Not half bad. Can't come up to Nell, though. No, can't do it! Well, I should shay not! Nell fine-lookin' girl! F—i—n—ine. You look damn bad longsider her, but by y'self ain't so bad. Have to do anyhow. Nell gone. On'y you left. Not half bad, though."

Maggie stood up.

"I'm going home," she said.

The mere boy started.

"Eh? What? Home," he cried, struck with amazement. "I beg pardon, did hear say home?"

"I'm going home," she repeated.

"Great Gawd, what hava struck," demanded the mere boy of himself, stupefied.

In a semi-comatose state he conducted her on board an up-town car, ostentatiously paid her fare, leered kindly at her through the rear window and fell off the steps.

Chapter XV

A forlorn woman went along a lighted avenue. The street was filled with people desperately bound on missions. An endless crowd darted at the elevated station stairs and the horse cars were thronged with owners of bundles.

The pace of the forlorn woman was slow. She was apparently searching for some one. She loitered near the doors of saloons and watched men emerge from them. She scanned furtively the faces in the rushing stream of pedestrians. Hurrying men, bent on catching some boat or train, jostled her elbows, failing to notice her, their thoughts fixed on distant dinners.

The forlorn woman had a peculiar face. Her smile was no smile. But when in repose her features had a shadowy look that was like a sardonic grin, as if some one had sketched with cruel forefinger indelible lines about her mouth.

Jimmie came strolling up the avenue. The woman encountered him with an aggrieved air.

"Oh, Jimmie, I've been lookin' all over fer yehs—," she began.

Jimmie made an impatient gesture and quickened his pace.

"Ah, don't bodder me! Good Gawd!" he said, with the savageness of a man whose life is pestered.

The woman followed him along the sidewalk in somewhat the manner of a suppliant.

"But, Jimmie," she said, "yehs told me ye'd—"

Jimmie turned upon her fiercely as if resolved to make a last stand for comfort and peace.

"Say, fer Gawd's sake, Hattie, don' foller me from one end of deh city teh deh odder. Let up, will yehs! Give me a minute's res', can't yehs? Yehs makes me tired, allus taggin' me. See? Ain' yehs got no sense. Do yehs want people teh get onto me? Go chase yerself, fer Gawd's sake."

The woman stepped closer and laid her fingers on his arm. "But, look-a-here—"

Jimmie snarled. "Oh, go teh hell."

He darted into the front door of a convenient saloon and a moment later came out into the shadows that surrounded the side door. On the brilliantly lighted avenue he perceived the forlorn woman dodging about like a scout. Jimmie laughed with an air of relief and went away.

When he arrived home he found his mother clamoring. Maggie had returned. She stood shivering beneath the torrent of her mother's wrath.

"Well, I'm damned," said Jimmie in greeting.

His mother, tottering about the room, pointed a quivering forefinger.

"Lookut her, Jimmie, lookut her. Dere's yer sister, boy. Dere's yer sister. Lookut her! Lookut her!"

She screamed in scoffing laughter.

The girl stood in the middle of the room. She edged about as if unable to find a place on the floor to put her feet.

"Ha, ha, ha," bellowed the mother. "Dere she stands! Ain' she purty? Lookut her! Ain' she sweet, deh beast? Lookut her! Ha, ha, lookut her!"

She lurched forward and put her red and seamed hands upon her daughter's face. She bent down and peered keenly up into the eyes of the girl.

"Oh, she's jes' dessame as she ever was, ain' she? She's her mudder's purty darlin' yit, ain' she? Lookut her, Jimmie! Come here, fer Gawd's sake, and lookut her."

The loud, tremendous sneering of the mother brought the denizens of the Rum Alley tenement to their doors. Women came in the hallways. Children scurried to and fro.

"What's up? Dat Johnson party on anudder tear?"

"Naw! Young Mag's come home!"

"Deh hell yeh say?"

Through the open door curious eyes stared in at Maggie. Children ventured into the room and ogled her, as if they formed the front row at a theatre. Women, without, bended toward each other and whispered, nodding their heads with airs of profound philosophy. A baby, overcome with curiosity concerning this object at which all were looking, sidled forward and touched her dress, cautiously, as if investigating a red-hot stove. Its mother's voice rang out like a warning trumpet. She rushed forward and grabbed her child, casting a terrible look of indignation at the girl.

Maggie's mother paced to and fro, addressing the doorful of eyes, expounding like a glib showman at a museum. Her voice rang through the building.

"Dere she stands," she cried, wheeling suddenly and pointing with dramatic finger. "Dere she stands! Lookut her! Ain' she a dindy? An' she was so good as to come home teh her mudder, she was! Ain' she a beaut'? Ain' she a dindy? Fer Gawd's sake!"

The jeering cries ended in another burst of shrill laughter.

The girl seemed to awaken. "Jimmie—"

He drew hastily back from her.

"Well, now, yer a hell of a t'ing, ain' yeh?" he said, his lips curling in scorn. Radiant virtue sat upon his brow and his repelling hands expressed horror of contamination.

Maggie turned and went.

The crowd at the door fell back precipitately. A baby falling down in front of the door, wrenched a scream like a wounded animal from its mother. Another woman sprang forward and picked it up, with a chivalrous air, as if rescuing a human being from an oncoming express train.

As the girl passed down through the hall, she went before open doors framing more eyes strangely microscopic, and sending broad beams of inquisitive light into the darkness of her path. On the second floor she met the gnarled old woman who possessed the music box.

"So," she cried, "'ere yehs are back again, are yehs? An' dey've kicked yehs out? Well, come in an' stay wid me teh-night. I ain' got no moral standin'."

From above came an unceasing babble of tongues, over all of which rang the mother's derisive laughter.

Chapter XVI

Pete did not consider that he had ruined Maggie. If he had thought that her soul could never smile again, he would have believed the mother and brother, who were pyrotechnic over the affair, to be responsible for it.

Besides, in his world, souls did not insist upon being able to smile. "What deh hell?"

He felt a trifle entangled. It distressed him. Revelations and scenes might bring upon him the wrath of the owner of the saloon, who insisted upon respectability of an advanced type.

"What deh hell do dey wanna raise such a smoke about it fer?" demanded he of himself, disgusted with the attitude of the family. He saw no necessity for anyone's losing their equilibrium merely because their sister or their daughter had stayed away from home.

Searching about in his mind for possible reasons for their conduct, he came upon the conclusion that Maggie's motives were correct, but that the two others wished to snare him. He felt pursued.

The woman of brilliance and audacity whom he had met in the hilarious hall showed a disposition to ridicule him.

"A little pale thing with no spirit," she said. "Did you note the expression of her eyes? There was something in them about pumpkin pie and virtue. That is a peculiar way the left corner of her mouth has of twitching, isn't it? Dear, dear, my cloud-compelling Pete, what are you coming to?"

Pete asserted at once that he never was very much interested in the girl. The woman interrupted him, laughing.

"Oh, it's not of the slightest consequence to me, my dear young man. You needn't draw maps for my benefit. Why should I be concerned about it?"

But Pete continued with his explanations. If he was laughed at for his tastes in women, he felt obliged to say that they were only temporary or indifferent ones.

The morning after Maggie had departed from home, Pete stood behind the bar. He was immaculate in white jacket and apron and his hair was plastered over his brow with infinite correctness. No customers were in the place. Pete was twisting his napkined fist slowly in a beer glass, softly whistling to himself and occasionally holding the object of his attention between his eyes and a few weak beams of sunlight that had found their way over the thick screens and into the shaded room.

With lingering thoughts of the woman of brilliance and audacity, the bartender raised his head and stared through the varying cracks between the swaying bamboo doors. Suddenly the whistling pucker faded from his lips. He saw Maggie walking slowly past. He gave a great start, fearing for the previously-mentioned eminent respectability of the place.

He threw a swift, nervous glance about him, all at once feeling guilty. No one was in the room.

He went hastily over to the side door. Opening it and looking out, he perceived Maggie standing, as if undecided, on the corner. She was searching the place with her eyes.

As she turned her face toward him Pete beckoned to her hurriedly, intent upon returning with speed to a position behind the bar and to the atmosphere of respectability upon which the proprietor insisted.

Maggie came to him, the anxious look disappearing from her face and a smile wreathing her lips.

"Oh, Pete—," she began brightly.

The bartender made a violent gesture of impatience.

"Oh, my Gawd," cried he, vehemently. "What deh hell do yeh wanna hang aroun' here fer? Do yeh wanna git me inteh trouble?" he demanded with an air of injury.

Astonishment swept over the girl's features. "Why, Pete! yehs tol' me—"

Pete glanced profound irritation. His countenance reddened with the anger of a man whose respectability is being threatened.

"Say, yehs makes me tired. See? What deh hell deh yeh wanna tag aroun' atter me fer? Yeh'll git me inteh trouble wid deh ol' man an' dey'll be hell teh pay! If he sees a woman roun' here he'll go crazy an' I'll lose me job! See? Yer brudder come in here an' raised hell an' deh ol' man hada put up fer it! An' now I'm done! See? I'm done."

The girl's eyes stared into his face. "Pete, don't yeh remem—"

"Oh, hell," interrupted Pete, anticipating.

The girl seemed to have a struggle with herself. She was apparently bewildered and could not find speech. Finally she asked in a low voice: "But where kin I go?"

The question exasperated Pete beyond the powers of endurance. It was a direct attempt to give him some responsibility in a matter that did not concern him. In his indignation he volunteered information.

"Oh, go teh hell," cried he. He slammed the door furiously and returned, with an air of relief, to his respectability.

Maggie went away.

She wandered aimlessly for several blocks. She stopped once and asked aloud a question of herself: "Who?"

A man who was passing near her shoulder, humorously took the questioning word as intended for him.

"Eh? What? Who? Nobody! I didn't say anything," he laughingly said, and continued his way.

Soon the girl discovered that if she walked with such apparent aimlessness, some men looked at her with calculating eyes. She quickened her step, frightened. As a protection, she adopted a demeanor of intentness as if going somewhere.

After a time she left rattling avenues and passed between rows of houses with sternness and stolidity stamped upon their features. She hung her head for she felt their eyes grimly upon her.

Suddenly she came upon a stout gentleman in a silk hat and a chaste black coat, whose decorous row of buttons reached from his chin to his knees. The girl had heard of the Grace of God and she decided to approach this man.

His beaming, chubby face was a picture of benevolence and kind-heartedness. His eyes shone good-will.

But as the girl timidly accosted him, he gave a convulsive movement and saved his respectability by a vigorous side-step. He did not risk it to save a soul. For how was he to know that there was a soul before him that needed saving?

Chapter XVII

Upon a wet evening, several months after the last chapter, two interminable rows of cars, pulled by slipping horses, jangled along a prominent side-street. A dozen cabs, with coat-enshrouded drivers, clattered to and fro. Electric lights, whirring softly, shed a blurred radiance. A flower dealer, his feet tapping impatiently, his nose and his wares glistening with rain-drops, stood behind an array of roses and chrysanthemums. Two or three theatres emptied a crowd upon the storm-swept pavements. Men pulled their hats over their eyebrows and raised their collars to their ears. Women shrugged impatient shoulders in their warm cloaks and stopped to arrange their skirts for a walk through the storm. People having been comparatively silent for two hours burst into a roar of conversation, their hearts still kindling from the glowings of the stage.

The pavements became tossing seas of umbrellas. Men stepped forth to hail cabs or cars, raising their fingers in varied forms of polite request or imperative demand. An endless procession wended toward elevated stations. An atmosphere of pleasure and prosperity seemed to hang over the throng, born, perhaps, of good clothes and of having just emerged from a place of forgetfulness.

In the mingled light and gloom of an adjacent park, a handful of wet wanderers, in attitudes of chronic dejection, was scattered among the benches.

A girl of the painted cohorts of the city went along the street. She threw changing glances at men who passed her, giving smiling invitations to men of rural or untaught pattern and usually seeming sedately unconscious of the men with a metropolitan seal upon their faces.

Crossing glittering avenues, she went into the throng emerging from the places of forgetfulness. She hurried forward through the crowd as if intent upon reaching a distant home, bending forward in her handsome cloak, daintily lifting her skirts and picking for her well-shod feet the dryer spots upon the pavements.

The restless doors of saloons, clashing to and fro, disclosed animated rows of men before bars and hurrying barkeepers.

A concert hall gave to the street faint sounds of swift, machine-like music, as if a group of phantom musicians were hastening.

A tall young man, smoking a cigarette with a sublime air, strolled near the girl. He had on evening dress, a moustache, a chrysanthemum, and a look of ennui, all of which he kept carefully under his eye. Seeing the girl walk on as if such a young man as he was not in existence, he looked back transfixed with interest. He stared glassily for a moment, but gave a slight convulsive start when he discerned that she was neither new, Parisian, nor theatrical. He wheeled about hastily and turned his stare into the air, like a sailor with a search-light.

A stout gentleman, with pompous and philanthropic whiskers, went stolidly by, the broad of his back sneering at the girl.

A belated man in business clothes, and in haste to catch a car, bounced against her shoulder. "Hi, there, Mary, I beg your pardon! Brace up, old girl." He grasped her arm to steady her, and then was away running down the middle of the street.

The girl walked on out of the realm of restaurants and saloons. She passed more glittering avenues and went into darker blocks than those where the crowd travelled.

A young man in light overcoat and derby hat received a glance shot keenly from the eyes of the girl. He stopped and looked at her, thrusting his hands in his pockets and making a mocking smile curl his lips. "Come, now, old lady," he said, "you don't mean to tel me that you sized me up for a farmer?"

A labouring man marched along; with bundles under his arms. To her remarks, he replied, "It's a fine evenin', ain't it?"

She smiled squarely into the face of a boy who was hurrying by with his hands buried in his overcoat pockets, his blonde locks bobbing on his youthful temples, and a cheery smile of unconcern upon his lips. He turned his head and smiled back at her, waving his hands.

"Not this eve—some other eve!"

A drunken man, reeling in her pathway, began to roar at her. "I ain' ga no money!" he shouted, in a dismal voice. He lurched on up the street, wailing to himself: "I ain' ga no money. Ba' luck. Ain' ga no more money."

The girl went into gloomy districts near the river, where the tall black factories shut in the street and only occasional broad beams of light fell across the pavements from saloons. In front of one of these places, whence came the sound of a violin vigorously scraped, the patter of feet on boards and the ring of loud laughter, there stood a man with blotched features.

Further on in the darkness she met a ragged being with shifting, bloodshot eyes and grimy hands.

She went into the blackness of the final block. The shutters of the tall buildings were closed like grim lips. The structures seemed to have eyes that looked over them, beyond them, at other things. Afar off the lights of the avenues glittered as if from an impossible distance. Street-car bells jingled with a sound of merriment.

At the feet of the tall buildings appeared the deathly black hue of the river. Some hidden factory sent up a yellow glare, that lit for a moment the waters lapping oilily against timbers. The varied sounds of life, made joyous by distance and seeming unapproachableness, came faintly and died away to a silence.

Chapter XVIII

In a partitioned-off section of a saloon sat a man with a half dozen women, gleefully laughing, hovering about him. The man had arrived at that stage of drunkenness where affection is felt for the universe.

"I'm good f'ler, girls," he said, convincingly. "I'm damn good f'ler. An'body treats me right, I allus trea's zem right! See?"

The women nodded their heads approvingly. "To be sure," they cried out in hearty chorus. "You're the kind of a man we like, Pete. You're outa sight! What yeh goin' to buy this time, dear?"

"An't'ing yehs wants, damn it," said the man in an abandonment of good will. His countenance shone with the true spirit of benevolence. He was in the proper mode of missionaries. He would have fraternized with obscure Hottentots. And above all, he was overwhelmed in tenderness for his friends, who were all illustrious.

"An't'ing yehs wants, damn it," repeated he, waving his hands with beneficent recklessness. "I'm good f'ler, girls, an' if an'body treats me right I—here," called he through an open door to a waiter, "bring girls drinks, damn it. What 'ill yehs have, girls? An't'ing yehs wants, damn it!"

The waiter glanced in with the disgusted look of the man who serves intoxicants for the man who takes too much of them. He nodded his head shortly at the order from each individual, and went.

"Damn it," said the man, "we're havin' heluva time. I like you girls! Damn'd if I don't! Yer right sort! See?"

He spoke at length and with feeling, concerning the excellencies of his assembled friends.

"Don' try pull man's leg, but have a heluva time! Das right! Das way teh do! Now, if I sawght yehs tryin' work me fer drinks, wouldn' buy damn t'ing! But yer right sort, damn it! Yehs know how ter treat a f'ler, an' I stays by yehs 'til spen' las' cent! Das right! I'm good f'ler an' I knows when an'body treats me right!"

Between the times of the arrival and departure of the waiter, the man discoursed to the women on the tender regard he felt for all living things. He laid stress upon the purity of his motives in all dealings with men in the world and spoke of the fervor of his friendship for those who were amiable. Tears welled slowly from his eyes. His voice quavered when he spoke to them.

Once when the waiter was about to depart with an empty tray, the man drew a coin from his pocket and held it forth.

"Here," said he, quite magnificently, "here's quar'."

The waiter kept his hands on his tray.

"I don' want yer money," he said.

The other put forth the coin with tearful insistence.

"Here, damn it," cried he, "tak't! Yer damn goo' f'ler an' I wan' yehs tak't!"

"Come, come, now," said the waiter, with the sullen air of a man who is forced into giving advice. "Put yer mon in yer pocket! Yer loaded an' yehs on'y makes a damn fool of yerself."

As the latter passed out of the door the man turned pathetically to the women.

"He don' know I'm damn goo' f'ler," cried he, dismally.

"Never you mind, Pete, dear," said a woman of brilliance and audacity, laying her hand with great affection upon his arm. "Never you mind, old boy! We'll stay by you, dear!"

"Das ri'," cried the man, his face lighting up at the soothing tones of the woman's voice. "Das ri', I'm damn goo' f'ler an' w'en anyone trea's me ri', I treats zem ri'! Shee!"

"Sure!" cried the women. "And we're not goin' back on you, old man."

The man turned appealing eyes to the woman of brilliance and audacity. He felt that if he could be convicted of a contemptible action he would die.

"Shay, Nell, damn it, I allus trea's yehs shquare, didn' I? I allus been goo' f'ler wi' yehs, ain't I, Nell?"

"Sure you have, Pete," assented the woman. She delivered an oration to her companions. "Yessir, that's a fact. Pete's a square fellah, he is. He never goes back on a friend. He's the right kind an' we stay by him, don't we, girls?"

"Sure," they exclaimed. Looking lovingly at him they raised their glasses and drank his health.

"Girlsh," said the man, beseechingly, "I allus trea's yehs ri', didn' I? I'm goo' f'ler, ain' I, girlsh?"

"Sure," again they chorused.

"Well," said he finally, "le's have nozzer drink, zen."

"That's right," hailed a woman, "that's right. Yer no bloomin' jay! Yer spends yer money like a man. Dat's right."

The man pounded the table with his quivering fists.

"Yessir," he cried, with deep earnestness, as if someone disputed him. "I'm damn goo' f'ler, an' w'en anyone trea's me ri', I allus trea's—le's have nozzer drink."

He began to beat the wood with his glass.

"Shay," howled he, growing suddenly impatient. As the waiter did not then come, the man swelled with wrath.

"Shay," howled he again.

The waiter appeared at the door.

"Bringsh drinksh," said the man.

The waiter disappeared with the orders.

"Zat f'ler damn fool," cried the man. "He insul' me! I'm ge'man! Can' stan' be insul'! I'm goin' lickim when comes!"

"No, no," cried the women, crowding about and trying to subdue him. "He's all right! He didn't mean anything! Let it go! He's a good fellah!"

"Din' he insul' me?" asked the man earnestly.

"No," said they. "Of course he didn't! He's all right!"

"Sure he didn' insul' me?" demanded the man, with deep anxiety in his voice.

"No, no! We know him! He's a good fellah. He didn't mean anything."

"Well, zen," said the man, resolutely, "I'm go' 'pol'gize!"

When the waiter came, the man struggled to the middle of the floor.

"Girlsh shed you insul' me! I shay damn lie! I 'pol'gize!"

"All right," said the waiter.

The man sat down. He felt a sleepy but strong desire to straighten things out and have a perfect understanding with everybody.

"Nell, I allus trea's yeh shquare, din' I? Yeh likes me, don' yehs, Nell? I'm goo' f'ler?"

"Sure," said the woman of brilliance and audacity.

"Yeh knows I'm stuck on yehs, don' yehs, Nell?"

"Sure," she repeated, carelessly.

Overwhelmed by a spasm of drunken adoration, he drew two or three bills from his pocket, and, with the trembling fingers of an offering priest, laid them on the table before the woman.

"Yehs knows, damn it, yehs kin have all got, 'cause I'm stuck on yehs, Nell, damn't, I—I'm stuck on yehs, Nell—buy drinksh—damn't—we're havin' heluva time—w'en anyone trea's me ri'—I—damn't, Nell—we're havin' heluva—time."

Shortly he went to sleep with his swollen face fallen forward on his chest.

The women drank and laughed, not heeding the slumbering man in the corner. Finally he lurched forward and fell groaning to the floor.

The women screamed in disgust and drew back their skirts.

"Come ahn," cried one, starting up angrily, "let's get out of here."

The woman of brilliance and audacity stayed behind, taking up the bills and stuffing them into a deep, irregularly-shaped pocket. A guttural snore from the recumbent man caused her to turn and look down at him.

She laughed. "What a damn fool," she said, and went.

The smoke from the lamps settled heavily down in the little compartment, obscuring the way out. The smell of oil, stifling in its intensity, pervaded the air. The wine from an overturned glass dripped softly down upon the blotches on the man's neck.

Chapter XIX

In a room a woman sat at a table eating like a fat monk in a picture.

A soiled, unshaven man pushed open the door and entered.

"Well," said he, "Mag's dead."

"What?" said the woman, her mouth filled with bread.

"Mag's dead," repeated the man.

"Deh hell she is," said the woman. She continued her meal. When she finished her coffee she began to weep.

"I kin remember when her two feet was no bigger dan yer t'umb, and she weared worsted boots," moaned she.

"Well, whata dat?" said the man.

"I kin remember when she weared worsted boots," she cried.

The neighbors began to gather in the hall, staring in at the weeping woman as if watching the contortions of a dying dog. A dozen women entered and lamented with her. Under their busy hands the rooms took on that appalling appearance of neatness and order with which death is greeted.

Suddenly the door opened and a woman in a black gown rushed in with outstretched arms. "Ah, poor Mary," she cried, and tenderly embraced the moaning one.

"Ah, what ter'ble affliction is dis," continued she. Her vocabulary was derived from mission churches. "Me poor Mary, how I feel fer yehs! Ah, what a ter'ble affliction is a disobed'ent chil'."

Her good, motherly face was wet with tears. She trembled in eagerness to express her sympathy. The mourner sat with bowed head, rocking her body heavily to and fro, and crying out in a high, strained voice that sounded like a dirge on some forlorn pipe.

"I kin remember when she weared worsted boots an' her two feets was no bigger dan yer t'umb an' she weared worsted boots, Miss Smith," she cried, raising her streaming eyes.

"Ah, me poor Mary," sobbed the woman in black. With low, coddling cries, she sank on her knees by the mourner's chair, and put her arms about her. The other women began to groan in different keys.

"Yer poor misguided chil' is gone now, Mary, an' let us hope it's fer deh bes'. Yeh'll fergive her now, Mary, won't yehs, dear, all her disobed'ence? All her t'ankless behavior to her mudder an' all her badness? She's gone where her ter'ble sins will be judged."

The woman in black raised her face and paused. The inevitable sunlight came streaming in at the windows and shed a ghastly cheerfulness upon the faded hues of the room. Two or three of the spectators were sniffling, and one was loudly weeping. The mourner arose and staggered into the other room. In a moment she emerged with a pair of faded baby shoes held in the hollow of her hand.

"I kin remember when she used to wear dem," cried she. The women burst anew into cries as if they had all been stabbed. The mourner turned to the soiled and unshaven man.

"Jimmie, boy, go git yer sister! Go git yer sister an' we'll put deh boots on her feets!"

"Dey won't fit her now, yeh damn fool," said the man.

"Go git yer sister, Jimmie," shrieked the woman, confronting him fiercely.

The man swore sullenly. He went over to a corner and slowly began to put on his coat. He took his hat and went out, with a dragging, reluctant step.

The woman in black came forward and again besought the mourner.

"Yeh'll fergive her, Mary! Yeh'll fergive yer bad, bad, chil'! Her life was a curse an' her days were black an' yeh'll fergive yer bad girl? She's gone where her sins will be judged."

"She's gone where her sins will be judged," cried the other women, like a choir at a funeral.

"Deh Lord gives and deh Lord takes away," said the woman in black, raising her eyes to the sunbeams.

"Deh Lord gives and deh Lord takes away," responded the others.

"Yeh'll fergive her, Mary!" pleaded the woman in black. The mourner essayed to speak but her voice gave way. She shook her great shoulders frantically, in an agony of grief. Hot tears seemed to scald her quivering face. Finally her voice came and arose like a scream of pain.

"Oh, yes, I'll fergive her! I'll fergive her!"

About Author

In 1896, Crane endured a highly publicized scandal after appearing as a witness in the trial of a suspected prostitute, an acquaintance named Dora Clark. Late that year he accepted an offer to travel to Cuba as a war correspondent. As he waited in Jacksonville, Florida for passage, he met Cora Taylor, with whom he began a lasting relationship. En route to Cuba, Crane's vessel the SS Commodore sank off the coast of Florida, leaving him and others adrift for 30 hours in a dinghy. Crane described the ordeal in "The Open Boat". During the final years of his life, he covered conflicts in Greece (accompanied by Cora, recognized as the first woman war correspondent) and later lived in England with her. He was befriended by writers such as Joseph Conrad and H. G. Wells. Plagued by financial difficulties and ill health, Crane died of tuberculosis in a Black Forest sanatorium in Germany at the age of 28.

At the time of his death, Crane was considered an important figure in American literature. After he was nearly forgotten for two decades, critics revived interest in his life and work. Crane's writing is characterized by vivid intensity, distinctive dialects, and irony. Common themes involve fear, spiritual crises and social isolation. Although recognized primarily for The Red Badge of Courage, which has become an American classic, Crane is also known for his poetry, journalism, and short stories such as "The Open Boat", "The Blue Hotel", "The Bride Comes to Yellow Sky", and The Monster. His writing made a deep impression on 20th-century writers, most prominent among them Ernest Hemingway, and is thought to have inspired the Modernists and the Imagists.

Early years

Stephen Crane was born on November 1, 1871, in Newark, New Jersey, to Jonathan Townley Crane, a minister in the Methodist Episcopal church, and Mary Helen Peck Crane, daughter of a clergyman, George Peck. He was the fourteenth and last child born to the couple. At 45, Helen Crane had suffered the early deaths of her previous four children, each of whom died within one year of birth. Nicknamed "Stevie" by the family, he joined eight surviving brothers and sisters—Mary Helen, George Peck, Jonathan Townley, William Howe, Agnes Elizabeth, Edmund Byran, Wilbur Fiske, and Luther.

The Cranes were descended from Jaspar Crane, a founder of New Haven Colony, who had migrated there from England in 1639. Stephen was named for a putative founder of Elizabethtown, New Jersey, who had, according to family tradition, come from England or Wales in 1665, as well as his great-great-grandfather Stephen Crane (1709–1780), a Revolutionary War patriot who served as New Jersey delegate to the First Continental Congress in Philadelphia. Crane later wrote that his father, Dr. Crane, "was a great, fine, simple mind," who had written numerous tracts on theology. Although his mother was a popular spokeswoman for the Woman's Christian Temperance Union and a highly religious woman, Crane wrote that he did not believe "she was as narrow as most of her friends or family." The young Stephen was raised primarily by his sister Agnes, who was 15 years his senior. The family moved to Port Jervis, New York, in 1876, where Dr. Crane became the pastor of Drew Methodist Church, a position that he retained until his death.

As a child, Stephen was often sickly and afflicted by constant colds. When the boy was almost two, his father wrote in his diary that his youngest son became "so sick that we are anxious about him." Despite his fragile nature, Crane was an intelligent child who taught himself to read before the age of four. His first known inquiry, recorded by his father, dealt with writing; at the age of three, while imitating his brother Townley's writing, he asked his mother, "how do you spell O?" In December 1879, Crane wrote a poem about wanting a dog for Christmas. Entitled "I'd Rather Have –", it is his first surviving poem. Stephen was not regularly enrolled in school until January 1880, but he had no difficulty in completing two grades in six weeks. Recalling this feat, he wrote that it "sounds like the lie of a fond mother at a teaparty, but I do remember that I got ahead very fast and that father was very pleased with me."

Dr. Crane died on February 16, 1880, at the age of 60; Stephen was eight years old. Some 1,400 people mourned Dr. Crane at his funeral, more than double the size of his congregation. After her husband's death, Mrs. Crane moved to Roseville, near Newark, leaving Stephen in the care of his older brother Edmund, with whom the young boy lived with cousins in Sussex County. He next lived with his brother William, a lawyer, in Port Jervis for several years.

His older sister Helen took him to Asbury Park to be with their brother Townley and his wife, Fannie. Townley was a professional journalist; he headed the Long Branch department of both the New-York Tribune and the Associated Press, and also served as editor of the Asbury Park Shore Press. Agnes, another Crane sister, joined the siblings in New Jersey. She took a position at Asbury Park's intermediate school and moved in with Helen to care for the young Stephen.

Within a couple of years, the Crane family suffered more losses. First, Townley and his wife lost their two young children. His wife Fannie died of Bright's disease in November 1883. Agnes Crane became ill and died on June 10, 1884, of meningitis at the age of 28.

Schooling

Crane wrote his first known story, "Uncle Jake and the Bell Handle", when he was 14. In late 1885, he enrolled at Pennington Seminary, a ministry-focused coeducational boarding school 7 miles (11 km) north of Trenton. His father had been principal there from 1849 to 1858. Soon after her youngest son left for school, Mrs. Crane began suffering what the Asbury Park Shore Press reported as "a temporary aberration of the mind." She had apparently recovered by early 1886, but later that year, her son, 23-year-old Luther Crane, died after falling in front of an oncoming train while working as a flagman for the Erie Railroad. It was the fourth death in six years among Stephen's immediate family.

After two years, Crane left Pennington for Claverack College, a quasi-military school. He later looked back on his time at Claverack as "the happiest period of my life although I was not aware of it." A classmate remembered him as a highly literate but erratic student, lucky to pass examinations in math and science, and yet "far in advance of his fellow students in his knowledge of History and Literature", his favorite subjects. While he held an impressive record on the drill field and baseball diamond, Crane generally did not excel in the classroom. Not having a middle name, as was customary among other students, he took to signing his name "Stephen T. Crane" in order "to win recognition as a regular fellow". Crane was seen as friendly, but also moody and rebellious. He sometimes skipped class in order to play baseball, a game in which he starred as catcher. He was also greatly interested in the school's military training program. He rose rapidly in the ranks of the student battalion. One classmate described him as "indeed physically attractive without being handsome", but he was aloof, reserved and not generally popular at Claverack. Although academically weak, Crane gained experience at Claverack that provided background (and likely some anecdotes from the Civil War veterans on the staff) that proved useful when he came to write The Red Badge of Courage.

In mid-1888, Crane became his brother Townley's assistant at a New Jersey shore news bureau, working there every summer until 1892. Crane's first publication under his byline was an article on the explorer Henry M. Stanley's famous quest to find the Scottish missionary David Livingstone in Africa. It appeared in the February 1890 Claverack College Vidette. Within a few months, Crane was persuaded by his family to forgo a military career and transfer to Lafayette College in Easton, Pennsylvania, in order to pursue a mining engineering degree. He registered at Lafayette on September 12, and promptly became involved in extracurricular activities; he took up baseball again and joined the largest fraternity, Delta Upsilon. He also joined both rival literary societies, named for (George) Washington and (Benjamin) Franklin. Crane infrequently attended classes and ended the semester with grades for four of the seven courses he had taken.

After one semester, Crane transferred to Syracuse University, where he enrolled as a non-degree candidate in the College of Liberal Arts. He roomed in the Delta Upsilon fraternity house and joined the baseball team. Attending just one class (English Literature) during the middle trimester, he remained in residence while taking no courses in the third semester.

Concentrating on his writing, Crane began to experiment with tone and style while trying out different subjects. He published his fictional story, "Great Bugs of Onondaga," simultaneously in the Syracuse Daily Standard and the New York Tribune. Declaring college "a waste of time", Crane decided to become a full-time writer and reporter. He attended a Delta Upsilon chapter meeting on June 12, 1891, but shortly afterward left college for good.

Full-time writer

In the summer of 1891, Crane often camped with friends in the nearby area of Sullivan County, New York, where his brother Edmund occupied a house obtained as part of their brother William's Hartwood Club (Association) land dealings. He used this area as the geographic setting for several short stories, which were posthumously published in a collection under the title Stephen Crane: Sullivan County Tales and Sketches. Crane showed two of these works to Tribune editor Willis Fletcher Johnson, a friend of the family, who accepted them for the publication. "Hunting Wild Dogs" and "The Last of the Mohicans" were the first of fourteen unsigned Sullivan County sketches and tales that were published in the Tribune between February and July 1892. Crane also showed Johnson an early draft of his first novel, Maggie: A Girl of the Streets.

Later that summer, Crane met and befriended author Hamlin Garland, who had been lecturing locally on American literature and the expressive arts; on August 17 he gave a talk on novelist William Dean Howells, which Crane wrote up for the Tribune. Garland became a mentor for and champion of the young writer, whose intellectual honesty impressed him. Their relationship suffered in later years, however, because Garland disapproved of Crane's alleged immorality, related to his living with a woman married to another man.

Stephen moved into his brother Edmund's house in Lakeview, a suburb of Paterson, New Jersey, in the fall of 1891. From here he made frequent trips into New York City, writing and reporting particularly on its impoverished tenement districts. Crane focused particularly on The Bowery, a small and once prosperous neighborhood in the southern part of Manhattan. After the Civil War, Bowery shops and mansions had given way to saloons, dance halls, brothels and flophouses, all of which Crane frequented. He later said he did so for research. He was attracted to the human nature found in the slums, considering it "open and plain, with nothing hidden". Believing nothing honest and unsentimental had been written about the Bowery, Crane became determined to do so himself; this was the setting of his first novel. On December 7, 1891, Crane's mother died at the age of 64, and the 20-year-old appointed Edmund as his guardian.

Despite being frail, undernourished and suffering from a hacking cough, which did not prevent him from smoking cigarettes, in the spring of 1892 Crane began a romance with Lily Brandon Munroe, a married woman who was estranged from her husband. Although Munroe later said Crane "was not a handsome man", she admired his "remarkable almond-shaped gray eyes." He begged her to elope with him, but her family opposed the match because Crane lacked money and prospects, and she declined. Their last meeting likely occurred in April 1898, when he again asked her to run away with him and she again refused.

Such an assemblage of the spraddle-legged men of the middle class, whose hands were bent and shoulders stooped from delving and constructing, had never appeared to an Asbury Park summer crowd, and the latter was vaguely amused.

— Stephen Crane, account of the JOUAM parade as it appeared in the Tribune

Between July 2 and September 11, 1892, Crane published at least ten news reports on Asbury Park affairs. Although a Tribune colleague stated that Crane "was not highly distinguished above any other boy of twenty who had gained a reputation for saying and writing bright things," that summer his reporting took on a more skeptical, hypocrisy-deflating tone. A storm of controversy erupted over a report he wrote on the Junior Order of United American Mechanics' American Day Parade, entitled "Parades and Entertainments". Published on August 21, the report juxtaposes the "bronzed, slope-shouldered, uncouth" marching men "begrimed with dust" and the spectators dressed in "summer gowns, lace parasols, tennis trousers, straw hats and indifferent smiles". Believing they were being ridiculed, some JOUAM marchers were outraged and wrote to the editor. The owner of the Tribune, Whitelaw Reid, was that year's Republican vice-presidential candidate, and this likely increased the sensitivity of the paper's management to the issue. Although Townley wrote a piece for the Asbury Park Daily Press in his brother's defense, the Tribune quickly apologized to its readers, calling Stephen Crane's piece "a bit of random correspondence, passed inadvertently by the copy editor". Hamlin Garland and biographer John Barry attested that Crane told them he had been dismissed by the Tribune, although Willis Fletcher Johnson later denied this. The paper did not publish any of Crane's work after 1892.

Life in New York

Crane struggled to make a living as a free-lance writer, contributing sketches and feature articles to various New York newspapers. In October 1892, he moved into a rooming house in Manhattan whose boarders were a group of medical students. During this time, he expanded or entirely reworked Maggie: A Girl of the Streets, which is about a girl who "blossoms in a mud-puddle" and becomes a pitiful victim of circumstance. In the winter of 1893, Crane took the manuscript of Maggie to Richard Watson Gilder, who rejected it for publication in The Century Magazine.

Crane decided to publish it privately, with money he had inherited from his mother. The novel was published in late February or early March 1893 by a small printing shop that usually printed medical books and religious tracts. The typewritten title page for the Library of Congress copyright application read simply: "A Girl of the Streets, / A Story of New York. / —By—/Stephen Crane." The name "Maggie" was added to the title later. Crane used the pseudonym "Johnston Smith" for the novel's initial publication, later telling friend and artist Corwin Knapp Linson that the nom de plume was the "commonest name I could think of. I had an editor friend named Johnson, and put in the "t", and no one could find me in the mob of Smiths." Hamlin Garland reviewed the work in the June 1893 issue of The Arena, calling it "the most truthful and unhackneyed study of the slums I have yet read, fragment though it is." Despite this early praise, Crane became depressed and destitute from having spent $869 for 1,100 copies of a novel that did not sell; he ended up giving a hundred copies away. He would later remember "how I looked forward to publication and pictured the sensation I thought it would make. It fell flat. Nobody seemed to notice it or care for it... Poor Maggie! She was one of my first loves."

In March 1893, Crane spent hours lounging in Linson's studio while having his portrait painted. He became fascinated with issues of the Century that were largely devoted to famous battles and military leaders from the Civil War. Frustrated with the dryly written stories, Crane stated, "I wonder that some of those fellows don't tell how they felt in those scraps. They spout enough of what they did, but they're as emotionless as rocks." Crane returned to these magazines during subsequent visits to Linson's studio, and eventually the idea of writing a war novel overtook him. He would later state that he "had been unconsciously working the detail of the story out through most of his boyhood" and had imagined "war stories ever since he was out of knickerbockers." This novel would ultimately become The Red Badge of Courage.

A river, amber-tinted in the shadow of its banks, purled at the army's feet; and at night, when the stream had become of a sorrowful blackness, one could see across it the red, eyelike gleam of hostile camp-fires set in the low brows of distant hills.

— Stephen Crane, The Red Badge of Courage

From the beginning, Crane wished to show how it felt to be in a war by writing "a psychological portrayal of fear." Conceiving his story from the point of view of a young private who is at first filled with boyish dreams of the glory of war and then quickly becomes disillusioned by war's reality, Crane borrowed the private's surname, "Fleming", from his sister-in-law's maiden name. He later said that the first paragraphs came to him with "every word in place, every comma, every period fixed." Working mostly nights, he wrote from around midnight until four or five in the morning. Because he could not afford a typewriter, he wrote carefully in ink on legal-sized paper, seldom crossing through or interlining a word. If he did change something, he would rewrite the whole page.

While working on his second novel, Crane remained prolific, concentrating on publishing stories to stave off poverty; "An Experiment in Misery", based on Crane's experiences in the Bowery, was printed by the New York Press. He also wrote five or six poems a day. In early 1894, he showed some of his poems or "lines" as he called them, to Hamlin Garland, who said he read "some thirty in all" with "growing wonder." Although Garland and William Dean Howells encouraged him to submit his poetry for publication, Crane's free verse was too unconventional for most. After brief wrangling between poet and publisher, Copeland & Day accepted Crane's first book of poems, The Black Riders and Other Lines, although it would not be published until after The Red Badge of Courage. He received a 10 percent royalty and the publisher assured him that the book would be in a form "more severely classic than any book ever yet issued in America."

In the spring of 1894, Crane offered the finished manuscript of The Red Badge of Courage to McClure's Magazine, which had become the foremost magazine for Civil War literature. While McClure's delayed giving him an answer on his novel, they offered him an assignment writing about the Pennsylvania coal mines. "In the Depths of a Coal Mine", a story with pictures by Linson, was syndicated by McClure's in a number of newspapers, heavily edited. Crane was reportedly disgusted by the cuts, asking Linson: "Why the hell did they send me up there then? Do they want the public to think the coal mines gilded ball-rooms with the miners eating ice-cream in boiled shirt-fronts?"

Sources report that following an encounter with a male prostitute that spring, Crane began a novel on the subject entitled Flowers of Asphalt, which he later abandoned. The manuscript has never been recovered.

After discovering that McClure's could not afford to pay him, Crane took his war novel to Irving Bacheller of the Bacheller-Johnson Newspaper Syndicate, which agreed to publish The Red Badge of Courage in serial form. Between the third and the ninth of December 1894, The Red Badge of Courage was published in some half-dozen newspapers in the United States.

Although it was greatly cut for syndication, Bacheller attested to its causing a stir, saying "its quality [was] immediately felt and recognized." The lead editorial in the Philadelphia Press of December 7 said that Crane "is a new name now and unknown, but everybody will be talking about him if he goes on as he has begun".

Travels and fame

At the end of January 1895, Crane left on what he called "a very long and circuitous newspaper trip" to the west. While writing feature articles for the Bacheller syndicate, he traveled to Saint Louis, Missouri, Nebraska, New Orleans, Galveston, Texas and then Mexico City. Irving Bacheller would later state that he "sent Crane to Mexico for new color", which the author found in the form of Mexican slum life. Whereas he found the lower class in New York pitiful, he was impressed by the "superiority" of the Mexican peasants' contentment and "even refuse[d] to pity them."

Returning to New York five months later, Crane joined the Lantern (alternately spelled "Lanthom" or "Lanthorne") Club organized by a group of young writers and journalists. The Club, located on the roof of an old house on William Street near the Brooklyn Bridge, served as a drinking establishment of sorts and was decorated to look like a ship's cabin. There Crane ate one good meal a day, although friends were troubled by his "constant smoking, too much coffee, lack of food and poor teeth", as Nelson Greene put it. Living in near-poverty and greatly anticipating the publication of his books, Crane began work on two more novels: The Third Violet and George's Mother.

The Black Riders was published by Copeland & Day shortly before his return to New York in May, but it received mostly criticism, if not abuse, for the poems' unconventional style and use of free verse. A piece in the Bookman called Crane "the Aubrey Beardsley of poetry," and a commentator from the Chicago Daily Inter-Ocean stated that "there is not a line of poetry from the opening to the closing page. Whitman's Leaves of Grass were luminous in comparison. Poetic lunacy would be a better name for the book." In June, the New York Tribune dismissed the book as "so much trash." Crane was pleased that the book was "making some stir".

In contrast to the reception for Crane's poetry, The Red Badge of Courage was welcomed with acclaim after its publication by Appleton in September 1895. For the next four months, the book was in the top six on various bestseller lists around the country. It arrived on the literary scene "like a flash of lightning out of a clear winter sky", according to H. L. Mencken, who was about 15 at the time. The novel also became popular in Britain; Joseph Conrad, a future friend of Crane, wrote that the novel "detonated... with the impact and force of a twelve-inch shell charged with a very high explosive." Appleton published two, possibly three, printings in 1895 and as many as eleven more in 1896. Although some critics considered the work overly graphic and profane, it was widely heralded for its realistic portrayal of war and unique writing style. The Detroit Free Press declared that The Red Badge would give readers "so vivid a picture of the emotions and the horrors of the battlefield that you will pray your eyes may never look upon the reality."

Wanting to capitalize on the success of The Red Badge, McClure Syndicate offered Crane a contract to write a series on Civil War battlefields. Because it was a wish of his to "visit the battlefield—which I was to describe—at the time of year when it was fought", Crane agreed to take the assignment. Visiting battlefields in Northern Virginia, including Fredericksburg, he would later produce five more Civil War tales: "Three Miraculous Soldiers", "The Veteran", "An Indiana Campaign", "An Episode of War" and The Little Regiment.

Scandal

At the age of 24, Crane, who was reveling in his success, became involved in a highly publicized case involving a suspected prostitute named Dora Clark. At 2 a.m. on September 16, 1896, he escorted two chorus girls and Clark from New York City's Broadway Garden, a popular "resort" where he had interviewed the women for a series he was writing. As Crane saw one woman safely to a streetcar, a plainclothes policeman named Charles Becker arrested the other two for solicitation; Crane was threatened with arrest when he tried to interfere. One of the women was released after Crane confirmed her erroneous claim that she was his wife, but Clark was charged and taken to the precinct. Against the advice of the arresting sergeant, Crane made a statement confirming Dora Clark's innocence, stating that "I only know that while with me she acted respectably, and that the policeman's charge was false." On the basis of Crane's testimony, Clark was discharged. The media seized upon the story; news spread to Philadelphia, Boston and beyond, with papers focusing on Crane's courage. The Stephen Crane story, as it became known, soon became a source for ridicule; the Chicago Dispatch in particular quipped that "Stephen Crane is respectfully informed that association with women in scarlet is not necessarily a 'Red Badge of Courage' ".

A couple of weeks after her trial, Clark pressed charges of false arrest against the officer who had arrested her. The next day, the officer physically attacked Clark in the presence of witnesses for having brought charges against him. Crane, who initially went briefly to Philadelphia to escape the pressure of publicity, returned to New York to give testimony at Becker's trial despite advice given to him from Theodore Roosevelt, who was Police Commissioner at the time and a new acquaintance of Crane. The defense targeted Crane: police raided his apartment and interviewed people who knew him, trying to find incriminating evidence in order to lessen the effect of his testimony. A vigorous cross-examination took place that sought to portray Crane as a man of dubious morals; while the prosecution proved that he frequented brothels, Crane claimed this was merely for research purposes. After the trial ended on October 16, the arresting officer was exonerated, and Crane's reputation was ruined.

Cora Taylor and the Commodore shipwreck

None of them knew the color of the sky. Their eyes glanced level and were fastened upon the waves that swept toward them. These waves were of the hue of slate, save for the tops, which were of foaming white, and all of the men knew the colors of the sea.

— Stephen Crane, "The Open Boat"

Given $700 in Spanish gold by the Bacheller-Johnson syndicate to work as a war correspondent in Cuba as the Spanish–American War was pending, the 25-year-old Crane left New York on November 27, 1896, on a train bound for Jacksonville, Florida. Upon arrival in Jacksonville, he registered at the St. James Hotel under the alias of Samuel Carleton to maintain anonymity while seeking passage to Cuba. While waiting for a boat, he toured the city and visited the local brothels. Within days he met 31-year-old Cora Taylor, proprietor of the downtown bawdy house Hotel de Dream. Born into a respectable Boston family, Taylor (whose legal name was Cora Ethel Stewart) had already had two brief marriages; her first husband, Vinton Murphy, divorced her on grounds of adultery. In 1889, she had married British Captain Donald William Stewart. She left him in 1892 for another man, but was still legally married. By the time Crane arrived, Taylor had been in Jacksonville for two years. She lived a bohemian lifestyle, owned a hotel of assignation, and was a well-known and respected local figure. The two spent much time together while Crane awaited his departure. He was finally cleared to leave for the Cuban port of Cienfuegos on New Year's Eve aboard the SS Commodore.

The ship sailed from Jacksonville with 27 or 28 men and a cargo of supplies and ammunition for the Cuban rebels. On the St. Johns River and less than 2 miles (3.2 km) from Jacksonville, Commodore struck a sandbar in a dense fog and damaged its hull. Although towed off the sandbar the following day, it was beached again in Mayport and again damaged. A leak began in the boiler room that evening and, as a result of malfunctioning water pumps, the ship came to a standstill about 16 miles (26 km) from Mosquito Inlet. As the ship took on more water, Crane described the engine room as resembling "a scene at this time taken from the middle kitchen of hades." Commodore's lifeboats were lowered in the early hours of the morning on January 2, 1897 and the ship ultimately sank at 7 a.m. Crane was one of the last to leave the ship in a 10-foot (3.0 m) dinghy. In an ordeal that he recounted in the short story "The Open Boat", Crane and three other men (including the ship's Captain) floundered off the coast of Florida for a day and a half before trying to land the dinghy at Daytona Beach. The small boat overturned in the surf, forcing the exhausted men to swim to shore; one of them died. Having lost the gold given to him for his journey, Crane wired Cora Taylor for help. She traveled to Daytona and returned to Jacksonville with Crane the next day, only four days after he had left on the Commodore.

The disaster was reported on the front pages of newspapers across the country. Rumors that the ship had been sabotaged were widely circulated but never substantiated. Portrayed favorably and heroically by the press, Crane emerged from the ordeal with his reputation enhanced, if not restored, after the battering he had received in the Dora Clark affair. Meanwhile, Crane's affair with Taylor blossomed.

Three seasons of archaeological investigation were conducted in 2002-04 to examine and document the exposed remains of a wreck near Ponce Inlet, FL conjectured to be that of the SS Commodore. The collected data, and other accumulated evidence, finally substantiated the identification of the Commodore beyond a reasonable doubt.

Greco-Turkish War

Despite contentment in Jacksonville and the need for rest after his ordeal, Crane became restless. He left Jacksonville on January 11 for New York City, where he applied for a passport to Cuba, Mexico and the West Indies. Spending three weeks in New York, he completed "The Open Boat" and periodically visited Port Jervis to see family. By this time, however, blockades had formed along the Florida coast as tensions rose with Spain, and Crane concluded that he would never be able to travel to Cuba. He sold "The Open Boat" to Scribner's for $300 in early March. Determined to work as a war correspondent, Crane signed on with William Randolph Hearst's New York Journal to cover the impending Greco-Turkish conflict. He brought along Taylor, who had sold the Hotel de Dream in order to follow him.

On March 20, they sailed first to England, where Crane was warmly received. They arrived in Athens in early April; between April 17 (when Turkey declared war on Greece) and April 22, Crane wrote his first published report of the war, "An Impression of the 'Concert' ". When he left for Epirus in the northwest, Taylor remained in Athens, where she became the Greek war's first woman war correspondent. She wrote under the pseudonym "Imogene Carter" for the New York Journal, a job that Crane had secured for her. They wrote frequently, traveling throughout the country separately and together. The first large battle that Crane witnessed was the Turks' assault on General

Constantine Smolenski's Greek forces at Velestino. Crane wrote, "It is a great thing to survey the army of the enemy. Just where and how it takes hold upon the heart is difficult of description." During this battle, Crane encountered "a fat waddling puppy" that he immediately claimed, dubbing it "Velestino, the Journal dog". Greece and Turkey signed an armistice on May 20, ending the 30-day war; Crane and Taylor left Greece for England, taking two Greek brothers as servants and Velestino the dog with them.

Spanish–American War

After staying in Limpsfield, Surrey, for a few days, Crane and Taylor settled in Ravensbrook, a plain brick villa in Oxted. Referring to themselves as Mr. and Mrs. Crane, the couple lived openly in England, but Crane concealed the relationship from his friends and family in the United States. Admired in England, Crane thought himself attacked back home: "There seem so many of them in America who want to kill, bury and forget me purely out of unkindness and envy and—my unworthiness, if you choose", he wrote. Velestino the dog sickened and died soon after their arrival in England, on August 1. Crane, who had a great love for dogs, wrote an emotional letter to a friend an hour after the dog's death, stating that "for eleven days we fought death for him, thinking nothing of anything but his life." The Limpsfield-Oxted area was home to members of the socialist Fabian Society and a magnet for writers such as Edmund Gosse, Ford Madox Ford and Edward Garnett. Crane also met the Polish-born novelist Joseph Conrad in October 1897, with whom he would have what Crane called a "warm and endless friendship".

Although Crane was confident among peers, strong negative reviews of the recently published The Third Violet were causing his literary reputation to dwindle. Reviewers were also highly critical of Crane's war letters, deeming them self-centered. Although The Red Badge of Courage had by this time gone through fourteen printings in the United States and six in England, Crane was running out of money. To survive financially, he worked at a feverish pitch, writing prolifically for both the English and the American markets. He wrote in quick succession stories such as The Monster, "The Bride Comes to Yellow Sky", "Death and the Child" and "The Blue Hotel".

Crane began to attach price tags to his new works of fiction, hoping that "The Bride", for example, would fetch $175.

As 1897 ended, Crane's money crisis worsened. Amy Leslie, a reporter from Chicago and a former lover, sued him for $550. The New York Times reported that Leslie gave him $800 in November 1896 but that he'd repaid only a quarter of the sum. In February he was summoned to answer Leslie's claim. The claim was apparently settled out of court, because no record of adjudication exists. Meanwhile, Crane felt "heavy with troubles" and "chased to the wall" by expenses. He confided to his agent that he was $2,000 in debt but that he would "beat it" with more literary output.

Soon after the USS Maine exploded in Havana Harbor on February 15, 1898, under suspicious circumstances, Crane was offered a £60 advance by Blackwood's Magazine for articles "from the seat of war in the event of a war breaking out" between the United States and Spain. His health was failing, and it is believed that signs of his pulmonary tuberculosis, which he may have contracted in childhood, became apparent. With almost no money coming in from his finished stories, Crane accepted the assignment and left Oxted for New York. Taylor and the rest of the household stayed behind to fend off local creditors. Crane applied for a passport and left New York for Key West two days before Congress declared war. While the war idled, he interviewed people and produced occasional copy.

In early June, he observed the establishment of an American base in Cuba when Marines seized Guantánamo Bay. He went ashore with the Marines, planning "to gather impressions and write them as the spirit moved." Although he wrote honestly about his fear in battle, others observed his calmness and composure. He would later recall "this prolonged tragedy of the night" in the war tale "Marines Signaling Under Fire at Guantanamo". After showing a willingness to serve during fighting at Cuzco, Cuba, by carrying messages to company commanders, Crane was officially cited for his "material aid during the action".

He continued to report upon various battles and the worsening military conditions and praised Theodore Roosevelt's Rough Riders, despite past tensions with the Commissioner. In early July, Crane was sent to the United States for medical treatment for a high fever. He was diagnosed with yellow fever, then malaria. Upon arrival in Old Point Comfort, Virginia, he spent a few weeks resting in a hotel. Although Crane had filed more than twenty dispatches in the three months he had covered the war, the World's business manager believed that the paper had not received its money's worth and fired him. In retaliation, Crane signed with Hearst's New York Journal with the wish to return to Cuba. He traveled first to Puerto Rico and then to Havana. In September, rumors began to spread that Crane, who was working anonymously, had either been killed or disappeared. He sporadically sent out dispatches and stories; he wrote about the mood in Havana, the crowded city sidewalks, and other topics, but he was soon desperate for money again. Taylor, left alone in England, was also penniless. She became frantic with worry over her lover's whereabouts; they were not in direct communication until the end of the year. Crane left Havana and arrived in England on January 11, 1899.

Death

Rent on Ravensbrook had not been paid for a year. Upon returning to England, Crane secured a solicitor to act as guarantor for their debts, after which Crane and Taylor relocated to Brede Place. This manor in Sussex, which dated to the 14th century and had neither electricity nor indoor plumbing, was offered to them by friends at a modest rent. The relocation appeared to give hope to Crane, but his money problems continued. Deciding that he could no longer afford to write for American publications, he concentrated on publishing in English magazines.

Crane pushed himself to write feverishly during the first months at Brede; he told his publisher that he was "doing more work now than I have at any other period in my life". His health worsened, and by late 1899 he was asking friends about health resorts. The Monster and Other Stories was in production and War Is Kind, his second collection of poems, was published in the United States in May. None of his books after The Red Badge of Courage had sold well, and he bought a typewriter to spur output. Active Service, a novella based on Crane's correspondence experience, was published in October. The New York Times reviewer questioned "whether the author of 'Active Service' himself really sees anything remarkable in his newspapery hero."

In December, the couple held an elaborate Christmas party at Brede, attended by Conrad, Henry James, H. G. Wells and other friends; it lasted several days. On December 29 Crane suffered a severe pulmonary hemorrhage. In January 1900 he'd recovered sufficiently to work on a new novel, The O'Ruddy, completing 25 of the 33 chapters. Plans were made for him to travel as a correspondent to Gibraltar to write sketches from Saint Helena, the site of a Boer prison, but at the end of March and in early April he suffered two more hemorrhages. Taylor took over most of Crane's correspondence while he was ill, writing to friends for monetary aid. The couple planned to travel on the continent, but Conrad, upon visiting Crane for the last time, remarked that his friend's "wasted face was enough to tell me that it was the most forlorn of all hopes."

On May 28, the couple arrived at Badenweiler, Germany, a health spa on the edge of the Black Forest. Despite his weakened condition, Crane continued to dictate fragmentary episodes for the completion of The O'Ruddy. He died on June 5, 1900, at the age of 28. In his will he left everything to Taylor, who took his body to New Jersey for burial. Crane was interred in Evergreen Cemetery in what is now Hillside, New Jersey.

Style and technique

Stephen Crane's fiction is typically categorized as representative of Naturalism, American realism, Impressionism or a mixture of the three. Critic Sergio Perosa, for example, wrote in his essay, "Stephen Crane fra naturalismo e impressionismo," that the work presents a "symbiosis" of Naturalistic ideals and Impressionistic methods. When asked whether or not he would write an autobiography in 1896, Crane responded that he "dare not say that I am honest. I merely say that I am as nearly honest as a weak mental machinery will allow." Similarities between the stylistic techniques in Crane's writing and Impressionist painting—including the use of color and chiaroscuro—are often cited to support the theory that Crane was not only an Impressionist but also influenced by the movement. H. G. Wells remarked upon "the great influence of the studio" on Crane's work, quoting a passage from The Red Badge of Courage as an example: "At nightfall the column broke into regimental pieces, and the fragments went into the fields to camp. Tents sprang up like strange plants. Camp fires, like red, peculiar blossoms, dotted the night.... From this little distance the many fires, with the black forms of men passing to and fro before the crimson rays, made weird and satanic effects." Although no direct evidence exists that Crane formulated a precise theory of his craft, he vehemently rejected sentimentality, asserting that "a story should be logical in its action and faithful to character. Truth to life itself was the only test, the greatest artists were the simplest, and simple because they were true."

Poet and biographer John Berryman suggested that there were three basic variations, or "norms", of Crane's narrative style. The first, being "flexible, swift, abrupt and nervous", is best exemplified in The Red Badge of Courage, while the second ("supple majesty") is believed to relate to "The Open Boat", and the third ("much more closed, circumstantial and 'normal' in feeling and syntax") to later works such as The Monster. Crane's work, however, cannot be determined by style solely on chronology. Not only does his fiction not take place in any particular region with similar characters, but it varies from serious in tone to reportorial writing and light fiction. Crane's writing, both fiction and nonfiction, is consistently driven by immediacy and is at once concentrated, vivid and intense. The novels and short stories contain poetic characteristics such as shorthand prose, suggestibility, shifts in perspective and ellipses between and within sentences. Similarly, omission plays a large part in Crane's work; the names of his protagonists are not commonly used and sometimes they are not named at all.

Crane was often criticized by early reviewers for his frequent incorporation of everyday speech into dialogue, mimicking the regional accents of his characters with colloquial stylization. This is apparent in his first novel, in which Crane ignored the romantic, sentimental approach of slum fiction; he instead concentrated on the cruelty and sordid aspects of poverty, expressed by the brashness of the Bowery's crude dialect and profanity, which he used lavishly. The distinct dialect of his Bowery characters is apparent at the beginning of the text; the title character admonishes her brother saying: "Yeh knows it puts mudder out when yes comes home half dead, an' it's like we'll all get a poundin'."

Major themes

Crane's work is often thematically driven by Naturalistic and Realistic concerns, including ideals versus realities, spiritual crises and fear. These themes are particularly evident in Crane's first three novels, Maggie: A Girl of the Streets, The Red Badge of Courage and George's Mother. The three main characters search for a way to make their dreams come true, but ultimately suffer from crises of identity. Crane was fascinated by war and death, as well as fire, disfigurement, fear and courage, all of which inspired him to write many works based on these concepts. In The Red Badge of Courage, the main character both longs for the heroics of battle but ultimately fears it, demonstrating the dichotomy of courage and cowardice. He experiences the threat of death, misery and a loss of self.

Extreme isolation from society and community is also apparent in Crane's work. During the most intense battle scenes in The Red Badge of Courage, for example, the story's focus is mainly "on the inner responses of a self unaware of others". In "The Open Boat", "An Experiment in Misery" and other stories, Crane uses light, motion and color to express degrees of epistemological uncertainty. Similar to other Naturalistic writers, Crane scrutinizes the position of man, who has been isolated not only from society, but also from God and nature. "The Open Boat", for example, distances itself from Romantic optimism and affirmation of man's place in the world by concentrating on the characters' isolation.

While he lived, Stephen Crane was denominated by critical readers a realist, a naturalist, an impressionist, symbolist, Symboliste, expressionist and ironist; his posthumous life was enriched by critics who read him as nihilistic, existentialist, a neo-Romantic, a sentimentalist, protomodernist, pointilliste, visionist, imagist and, by his most recent biographer, a "bleak naturalist." At midcentury he was a "predisciple of the New Criticism"; by its end he was "a proto-deconstructionist anti-artist hero" who had "leapfrogged modernism, landing on postmodernist ground." Or, as Sergio Perosa wrote in 1964, "The critic wanders in a labyrinth of possibilities, which every new turn taken by Crane's fiction seems to explode or deny."

One undeniable fact about Crane's work, as Anthony Splendora noted in 2015, is that Death haunts it; like a threatening eclipse it overshadows his best efforts, each of which features the signal demise of a main character. Allegorically, "The Blue Hotel," at the pinnacle of the short story form, may even be an autothanatography, the author's intentional exteriorization or objectification, in this case for the purpose of purgation, of his own impending death. Crane's "Swede" in that story can be taken, following current psychoanalytical theory, as a surrogative, sacrificial victim, ritually to be purged.

Transcending this "dark circumstance of composition," Crane had a particular telos and impetus for his creation: beyond the tautologies that all art is alterity and to some formal extent mimesis, Crane sought and obviously found "a form of catharsis" in writing. This view accounts for his uniqueness, especially as operative through his notorious "disgust" with his family's religion, their "vacuous, futile psalm-singing". His favorite book, for example, was Mark Twain's Life on the Mississippi, in which God is mentioned only twice—once as irony and once as "a swindle." Not only did Crane call out God specifically with the lines "Well then I hate thee / righteous image" in "The Black Riders" (1895), but even his most hopeful tropes, such as the "comradeship" of his "Open Boat" survivors, make no mention of deity, specifying only "indifferent nature." His antitheism is most evident in his characterization of the human race as "lice clinging to a space-lost bulb," a climax-nearing speech in "The Blue Hotel," Ch. VI. It is possible that Crane utilized religion's formal psychic space, now suddenly available resulting from the recent "Death of God", as a milieu for his compensative art.

Novels

Beginning with the publication of Maggie: A Girl of the Streets in 1893, Crane was recognized by critics mainly as a novelist. Maggie was initially rejected by numerous publishers because of its atypical and true-to-life depictions of class warfare, which clashed with the sentimental tales of that time. Rather than focusing on the very rich or middle class, the novel's characters are lower-class denizens of New York's Bowery. The main character, Maggie, descends into prostitution after being led astray by her lover. Although the novel's plot is simple, its dramatic mood, quick pace and portrayal of Bowery life have made it memorable. Maggie is not merely an account of slum life, but also represents eternal symbols. In his first draft, Crane did not give his characters proper names. Instead, they were identified by epithets: Maggie, for example, was the girl who "blossomed in a mud-puddle" and Pete, her seducer, was a "knight". The novel is dominated by bitter irony and anger, as well as destructive morality and treacherous sentiment. Critics would later call the novel "the first dark flower of American Naturalism" for its distinctive elements of naturalistic fiction.

Written thirty years after the end of the Civil War and before Crane had any experience of battle, The Red Badge of Courage was innovative stylistically as well as psychologically. Often described as a war novel, it focuses less on battle and more on the main character's psyche and his reactions and responses in war. It is believed that Crane based the fictional battle in the novel on that of Chancellorsville; he may also have interviewed veterans of the 124th New York Volunteer Infantry Regiment, commonly known as the Orange Blossoms, in Port Jervis, New York. Told in a third-person limited point of view, it reflects the private experience of Henry Fleming, a young soldier who flees from combat. The Red Badge of Courage is notable in its vivid descriptions and well-cadenced prose, both of which help create suspense within the story. Similarly, by substituting epithets for characters' names ("the youth", "the tattered soldier"), Crane injects an allegorical quality into his work, making his characters point to a specific characteristic of man. Like Crane's first novel, The Red Badge of Courage has a deeply ironic tone which increases in severity as the novel progresses. The title of the work is ironic; Henry wishes "that he, too, had a wound, a red badge of courage", echoing a wish to have been wounded in battle. The wound he does receive (from the rifle butt of a fleeing Union soldier) is not a badge of courage but a badge of shame.

The novel expresses a strong connection between humankind and nature, a frequent and prominent concern in Crane's fiction and poetry throughout his career. Whereas contemporary writers (Ralph Waldo Emerson, Nathaniel Hawthorne, Henry David Thoreau) focused on a sympathetic bond on the two elements, Crane wrote from the perspective that human consciousness distanced humans from nature. In The Red Badge of Courage, this distance is paired with a great number of references to animals, and men with animalistic characteristics: people "howl", "squawk", "growl", or "snarl".

Since the resurgence of Crane's popularity in the 1920s, The Red Badge of Courage has been deemed a major American text. The novel has been anthologized numerous times, including in the 1942 collection Men at War: The Best War Stories of All Time, edited by Ernest Hemingway. In the introduction, Hemingway wrote that the novel "is one of the finest books of our literature, and I include it entire because it is all as much of a piece as a great poem is."

Crane's later novels have not received as much critical praise. After the success of The Red Badge of Courage, Crane wrote another tale set in the Bowery. George's Mother is less allegorical and more personal than his two previous novels, and it focuses on the conflict between a church-going, temperance-adhering woman (thought to be based on Crane's mother) and her single remaining offspring, who is a naive dreamer. Critical response to the novel was mixed. The Third Violet, a romance that he wrote quickly after publishing The Red Badge of Courage, is typically considered as Crane's attempt to appeal to popular audiences. Crane considered it a "quiet little story." Although it contained autobiographical details, the characters have been deemed inauthentic and stereotypical. Crane's second to last novel, Active Service, revolves around the Greco-Turkish War of 1897, with which the author was familiar. Although noted for its satirical take on the melodramatic and highly passionate works that were popular of the nineteenth century, the novel was not successful. It is generally accepted by critics that Crane's work suffered at this point due to the speed which he wrote in order to meet his high expenses. His last novel, a suspenseful and picaresque work entitled The O'Ruddy, was finished posthumously by Robert Barr and published in 1903.

Short fiction

Crane wrote many different types of fictional pieces while indiscriminately applying to them terms such as "story", "tale" and "sketch". For this reason, critics have found clear-cut classification of Crane's work problematic. While "The Open Boat" and "The Bride Comes to Yellow Sky" are often considered short stories, others are variously identified.

In an 1896 interview with Herbert P. Williams, a reporter for the Boston Herald, Crane said that he did "not find that short stories are utterly different in character from other fiction. It seems to me that short stories are the easiest things we write." During his brief literary career, he wrote more than a hundred short stories and fictional sketches. Crane's early fiction was based in camping expeditions in his teen years; these stories eventually became known as The Sullivan County Tales and Sketches. He considered these "sketches", which are mostly humorous and not of the same caliber of work as his later fiction, to be "articles of many kinds," in that they are part fiction and part journalism.

The subject matter for his stories varied extensively. His early New York City sketches and Bowery tales accurately described the results of industrialization, immigration and the growth of cities and their slums. His collection of six short stories, The Little Regiment, covered familiar ground with the American Civil War, a subject for which he became famous with The Red Badge of Courage. Although similar to Crane's noted novel, The Little Regiment was believed to lack vigor and originality. Realizing the limitations of these tales, Crane wrote: "I have invented the sum of my invention with regard to war and this story keeps me in internal despair."

The Open Boat and Other Tales of Adventure (1898) contains thirteen short stories that deal with three periods in Crane's life: his Asbury Park boyhood, his trip to the West and Mexico in 1895, and his Cuban adventure in 1897. This collection was well received and included several of his most critically successful works. His 1899 collection, The Monster and Other Stories, was similarly well received.

Two posthumously published collections were not as successful. In

August 1900 The Whilomville Stories were published, a collection of thirteen stories that Crane wrote during the last year of his life. The work deals almost exclusively with boyhood, and the stories are drawn from events occurring in Port Jervis, where Crane lived from the age of six to eleven. Focusing on small-town America, the stories tend toward sentimentality, but remain perceptive of the lives of children. Wounds in the Rain, published in September 1900, contains fictional tales based on Crane's reports for the World and the Journal during the Spanish–American War. These stories, which Crane wrote while desperately ill, include "The Price of the Harness" and "The Lone Charge of William B. Perkins" and are dramatic, ironic and sometimes humorous.

Despite Crane's prolific output, only four stories--"The Open Boat", "The Blue Hotel", "The Bride Comes to Yellow Sky", and The Monster—have received extensive attention from scholars. H. G. Wells considered "The Open Boat" to be "beyond all question, the crown of all his work", and it is one of the most frequently discussed of Crane's works.

Poetry

Many red devils ran from my heart

And out upon the page.

They were so tiny

The pen could mash them.

And many struggled in the ink.

It was strange

To write in this red muck

Of things from my heart.

— Stephen Crane

Crane's poems, which he preferred to call "lines", are typically not given as much scholarly attention as his fiction; no anthology contained Crane's verse until 1926. Although it is not certain when Crane began to write poetry seriously, he once said that his overall poetic aim was "to give my ideas of life as a whole, so far as I know it". The poetic style used in both of his books of poetry, The Black Riders and Other Lines and War is Kind, was unconventional for the time in that it was written in free verse without rhyme, meter, or even titles for individual works. They are typically short in length; although several poems, such as "Do not weep, maiden, for war is kind", use stanzas and refrains, most do not. Crane also differed from his peers and poets of later generations in that his work contains allegory, dialectic and narrative situations.

Critic Ruth Miller claimed that Crane wrote "an intellectual poetry rather than a poetry that evokes feeling, a poetry that stimulates the mind rather than arouses the heart". In the most complexly organized poems, the significance of the states of mind or feelings is ambiguous, but Crane's poems tend to affirm certain elemental attitudes, beliefs, opinions and stances toward God, man and the universe. The Black Riders in particular is essentially a dramatic concept and the poems provide continuity within the dramatic structure. There is also a dramatic interplay in which there is frequently a major voice reporting an incident seen ("In the desert / I saw a creature, naked, bestial") or experienced ("A learned man came to me once"). The second voice or additional voices represent a point of view which is revealed to be inferior; when these clash, a dominant attitude emerges.

Legacy

In four years, Crane published five novels, two volumes of poetry, three short story collections, two books of war stories, and numerous works of short fiction and reporting. Today he is mainly remembered for The Red Badge of Courage, which is regarded as an American classic. The novel has been adapted several times for the screen, including John Huston's 1951 version. By the time of his death, Crane had become one of the best known writers of his generation. His eccentric lifestyle, frequent newspaper reporting, association with other famous authors, and expatriate status made him somewhat of an international celebrity. Although most stories about his life tended toward the romantic, rumors about his alleged drug use and alcoholism persisted long after his death.

By the early 1920s, Crane and his work were nearly forgotten. It was not until Thomas Beer published his biography in 1923, which was followed by editor Wilson Follett's The Work of Stephen Crane (1925–1927), that Crane's writing came to the attention of a scholarly audience. Crane's reputation was then enhanced by faithful support from writer friends such as Joseph Conrad, H. G. Wells and Ford Madox Ford, all of whom either published recollections or commented upon their time with Crane. John Berryman's 1950 biography of Crane further established him as an important American author. Since 1951 there has been a steady outpouring of articles, monographs and reprints in Crane scholarship.

Today, Crane is considered one of the most innovative writers of the 1890s. His peers, including Conrad and James, as well as later writers such as Robert Frost, Ezra Pound and Willa Cather, hailed Crane as one of the finest creative spirits of his time. His work was described by Wells as "the first expression of the opening mind of a new period, or, at least, the early emphatic phase of a new initiative." Wells said that "beyond dispute", Crane was "the best writer of our generation, and his untimely death was an irreparable loss to our literature." Conrad wrote that Crane was an "artist" and "a seer with a gift for rendering the significant on the surface of things and with an incomparable insight into primitive emotions". Crane's work has proved inspirational for future writers; not only have scholars drawn similarities between Hemingway's A Farewell to Arms and The Red Badge of Courage, but Crane's fiction is thought to have been an important inspiration for Hemingway and his fellow Modernists. In 1936, Hemingway wrote in The Green Hills of Africa that "The good writers are Henry James, Stephen Crane, and Mark Twain. That's not the order they're good in. There is no order for good writers." Crane's poetry is thought to have been a precursor to the Imagist movement, and his short fiction has also influenced American literature. "The Open Boat", "The Blue Hotel", The Monster and "The Bride Comes to Yellow Sky" are generally considered by critics to be examples of Crane's best work.

Several institutions and places have endeavored to keep Crane's legacy alive. Badenweiler and the house where he died became something of a tourist attraction for its fleeting association with the American author; Alexander Woollcott attested to the fact that, long after Crane's death, tourists would be directed to the room where he died. Columbia University Rare Book and Manuscript Library has a collection of Crane and Taylor's personal correspondence dating from 1895 to 1908. Near his brother Edmund's Sullivan County home in New York, where Crane stayed for a short time, a pond is named after him. The Stephen Crane House in Asbury Park, New Jersey, where the author lived with his siblings for nine years, is operated as a museum dedicated to his life and work. Syracuse University has an annual Stephen Crane Lecture Series which is sponsored by the Dikaia Foundation.

Columbia University purchased much of the Stephen Crane materials held by Cora Crane at her death. The Crane Collection is one of the largest in the nation of his materials. Columbia University had an exhibit: 'The Tall Swift Shadow of a Ship at Night': Stephen and Cora Crane, November 2, 1995 through February 16, 1996, about the lives of the couple, featuring letters and other documents and memorabilia. (Source: Wikipedia)

CPSIA information can be obtained
at www.ICGtesting.com
Printed in the USA
LVHW090014191119
637710LV00016B/573/P

9 789353 839253